War and Imagination

War and Imagination

Perspectives from the *Hudson Review*

Edited by Ronald Koury

With an Introduction by David Mason

Syracuse University Press

First Edition 2024

24 25 26 27 28 29 6 5 4 3 2 1

∞ The paper used in this publication meets the minimum requirements of the American National Standard for Information Sciences—Permanence of Paper for Printed Library Materials, ANSI Z39.48-1992.

For a listing of books published and distributed by Syracuse University Press, visit https://press.syr.edu.

ISBN: 9780815611677 (paperback)
9780815657132 (e-book)

Library of Congress Cataloging-in-Publication Data

Names: Koury, Ronald, editor. | Mason, David, 1954- writer of introduction.
Title: War and imagination : perspectives from the Hudson Review / edited by Ronald Koury ; with an introduction by David Mason.
Other titles: Hudson review.
Description: First edition. | Syracuse, New York : Syracuse University Press, 2024. | Includes bibliographical references.
Identifiers: LCCN 2024005194 (print) | LCCN 2024005195 (ebook) | ISBN 9780815611677 (paperback) | ISBN 9780815638452 (hardback) | ISBN 9780815657132 (ebook)
Subjects: LCSH: War in literature. | War and literature. | LCGFT: Essays. | Literary criticism.
Classification: LCC PN56.W3 W3256 2024 (print) | LCC PN56.W3 (ebook) | DDC 809/.93358—dc23/eng/20240202
LC record available at https://lccn.loc.gov/2024005194
LC ebook record available at https://lccn.loc.gov/2024005195

Manufactured in the United States of America

To Gary Langley, whose idea this was

Photograph by Jane Bishop

Ronald Koury, a graduate of Columbia College with a degree in English, joined the *Hudson Review* in 1981 and has been its managing editor since 1985. He has been a speechwriter for the delegation of the Permanent Mission of the Kingdom of Bhutan to the United Nations. He is the editor of two previous Syracuse University Press books: *Literary Awakenings: Personal Essays from the* Hudson Review (2017) and *Places Lost and Found: Travel Essays from the* Hudson Review (2021). He lives in New York.

Contents

Part Six. Fiction

Foreword

Ronald Koury

"War is what happens when language fails," wrote Margaret Atwood. And according to Winston Churchill, "The story of the human race is war. Except for brief and precarious interludes, there has never been peace in the world, and before history began, murderous strife was universal and unending." As we see with current international events, especially but not exclusively in Ukraine and the Middle East, war remains front and center, not just in the news, but in our lived relations.

Like most, my family is no stranger to war. During the Civil War, one of my ancestors, a Union soldier, died at the age of nineteen in a horrible Confederate prison, never knowing his son. Also at nineteen, my great-uncle Freddy died during World War II, in the Pacific Theater, when a Japanese kamikaze pilot crashed into the ship on which he served, the USS *Princeton*. My great-grandmother, on hearing the news, had a stroke and died.

The work in this book—poetry, memoirs, letters, fiction—is culled from sixty years of the *Hudson Review*. The writers are from diverse backgrounds and cultures, with a rich variety of material covering wide-ranging aspects of war and how combatants and civilians alike are affected. The foundation stone was Joseph Bennett's "Cambodian Diary," which prompted a friend to suggest I put together this anthology. The collection takes in a number of wars. I specifically wanted it to conclude with Cary Holladay's beautiful story "The Bridge," because it encapsulates so many of the themes of the book and because its central image is a wonderful metaphor. As Cary wrote to me about the actual structure, "I kept thinking of the bridge as it is today, which is several iterations past the initial rebuilding; and its predecessor that went up in flames, and all the while, the river kept flowing."

I am immensely grateful to David Mason, who wrote the thoughtful, comprehensive, insightful introduction. It is an essay in itself.

There are so many to whom I wish to express my gratitude. Among my colleagues, first, to *Hudson Review* editor Paula Deitz, a mentor and friend, who guided me in this project from beginning to end. Zach Wood was an ace with production. Katherine Seger was invaluable in helping to prepare the manuscript and with the copyediting, aided in the latter by our talented intern Evelyn Finn-Wilson.

At Syracuse, I could not ask for a more ideal group of people. Acquisitions Editor Deborah Manion was ever enthusiastic, ever encouraging, someone I have come to consider a good friend over the years. Her worthy successor Kelly Balenske has been with me every step of the way. Thanks also to Marcia Hough, the world's best copy editor. I am fortunate to have Jackson Adams handling publicity/promotion. I owe a real debt of gratitude to Lynn Wilcox for her inspired cover design. And warmest thanks to Miranda Baur for seeing me over the finish line.

Deepest appreciation to Michael A. Boyd for his generosity in supporting this anthology, his fourth for the *Hudson Review*.

Last but not least, my thanks to the writers. I love the thought that this book allows their work a second life.

Introduction

David Mason

I know little of war, but that has not kept me from writing about it. The imagination goes where it goes. This remains true for soldiers and non-soldiers alike. A writer's job is to reveal, which is not the same as the lawyer's job, to persuade. Some veterans of war deride the writing of non-veterans, but all writers, no matter what their backgrounds might be, face the same problems when it comes to telling stories—how to make them live on the page. Both war and imagination involve us in the unimaginable, the unrealness of reality.

This has always been true. Many ancient writers, such as Sophocles in Greece and Lu Chi in China, were also soldiers. But the greatest poet of war was Homer, and of "him" or "them"—depending on how the *Iliad* was composed—we know nothing. We only have the poem, and it is enough.

No matter who writes them, our stories of war are not war itself. Oliver Stone's 1986 movie, *Platoon*, has been praised for its realism, and I remember being shocked by its climactic battle, yet the movie is also identical in many ways to dozens of other war movies. There is a unit of soldiers slowly getting picked off by an unseen enemy, with parables of good and evil, innocence of experience thrown into the mix. In one cliché scene a soldier shows his buddies a photo of his girlfriend, and you know that's the guy who gets killed in the next firefight. Within minutes, the poor fellow is gasping his last. Yet clichés relate to things that really do happen. My father remembered a buddy after the battle of Iwo Jima showing a photo of his wife and tearfully saying he was afraid he would never see her again. He didn't. A kamikaze killed him weeks later at Okinawa. *Platoon* pioneered new technologies to convey "combat realism," but in its storytelling it is hardly more real than any other war or coming-of-age flick. The imagination must also get its due.

How we write about war, then, is as problematic as how we write about anything else and is influenced by all that has been written (and filmed or staged) before us. The critic and historian Paul Fussell understood this when he composed his masterpiece, *The Great War and Modern Memory* (1975). His preface to the first edition begins, "This book is about the British experience on the Western Front from 1914 to 1918 and some of the literary means by which it has been remembered, conventionalized, and mythologized. It is also about the literary dimensions of the trench experience itself. Indeed, if the book had a subtitle, it would be something like 'An Inquiry into the Curious Literariness of Real Life.'"

We all know what it's like to imagine we are part of a story. How many soldiers, going off to battle—an actual experience that in itself might obliterate anything remotely resembling rationality—have thought of themselves as characters in a book or a movie?

This is the kind of thinking illuminated by writer Tim O'Brien, who served in Vietnam from 1969 to 1970, the period of the My Lai Massacre. A version of that terrible event eventually became the central nightmare of his novel *In the Lake of the Woods* (1994). His collection of stories, *The Things They Carried* (1990), meditates on the problem of war and imagination, particularly in "How to Tell a True War Story," where a traumatized narrator explodes the genres of both fiction and criticism:

> In any war story, but especially a true one, it's difficult to separate what happened from what seemed to happen. What seems to happen becomes its own happening and has to be told that way. The angles of vision are skewed. When a booby trap explodes, you close your eyes and duck and float outside yourself. When a guy dies, . . . you look away and then look back for a moment and then look away again. The pictures get jumbled; you tend to miss a lot.

> And then afterward, when you go to tell about it, there is always that surreal seemingness, which makes the story seem untrue, but which in fact represents the hard and exact truth as it seemed.

This is what Joseph Conrad, Ford Madox Ford, and their friend Stephen Crane meant by "impressionism," a literary technique approximating the symptoms of shock, which has influenced later writers about war, though arguably we find it in Homer and Tolstoy as well. The imagistic manner of impressionist writing conveys not just events themselves, but how those events are perceived in the mind. O'Brien's story returns to the deaths of boys on patrol:

> Four guys go down a trail. A grenade sails out. One guy jumps on it and takes the blast, but it's a killer grenade and everybody dies anyway. Before they die, though, one of the dead guys says, "The fuck you do that for?" and the jumper says, "Story of my life, man," and the other guy starts to smile but he's dead.

O'Brien gives us a master class in writing. Dialogue should catch a character's particular syntax. The dying soldier in shock does not say, "What the fuck did you do that for?" but "The fuck you do that for?" He could be asking God as much as his fellow GI. The hero who has attempted to save his friends dies on a cliché: "Story of my life, man." And the moment between life and death is conveyed by a dying smile.

"In the end," O'Brien writes,

> a true war story is never about war. It's about the special way that dawn spreads out on a river when you know you must cross the river and march into the mountains and do things you are afraid to do. It's about love and memory. It's about sorrow. It's about sisters who never write back and people who never listen.

It's about life, the vast and short and incomprehensible experience that ends for all of us before we really apprehend its meaning.

The *Hudson Review* is a war baby. Two of its three founders, Frederick Morgan and Joseph Bennett, served in uniform during World War II. This collection of writing from the magazine contains

Frederick Morgan's powerful editorial for the Spring 1968 issue, which begins, "The *Hudson Review* published its first issue twenty years ago, in the aftermath of World War II and Hiroshima, when a generation was first becoming aware of its literally infinite potential for ruin." War and all that it pertains to had given these editors a sense of purpose. "Now, in 1968," Morgan continues, "sickened additionally by an odious and unjust war, the nation is rapidly approaching a fateful self-confrontation." His words are prophetic. America's wars have not abated. Old men have not become wiser. Young men and women have been swept up in the fervor of an abstract cause, learning as all soldiers must that war is a factory of irony, simultaneously beautiful and obscene.

Morgan's editorial asks, "Of what use are literature and the arts at such a time?" His answer insists upon the journal's independence from fashion. The arts "will serve best if they perform their traditional function . . . to keep our minds and sensibilities alert and honest, and our imaginations free." The arts, including literature, have a social purpose, always endangered by conformity: "A society depends on its artists to give it its full scope of intellect and feeling." Morgan finds it appalling that universities, prizes, and fellowships too often reinforce mediocrity rather than challenging it—a situation that remains true, if not worse, today. He defends the unpopular, the difficult, and promotes good criticism as a way of keeping the arts fit for purpose: " . . . the problem is to pick out the genuine artist from the frauds and second-raters, the true talent from the inflated reputations, the valid insight from the spurious." The *Hudson Review* has always provided a home for honest criticism, as well as good fiction, nonfiction, poetry, and drama. And in more than seven decades, what an amazing swathe of writers the review has harvested, all writing out of that same commitment to independence and excellence, that same belief in good writing, which pays respect to the beauties and complexities of life.

This is a book about war and wartime seen from multiple points of view—civilian and soldier, poet, essayist, critic and fiction writer—from several languages, times, and cultures. Previous volumes in this series have focused on the review's legacy of publishing translations and travel writing. Once again, Managing Editor Ron Koury has had a lot of great writing to choose from. I am struck by how rich and varied the book is. Everything in it rewards reading and will send you looking for more work by its authors, some of whom are not as well-known as they deserve to be.

I have made "war and imagination" my theme, so it is fitting that the first prose we read in the book may well blur the line between fiction and fact. Since it was published in book form in 1974, the authenticity of "Last Letters from Stalingrad" has been questioned. A few critics have felt that the literary sensibility of the letters' authors is too unified for us to believe they are real documents from German soldiers trapped in a besieged city. According to their translators, "When, in January 1943, the last plane out of Stalingrad landed in Novo-Cherkask, seven bags of mail were seized. The letters were opened; address and sender's name were removed. Then they were classified by content and general tenor, tied into neat bundles and sent to the Army High Command." The letters were at first used to ascertain the morale of German troops, but it quickly became apparent that morale was low and faith in their commanders nonexistent. Of the two million casualties at Stalingrad (1942–43), eight hundred thousand were German. According to some statistics, only six thousand German soldiers survived the battle and their internment in Soviet prison camps. However these letters were handled, transcribed, used and neglected—finally trashed by Goebbels as "unbearable," the same word used to designate the Jews—they are haunting documents. The German Army had captured much of the city but now found itself surrounded and cut off. Soldiers knew their invasion of the Soviet Union was failing and could imagine what their own fates might be. "I always thought in light-years," one writes, "but I felt in seconds." Ironically, such a soldier might have been influenced by reading Tolstoy. He sounds like a Tolstoy hero when he writes,

> Monica, what is our life compared to the many million years of the starry sky! On this beautiful night, Andromeda and Pegasus are

> right above my head. I have looked at them for a long time; I shall be very close to them soon. . . . The stars are eternal, but the life of man is like a speck of dust in the Universe.

He finishes, "I should have liked to count stars for another few decades, but nothing will ever come of it now, I suppose."

If I remain convinced by these letters, it is partly because of the simple and homely musings of their authors, who stumble into profundity. The men talk about their trades, their families, their feelings of incompleteness, and whether or not they are ready for death. One is a pianist who has lost fingers to frostbite and mourns his gift as much as his life. Several of them curse Hitler and his minions for what they have done to Germany. Quite a few offer their own versions of war's irony:

> You were supposed to die heroically, inspiringly, movingly, from inner conviction and for a great cause. But what is death in reality here? Here they croak, starve to death, freeze to death—it's nothing but a biological fact like eating and drinking. They drop like flies; nobody cares and nobody buries them. Without arms or legs and without eyes, with bellies torn open, they lie around everywhere. One should make a movie of it; it would make "the most beautiful death in the world" impossible once and for all. It is a death for beasts; later they will ennoble it on granite friezes showing "dying warriors" with their heads or arms in bandages.

How often have words like these been written? We see such sentiments in literary works from Homer to the present day. We know from Marilyn Nelson's memoir in this book that the ironies of war are taught honestly to cadets at West Point, some of whom will go out to repeat them in the next war. What does this tell us about human beings and their endless capacity for the deception of others and themselves? Wilfred Owen's "old lie" of patriotism just goes on and on. The Greeks understood this. War does not end in Homer's *Odyssey* until the goddess Athena steps in and calls a halt to the fighting. Human beings appear to be incapable of living for long in peace.

War makes philosophers out of soldiers, who often strive to understand why things are thus and not otherwise. "In Stalingrad," one of the German soldiers writes to his father, " . . . to put the question of God's existence means to deny it. . . . I have searched for God in every crater, in every destroyed house, on every corner, in every friend, in my foxhole and in the sky. God did not show Himself, even though my heart cried for Him." Another prepares his young wife to deal with widowhood:

> Gertrude and Claus need a father. Don't forget that you must live for the children, and don't make too much fuss about their father. Children forget quickly, especially at that age. Take a good look at the man of your choice, take note of his eyes and the pressure of his handshake, as was the case with us, and you won't go wrong.

Still another soldier offers that "all in all, life was beautiful once, so these days have to be endured calmly." A few soldiers write details of combat as brutal as anything you might see in a lurid movie, but most are concerned with finding or making meaning in their time of despair. These are the letters of the condemned and the damned, yet they are achingly beautiful.

Joseph Bennett's "A Cambodian Diary" was published in 1971, just months before his death from leukemia, age fifty, in Perth, Australia, where he had flown from Southeast Asia for treatment. A poet and novelist as well as a cofounder of the review, Bennett wrote superbly. As journalism, travel writing, and political invective, this piece deserves comparison to George Orwell and James Fenton. At the time of his writing, Cambodia was a sort of quasi-communist Shangri-la between the American-inspired corruption in Thailand and the war in Vietnam. By the time the piece was published, the situation had changed. Lon Nol had ousted Prince Sihanouk, who was to some degree Mao's puppet, and Cambodia lurched toward civil war, Pol Pot, the Khmer Rouge, and the killing fields. Bennett wittily and somewhat dispassionately reports the state of things under Sihanouk, the pros and cons of a safe, nonindustrial society where the influence of Chinese communism could not be entirely avoided. For a while, Sihanouk played the Americans against the Chinese, preserving his own and his country's independence, but corruption of one sort or another proved inevitable. Eventually, millions died.

Bennett writes with affection for people and a keen eye for their foibles, as well as contempt for the leaders who get them in such trouble. He can summon up a satirical mood when it suits him:

> All these America-created, America-obsessed cities, Tokyo, Seoul, Taipei, Bangkok, Saigon, have in common a smog that strangles and burns the lungs, product of the exhaustion of so many motors into a naturally damp, sluggish atmosphere, sitting inland in bowls where air can scarcely arrive. In Taipei, Seoul, and Saigon the filth piles up among the flashing new motors, crawling atop each other's backs. . . . At the trail's end lie Las Vegas and Miami, where they all want to go when they die, living off money piled up in Switzerland.

This is the polluted effluvium of America's wars, the money pumped into abstract causes and siphoned off by newly minted oligarchs. As I write, according to news reports, a son of the former defense minister of Afghanistan is buying a multimillion-dollar mansion in Beverly Hills.

Turning from Bennett's elegant prose about corruption, from which there is little escape except to the monkish realms of Angkor Wat, we find one of history's original middlemen, the charismatic traitor and double agent, Alcibiades, in John Finlay's meditation on the perils of egoism in a time of civil war:

> Alcibiades drank the black broth and ate the stale bread of the Spartan mess hall when he lived there in exile from an Athens which had sentenced him in absentia to death—"I'll show them I'm still alive," he is related to have then said. He wore his hair long and untrimmed in the Spartan way, took cold baths and then robed himself in the coarse, homespun cloak of a Spartan aristocrat. He sweated through all the manly exercises. For someone so much a victim of a multitude of passions this ascetical regimen must have

> been the last novelty. But he adapted himself with equal facility and abandonment to the manners of other cultures. In Thrace he outdrank them all in the drunk place. In "horse-breeding" Thessaly he was more of a centaur than the natives. While he lived in Asia Minor he was luxuriant and indulged in the pomps and the ostentations of an Eastern satrap. . . . His entire life seemed only a succession of brilliantly maintained but quickly discarded exteriors, a series of costumes and cosmetics such as a figure in the haunting transvestite dream he had just before he died. . . .

Alcibiades advocated for the Athenian invasion of Sicily, which turned out to be as disastrous as America's wars in Iraq and Afghanistan, then he betrayed the very people he had pushed into the disaster. Claiming to love Socrates, he had a hand in creating the society that put the philosopher to death. Socrates comes to represent the wisdom that dies when a country goes to war—kind and sociable and relatively humble before the mysteries. Alcibiades is the survivor-ego—that is, of course, until his own assassination.

I begin to see the ways each piece of writing collected in this book is connected. The pieces talk to each other, as when Marilyn Nelson, who describes herself in "Aborigine in the Citadel" as "a fat, inexorably aging, California laid-back, funky, left-leaning, dread-locked Aframerican woman poet" brings the peace-loving traditions of poetry and meditation to cadets at West Point. Her memoir calls to mind the one occasion I taught a class at the Air Force Academy in Colorado Springs. The major who hosted me, a Seamus Heaney scholar, walked me over to a window facing the campus quad and the chapel, which resembled a bunch of jets stacked in a row like dominoes. As we stood looking out on that vacancy, he asked me, "What's wrong with this picture?" Though the campus architecture was a modernist nightmare, I said I saw nothing wrong with it. "There's no place to sit," he said. "No benches, no shade trees, no lawn to dream on. These cadets are scheduled from dawn to lights out with no breaks of any kind. How can we really say they're getting educated?" Nelson's students tell her that the minutes of silent meditation with which she begins her class are the best time in their day. "The method I am trying to teach requires time and quiet. And these are in short supply at West Point."

I remember war veterans like the poet Anthony Hecht, who at one point confessed he was prepared to shoot an officer rather than obey an insane order—luckily the order was rescinded in time. What does it mean to treat soldiers as drones or myrmidons rather than human beings? Nelson writes about needing

> To see soldiers not as uniformed, muscle-bound GI Joe skinheads, but as volunteer firefighters willing to enter a heat-blinding inferno to rescue a terrified child still clutching the burnt match. I hope meditation will help my cadets recognize, even disobey, stupid and unjust orders, and to give wise and considerate ones. . . . I hope they will be soldiers who live with the humanist values kept alive by the poets, aborigines, and fools who refuse to close the door on our inner wilderness, with its echoing silence. We, after all, are crazy. We bring the verdant underworld jungle of absurd and necessary values into the marketplace, into the classroom, in this white man's world, even—as crazy as it seems—into the citadel.

Many of the pieces in this book reflect the experience of civilians, who now comprise the majority of casualties in war. The physicist and historian Abraham Pais writes, in "'The Impossible Real,'" of his survival of the Holocaust, hidden by virtuous friends who put their own lives at risk. At one point he huddled in a house almost next door to the attic in which Anne Frank and her family hid—an indication of the peril he faced. "I feel that common language is inadequate to those events, which were too singular to be described by such terms as horror, tragedy, disaster." That is, of course, precisely the purpose of much literature—to give voice to unspeakable things, to attempt to say what cannot be said. Meticulously, Pais re-creates the vanished camp in which his sister was gassed at age twenty-three. He also relates his own arrest in the final weeks of the war, and how narrowly he missed execution, a fate suffered by one of his friends. Like all good writers, he notices the contradictions in his experience:

"About happiness in prison. From that period I have learned that even in times of misery there are good days and bad days."

Louis Simpson's memoir "Soldier's Heart" appeared in 1997, one of dozens of contributions he made to the journal over his lifetime. Simpson served in the 101st Airborne Division and "saw action" many times, including at the Battle of the Bulge. Among our best poets of World War II, along with figures like Richard Wilbur, Anthony Hecht, and Samuel Menashe, he brought a soldier's irony to his vision of civilian life. His memoir is distinguished by an honest anger as he details his mental breakdown and hospitalization after the war. Simpson saw a black patient in the mental ward beaten to death by guards and came to understand the hypocrisy and racism of the civilian society he was trying to reenter, a society in which he would always feel an outsider, even when he won the Pulitzer Prize for poetry.

The poems included in this book range from despair and grief to a kind of hope at what survives humanity's murderous tendencies. Ron Koury has chosen as his epigraph a very fine poem, "Halabja," by Nina Bogin, an American who has lived in Europe for many years. The title refers to a chemical attack perpetrated against Kurdish people by the forces of Saddam Hussein on March 16, 1988. Between 3,200 and 5,000 men, women, and children are reported to have died. Bogin does not write as a journalist or lawyer in the case, but instead moves lyrically to the impossible truth: "No gods, no men come forward. Only children / with the faces of angels, and they are dead." Bogin's poem "Yugoslavia in Ruins" heads up the poetry section of this book, and here again impressionism and shock predominate with "words / broken on every crag of these forsaken outposts."

"The Miracle of Camp 60," by the late Anne Stevenson, a poet not known for sentimentalizing anything, tells a remarkable story. Italian prisoners of war, held at Lamb Holm in Orkney, off the north coast of Scotland, took the detritus of war—cement, barbed wire, two Nissen huts laid end to end—and fashioned a beautiful chapel. One of the prisoners, an artist named Domenico Chiocchetti, painted the interior Madonna and other works. As the narrator says, "We wept for sadness and joy because from memory / we had made in our ugly camp a dream of Italy." Like the German soldiers writing home from Stalingrad, these men did not care about causes, about great leaders and notions of imperial gain. They were as human as the British soldiers who had captured them in North Africa.

> Chiocchetti did not come home with us.
> He stayed to complete his font, and when I met him in Moena—
> many many years later—he told me he, too, felt guilty.
> But guilt is not right, he said, for art is joy.
> Short is our suffering in this life, joy is forever.

So why do we go to war? Why do young men and women continually put themselves in such absurd positions, where the arts seem a distant luxury? The excerpt from John Ridland's fine translation of the Middle English classic, *Sir Gawain and the Green Knight*, offers its own ironic take on notions of nobility and courage, the height of egotism and the way experience brings it down. "Knives," a poem by Maria Terrone, underlines the doubleness of objects, tools used in both war and peace, while Maxine Kumin's poems deal with deadening bureaucratic responses to terrorism. All of these works pit individual incredulity against the group mind, the hive mind that blunders into war.

Abraham Pais's Holocaust memoir began in the Jewish shrine of remembrance at Yad Vashem, but he does not mention the only poetry inscribed within. These are the concluding lines of "Préface en Prose," by Benjamin Fondane, who was gassed at Auschwitz-Birkenau in 1944, given here in the translation of John Balaban and Donka Farkas:

> But a day will come, for sure, when this poem
> will lie before you, asking nothing.
> Leave it. Leave it. It's just an outcry.
> You can't turn that into a poem.
> (Will I have time to polish this?)
> But when you tread on this clutch of nettles

> that was once me, reading this in some other century
> like an outdated story, remember that I was innocent
> and that like you, mortals of your day, I too
> had a face marked by anger, and by pity, and by joy.
>
> A man's face, quite simply.

Writing is alchemy. The words have no meaning until they are invested with purpose in the alembic of imagination, where they might join the most beautiful and enduring remnants of our species.

How we write about war concerns the critic Brooke Allen, whose reviews often represent the multiple ways in which a literary journal positions itself in relation to the world. Here, she takes up the American Revolution through the lens of a single prose history and skeptically examines its thesis. Allen upholds one of the values imparted by Morgan in his 1968 editorial—the importance of criticism to keep the arts real and help them avoid the pitfalls of propaganda.

Finally, we have an extraordinary set of fictions, all of which speak to the issues raised in the book so far. Two scholars, Nicholas Moschovakis and David Roessel, discovered an unpublished short story by Tennessee Williams, "In Spain There Was Revolution," and brought it to the review. Williams apparently wrote the story in about 1936, when he could hardly have known its full ironies. It focuses on young lovers at a summer camp in America, blissfully unaware of the direction in which the world is headed. Yet Williams seems to have sensed the coming catastrophe, rather as Auden did in his most prophetic poems. So the imagination knows things that have not yet dawned on the rational mind.

Which leads us to the utter greatness of Tolstoy, whose storytelling survives in any translation, here in the one by Richard Pevear and Larissa Volokhonsky. We are given three major sections from *War and Peace*: the Battle of Austerlitz, Natasha Rostov's first ball and the glimmerings of her romance with Prince Andrei, and the last days of Petya Rostov during the French retreat. All the ironies of war are here, the psychology of young men fuddled by ideals and confronting ugly realities, the grandeur and chaos of battle strangely matched by the peacetime conflicts of the heart. I had not read these passages since I was a nineteen-year-old fisherman in Alaska, and once again I was besotted, swept along in the tide of story. As I've already noted, a lot of great writing about war seems to echo Homer and Tolstoy, and this must be because they got so many things so right, particularly the way heroism and absurdity coexist, the way war becomes irony's playground. Austerlitz begins quite literally in a fog, so the armies arrayed against Napoleon have no idea how close his troops have come to them. For much of the battle, no one knows who is killing whom—an impression Homer sometimes gives as well. As Jean Renoir would demonstrate in his great film, *Grand Illusion* (1937), there is also the class struggle, the way officers treat each other as fellow aristocrats even as they set out to kill one another. Manners in war parallel the manners of the fancy ball in which Natasha dances with her prince. And in the later scenes, poor Petya Rostov is just too young, too enthusiastic, to believe he is riding straight to his death. I cannot imagine Ernest Hemingway or even Tim O'Brien writing without the influence of Tolstoy. There may be differences of nationality, class, and manners, but the psychology of war, the impressionism of writing, and the way heroes and fools can meet identical ends, are the same.

For most of Wendell Berry's story, "A Desirable Woman," war is a "distant mutter of thunder." Berry gives us an intimate portrait of a marriage and the whole agrarian community surrounding and sustaining it. He also gives us a kind of love outside the marriage, which is not an infidelity, but an enlargement, as the wife considers it, "for all love must begin without knowledge. Perhaps, she thought, it is itself a kind of knowledge." Berry's psychology is religious in the best sense, steeped in ritual and mystery—again, seeming to express the inexpressible—and he brings his story to one of the most beautiful endings I have ever read.

The Spanish Civil War returns in "Hunting in July," a story by Julián Ríos. Born in 1941, Ríos is part of the generation of Spanish writers who came of age under Franco's dictatorship, so fiction becomes an attempt to understand events of another time. His story owes much to Ambrose Bierce's "An Occurrence at Owl Creek Bridge," and also "The Secret Miracle," an homage to Bierce by Jorge Luis Borges—both exploring the psychology of death. Postwar Japan and the struggle to survive during the American occupation are the background for "Allegiance" by Japanese writer Asako Serizawa. Here a husband and wife must navigate the aftermath of the firebombing of Japanese cities, the loss of their son, and their own guilt at having failed to resist sufficiently the wartime ethos of their country.

Luke Mogelson's gripping story "Kids" brings us closer to the present as we follow a unit of American soldiers in Afghanistan. Mogelson, a prominent war correspondent for the *New York Times* and the *New Yorker*, spent several years in Kabul and writes about his lieutenant narrator and a platoon of soldiers as if he had been one of them. He writes dialogue with the terse panache of Tim O'Brien and gets the lingo and manners of the men, such as the overweight machine gunner, Corporal Kahananui:

> He'd fallen for the SAW the first time he felt it chugging in his arms, spraying metal down the range at Benning. Call it an affinity, like the fat kid who chooses tuba. During a tiff, he could fix a jam, reload a belt, or jury-rig a broken drum with hardly a hiccup in his surgically directed devastation. He had achieved that intuitive communion with his weapon that every rifleman aspires to. It was humbling—it was truly a delicious treat—to watch him work.

As you might have noticed, Mogelson's narrator has a few issues. He misreads his men and for a time is hated by them. He doles out punishment unfairly and partly causes a man's death and is in turn relieved when a new recruit fucks up even more than he has. He doesn't even understand that the recruit is a Jew, who might not appreciate being sent to a chaplain for counsel. We see this unit undergoing trauma and confusion about who is and is not an enemy combatant, yet Mogelson knows that those who survive will be telling different stories when they get back home, some of them deeply changed, others deep in denial.

Trauma is also the subject of Lara Prescott's story, "Those Who Burn," which follows civilians through an unnamed city under siege, dodging sniper fire as they search for food. It is, like Tim O'Brien's stories, about all the things that can and cannot be carried through this life.

And then we come to "The Bridge," the final story in this book, in which Cary Holladay conveys a novel's worth of characters during the American Civil War. Holladay's bridge over the Rapidan River becomes, like so many other locations in this book, liminal, between one state of being and another—between appearance and reality, past and present, North and South, man and woman, war and peace. The very contradiction in the term "civil war" comes to bear on this, as well as all the dreams and expectations and losses of her characters, their projections into a future some of them will not live to see.

As I said at the beginning, both war and imagination involve us in the unimaginable, the unrealness of reality. Reality and imagination cannot fully be distinguished from each other. I'm thinking of Lily Briscoe, the artist in Virginia Woolf's *To the Lighthouse*, who in the aftermath of World War I finds herself trying to complete a painting she had begun before the war. "So much depends," she thinks, looking out to sea where her friends may or may not be reaching the hoped-for lighthouse in their boat, "upon distance: whether people are near us or far from us. . . ." All writing, all art, grapples with that distinction. The literature in this book changes our perspectives upon war, seeing it at a distance and close up, as the perplexing mystery it remains, no matter who lives it, or how.

War and Imagination

Halabja

Nina Bogin

Halabja, tonight the silence of the world
is so heavy above you

that the stars
slow their burning and gaze

at the emptiness, the terrible grass
whitening the fields.

Flocks of sheep on the hillsides, children
in their embroidered shirts,

women, men, wrapped in each other's arms
as if the whole world had lain down to sleep—

what is this day that begins with the singing
of all days, the bread, the milk, the heated pan,

the tree branch swinging
in the wind, the one bird

perched at the crown? It is the day
when history turns its back,

when the old laws
turn to ash in the grazing lands.

No gods, no men come forward. Only children
with the faces of angels, and they are dead.

Summer 1994

Part One

Editorial

Editorial

Frederick Morgan

The *Hudson Review* published its first issue twenty years ago, in the aftermath of World War II and Hiroshima, when a generation was first becoming aware of its literally infinite potential for ruin. This potential, along with its opposite, still remains. Industrial and technological progress has more and more forbiddingly taken the aspect of that "diseased commotion, moral and physical" which Poe believed could be purified only by cosmic fire. The greatest economic boom in history has only intensified the destruction of our countryside, the fouling of our environment, the alienation of our urban poor, the disaffection of our young. Now, in 1968, sickened additionally by an odious and unjust war, the nation is rapidly approaching a fateful self-confrontation. It will require all its honesty and intelligence if it is to survive, and help the world survive, the next quarter-century.

Of what use are literature and the arts at such a time? They will serve best if they perform their traditional function—which is, putting it only in part and much too simply, to keep our minds and sensibilities alert and honest, and our imaginations free. To help us remain open to possibility, and at the same time emotionally and intellectually responsible in the face of ideas and events. A society depends on its artists to give it its full scope of intellect and feeling. But whereas twenty years ago there was danger of good artists going unrecognized, the situation today is radically different. The universities and foundations have done their work all too well. A host of mediocrities (along with the few of real talent) is maintained on the near-permanent subsidy of fellowships and grants. At the same time, literature, in the wake of the visual arts, is being gradually absorbed by public relations. Commerce, which once rejected art, now hugs it in deadly embrace. With the connivance of the middlemen, artists are promoted as personalities; they are interviewed, gossiped about; they become celebrities. And from the standpoint of both promoters and public, it matters little, in fact is in many ways preferable, that their works not be understood. In this superflux, the problem is to pick out the genuine artist from the frauds and second-raters, the true talent from the inflated reputations, the valid insight from the spurious. This is the traditional mission of criticism, and it has never been more important than it is today.

Artists are necessary for the health of society, and criticism is necessary for the health of art. Today, there are at work, in unusually large number, forces that would pervert art and stifle responsible criticism. Under the circumstances it is all the more imperative for an independent literary review to exercise its lonely prerogatives: of remaining accessible to the new and unexpected, of joining no coterie (or even "establishment") of log-rollers and adulators, and of maintaining the cleansing function of criticism as the revealer and scourge of fraud.

Spring 1968

Part Two

Letters

Last Letters from Stalingrad

Translated by Franz Karl Schneider
and Charles Gullans

The letters and fragments of letters that follow were originally published in Germany in 1954 by the C. Bertelsmann Verlag (now Sigbert Mohn Verlag), Guetersloh, under the title Letzte Briefe aus Stalingrad. *The following note appeared as a postscript to the German edition:*

> *A full account of the fate of these letters would make a fantastic tale of overorganization—of a military and party bureaucracy gone mad with censorship, snooping and analytical and documentary zeal. From the day they were flown out of the Stalingrad trap, the letters passed through serried ranks of bureaus. They were to be used to "ascertain the morale of the troops"; an order was issued from Hitler's headquarters that they were to be impounded. The order went to the Army High Command and from there to the central censorship bureau of the army postal system. When, in January 1943, the last plane out of Stalingrad landed in Novo-Cherkask, seven bags of mail were seized. The letters were opened; address and sender's name were removed. Then they were classified by content and general tenor, tied into neat bundles and sent to the Army High Command.*
>
> *The Bureau of Army Information took care of the statistical breakdown of "troop morale," dividing it into five rubrics. This was the resulting "picture":*

A-Positive Attitude towards the Leadership	. . . . . *2.1%*
B-Doubtful " " " "	. . . . . *4.4%*
C-Negative " " " "	. . . . *57.4%*
D-Actively Opposed	. . . . . *3.4%*
E-Indifferent	. . . . *33.0%*

After having been processed and "taken cognizance of," the letters, along with other Stalingrad documents such as orders from Hitler, field orders, reports and radio messages—all in all about 1100 lbs. of paper—were placed in the custody of the Army Press Corps, whose assignment it was to write a documented account of the Battle of Stalingrad. The German Supreme Command hoped to find itself exculpated, but the language of the documents was unmistakably clear. So the book was suppressed; Goebbels decided that it was "unacceptable to the German nation." [The German word here is "untragbar," *which literally means "unbearable." In the stark simplicities of Nazi jargon and thinking it therefore meant "exterminable." The Jews also were* "untragbar."*]*

Ultimately, authenticated copies of the letters found their way into the army archives in Potsdam. From there they were removed a few days before the fall of Berlin and preserved for posterity."

1

. . . My life has changed in nothing; it is now as it was ten years ago, blessed by the stars, avoided by men. I had no friends, and you know why they wanted to have nothing to do with me. I was happy when I could sit at the telescope and look at the sky and the world of stars, happy as a child that is allowed to play with the stars.

You were my best friend, Monica. Yes, you read correctly, you were. The time is too serious for jokes. This letter will take two weeks to reach you. By then you will already have read in the papers what has taken place here. Don't think too much about it, for in reality everything will have ended differently: let other people worry about setting the record straight. What are they to you or me? I always thought in light-years, but I felt in seconds. Here, too, I have much to do with the weather. There are four of us and, if things were to continue the way they are now, we would be content. What we do is very simple. Our job is to measure temperatures and humidity, to report on cloud ceilings and visibility. If some bureaucrat read what I write here, he would have a fit . . . violation of military security. Monica, what is our life compared to the many million years of the starry sky! On this beautiful night, Andromeda and Pegasus are right above my head. I have looked at them for a long time; I shall be very close to them soon. My peace and contentment I owe to the stars, of which you are the most beautiful to me. The stars are eternal, but the life of man is like a speck of dust in the Universe.

Around me everything is collapsing, a whole army is dying, day and night are on fire, and four men busy themselves with daily reports on temperature and cloud ceilings. I don't know much about war. No human being has died by my hand. I haven't even fired live ammunition from my pistol. But I know this much: the other side would never show such a lack of understanding for its men. I should have liked to count stars for another few decades, but nothing will ever come of it now, I suppose.

2

. . . I took out your picture once again and looked at it for a long time. I remember the experience we shared that lovely summer evening in the last year of peace, when we walked home through the blooming valley towards our house. When we found each other for the first time, only the voice of the heart spoke in us; later it was the voice of love and happiness. We talked about ourselves and about the future which lay before us like a many-colored carpet.

That gay carpet is no longer there. The summer evening is no longer there, and neither is the blooming valley. And we are no longer together. Instead of the carpet there is now an endless white field, there is no more summer, but only winter, and there is no future, at least not for me, and consequently not for you either. All this time I had a feeling which I could not explain, but today I know that it was anxiety about you. I felt, despite the distance of many thousand kilometers, that it was the same with you. When you receive this letter, listen intently to it, perhaps you will hear my voice then. They tell us that our struggle is for Germany. But there are only a few here who believe that this meaningless sacrifice could be of use to our country.

3

. . . You must get that out of your head, Margaret, and you must do it soon. I would even advise you to be ruthless about it, for your disappointment will be less. In every one of your letters I sense your desire to have me home with you soon. It isn't strange at all that you are looking forward to it. I too am waiting and longing for you passionately. That is not so much what disturbs me, but rather the unspoken desire I read between your lines to have not only the husband and lover with you again, but also the pianist. I feel that very distinctly. Is it not a strange confusion of feeling that I, who should be most unhappy, have resigned myself to my fate, and the woman who should have every reason to be thankful that I am still alive (at least so far) is quarreling with the fate that has struck me?

At times I have the suspicion that I am being silently reproached, as if it were my fault that I can play no longer. That's what you wanted to hear. And that's why you kept probing in your letters for the truth which I would have much preferred to tell you in person. Perhaps it is the will of destiny that our situation here has come to a point which permits no excuses and no way out. I do not know whether I shall have a chance to talk to you once more. So it is well that this letter should reach you, and that you know, in case I should turn up some day, that my hands are ruined and have been since the beginning of December. I lost the little finger on my left hand, but worse still is the loss of the three middle fingers of my right hand through frostbite. I can hold my drinking cup only with my thumb and little finger. I am quite helpless; only when one has lost his fingers does one notice how much they are needed for the simplest tasks. The thing I can still do best with my little finger is shoot. Yes, my hands are wrecked. I can't very well spend the rest of my life shooting, simply because I'm no good for anything else. Perhaps I could make out as a game warden? But this is gallows humor; I only write it to calm myself.

Kurt Hahnke, I think you remember him from the Conservatory in '37, played the Appassionata a week ago on a grand piano in a little side street close to Red Square. Such things don't happen every day. The grand piano was standing right in the middle of the street. The house had been blown up, but feeling sorry for the instrument, they must have got it out beforehand and put it in the street. Every passing soldier hammered away at it. I ask you, where else can you find a place with pianos in the streets? As I said, Kurt played incredibly well on January 4. He will be in the very front line soon.

Excuse me; here I am using the word "front line" instead of "first rank,"[1] such is the influence of war on us. If the boy gets home, we will soon hear about him. I certainly shall never forget these hours—the kind of audience and the situation were unique. Pity that I am not a writer, so that I could describe how a hundred soldiers squatted around in their greatcoats with blankets over their heads. Everywhere there was the sound of explosions, but no one let himself be disturbed. They were listening to Beethoven in Stalingrad, even if they didn't understand him. Do you feel better now that you know the full truth?

4

. . . Just don't bother me with your well-meant advice. Don't you know what kind of situation you'll get me into? The way you go on! You wouldn't have done it; you would have known how to do it! Things should have been done in such and such a way, etc., etc.! What is all that supposed to mean? You know that I am of your opinion and that we talked more about it than was safe. But you don't put that sort of thing in writing! Do you think the others are idiots?

If *I* write now, it is because I know that nothing can happen to me, and I took the precaution to leave off my name and return

1. The confusion is between *vordersten Front* and *vordersten Reihe*, the first of which refers to the line of combat and the second to artistic eminence.

address; moreover, you will receive this letter in the agreed-on way. Even if anybody knew who wrote this letter, I couldn't be safer any place than in Stalingrad. It is so easy to say: Put down your weapons. Do you think the Russians will spare us? You are an intelligent man, so why don't you also demand that your friends refuse to produce ammunition and war materiel?

It is easy to give good advice; but it just won't work the way you think it will. Liberation of nations, nonsense. Nations remain the same. Their rulers change, and bystanders will keep arguing for liberating the people from their respective rulers. The time to act was in 1932; you know that very well. Also, that we let the moment go by. Ten years ago, the ballot would still have done the trick. Today, all it will cost you is your life.

5

. . . This morning in the division command post, Hannes persuaded me to write to you after all. For a whole week I have avoided writing this letter; I kept thinking that uncertainty, painful though it is, still keeps a glimmer of hope alive. I was the same way in thinking about my own fate; every night I went to sleep not knowing how the scales might tip—whether we would get help here or would be destroyed. I didn't even try to come to any final conclusion, to resolve the doubt. Perhaps from cowardice. I might have been killed three times by now, but it would always have been suddenly, without my being prepared. Now things are different; since this morning I know how things stand; and since I feel freer this way, I want you also to be free from apprehension and uncertainty.

I was shocked when I saw the map. We are entirely alone, without help from outside. Hitler has left us in the lurch. If the airfield is still in our possession, this letter may still get out. Our position is to the north of the city. The men of my battery have some inkling of it, too, but they don't know it as clearly as I do. So this is what the end looks like. Hannes and I will not surrender; yesterday, after our infantry had retaken a position, I saw four men who had been taken prisoner by the Russians. No, we shall not go into captivity. When

Stalingrad has fallen, you'll hear and read it. And then you'll know that I shall not come back.

6

. . . It is perfectly useless to rebel against it; I would most certainly find a way out if there were one. Of course, I have tried everything to escape from this trap, but there are only two ways left: to heaven or to Siberia. Waiting is the best thing, because, as I said, the other is useless. At home some people will congratulate themselves on being able to keep their chairs, both easy and academic, and in many newspapers you will find beautiful, high-sounding words in big black borders. They will always pay us due honor. Don't be taken in by this idiotic to-do. I am so furious that I could smash everything in sight, but never in my life have I been so helpless.

I continually tell myself one thing: stay healthy, and you will survive the most difficult times. Health is the prerequisite for my return home. I will not resign my chair at home. When you meet my colleagues, tell them so, exactly as I write it. The higher the chair, the harder you fall.

7

. . . You are the wife of a German officer; so you will take what I have to tell you, upright and unflinching, as upright as you stood on the station platform the day I left for the East. I am no letter writer and my letters have never been longer than a page. Today there would be a great deal to say, but I will save it for later, i.e., six weeks if all goes well and a hundred years if it doesn't. You will have to reckon with the latter possibility. If all goes well, we shall be able to talk about it for a long time, so why should I attempt to write much now, since it comes hard to me. If things turn out badly, words won't do much good anyhow.

You know how I feel about you, Augusta. We have never talked much about our feelings. I love you very much and you love me, so you shall know the truth. It is in this letter. The truth is the knowledge that this is the grimmest of struggles in a hopeless situation. Misery, hunger, cold, renunciation, doubt, despair and horrible death. I will say no more about it. I did not talk about it during my leave either, and there's nothing about it in my letters. When we were together (and I mean through our letters as well), we were man and wife, and the war, however necessary, was an ugly accompaniment to our lives. But the truth is also the knowledge that what I wrote above is no complaint or lament but a statement of objective fact.

I cannot deny my share of personal guilt in all this. But it is in a ratio of 1 to 70 millions. The ratio is small; still, it is there. I wouldn't think of evading my responsibility; I tell myself that, by giving my life, I have paid my debt. One cannot argue about questions of honor.

Augusta, in the hour in which you must be strong, you will feel this also. Don't be bitter and do not suffer too much from my absence. I am not cowardly, only sad that I cannot give greater proof of my courage than to die for this useless, not to say criminal, cause. You know the family motto of the von H——'s: "Guilt recognized is guilt expiated."

Don't forget me too quickly.

8

. . . Again I am writing a short letter, although I wrote one to you and a second one to Hans Mullner only yesterday. You certainly can't complain about lack of mail. A buddy will take this one along. I wish Grandmother a happy 74th birthday, and I am sorry that I cannot eat a piece of her cake. Can you get the things you need to bake a cake? No cake for us, but once we are out of here, we'll have everything again; until then we simply have to tighten our belts. Go to the savings bank, take out fifty marks, and buy Grandmother a present. She is to enjoy herself. The Bergers probably have some coffee left, her husband being with the port administration. If they have some, they will certainly give it to you. You just tell them it's for the birthday party. In my time I have done the Bergers many favors.

I am writing nothing but nonsense. But nonsense is better than no mail at all. And you never know if the next bullet won't have your name on it. But don't be afraid for us. I am sure we'll get out of here, and then we'll all go home on leave for four weeks. It's very cold here now; do you have snow, too? We don't have to strew any sand here; everyone has to look out so he doesn't fall.

9

. . . Around me everything is confused, so that I don't know how to begin. Wouldn't it be better to start at the end?

Dearest Anne, you will probably be surprised to receive such a relatively funny letter. But if you take a closer look, you'll find that the letter is not funny at all. You always used to take me for a philistine, and I have to concede you a point—for example, in the way I stowed my lunch into my briefcase. One sandwich on the right, one on the left, and on top of them I put the apples, and on top of that the thermos bottle. The bottle had to lie across the apples, so that it would not melt the butter. It was a—how did Uncle Herbert always call it?—a tranquil time. Today I am not a philistine anymore. You should see how I go to my "place of employment." It is cozy and warm in our bunker. We have dismantled a few trucks and rerouted the pieces to our stove. It's strictly against regulations, but that is the least of our worries.

My "place of employment" is right next door, as I already wrote you a few days ago. It too is a bunker, in which a captain lived a short while ago. Here I am telling you in great detail how things look around here, and all the time I want to write about something entirely different. Then again, I don't want to, but it is advisable and even of some importance that I do write about it. I don't want to cause you unnecessary anxiety, but things are supposed to be pretty murky here. You hear it from all sides. We are stationed a long way behind the lines; once in a while we hear a shot. If it weren't for that, we wouldn't be reminded of the war at all. As things are right now, I could stand it for another hundred years. But not without you. And it won't last that long anyway; we expect to get out of here any day. But this hope doesn't fit in with the rumors.

The army has been surrounded now for seven weeks, and it can't last another seven. My leave was already due in September, but it didn't come through. I consoled myself with the others, who also had to kiss their leaves good-bye. Yesterday morning the word was that one-third of us are going home on leave towards the end of January. The master sergeant from the staff company claims to have heard it. Or it may take a few days longer than that. Nobody really knows what is up around here. I haven't been with you for eight months now; a few days won't make any difference. Unfortunately I won't be able to bring you much, but I'll see what I can do in Lemberg. I am looking forward to a real day on leave, and even more to seeing you and Mother again. When you receive the telegram, send news to Uncle Herbert immediately. It is good to be looking forward to something; I live on this anticipation, especially since yesterday morning. Every day I mark off a day on my calendar, and every mark means that I am a day closer to you.

10

. . . You are my witness that I never wanted to go along with it, because I was afraid of the East, in fact of war in general. I have never been a soldier, only a man in uniform. What do I get out of it? What do the others get out of it, those who went along and were not afraid? Yes, what are we getting out of it? We, who are playing the walk-on parts in this madness incarnate? What good does a hero's death do us? I have played death on the stage dozens of times, but I was only playing, and you sat out front in plush seats, and thought my acting authentic and true. It is terrible to realize how little the acting had to do with real death.

You were supposed to die heroically, inspiringly, movingly, from inner conviction and for a great cause. But what is death in reality here? Here they croak, starve to death, freeze to death—it's nothing but a biological fact like eating and drinking. They drop like flies; nobody cares and nobody buries them. Without arms or legs and without eyes, with bellies torn open, they lie around everywhere. One should make a movie of it; it would make "the most beautiful death in the world" impossible once and for all. It is a death fit for beasts; later they will ennoble it on granite friezes showing "dying warriors" with their heads or arms in bandages.

Poems, novels, and hymns will be written and sung. And in the churches they will say masses. I'll have no part of it, because I have no desire to rot in a mass grave. I have written the same thing to Professor H——. You and he will hear from me again. Don't be surprised if it takes a while, because I have decided to take my fate into my own hands.

11

. . . Today O—— and I are enjoying a wonderfully quiet evening. For once everybody is sitting around across the street and not here. The Russians are quiet, and we were able to close up shop early. A good bottle of Cordon Rouge drunk peacefully in the evening made us feel especially good.

I read Binding's war diary and some other things. How incredibly well this man echoes what moves and touches us out here. He purges the experience of all that is false and irrelevant. Only the crucial things radiate from his mind, from his words.

We expect nothing any more of great decisions that would have to be made . . . by the men on top. Whether time will not outrun these decisions anyhow, no one can say! But there is nothing else for us to hope for. The only thing that *has* been done until now has been fearfully violent fighting over Hill X inside and outside the city. Generals and colonels have played with the possibility that this hill, of all things, might be a turning point in world history! And not only generals!

Every day a few positions are taken; every day, the enemy or we, depending on who happens to be holding them at the time, are thrown out again! Neither the enemy nor we have so far had sense enough to decide to take only what can be held.

One can safely say that with little things it is the same as with big things! This perpetual activity without result demands an indolence or an endurance which is almost impossible to muster, and since it consists only in waiting, it wears you out.

Soon it will be ten o'clock. I want to sleep as much as I still can. The more you sleep, the less you feel the hunger. And hunger is not pleasant, it's cruel.

All my love to you.

12

. . . Well, now you know that I shall never return. Break it to our parents gently. I am deeply shaken and doubt everything. I used to be strong and full of faith; now I am small and without faith. I will never know many of the things that happen here; but the little that I have taken part in is already so much that it chokes me. No one can tell me any longer that the men died with the words "Deutschland" or "Heil Hitler" on their lips. There is plenty of dying, no question of that; but the last word is "mother" or the name of someone dear, or just a cry for help. I have seen hundreds fall and die already, and many belonged to the Hitler Youth as I did; but all of them, if they still could speak, called for help or shouted a name which could not help them anyway.

The Führer made a firm promise to bail us out of here; they read it to us and we believed in it firmly. Even now I still believe it, because I have to believe in something. If it is not true, what else could I believe in? I would no longer need spring, summer, or anything that gives pleasure. So leave me my faith, dear Greta; all my life, at least eight years of it, I believed in the Führer and his word. It is terrible how they doubt here, and shameful to listen to what they say without being able to reply, because they have the facts on their side.

If what we were promised is not true, then Germany will be lost, for in that case no more promises can be kept. Oh, these doubts, these terrible doubts, if they could only be cleared up soon!

13

. . . Unfortunately, the Christmas I have to tell about was not beautiful, but we were comfortably warm. Our position is right on the banks of the Volga. We got hold of some rum; it was thin but tasted marvelous. My buddy brought something with him from division headquarters: ham and meat-jelly. I suppose he swiped it from the kitchen, but it tasted magnificent, and they have more, else he couldn't have swiped it. Bread is mighty scarce. So we made pancakes: flour, water, salt, and underneath it ham in the pan. The flour wasn't exactly homegrown either.[2] This is the fourth Christmas since the war started, but this time was the saddest of all. We will have to make up for it all when the war is over, and I hope that next year we can celebrate Christmas at home.

We have been in Stalingrad for three months now and still have not made any headway. It is rather peaceful here, but on the other side, on the steppes, they are fighting. The fellows there don't have it as good as we do. But that's their bad luck. Perhaps it will be our turn soon, because their losses are heavy. But the best thing is not to think about it. And yet you keep thinking about it; if you haven't anything to do for 24 hours but daydream, your thoughts turn towards home. Did all of you think of me on Christmas Eve? I had such a strange feeling, and it sometimes does happen that you feel it when someone thinks of you.

14

. . . The time has come for me to send you greetings once more, and to ask you to greet once more all the loved ones at home.

The Russians have broken through everywhere. Our troops, weakened by long periods of hunger without possibility of (*illegible*), engaged in the heaviest fighting since the beginning of this battle, without a day's relief, and in a state of complete physical exhaustion, have performed heroically. None of them surrenders! When bread, ammunition, gasoline and manpower give out, it is, God knows, no victory for the enemy to crush us!

We are aware that we are the victims of serious mistakes in leadership; also, the wearing down of the fortress Stalingrad will cause most severe damage to Germany and her people. But in spite of it, we still believe in a happy resurrection of our nation. Truehearted

2. In other words, they stole it.

men will see to that! You will have to do a thorough job in putting all madmen, fools, and criminals out of business. And those who will return home will sweep them away like chaff before the wind. We are Prussian officers and know what we have to do when the time comes.

In thinking over my life once more, I can look back on it with thankfulness. It has been beautiful, very beautiful. It was like climbing a ladder, and even this last rung is beautiful, a crowning of it, I might almost say a harmonious completion.

You must tell my parents that they should not be sad; they must remember me with happy hearts. No halo, please; I have never been an angel! Nor do I want to confront my God as one; I'll manage it as a soldier, with the free, proud soul of a cavalryman, as a *Herr*! I am not afraid of death; my faith gives me this beautiful independence of spirit. For this I am especially thankful.

Hand my legacy on to those who come after us: raise them to be *Herren*![3] Severe simplicity of thought and action! No squandering of energies!

Be especially loving with my parents and so help them get over the first grief. Put up a wooden cross for me in the park cemetery, as simple and beautiful as Uncle X's.

Maintain Sch—— as the family seat of the X's. That is my great wish. In my writing desk is a letter in which I recorded my wishes during my last leave.

So, once more, I turn to all of you, dear ones. My thanks once more, for everything, and hold your heads high! Keep on!

I embrace all of you!

15

. . . If there is a God, you wrote me in your last letter, then He will bring you back to me soon and healthy; you went on: a human being like you, who loves animals and flowers and does no harm to

3. This term, which might be translated as "gentlemen," is used here in a special and emphatic sense. It means "noblemen," and beyond that, men who are their own masters.

anyone, who loves and adores his wife and child, will always have God's protection.

I thank you for these words, and I always carry this letter with me in my *brustbeutel*.[4] But, dearest, if your words are weighed now and you make the existence of God dependent upon them, you will have to make a difficult and great decision. I am a religious man, you always were a believer, but this will have to change now if we accept the consequences of the conviction which we held up to now, because something has happened which has overthrown everything in which we believed. I am searching for words to tell you. Or have you guessed already? I find a rather strange tone in your last letter of December 8. Now it is the middle of January.

This will be my last letter for a long time, perhaps for ever. It will be taken along by a friend who has to go to the airfield, because it is said that tomorrow the last plane will fly out of the pocket. The situation has become untenable. The Russians are within three kilometers of our last airfield, and once this is lost, not a mouse will get out, not to mention me. Of course, hundreds of thousands of others won't get out either. But it is small comfort to have shared your own destruction with others.

If there is a God. Over there on the other side many ask the same question, perhaps millions in England and France. I don't believe any longer that God can be good, for then he would not permit such great injustice. I don't believe in it anymore, for he would have enlightened the minds of those people who began this war and always talked of peace and the Almighty in three languages. I don't believe in God anymore, because he betrayed us. I don't believe anymore, and you must see how you can come to terms with your faith.

16

. . . On the evening before the holy day, in a hut which was still fairly intact, eleven soldiers celebrated in quiet worship. It was not easy to

4. A small leather pouch fastened to a thong around the neck.

find them in the herd of the doubting, hopeless, and disappointed. But those I found came happily and with a glad and open heart. It was a strange congregation which assembled to celebrate the birthday of the Christ Child. There are many altars in the wide world, but surely none poorer than ours here. Yesterday the box still held anti-aircraft shells; today my hand spread over it the field-grey tunic of a comrade whose eyes I closed last Friday in this very room. I wrote his wife a letter of consolation. May God protect her.

I read my boys the Christmas story according to the gospel of Luke, chapter 2, verses 1–17; gave them hard black bread as the holy sacrifice and sacrament of the altar, the true body of our Lord Jesus Christ, and entreated the Lord to have pity on them and to give them grace. I did not say anything about the fifth commandment. The men sat on footstools and looked up to me from large eyes in their starved faces. They were all young, except one, who was 51. I am very happy that I was permitted to console their hearts and give them courage. When it was over, we shook each other's hands, took down addresses, and promised to look up relatives and tell them about our Christmas Eve celebration in 1942, in case one of us should return home alive.

May God hold his hands over you, dear parents, for now the evening is at hand, and we will do well to set our house in order. We will go into the evening and the night calmly, if it is the will of the Lord of the world. But we do not look into a night without end. We give our life back into the hands of God; may He be merciful when the hour has come.

17

. . . In Stalingrad, to put the question of God's existence means to deny it. I must tell you this, Father, and I feel doubly sorry for it. You have raised me, because I had no mother, and always kept God before my eyes and soul.

And I regret my words doubly, because they will be my last, and I won't be able to speak any other words afterwards which might reconcile you and make up for these.

You are a pastor, Father, and in one's last letter one says only what is true or what one believes might be true. I have searched for God in every crater, in every destroyed house, on every corner, in every friend, in my foxhole, and in the sky. God did not show Himself, even though my heart cried for Him. The houses were destroyed, the men as brave or as cowardly as myself, on earth there was hunger and murder, from the sky came bombs and fire, only God was not there. No, Father, there is no God. Again I write it and know that this is terrible and that I cannot make up for it ever. And if there should be a God, He is only with you in the hymnals and the prayers, in the pious sayings of the priests and pastors, in the ringing of the bel1s and the fragrance of incense, but not in Stalingrad.

18

. . . It's enough to drive me mad, dear Helmut; here I have a chance to write and I don't know to whom. A thousand poor devils who are lying in their holes up front and have no suspicion of such a chance would envy me and give me a year's pay for it. A year ago we still were sitting in Jüterbog together, cramming "military science." And now I sit right in the middle of the shit and don't know what to do with all that trash. But it is just the same with everybody else around here. It is an idiotic situation. If you should ever notice the name "Zaritza" in the OKW-report[5] (just possibly they might happen to tell the truth someday), then you'll know where I am. Do we live on the moon, or do you? We sit in the mud with 200,000 men, with nothing but Russians all around us, and are not permitted to say that we are encircled, completely and without hope.

I received your letter on Monday, today is Sunday, a real holiday. Above all, I would like to comment on the words with which you congratulated me for having been given front-line duty. I have just read "Gneisenau" (not everybody has time to do that) and would like

5. *Oberkommando der Wehrmacht*, Supreme Command of the Armed Forces.

to quote you a sentence which he wrote to Beguelin after the defense of Kolberg:

> . . . On reading this news, I thought that they might have heard the thunder of our cannon and might send up prayers for our salvation. There were days when the earth shook, and I behaved like a gambler who bravely puts up his last louis d'or in the hope that his luck will turn. For there was a time once when I had ammunition for only fourteen days, and yet I could not decrease my fire for fear the enemy would become aware of my lack of ammunition. It is a scandal how badly this fortress was provided.

Ah, dear boy, those were the days. Gneisenau should have heard the rocket salvos, and the discharge of 200 guns per kilometer. Not only he, but you too, and then you wouldn't be in such a hurry to come "up front." Don't be peeved now. I don't want to shatter your faith in your own bravery, but here it would do no good. Here the brave and the cowards die in one hole without a chance of defending themselves. If just once we had had ammunition for "only" 14 days, man! would we have had fun with the fireworks! My battery has just 26 rounds left, that's all, and there will be no more. Since you are one of the disciples of St. Barbara,[6] you can draw your own conclusions. Here I am: still in one piece, with a fairly normal pulse, a dozen cigarettes, had soup day before yesterday, liberated a canned ham today from a supply bomb (there is no more regular distribution; everyone is on his own), am squatting in a cellar, burning up furniture, 26 years old and otherwise no fool, one of those who was mighty keen on getting his bars and yelled "Heil Hitler" with the rest of you; and now it's either die like a dog or off to Siberia. That wouldn't be so bad. But to know that it is done for something utterly senseless makes me see red.

But let them come. The third still has 26 rounds and their commander an 08 with six shiny bullets. It is time to finish; "vespers" are coming, time to crawl a little deeper into the earth. Dear old boy,

6. The patron saint of artillery.

you can save yourself an answer to this letter, but think of my lines in, let's say, two weeks. You don't have to be clairvoyant to foresee the end. What it will actually be like, you'll never know.

19

. . . I just heard at the Command Post that mail is going out. I hope you can read what I am writing. There is no better paper available here. But the main thing is what is on it. And it's getting dark too. I have been detailed as a motorcycle courier and get around a lot. Otherwise I wouldn't have known that we are allowed to send letters. I am still doing pretty well; I hope the same is true of you. Except that riding around in ice and snow is no picnic. Guess who I ran into? The son of Gründel, the merchant. He is in the depot. He will be sitting pretty for a long time yet. In this way I got a can of pork and two loaves of bread. We are not allowed to send packages, otherwise I would send you the can. But then, I won't mind eating it myself either. How is little Marie doing and how are the folks? I haven't got a letter for a long time now. The last one came two weeks ago, from Richard. Now I have to finish, because it is already dark, and I still have ten kilometers to go.

20

. . . I have written to you twenty-six times from this damned city, and you answered me with seventeen letters. Now I shall write just once more and then never again. There, I said it. For a long time I thought about how I should formulate so fateful a sentence so that it would say everything and still not hurt too much.

I am saying good-bye to you, because since this morning the issue is settled. I will not comment on the military situation in my letter; it is clear-cut and completely up to the Russians. The only question is how long we will be around. It may last a few more days or just a few hours. Our whole life together is there for us to see. We have honored and loved each other, and waited for each other now for two years. It is good that so much time has passed. It has increased the anticipation of reunion, to be sure, but also in large measure helped to make us strangers. And time will have to heal the wounds of my not coming back.

In January you will be twenty-eight. That is still very young for such a good-looking woman, and I am glad that I could pay you this compliment again and again. You will miss me very much, but even so, don't withdraw from other people. Let a few months pass, but no more. Gertrud and Claus need a father. Don't forget that you must live for the children, and don't make too much fuss about their father. Children forget quickly, especially at that age. Take a good look at the man of your choice, take note of his eyes and the pressure of his handshake, as was the case with us, and you won't go wrong. But above all, raise the children to be upright human beings who can carry their heads high and look everybody straight in the eye. I am writing these lines with a heavy heart. You wouldn't believe me if I said that it was easy, but don't be worried, I am not afraid of what is coming. Keep telling yourself, and the children also when they have grown older, that their father never was a coward, and that they must never be cowards either.

21

. . . This terrible confusion has been going on for eleven days now. Today I can send you a few lines just once more. I hope that you received all the rest in good condition. I have been spared nothing either. But still, all in all life was beautiful once, so these days have to be endured calmly.

We have been pushed entirely into the city. This damned city! If only the end would come soon! Then, as I wrote before: "Let me go on my way contentedly. . . ."[7]

Farewell!

22

. . . Dearest, I think of you all the time. Today, standing in the chow line I thought of you again. Of the wonderful food you used to cook.

7. A line from a hymn, so the meaning is resignation to the will of God.

My socks are in shreds, too, and I can't get rid of my cough any more. No pills are available for it. You could send me cough syrup, but don't use any glass bottles. Have you caught cold too? Always put on something good and warm. Do you have enough coal? Just go and see Al——, he got lumber from me for his furniture. Let him give you coal for it now. I hope Uncle Paul has nailed the weather stripping to your windows; otherwise it will be too late for it this year. I did not celebrate Christmas here. I was on the road with the car, and we got stuck in the snow because we went the wrong way. But we soon got out again. I have decided that next year we will celebrate a real Christmas, and I am going to give you a beautiful present.

It is not my fault that I can't give it to you now. The Russians are all around us, and we won't get out again until Hitler gets us out. But you must not tell that to anyone. It is supposed to be a surprise.

23

. . . We have had to swallow a lot; will swallow this too! Stupid situation. You might say, devilishly difficult. Beats me how we are to get out of here. Not really my business, though. We marched in here on orders, shoot on orders, starve on orders, die on orders, and will march out again, all on orders. Could have marched out a long time ago, except the grand strategists haven't come to an agreement yet. Soon it will be too late, if it isn't already. One thing is sure, we'll march once again on orders. In all probability in the direction originally planned, but without weapons and under a different command.

Kemner of the heavies right next to us has been shooting craps with Helms . . . Pay gone, watch, ring and an IOU, even his piano in home sweet home. Around here people get the most idiotic ideas. Am curious about the legal title to that gambled-away piano. Little Fatso won back his watch and ring. Perhaps he will win the summerhouse tomorrow. But if both kick off, how will the estates be probated? Would have liked to know all that, but there won't be any time. Am ignorant of many things, will probably get over that too. As I said at the beginning, we've had to swallow a lot. Tell it to Egon. Title: "Troubles of a Second Lieutenant in Stalingrad." When the chips are down—seems to me that will be soon—we'll be in there shooting. Shoot guns even better than craps.

24

. . . Now that I know where I stand, I release you from your vow. This has not been easy for me to do, but the differences between us were too great. I looked for a wife with a generous heart, but it wasn't supposed to be that generous. I have written to Mother already and told her what she has to know. Please spare me the trouble of naming the witnesses and mentioning the circumstances which gave me proof of your infidelity. I feel no hatred for you; rather I advise you to choose good grounds for divorce and speed up the procedure. I have written to Dr. F—— that I agree to a divorce. And if I am back home six months from now, I do not wish to be reminded of you by anything.

I shall pass up my leave in February or March.

25

. . . Just now the master sergeant told me that I cannot go home for Christmas. I told him that he has to keep his promise, and he sent me to the captain. The captain told me that others had wanted to go on leave for Christmas too, and that they too had promised it to their relatives without being able to keep the promise. And so it wasn't his fault that we couldn't go. We should be glad that we were still alive, the captain said, and the long trip wouldn't be good in the cold winter anyhow.

Dear Maria, you must not be angry now because I cannot come on leave. I often think of our house and our little Luise. I wonder if she can laugh already. Do you have a beautiful Christmas tree? We are supposed to get one also, if we don't move into other quarters. But I don't want to write too much about things here, otherwise you'll cry. I'll enclose a picture; I have a beard in it; it is already three months old and was taken in Kharkov by a friend. A lot of rumors are going around here, but I can't figure them out. Sometimes I am afraid we will not see each other again. Heiner from Krefeld told me that a man must not write this; it only frightens his relatives. But what if it's true!

Maria, dear Maria, I have only been beating around the bush. The master sergeant said that this would be the last mail because no more planes are leaving. I can't bring myself to lie. And now, nothing will probably ever come of my leave. If I could only see you just once more; how awful that is! When you light the candles, think of your father in Stalingrad.

26

. . . I still must tell you that we went to the movies on Thursday. It was not a regular show, otherwise you might think that we have more time than we know what to do with. We saw *Geier-Walli*, all sat on the floor on their helmets or squatting like Negroes. It is a very nice film. You wrote me that I should be careful with girls. But, Maria, there aren't any girls around here. We were all by ourselves, close to two hundred men. The movie came from the propaganda company. They play in the barn every evening; only yesterday, so I have heard, the Russians fired into the village. I had planned to see *Geier-Walli* earlier in Dresden and Hanover; but I couldn't make it then. In Stalingrad I finally succeeded and saw *Geier-Walli*. What a joke. If I go on leave, I am going to see *Geier-Walli* in a real movie house. I hope they will play the film in Dresden. Even in the barn the film was quite beautiful. Only the sound couldn't be heard properly, and then the others made so many jokes, and smoked so much, you couldn't see anything for smoke. Some also used the show to get warm and to get some sleep. *Geier-Walli* in Stalingrad. I'll never forget it.

27

. . . What a misfortune that there had to be a war! The beautiful villages fell victim to it and were destroyed. And the fields are not tilled anywhere. And the worst is that so many people have died. Now they lie buried in enemy country. What a great misfortune this is! But you should be glad that the war is in a country far away and not in our beloved German homeland. It must not ever come there and increase the misery! You must be real thankful for that and thank the Lord on your knees. We are standing here on the banks of the Volga and keep watch. For you and our home. If we did not stand here, the Russians would break through and demolish everything. They are very violent and many millions strong. They are not bothered by the cold. But we are terribly cold.

I am lying in a hole dug in the snow, and it's only in the evening that I can slip into a cellar for a few hours. You wouldn't believe how good that is. We are on guard, so you don't need to be afraid. But we are getting fewer and fewer all the time, and if things continue this way, soon there won't be anyone here. But Germany has many more soldiers, and they will all fight for their country. We all wish that there will be peace soon and that we shall be victorious. That is the main thing. Keep your fingers crossed!

28

. . . Even for me this letter is difficult, how much more difficult will it be for you! Unfortunately, there won't be any good news in this letter. And it hasn't been improved by my waiting ten days either. The situation has now become so bad we fear we'll soon be completely cut off from the outside. Just now we were assured that this mail will definitely get out. If I knew that there would be another opportunity, I would wait still longer. But that is just what I don't know; so, for better or for worse, I have to come out with it. For me the war is over.

I am in the field hospital in Gumrak, waiting to be transported home by plane. Although I am waiting with great longing, the date is always changed. *That* I will be coming home is a great joy for me and for you, my dear. But the condition in which I'll get home won't be any joy to you. I am in complete despair when I think of lying before you as a cripple. But you must know sometime that my legs were shot off.

I'll be quite honest in writing about it. The right leg is totally shattered and amputated below the knee. The left one is amputated in the thigh. The doctor thinks that with prosthesis I should be able to get around like a healthy man. The doctor is a good man and means well. I hope he is right. Now you know before you see me. Dear Elise, if I only knew what you are thinking. I have time all day long to think of nothing but that. Often my thoughts are with you. Sometimes I have also wished that I were dead, but that is a serious sin and one must not say such a thing.

Over eighty men are lying in this tent; but outside there are countless men. Through the tent you can hear their screaming and moaning, and no one can help them. Next to me lies a sergeant from Bromberg, shot through the groin. The doctor told him he would be returned home soon. But to the medic he said, "He won't last until evening. Let him lie there until then." The doctor is such a good man. On the other side, right next to me against the wall, lies a soldier from Breslau who has lost an arm and his nose, and he told me that he wouldn't need any more handkerchiefs. When I asked him what he would do if he had to cry, he answered me, "No one here, you and me included, will have a chance to cry anymore. Soon others will be crying over us."

29

. . . Axel is writing this letter for me. His real name isn't Axel at all but Lachmann, and he comes from Königsberg. But we call him Axel. My arm is propped up and wrapped in thick bandages, so I cannot write. I'll soon be home, the doctor told me, and I am looking forward to it very much. There is a little piece missing on my arm, the doctor said that too. Only the funny thing is that I cannot move my fingers. As a gardener I need my fingers. The soil here is very rich and soft. We sure could use some of that in Lüneburg.[8] There is snow outside, you can't see the soil. Four days ago I lay in a hole a yard deep, and all day long I observed the soil; good soil for wheat,

8. The country around Lüneburg has very poor, sandy soil.

naturally there was no trace of fertilizer; the steppes produce their own. In this hole I got scared. Today I laugh about it. I don't have a very comfortable bed, but once I am home I'll laugh even more. And all of you will laugh with me.

30

. . . I have received your answer. You will hardly expect thanks for it. This letter will be short. I should have known better when I asked you to help me. You always were and you remain forever "righteous." This wasn't unknown to either Mama or me. But we could hardly expect that you would sacrifice your son to "righteousness." I asked you to get me out of here because this strategic nonsense isn't worth biting the dust for. It would have been easy for you to put in a word for me, and the appropriate order would have reached me. But you don't understand the situation. Very well, Father.

This letter will not only be short, but also the last one I write you. I won't have any more opportunities to write to you, even if I wanted to. It is also unimaginable that I should ever stand face to face with you again and have to tell you what I think. And because neither I in person nor another letter will ever speak to you again, I will once more recall to you your words of December 26: "You became a soldier voluntarily; it was easy to stand under the flag in peacetime, but difficult to hold it high during the war. You will be faithful to this flag and be victorious with it." These words were much clearer than the position you have taken during the last few years. You will have to remember them, because the time is coming when every German with any sense will curse the madness of this war. And you will see how empty are those words about the flag with which I was supposed to be victorious.

There is no victory, Herr General; there are only flags and men that fall, and in the end there will be neither flags nor men. Stalingrad is not a military necessity but a political gamble. And your[9] son

9. From this point to the end, he uses the formal mode of address in speaking to the man who was his father but who has now become a mere general.

is not participating in this experiment, Herr General! You blocked his way to life; he will choose the second way, which also leads to life, but in an opposite direction and on the other side of the front. Think of your words, and I hope that, when the whole show collapses, you will remember the flag and stand by it.

31

. . . How many letters have I written up to now? Thirty-eight according to my calculation, today's included. In August you wrote me that you keep a mail book, a real file of pen pals with their addresses and peculiarities, the dates you became acquainted with them, and how the friendships fared. It amused me greatly. Did you add the picture which I sent you to your file? My mail book is too inaccurate; your bookkeeping is probably better than the little marks I make in my pocket calendar. After all it doesn't really matter whether I wrote you 36 or 37 letters. I am number five among your pen pals. It must be very interesting to read all the letters you have received. They come from all theatres of the war, don't they? When the war is over, you will have a magnificent volume of memoirs in letter form. This year, at Christmas, we wanted to meet each other for the first time in Karlsruhe. Nothing came of it. The future also looks bleak to me, very bleak. I see almost no hope.

Thank God, I have gotten around to saying it. There won't be any meeting; even the date for the coming year can't be kept. Dear girl, what a fizzle! The stupid thing is that all one can do is look on; that's what's slowly driving me crazy. If only I had toddled off for home in September, when I caught that shrapnel in my arm. But I wanted to be around when we captured Stalingrad, and I have often regretted this crazy idea since.

They were pretty funny letters you received from me; I have always been a joker, as you can testify. But jokes won't help us along now; things are getting serious.

What will you write down in column six of your mail book? In any case, don't write "He died for Greater Germany," etc., for that wouldn't be true. Write "for Hanna on such and such a date," for all I care. I hope you won't find this tone frivolous. I mentioned your other pen pals. One of these days, a few of them will go out of commission too. But their circumstances are different. They will just stop writing all of a sudden. Their letters will just stop coming. But I give you formal notice. Fräulein Hanna, this is more or less my last letter, as it were. Farewell. The hope of seeing each other someday is being sacrificed to this idiotic and totally one-sided struggle. Farewell, and as a good-bye my thanks for the time which you have lovingly devoted to me. At first I meant to write "wasted," but I thought better of it. It was not a waste of time, I got a great deal of pleasure from your letters.

32

. . . Today I talked to Hermann. He is south of the front, a few hundred yards from me. Not much is left of his regiment. But the son of baker B—— is still with him. Hermann still had the letter in which you told us of Father's and Mother's death. I talked to him once more, for I am the elder brother, and I tried to console him, though I too am at the end of my rope. It is good that Father and Mother will not know that Hermann and I will never come home again. It is terribly hard that you will have to carry the burden of four dead people through your future life.

I wanted to be a theologian, Father wanted to have a house, and Hermann wanted to build fountains. Nothing worked out that way. You know yourself what the outlook is at home, and we know only too well what it is here. No, those things we planned certainly did not turn out the way we imagined. Our parents are buried under the ruins of their house, and we, though it may sound harsh, are buried with a few hundred or so men in a ravine in the southern part of the pocket. Soon these ravines will be full of snow.

33

. . . When I come to think about it, it was only here that I began to reflect on my environment, but without any positive results. One should reflect often, but it takes time. Basically, this would not be too bad, for I never had so much time as in this war, and especially here in Stalingrad. A few days ago I talked to the chaplain, and we had a long conversation together. But we did not really agree with each other, for it seemed to me that suffering is greater than the possibility of assuaging it. The chaplain thought that there we had reached a point where philosophy has to end and religion begin. One of us is surely right. But I ask myself: what difference does it make? I am continually thinking; I brood and sit in my bunker for hours.

Most esteemed Herr Geheimrat! We have no need to discuss private matters, and I am very glad not to be involved in family ties like my comrades. Those surely must be terrible and torturing thoughts, which could drive a man to despair. Those perpetual anxieties about wife and child and whatnot. Every day I hear what they are talking about; sometimes it is tragic, sometimes ridiculous to see how seriously they take everything, most of all themselves. Some talk about their business and wonder if their houses are damaged, others are full of worries about their packages on the way to and from home. And I pondered what those packages leaving Stalingrad could possibly contain. A fellow from Lüdenscheid who is stationed with me asks in every letter about his cat! Grotesque! Money, job, position, property. But above all the fear about their personal fate. And they write about this fear in many of their letters. I feel disgusted when I see how they behave.

Just an hour ago, a captain who shares the bunker with me asked if I had heard of the Russian breakthrough in the north. As if that could change the situation. Everywhere they are pulling together towards the center of the pocket, but the haste with which they do so raises the suspicion that they are looking for a way out. But there is no way out that they would find acceptable. Their thinking and their common sense, insofar as they have any, is destroyed by fear. And they don't even notice how ridiculous and unmanly their behavior is.

My field of vision extends only about a hundred yards and covers approximately a hundred men. They are all alike; namely, cowardly. Once in a while someone comes slithering down the hill or limping from the front line. And starts shaking his head in wonder when he sticks his nose in here. With these people here we cannot win a war, let alone this war. It's lucky that the men on the line behave differently from this pitiful bunch of leftover staffs with their confusion of functions. I ask myself what kind of role I ought to be playing. Am I brave, or whatever one is to call it? Am I brave because I don't run back and forth from shelter to shelter, cackling like a scared chicken? Am I brave because I don't hunt for rumors and spread them, because I sleep well at night and don't make speeches about what I'll be doing on this or that day?

Herr Geheimrat! Stalingrad is a great education for the German people; too bad that those who are getting this object lesson will hardly be able to make use of it later. One should preserve the results. I am a fatalist. My personal needs are so small that the moment the first Russian comes in here I can pick up my bag and start walking. I won't shoot; why should I? Just to kill one or two people I don't know? I shall not even shoot myself, why should I? Would it be doing a service to anyone, perhaps Herr Hitler? I have learned more during my four months of war here than I could have learned in a lifetime, even if I lived to be a hundred. The only thing I regret is that I am compelled by circumstance to spend my last days in such wretched company.

34

. . . Nobody knows what will happen to us now, but I think this is the end. Those are hard words, but you must understand them the way they are meant. Times are different now from the day when I said good-bye and became a soldier. Then we still lived in an atmosphere which was nourished by a thousand hopes and expectations of everything turning out well in the end. But even then we were hiding a paralyzing fear beneath the words of farewell which were to console us for our two months of happiness as man and wife. I still remember one of your letters in which you wrote that you just wanted to bury your face in your hands in order to forget. And I told you then that all this had to be and that the nights in the East were much darker and more difficult than those at home.

The dark nights of the East have remained, and they have turned much darker than I had ever anticipated. In such nights one often listens for the deeper meaning of life. And sometimes there is an answer. Now space and time stand between us; and I am about to step over the threshold which will separate us eternally from our own little world and lead into that greater one which is more dangerous, yes, even devastating. If I could have made it through this war safely, I would have understood for the first time what it means to be man and wife in its true and deepest sense. I also know it now—now that these last lines are going to you.

35

. . . During the last few nights I have wept so much that it seems unbearable even to myself. I saw one of my fellow soldiers weep also, but for a different reason. He was weeping for the tanks he lost; they were his whole pride. And though I don't understand my own weakness, I do understand how a man can mourn dead war materiel. I am a soldier and I am prepared to believe that tanks are not inanimate materiel to him. But everything considered, the remarkable fact is that two men weep at all. I was always susceptible to tears. A moving experience or a noble action made me weep. It could happen in the movie theater, when I read a book, or saw an animal suffer. I cut myself off from external circumstances and immersed myself in what I saw and felt. But the loss of material goods never bothered me. Therefore, I would have been incapable of weeping about tanks which, when they ran out of gas, were used in the open steppes as artillery and thus easily shot to bits. But seeing a fine man, a brave, tough and unyielding soldier cry like a child over them—that did make my tears flow in the night.

On Tuesday I knocked out two T-34s with my mobile anti-tank gun. Curiosity had lured them behind our lines. It was grand and impressive. Afterwards I drove past the smoking remains. From a hatch there hung a body, head down, his feet caught, and his legs burning up to his knees. The body was alive, the mouth moaning. He must have suffered terrible pain. And there was no possibility of freeing him. Even if there had been, he would have died after a few hours of torture. I shot him, and as I did it, the tears ran down my cheeks. Now I have been crying for three nights about a dead Russian tank driver, whose murderer I am. The crosses of Gumrak shake me and so do many other things which my comrades close their eyes to and set their jaws against. I am afraid I'll never be able to sleep quietly, assuming that I shall ever come back to you, dear ones. My life is a terrible contradiction, a psychological monstrosity.

I have now taken over a heavy anti-tank gun and organized eight men, four Russians among them. The nine of us drag the cannon from one place to another. Every time we change position, a burning tank remains on the field. The number has grown to eight already, and we intend to make it a dozen. However, I have only three rounds left, and shooting tanks is not like playing billiards. But during the night I cry without control, like a child. What will all this lead to?

36

. . . A year ago, your letter came to a stranger who was alone in this world. I picked it up, and during the long winter days I listened to the heartbeat which spoke to me in it: the heartbeat of the farmers and animals, the plants and the mountaintops, the thunder of the spring storm and the avalanches.

You always wrote that your letters were meant to give the "unknown soldier" stimulation, strength, courage and faith. Today, I have to tell you that I did draw stimulation, strength and even courage from them. But faith—faith in the good cause—is dead, as dead as I, together with a hundred thousand others, will be a month from now.

I am writing you today for two reasons. First, because according to military custom, the unknown soldier to whom you wrote a year ago has to give notice of his departure, which I now do. And second, because I assume that you will now begin to write to a new stranger, so as to give him strength, stimulation, and courage. And faith.

Miss Adi, this is the most important reason. One can perhaps show faith on paper, but if it is, as here in this devastated city on the Volga, put on sale and hawked around; if one realizes as one does here, that one's faith in the good cause was time needlessly wasted, then one is bound to warn everybody against persuading another to this faith!

37

. . . They told us this morning that we could write. Just once more, I say, for I know definitely that it will be the last time. You know that I always wrote to two people, two women, to the "other one" and you. And to you most infrequently. I have been very distant from you; Carola was closer to me than you during those last years. We don't want to go over how it happened and why it had to turn out that way. Today, however, when fate gives me the choice of writing to one person only, my letter goes to you, who have been my wife for six years.

It will do you good to learn that the last letter of the man whom you loved is directed to you. I simply could not manage to write Carola and ask her to give you my regards. So I am asking you, dear Erna, in this hour which contains my last wish: be generous and forgive the wrong I have done you in life. Go to her (she lives with her parents) and tell her that I owe her a great deal, and that I greet her through you, my wife. Tell her that she meant a lot to me during these last days, and that I often thought about what would happen after my return home. But tell her also that you were more to me and that, although I am very sad not to be returning home, in a way I am glad to be compelled to take this road, since it will save the three of us ghastly tortures.

Is God greater than fate? I am perfectly composed, but you don't know how difficult it is to say in one hour everything that still needs saying. There is such a vast deal still to be written, but because it is so much, one must know when to stop, take pen from paper and put it away. Just as I now put my life away.

Of my company, only five men are still around. Wilmsen among them. The others are all . . . all grown too tired. Isn't that a nice euphemism for the horror? But what is the point of talking about that now, and what good would it do you to know about it? So keep me alive in your memory as the man who recalled only at the very end that he is your husband and who asks your forgiveness; more, asks you to tell everyone you know, Carola included, that I found my way back to you at the moment which will take you away from me forever.

38

. . . I wanted to write you a long letter, but my thoughts constantly disintegrate like houses which collapse under shellfire. I still have ten hours, then this letter has to be turned in. Ten hours is a long time for people who are waiting, but short for those in love. I am not nervous at all. Actually, it is here in the East that I have for the first time become really healthy; I don't have colds and sniffles any more; that is the only good the war has done me. It gave me something else, the realization that I love you. It is strange that people value things only when they are about to lose them. The vast distance is spanned by the bridge from heart to heart. By that bridge I wrote you about our daily round and the world in which we live here. I meant to tell you the truth when I returned, and then we would never have talked about the war again. Now you will learn the truth beforehand, the last truth. Now I can write no more.

As long as there are shores, there will always be bridges. We should have the courage to walk on them. One bridge leads to you, the other to eternity; at the very end they are the same for me.

Tomorrow I shall set foot on the last bridge. That is the literary way of saying "death," but as you know, I always liked to express things figuratively, because I took pleasure in words and sounds. Give me your hand, so that crossing it won't be so hard.

39

. . . Dearest Father, the division has been trimmed down for the big battle, but the big battle won't take place. You will be surprised that I write to you and in care of your office. But what I have to say in this letter can only be said among men. You will transmit it to Mother in your own way. The word is out that we can write today. For one familiar with the situation that means that we can do it just once more.

You are a colonel, my dear Father, and a member of the general staff. So you know what this means, and I needn't go into explanations which might sound sentimental. This is the end. It will last perhaps another week, I think, then the game's up. I do not want to look for reasons which one could marshal for or against our situation. The reasons are now altogether unimportant and pointless. But if I am to say anything about them, it is this: Do not look to us for an explanation of the situation, but to yourselves and to the man[10] who is responsible for it. Don't knuckle under—you, Father, and all those who think like you. Be on guard, so that a greater disaster does not overtake our country. The hell on the Volga should be a warning to you. I beg you, don't brush off this experience.

And now a remark about the present. Of the whole division only 69 men are still in fighting condition. Bleyer is still alive, and so is Hartlieb. Little Degen lost both his arms; he will probably be in Germany soon. It is also the end for him. Ask him for any details you would like to know. D—— has lost all hope. I would like to know what he is thinking at times of the situation and its consequences. We still have two machine guns and 400 rounds of ammunition. One mortar and ten shells. Besides that, only hunger and fatigue. Without waiting for orders, Berg broke out with twenty men. Better to know in three days how things will end, than in three weeks. Can't blame him.

And now to personal matters. You can be sure that everything will end decently. It is a little early at thirty, I know. No sentiments. Handshake for Lydia and Helene. Kiss for Mother (be careful, old man, think of her heart trouble), kiss for Gerda, regards to all the rest. Hand to helmet, Father. First Lieutenant—respectfully gives notice of departure.

Autumn 1961

10. Hitler.

Part Three

Essays

A Cambodian Diary

Joseph Bennett

August 1969

Approached from either side, the country is an oasis of quiet and contentment in the midst of an America-wracked area. To the west is the harsh cacophony of Bangkok with its screaming tires, its traffic jams, its blaring Miami hotels, its hordes of restless GIs on leave, surging the pavement, renting cars—Bangkok a vast jukebox, gimcrack plaster temples, miles of whores—military vehicles everywhere, the consciousness of American power cresting higher and higher, in a total aimlessness, seeking some vast combustion . . . the planes streaking overhead . . .

From this exercise in the dynamics of waste and the havoc of sensibility, the destruction of composure, of analysis, of stance, the unbalancing of poise—the Pentagon relaxing in Las Vegas, the astronauts on holiday . . . to drop down from the skies in a peaceful little airliner marked "Royal Air Cambodge," and to drop into that "royaume," is to awaken in green fields, beside murmuring brooks, from a nightmare, and to be told and to be comforted that it was all a dream, that it wasn't true; there can't be a Bangkok, there is no America; America is still tree-shaded, the first automobiles, perhaps, being tested on rural roads in Ohio—

To have an artist for a ruler is a novel experience for a nation, even a small one—we are familiar with Nero's histrionics, with Churchill's easel, with Eisenhower's palette; are aware that Hitler was once a sign painter—Mao a female impersonator on the classical stage—of all these Nero alone had ambitions of professional status, wept over his accomplishments—the others, a means of relaxation, or an earlier method of making a living—

His Highness Prince Norodom Sihanouk, uniting in his person the royal lines of Sisowath and Norodom, claiming descent from the Khmer kings who fled from Angkor to escape the Siamese incursions of the fifteenth century, the two royal families settling in the plain of the Mekong and then finally, prodded by the French, by this little stupa on a hillock by a bend where the Tonle Sap is joined to the all-flooding Mekong—hoping that history will ignore them—

The Siamese to the west the traditional enemy, gnawing, devouring, pushed in turn by the demonic Burmese warlords; to the east, the Chinese in their Annamese form, less disturbing, more debilitated—the royal families, all descended from King Ang-Duong, were taken up and made much of by the French, who, using Siam as a neutral stretch of ground for their struggle with the British colonial power, in 1907 wrested the western part of the Khmer territories from the Siamese at the conference table.

This was ostentatiously restored to the Sisowaths and the Norodoms; and since it contained the ancient Khmer capital of Angkor, once again, after five hundred years, the Khmers had a consciousness of national and dynastic identity.

Sihanouk had an excellent education and returned to Cambodia a devotee of the beaux arts.

His portrait greeted you in the small, relaxed airport buildings; there was an intimacy among the staff, a familial relationship—quiet, calm, happy, and effortless—papers were meant to be stamped, not pored over or puzzled out—the important thing was the smile—no American military were allowed in the country, no representative or employee of American government, there was no embassy or legation—all believed in serenity, in a tenor of life, no struggle—a well-regulated kingdom.

From the secluded, sylvan, inactive (no American airlines) airport, a miniature bus set out alone on the lonely road.

Automobiles seemed to have been abolished; there were bicycles and carts, a few lorries; the trees arched overhead, leaves rustled—where were the clogged superhighways leading to the Bangkok airport? There seemed to be one or two factories, inactive, deserted, entrepôts of brick and lime, and then, inside the town, broad Haussmann avenues, broken into four, sometimes six, paths for vehicles through the interconnecting parallel courses of trees.

The mound, with its stupa and plaque commemorating the return of Angkor to the Norodoms and Sisowaths, rose modestly from a great circle of verdure and trees at the end of one of these placid, trafficless promenades; an occasional cycle-carriage, a single horse-cart punctuated the view. The flowers rustled.

The royal families own a few Peugeots; there are a few more for the government; the Chinese (here Vietnamese) who own the shops and control trade do not own cars; they dwell, as Chinese do throughout the southeast, in the center of the bazaars, above their godowns and shops. They will hire a cycle-carriage, for a short distance, a shade carefully drawn above their heads, their soft and sensitive skins. It is not that Prince Sihanouk officially discourages cars; it is just that there aren't any of them; there is no reason for them; employees of the American government, no matter how innocuous their function, are prohibited from entering the country.

Note that the diplomats refrain from using their own vehicles, except for official functions. All respect the Prince's desire to keep his manicured garden capital free of exhaust gases and the snarl of the internal combustion engine; he wants the flowers to grow, the children to breathe. Vespas and motorbikes are his special dislike, sources of pollution and racket, immense harm in small packages, reminders of that Japan he found so disturbing on his sole visit. Composure is everything. No one is hurried. Can this be a dictatorship?

Japanese goods are not flaunted. Japanese transistors do not blare out rock music and news; there are no glitter-yarn shirts. There is not even any press. Once a week a French-language bulletin gives snippets of information from the world outside; many of these are encomiastic references to Peking or to that lovable, sweet-tempered, sugar-coated, toothsome sweetheart-of-the-masses, the former female impersonator of the Chinese classical theater, Mao Tse-tung, who has one of the tree-lined Champs-Élysées French avenues named after him: Rue de Mao Tse-tung.

Thus filtered out, the world recedes; what is happening in Cambodia? Prospects for the rice harvest, new outrages: another downed American plane on the Cambodian side of the border. There is the schedule of the dance rehearsals and recitals for the week at the Palace, where his mother the Queen (a Sisowath) resides. He is only a Prince. There are the plans of his niece, the prima ballerina of the Royal Ballet, for the next full-moon performances at Angkor. The Prince can occasionally be seen, rushing in his Peugeot, to the new multi-unit hotel he is building by the Quatre-Bras of the rivers, each individual unit in traditional gilded Cambodian, peaked temple-roof style. There will of course be no Muzak in the hotel; one or two musicians, traditionally garbed, will be on hand with padded sticks to strike odd tones from a set of gongs duplicating those in his mother's palace.

No Western radio music is allowed: the sole radio station for the country strikes these same gongs at all times of day, interspersed with temptress-voiced singsongs of ancient Cambodian folktales couched in the phraseology of the former Khmer court, kings strutting on high terraces of Angkor temples; and the soft, effortless music that accompanies the universal village steps of the Ram Vong, where the couples circle, shuffling, but never touch.

There is no news, not even of Mao Tse-tung, who is expected to be contented with his Avenue and behave as a properly propitiated demon. The Prince, whose mother's father preceded him as King, wants nothing discordant. He supervises the gilding of each temple-peaked point on the roofs of his hotel. He did not build his beautiful capital to be corroded and soiled by the fumes of the internal combustion engine, its umbrella-shielded orange monks to be stricken at their meditations and their strolling by its crackle. The Chinese embassy, prudently, grateful for its Mao-avenue, walks or uses cycle-carriages; the Chinese have no individual cars.

There are few jails in Cambodia, laid to the fact that the French built no schools; thus the Khmers did not learn enough to want something enough (a motor, a radio) to steal it; it is a rice-exporting country, thus everyone has more than enough to eat; the Chinese (Vietnamese) do all the storekeeping (how degrading, how tedious, impossible to keep standing at it) chores, what is there to buy (no Japanese watches are allowed in), therefore why steal money from the Chinese (no Khmers have money) since they have nothing in their stores for you to buy with the money? A few kerosene lamps, and stoves, textiles from France—

Banned is the Seiko, the thick, heavy day-and-date automatic watch; banned also is the instruction of the Japanese martial arts: no karate, no judo. The youngsters grow up knowing only a little Thai-style kickboxing. There are no firearms—the so-called army, productive of generals of the Sisowath and Norodom families, can scarcely get a bullet inside its guns. Unofficially the dictator prefers the "troops"—a gang of harmless, wandering peasants—to exercise with blanks.

Sometimes prisoners forget to leave jail, form an attachment to the cook; or jailers forget to watch them, leaving the door open. They wander out to their families, have another baby, wander back at mealtimes.

Gauloises are preferred, but American cigarettes trickle in through the borders. A whole village will suddenly sport GI green gear, sturdy new expensive clothing, captured by the Viet Cong or pried loose from PX stores. In the center of the riverbank monumental avenue, a pile of crashed American plane-fuselage-junk, and tank-junk, and artillery-junk, growing daily, makes an impressive sight for the Chinese embassy to comment upon and write to Mao about; Cambodia suffering under the heel of the American oppressor.

Mao is his problem, Sihanouk is after all a monarch; Mao was not very sympathetic to the survivors of the Ch'ing dynasty; its senior member, the last of the Manchus, washes floors in Shanghai and makes public confessions; the family of Bao Dai, "Empereur d'Annam," are proscribed as enemies of the revolution. Sihanouk waves his Gauloises. He wears excellently tailored suits.

Each year the Queen comes to life with the Reversal of the Waters. This is when Mother has her moment. Kept in storage the rest of the time (someone, alive and real, has to be used for living in the palace), smiling at dance recitals, encouraging all her great-nieces to take up ballet, she seems to have been made into the Spirit of the Mekong. During the rainy season, the south-flooding Mekong thrusts its waters northward up into the channel of the Tonle Sap, swelling its lake to triple the normal size. Regulated by the full moon at the end of October and the beginning of November, the Mekong, when the Queen speaks to it, bobbling on Her Floating House, reverses itself and begins to flow southward again, back down the Tonle Sap, in its normal direction. The waters have subsided, the rains have ended. The Quatre-Bras, where this hydraulic drama takes place, is before her palace, and she is annually hoisted out on her great gilt throne and placed on Her Floating House, to remain there until the water is duly returning.

Her portrait is everywhere, cross-ankled on that gilded throne. Can one imagine Stalin's mother, or Hitler's, or Franco's, in every tobacco shop, smiling, and once a year in charge of the local equivalent of May Day?

Prince Sihanouk's wife is an actress; the film festival, organized by Sihanouk and with himself on the panel of judges, has awarded the prize to films produced and directed by His Highness and starring his Princess Monique, in each year of its two-year existence.

There are the "auberges royales," architectural (and heavily traditionalist) caprices of his younger days; an attempt has been made to make them into hotels. One, at Siem Reap, is Rockefeller Center modern in feeling, with rooms modeled on that of an airport of the 1930s; the Marine Air Terminal at LaGuardia gives an idea of what was in mind. On the treeless heights of Bokor, 3,200 feet above the sea, is a hewn-stone, rustic, iron grillwork villa, a tropical ski lodge two thousand miles from the nearest snow. No one ever seems to have stayed there, and now the traveler is forced to sleep in a few grisly rooms above a lugubrious casino where the Chinese shopkeepers of Phnom-Penh eat greasy Chinese food and play at dice and roulette. But at Kep (charming, French colonial, reminiscent of a Biscay summer resort) the bungalows use as their restaurant a fine, open, airy colonnaded pavilion, in Beaux-Arts style, perfectly suited to the view, terrain landscaped all the way to the sea.

Bungalows, bungalows, bungalows—before his obsession with individual, gilded, Cambodian peaked-roof temples for tourists, the Prince felt they should have bungalows, not individual (except at Kep) but connected, highly utilitarian, heavily plumbed, disturbingly and thrashingly air-conditioned. When he realized that he had a gold mine at Angkor (accompanying the pale, fragile nun, renouncer of the world, tragedy-afflicted Mrs. Onassis), he decided he could make them pay for his personal taste as well; they would sleep on Cambodian temple-styled beds if he so wished. There was no reason too why tourists should not enjoy Sihanouk-made films; one of these was shown every night at Angkor just before the Prince's niece began her ballet across the way; another was of the ballet itself.

The Phnom-Penh museum is room after room of carefully labeled sculptures; detailed monographs of each section of the collection come off the press. Nobly housed in a red palace in purest peaked-roof style, the museum is allowed no electricity; all must be seen naturally. There are no guards, no watchers, no latrines; a lone typewriter clicks sporadically in some research office far off to the side. Like the Cairo museum (untouched for political reasons), the Phnom-Penh museum shows what can be done to instruct the seeker after knowledge when there are no glamorously high-paid theatrical, narcissistic personalities constantly shaking it up, issuing earsets, suppressing detailed historical labelings, and keeping the bulk of the collections in the basement so that the selected items can be mounted singly as if for open-air elephant-assisted performances of grand opera. The curator actually did spend his time adding items to the collection and lining them up side by side; he never had a "happening" in his museum; there is not even a toilet, much less a tearoom.

The minibus threading the vast, empty avenues, with its eye on the spire of the stupa, ducked in among the trees; an Australian or two got out; we were at the hotel, a heavy, outflung construction of French colonial days, at one time very stately quarters for senior French military officers. Here a shallow, warm swimming pool was set down in the back with several couples of sophisticated Parisian young moderns, slipping back and forth between argots; they were not tourists, they had no interest in archaeology. Plop! one dives into the pool, nearly breaking his nose on the bottom, which is five feet at most; the others cheer derisively. They are always there during the hot hours.

The sun slants down over the Phnom; the trees rustle, the flowers sparkle—one glides down the vast avenue, as down the arcades of a forest, noiseless, around the darkening mound with its stupa, admiring the bright terra-cottas with which the French commemorated the return of Angkor to the Norodoms and Sisowaths—one can climb that stupa of the Phnom, through a side garden, and then descend the eastern approach, with its Angkor naga serpents carved in stone on the rails, and on past an ornate, embowered royal building to the riverfront. There is a vast bridge, too far to the north to be of use to anyone, leading nowhere, another monument to the Prince, built with the hopeful funds of some friendly, rich power.

There is the Independence Monument, one of the *meru* towers of Angkor Wat placed atop the Arc de Triomphe, on Norodom Sihanouk Avenue, next to the Norodom Sihanouk museum; this last filled exclusively with gifts made to the Chief of State, stamp collections, autographed photos.

But the greatest monument to the Prince's diplomacy was Sihanoukville, with its highway, built with $35,000,000 in American funds. The Cardamom chain cuts off Phnom-Penh, a river port, from the sea. Sihanoukville provided an artificial harbor, capable of unloading four modest-sized freighters at once. The first freighters to berth at the port were not US, but Mao Chinese. As soon as he had the key to the port in his pocket, the ungrateful Prince expelled the American ambassador, closed the embassy, and in effect diverted the port and its 135-mile highway to the purpose of supplying the Viet Cong with arms. The four small ships were always unloading there, brimful of tanks and guns, while others waited their turn offshore. The flags tended to be British, though the supplies came from Canton and Shanghai and Odessa; another problem for the beleaguered Washingtonians.

How did Sihanouk survive? His problem was Mao: as helpless a plaything in Mao's paws as Hong Kong or Macao, he had to prove the usefulness of his independence to the ex-theatrical transvestite. What was the point of tying up divisions of Hanoi troops to hold the country down (the Khmers hate the Annamese-Vietnamese almost as much as they hate the Siamese) when the grateful and obliging Prince would get the port built at US expense and keep it free and open for the flood of supplies to reach the Viet Cong effortlessly and safely? As the Prince pointed out in Peking and Hanoi, if they took over his country, the Americans would quickly bomb into uselessness the vulnerable artificial port, open on a flat peninsula, and the deeply rock-cut highway. The compromise was arrived at: the supplies flowed through the port and the highway to the east to the Viet Cong; and the rest of the country remained free, adoring their Samdech for so cleverly preserving them. For their part, the Viet Cong remained strictly within the boundaries of the territory assigned them in the east and did not engage in political activity.

Wise also, the Prince, in not creating an army, merely a few thousand stumbling, well-fed peasants to provide an excuse for distributing generalships to the royal houses. Had he established a military force, Mao would have moved, for the possibility of its use by the Americans would then become a factor. By this means, a miraculous set of external political circumstances acted to confirm the already non-militant nature of the Khmers and make their country one as if shaded by an orange parasol from the destructive turmoil and violence of the American satellites to the west and east. Thus not even karate or judo. Thus the pile of American military junk, constantly being added to, on the riverbank boulevard. Especially favored were the tailpieces of American planes, with resplendently repainted USAF markings, and helicopter rotor vanes, khaki green. This was to convince the nodding and approving, hand-rubbing and contented Mao diplomats that all was well, that the dutiful Khmers were seizing the naughty American war-folk who strayed over.

As well, the happy Khmers were preserved from contact with nonuniformed employees of the US Government, saved from having a US Embassy gassing away its motor fumes and portentous bumptious pettifoggery, its Congressmen and libraries, its photos of astronauts, its masters of the democratic style of social greeting. Mao would have become suspicious and closed in. Not even an agriculture expert, a public health official, or a cultural lecturer could get past the barrier. The Khmer tradition was enforced and purified by the shadow of Mao and Hanoi. French, too, remained the language.

The whores, lovely slit-skirt Chinese (never Khmer) butterflies, featuring black silk and skins whitened with powder, long black hair, confined themselves discreetly to the ambience of the Café de Paris and the Venise—they were luxury whores, tinkling in their French, and witty and gentle and regulated. They were not allowed to have drinks; they did not appear on the streets, swaying blaring transistor radios (Bangkok, Saigon); they were visible only at night. A lower echelon, equally well regulated, fluttered to nest in the evening in the two floating restaurants on the river, much favored by the Australian do-gooders and helpers, who were unused to such simplicity and refinement. Arrangements were subtle, discreet, and sufficiently clandestine; nothing could be noticed. A smile, the departure of a couple to a villa distant, dimly lit among trees.

The Australians on these aid-to-Cambodia (dams, health, electricity, seeds) missions were overwhelmed; most had never seen Europe; most had been married young to mates selected for health, strength, and good character. They began to disguise the dates of their home leaves; the place to spend one's home leave was in a villa; none of these charming creatures would think of being exposed to the glaring public entranceway of the hotel, though there were bungalows—

The hotel, in its bulk, featuring large and solid suites that had been the quarters of the military French, had in all twenty flimsy, jerry-built bungalows thickly massed flank-to-flank in the area of that warm pool, with its expensive and uninspired restaurant (the sophisticated Parisians used it only for breakfast and sandwiches). I learned which of the two exits (east-west) was the most private, which bungalows had the best furniture, which the most rooms. Night-butterflies could occasionally be seen, faces muffled and veiled, only the white skin, or a jewel in the hair, or a flower visible.

These lovely creatures disdained any Australian who drank, who smoked, or who raised his voice. Quickly the Australians learned to emulate the young poolside sophisticated Parisians, and at night the twittering of the lovely spidery creatures in and out of all twenty bungalows was as natural and delightful a sight as the nocturnal egress of night-flying birds from their daytime homes inside the vast four-faced ruins of Angkor. They would not enter automobiles, whether to arrive or leave, too public—the noise of motors, the glare of lights, the clack of doors, the noise of the starter. The carriages waited in files, silently. These ladies were skilled and took pride in their professional accomplishments, insisted upon high health standards; the portrait of our *Samdech* which each bungalow contained over its dresser looked down on extraordinary scenes when successful, middle-aged high-income Australian officials became debutants in acts so far unknown in the temperate Antipodes.

The carriage glides along the riverbank, and it is sunset. Where in other Asian countries most government employees are set at desks, to confound and confuse, here the bureaucrats seem to have been liberated at their various salary levels, so that all can become gardeners—literally, it is true, the Government offices (my constant one: Ministère de Sécurité Nationale) are almost understaffed. The royal families are supposed to become generals, not bureaucrats. So this vast sea of flowers undulates along the riverbank after one leaves the Port des Bateaux—there is a "Port de Phnom-Penh": it handles goods coming down the Mekong from Kratie and the north and river steamers.

The long and graceful lines of the Queen's moderately sized palace rise up in the dark; people are walking in small groups along the river; there is not a motor in sight to the south or the north along this huge planted esplanade. . . .

But there is a Chinese (Vietnamese) population as well—all those shops are owned and manned; the retail, the wholesale trade of the country is in their hands. To satisfy them, well out of the Queen's angle of view to the south, the Casino pulsates with light, surrounded by food stalls. Inside the same Chinese faces pore over the crushingly lighted gambling tables as in Bangkok and Saigon, Singapore and Hong Kong; this is the only recreation the Chinese allows himself, a holiday of the abacus, an amusement based on calculation; never sports or physical exercise. Their lusts are short and sharp, like the opening and clicking of a shutter camera, behind their lensed glasses, and they are lusts of money, briefly revealed. No Khmer faces (broad foreheads, wide cheekbones) are in the Casino—the Khmers are too poor; they are mainly dancers and flute players, gong ringers; they don't like bright lights, only faint single flame lamps flickering out of doors reflect their faces, listening to soft dissonances. The Chinese inside the Casino move like automatons, greeting, calculating each other, spotlessly clean; with clothing carefully pressed and creased; no dust on their shoes, for they will not walk, even more than a hundred feet outside their shops.

In Phnom-Penh as the river turns black the wind seems to push you forward; the horns of the Queen's prang-roofed palace now stand out against the dry stars; star-fields appear. A Chinese temple near the foot of the monumental bridge goes bang-out with explosions and rockets, crackers and sparklers; the staid merchants alight from their carriages; ignite their incense sticks; rotate their wheels; revere their ancestors. The temple yard mills with Khmer poor, ragged and bright; there seems no reason not to go around the river parks all night. Next day in the town there are sidewalk cafes everywhere, with the round tables of Paris; tea, coffee, the pressed citron, in the busiest quarters, by the markets; one watches the life; there is great sweetness in the air.

A long Peugeot station wagon, with the customary eleven passengers, lumbers beside the Tonle Sap River for the five hours' run to Siem Reap; one eats dried lotus heads at the ferry; none of the villages on the route have been disturbed or harmed. Crossing at last a carved stone snake-balustraded bridge built by the monarch of the Bayon and Angkor Thom, one enters the Angkor country. The whirr of the Prince's air conditioners grips one in its deep freeze; the bungalows are utilitarian luxury and situated in the high silk-cotton trees. A dining room clatters with the voices of all Europe, seen from the outside.

I stumble out in the dark. There are no lights across the road. There is a wide, vast, endless moat. A raised causeway leads across it. This is very long. Then there are difficult steps up onto a stone porch.

On the other side, through the stone porch, one stumbles downward. All light from the road has been cut off by the great closed length of the porch. I blunder ahead. An endless causeway leads on and on, snakes wriggling in stone as balustrades to either side; occasionally, seven heads, arranged fan-shaped, arise to ornament it. Dim small buildings, like islands, rise up from the empty lakes to either side. Far off, high up, is a tiny light, flickering, yellowish in the darkness. Stars punctuate.

A corner of the red rising moon stares out from the shoulder of the black hill ahead. I am walking down the full distance of the causeway, and the moon moves out further and further to the right; it is free of the hilltop and strong, vastly distant. I fall under the shadow of a long high portico stretching to either side. I am up against some steps, hard and high, uneven and treacherous. Under the portico, small courts to either side, smudged with starlight, heavily galleried with stone. Up and up. Another court, squeezed together, short, obliterated by the huge mass overhanging it, small raised buildings to either side.

The final stairs hit your nose, colossal, meant for a race of gods.

With the four other high ghostly towers at the corners of the topmost court, the central tower overhangs the earth like a celestial plane. It is a surface bearing the gods, and their servants, the kings, above all that level of unlighted, intersected rice fields.

The courts at the top begin to form shadows in the moonlight. The cusps ascending the towers begin to take form. In the rice fields the heads of sheaves rise and stir. The sandstone, deeply carved, resists the moonlight. The core of this monument is sand, held in, incompressible, by stone embankments and blocks. If the sand spreads out at the base, the roofs, the cloud city will collapse.

Now down the long descending galleries and steps, the passages, the stairs meant for giants. The public was barred; the rice cultivators worshipping the kings above. The Khmer deities spoke in elevated tones, addressing each other across vast stages, referring in elaborate circumlocutions only to the most dry and uplifting subjects: narrations of their ancestry from the gods; of the assistance of Krishna in battle; of their hurling axes, their chariots, their horses, their fire processions. On these platforms, amid such elocutions, they moved beneath ceremonial parasols, held by highly placed priestly relatives.

It was a short trip, swayed over by long-handled, bending fans, from temple to wooden palace and palace to temple again.

The delicate, airy light buildings of their residence were set up on piles, among the cool, high trees, surrounding ornamental lakes, tiered with water plants and fish carven in stone.

The moon is rising outside. It leads away, along the long pool, the shape of Angkor Wat across the water receding huge and hollow with gray detail, defined in the glare. It leads along the road into the forest. There is a high mound, touched by moonlight, to the left.

Across an immense moat, huge solid walls rise, endless in the distance. It is Angkor Thom, an enormous, moonstruck city. The moon seems to have heat, beating down on this empty metropolis, this cubic jungle fortress.

The great gate looms; above its corbel the front face is crowned with a high, receding tower. The east and west faces appear in sharp profile of nose and eyes and lips. The Bodhisattva of the current cycle, Avalokiteshvara, extends the protection of his gaze. His faces are everywhere the same; the faces too of the broad-browed, flat-cheeked Khmer peasants of the region. Elephants feed on stone lotuses on each side of the gate, their sculptured trunks dipping low to sway over this celestial fodder.

The long central roadway leads forward, inside the walls, under the archway of the high trees.

The grayishness, the whitishness ahead takes on a slight blur, a slight complication; there is a subtle darkness within the whiteness. It is a low mass, rising above the trees, with a tower or cone, all whitish-gray, scarcely distinguishable in the white haze which drowns all contours.

Dimly the faces begin to appear, lower down. The building is long, with a central tower; the smaller towers sprout with faces seeing in all four directions. It is Avalokiteshvara, guarding the city, at its heart. Axes radiate to the four walls and the five gates.

This cathedral of protection is tied to the human; the preservative, the paternal, are sought by this Buddhist monument. These gentle faces of death offer recourse, soundlessly from their stone lips. Annulling reassurances, deadening of pain; a vast, multiple, gray-stone anesthesis.

A mile to the east, at the gate of the dead, the same faces stare out. Those who go out of the city carried on pairs of shoulders are reassured, as they are burnt in the jungle; their smoke arising as the scent of perfume to the blank lips. To lose identity beneath the devouring horizontal gaze.

Here at the Bayon we are at the heart of the realm of the weeping king, Jayavarman, and his ameliorating four-faced god; it is very late, almost at the end of empire. In the reliefs below, the King destroys the fleets and armies of the Chams; but above, the stone faces of Avalokiteshvara proclaim: it is vain, it is vain.

On the moon-viewing platforms one wanders at the base of the face-studded thick spires. Black lichens cover plump noses, thick lips, staring out smiling into a jungle which steams with moonlight. The trees, with dry, immobile leaves, rise high around the clearing. One looks out at the bright, foaming jungle, listening for the call of a bird, which does not come. The cold black stone lips rise, waiting to be kissed, in the flashing sky.

Jayavarman, who made this, sits softly in the Phnom-Penh museum, late Egyptian, smiling, Saite, of the period of the delta invasions. His platform was not meant for day viewing. The trees crackle, soundlessly, in the light; their hazy density, million-leaved, shimmers like dry snow.

Returning, one sees Angkor Wat arise from its sea, black, blocking out the sky. The superhuman dimension crushes, of this Hindu archaeological skyscraper. Angkor Wat never wholly returned to the jungle; monks kept coming, bringing Buddha statues. The peasants went to its summit in times of peril.

In the Phnom-Penh museum, the statue of Lokeshvara, that looked out from the Gate of the Dead to the smoke of the burning places, concentrates inward, savoring the thoughts of polarized divinity. Along with the statue of Jayavarman, these carvings were taken erect, square-shouldered, through the moonlit jungle, on a journey over roads and lakes, to sit in the wooden, prang-roofed palace, in a quiet, somnolent city of slow vehicles and wide parks. The statues, accustomed to gaze over the jungle, over those wisps of smoke, dominate the museum, burgeoning with suppressed moonlight; their silence becomes overpowering.

Back at the foot of Angkor Wat, troubled by the gigantesque, the tiny lights of the Prince's bungalows twinkle. In a few hours I am back out again, in the trees, prepared for heat. The pedals and chain of my bicycle creak; the trees are monotonous, the road vibrates with heat. At last, the road swings to the left, past ruined towers of brick, and I approach the sheet of water of Sras Srang, terraced and lion-surmounted, serpent-railed.

A woman sits across the road from the long side of the lake, selling food and tea; behind her, stretching back from the road, is a group of houses. They are wooden, raised on stilts, covered with palm thatch; sleeping mats of coconut straw; two wooden chairs, the best of which is permanently occupied by the mother of the food-vendor, corpulent, nodding, inarticulate. Cooking is done on the ground below; sanitation is among the trees. The grandmother is house-owner and owner of their small strip of rice field. The grandfather and father are dead; the house is a matriarchy; the work of the rice field is done by a grown grandson and the mother and sisters; this is the heart of the dry season; there is no work to do.

I want to shift from the Prince's bungalows with their clatter of languages. The Japanese guests wear kimonos and bathe, interminably, in their rooms. They are not popular, in spite of their heavy expenditure and full use of every rentable auxiliary, their constant requirement for guides. The occupation was harshly severe, and since the Japanese were committed to their Thai allies, the Khmers were identified as an inferior, subject race. The Japanese, before Pearl Harbor, in March 1941, awarded the western part of Cambodia to their Siamese allies; and in 1942, all of Laos; the Siamese, who had been driven out in 1907, once again occupied Angkor. In 1907, the Khmers tore down the citadel which the Siamese built in the center of Siem Reap with stones taken from the staircases of the Phnom Bakheng, a ninth-century temple; in 1941 they saw the Siamese return in full concert with their Japanese allies. Following this, the Japanese awarded Thailand the four northern states of Malaysia and the two eastern Shan states of Burma.

Japan is no longer the Thai military ally; instead, Thailand has the United States in its place; together, the two partners work at the grand design of pacifying Indo-China. Cambodia, squeezed between the twin American outposts of Bangkok and Saigon, sees the Japanese and the Thais, who raped it in World War II, now the favored pets of American power; it sees the Japanese returning, not as warlords to set them at forced labor in construction gangs in the death-jungles of West Thailand (the Burma railway) and Tongking (the Red River above Hanoi), but as luxurious lords of creation who live in the fine hotels surrounded by expensive appliances and treated with deference by the swarms of servitors of the tourist industry.

Of all the Asian national groups, only the Thais were able to profit from the full favor and protection of their Japanese allies, followed by heavy subsidization from America. Switching away from Japan just in time in 1945; since 1952, convincing Washington that the Korean problem was being duplicated in Hanoi, they have made Thailand the funnel for pouring untold quantities of money into the Indo-China pacification. The corrupt and heavy-handed military dictatorship in Thailand is skilled in only one accomplishment: extracting money from its frightened, gargantuan, lavish, and helpless ally in Washington. Individual fortunes among the generals, in Switzerland, vary from twenty to a hundred million dollars. When games of dominoes are mentioned, it is Bangkok that is meant that might fall.

At Sras Srang the family of Oeur Sam Bath shelters me. Excursions spring up: to the great lake, with its fishponds and stilt villages; to the vastness of the northern jungle; to a pool from which arises an immense lotus of stone and a flying horse to whom cling those it saves; this is Avalokiteshvara. Sunsets are followed by dinner in Siem Reap as the moon gets older and more feeble; the Apsara restaurant turns out to be the place where the good cooking is; small, an exterior blackboard, and giant winged cockroaches, like bullets, which roar directly into your mouth and eyes, falling on your plate. I return to the great monuments later at night; then it becomes necessary to view them in starlight, and a new, more delicate effervescence is detected.

More and more I come to live in the ruins, watching the change of light, becoming a troglodyte. At Ta Prohm the four faces have umbrellas . . . of trees sprouting above their heads; slender tendrils of vines attach themselves with tiny adhesive feelers, shooting across lintels and sticking there; then digging in deeper and deeper, etching their lines through the stone balustrades of the windows, wearing themselves through the noses and chins and tiara-headdresses of Apsara maidens. Stones are lifted and cracked off their bases; the green gloom turns to black. Then to walk back without a cycle to my stilt-house from the fading, inking, undersea labyrinth, along a road shared by a shepherd of thin brown ducks (controlled by a long slender wand, with a rag at its end, held by an infant of five)—to walk beside the water-sheet, gazed at by tall-forelegged lions, of Sras Srang—to eat rice at the roadside stand—not to go into the leisurely, Frenchified rhythm of dances and restaurant at Siem Reap—this is to find the even level of peasant life.

Then to sit by the lions of Sras Srang and watch the stars press their light on that slowly shrinking basin, the grandeur of the day forgotten, the gods put to sleep without a moon, gazing alone into their jungle through the veil of vines and branches—

A return to Phnom-Penh; an exploration of the west bank of the river. Even though it is the dry season, the Mekong is full and miles wide. In the villages, the idleness of the dry season; the only motor sound is an occasional chug as an antiquated, dwarfed river steamer struggles up the giant flow of the Mekong . . . time stops, the trees grow. The population is thinly scattered, even here so close to the capital; Phnom-Penh sits easily in this hinterland; there is no harsh change between city and country; the green of the forests and the rice fields becomes the green of the parks and the gardens . . .

Approached from the other side, it seems that this country is enfolded in a crystal mountain, far apart from the convulsions and unnatural tremors, like a pool of slowly boiling volcanic mud, of its neighbor to the east. In the central avenue before the Parliament, the National Assembly, rises the newly erected symbol of Saigon: two immense, roughly clad cement soldiers, full of reinforcing iron, an expression of delight on their features; helmets askew, their shoulders twist and the bodies strain their haunches above monstrous squat legs to thrust an imaginary bayonet into the entrails of thin air; the whole is a movie-palace come-on for the exhibition of a sadistic film.

All these America-created, America-obsessed cities, Tokyo, Seoul, Taipei, Bangkok, Saigon, have in common a smog that strangles and burns the lungs, product of the exhaustion of so many motors into a naturally damp, sluggish atmosphere, sitting inland in bowls where air can scarcely arrive. In Taipei, Seoul, and Saigon the filth piles up among the flashing new motors, crawling atop each other's backs, newly imported from Japan; sewage or water supply is scarcely a consideration. At the trail's end lie Las Vegas and Miami, where they all want to go when they die, living off money piled up in Switzerland.

One longs for the austerity of a Marx or an Engels, even of a Lenin; one realizes why Marx and Engels have lost; everywhere the peoples move toward electronically amplified sound, join in the giant rhythm of the motors, of speed, of elevators, the wild spurt of the demons which are exclusively Western, and for which the principles of the Revolution, and its blood, are meaningless. The communal, sharing, austere balancing of society seems ridiculous and strangling; the deferring of individual aims to a mass purpose, intolerable. In India at the temples of Puri and Konarak I am surrounded by a crowd of young Russians; they want to know about Japan, about its department stores, its escalators, its hairdressers; its motors and Hondas and Yamahas and tape recorders, its video screens and electronic doors. Because of my nationality, I am an ambassador of Las Vegas and Miami, the capitals of the future. The children have been let out of the libraries, sterile with political theory, and the factories, heavy with production of machine tools, let away from the gaze of the portraits of Lenin, to a kaleidoscope of neon and flesh and movement that must be at random, without purpose, the exhaustion of the day. There are no more enemies; there are no more classes; there is one more day. One admires the purposefulness and the focusing upon aims of the revolutionary leaders. Now, stranded by history, they are Easter Island heads above the treeless grass, their black granite heads and monumental beards (the only heritage they have left the young) are as effective a world force today as say, the teachings of Matthew Arnold or Thomas Carlyle.

Their greatness lay not in their teachings, which are probably as much rubbish as Las Vegas and Miami proclaim them to be, but in their ability to hypnotize whole populations, however briefly, into the illusion that there is such a thing as communal purpose and a justification for the organization of society. Like the experiment of Cromwell and the Roundheads, the interlude between cutting off the head of the king and the Restoration of the monarchy was very brief.

The Puritanism of the great revolutionary leaders has not survived their death; Mao's hysterical and irrational gyration is motivated by his realization that he is an anachronism, an Easter Island head left stranded by the tide. The Bible and the Handbook of Kapital alike have been forgotten.

The extraordinary thing was that, like the monsters and the miracles of the Old Testament, the text of Marx could be believed at all, so contrary is it to human nature, so demanding, so disciplining, meant for a society of martyrs and ascetics. That a doctrine of such superhuman austerity could be accepted as the formal article of belief for a large section of the world's population is one of the riddles of history, like the jihads of the Muslims, the Crusades, the diaspora of the Israelites, all examples of the power of the Book. The rise and fall of the book of Marx is another example of the power of faith to cause, for short periods of time, the masses to act contrary to their natures, their expectations, their comforts, and their amusements. The next generation finds itself deceived. That Las Vegas was to be the alternative to *Das Kapital* Marx could never have dreamed; too Puritanical and too obsessed; Sodom and Gomorrah he was aware of, but that problem had been solved, in another system. Their triumph over the theories of this bearded prophet was as the triumph of the golden calf; the people of Israel turned back to the worship of idols.

The cement statue is the focus of Saigon; whores, pimps, petty criminals, and swindlers swarm about it by day and night. The hard-faced whores on platform plastic slippers eye those lower-echelon beneficiaries of Washington's largesse who are not able to get away to Bangkok, or who have just come back. All this revenue is being drained upwards, to higher receptacles; the intake is enriching those already in power. Even for an evening the higher military will fly to Bangkok; this Saigon is not Las Vegas, merely a gate into the hall of judgment of the dead.

The whores weigh the hearts and find them worth nothing; street after street resound with the thud of artillery barrages after dark. By a river jammed with barges and steel ships one can sit, threading the barbed wire, and watch the police and the helmeted military crash by, in jeeps and armed cars and snarling motorcycles. An explosion in the distance. Tinkling of glass; no one moves. American is spoken everywhere. A hotel on the waterfront announces with banners a congress of Buddhist monks from the Buddhist countries: Ceylon, Thailand, Laos, Burma (none from Cambodia). Orange- and yellow-robed shaven heads pass by in the lobby, umbrellas folded, by the registration desk. I find one who can speak Sinhalese from the Siamese seminary in Kandy. His expenses have been paid by the US Government, with the Vietnamese Government as the paying agent; it is a cultural front for the breaking-down military machine. They waited in Bangkok, putting up at the Wats, for an idle civilian transport. They are warned not to stray from their watchful protectors, lest they be bombed, maimed, or robbed. They look on, fragile, terrified, thinking of their rice bowls in their various jungles, as lost and as high-stemmed as storks on a lake of boiling pitch.

Another hotel, advertised as the largest, the most cubical, modern, stands somewhat away from the center, on a patrolled avenue, listless Chinese at the reception. It turns out to be the temporary haven where low-ranking GIs take their whores; thus the low rates are geared to a brief occupancy. It is like a lost prison compound, or the Federal fort on the Dry Tortugas of the Florida Keys—row after row of plastered brick cells, doors slamming, cracked washbasins being banged to encourage the dribbling of faucets; the whores are blank-faced; the GIs are sullen; it is all very expensive; there is no pleasure, only mechanical relief in a process like urination; the Chinese, scrutable, rest on their chairs in the reception below, counting their receipts; their sons man the paying windows; all eyes gleaming with money, intent on the hard green currency.

The lights go off, then on; there is a dull, huge thud in the distance; two GIs relieved of their bladder pressures and their purses decide to fight; they bang briefly in one of the lower corridors of the huge hexagon but give it up; their echoes resound for a while. Their hands drop to their sides, they stand in the corridors, blank, having nowhere else to go; there is the dull clatter, and shifting, in the rooms. All wait for the tolling of some bell which will release them from present misery, but the roofs press down, squeezing the air. The senior Chinese, wisp-bearded in a jacket of braided and raised black silk, sits on his throne like Minos, describing with his tail the number of circles each must descend; they ascend to the proper ring; each enters his cell. There is no screaming. The whores are expert, lifeless. Medical stations lie in a lower circle. Whores who hope to feed (there are no dining places) with their bladder partners wait outside, while burning chemicals are applied to the animals' parts. Killing is easier than this, and more joyous, the statue with the upraised blade proclaims. The Parliament sits there like a travesty, as if discussions, dispute, voting, proposals, had any meaning. Generals pass, with slit-eyed faces, stiff, bespectacled, in staff cars, guarded. It is hard to tell which side they are on; of course they are on "our" side, but tomorrow, or tonight, they may be on the other side, if it profits. They calculate the odds, their minds, like those of their Bangkok confreres, on Switzerland.

At night, above the second most expensive hotel, the roof, formerly a pleasure resort, is just high enough to cut off the view of the statue. It is not raining, merely threatening; around the brown-glowing horizon, which must reach rice fields somewhere, electric and military flashes fan up; the dull boom goes on; there must be a war near at hand. One sleeps by this rhythm, everything double-locked and padlocked. In the marble lobby of the office building facing the statue, a tout offers to change twenty dollars at double the official rate; the wad of notes stuffed with worthless denominations is pushed into the palm; the light goes out; the men flee, grasping the $20 bill. The brown light of day outside in the smog is a different type of night; the traffic grates; motors of all sizes spit and snap and dissolve the atmosphere; the eyes and lungs burn; one longs for night to fall, real night, not this false, sweating, wavering light, drawn from somewhere deep in the pavement; the sky drops down forever.

The long avenues have the remains of trees, tall giants whose leaves are without juice or greenness, dying from fumes, the Champs-Élysées, planted by the French. Trees ringed with barbed wire; military traffic, military police pass by. In the remains of a public park are a museum, a botanical garden, a zoo, discredited and deteriorating; the few remaining animals cough in the carbon gases muffling the city. There must be rice fields, peasants, somewhere. In this asphalted area, heaving and cracking atop a lake of pitch, the vehicles crawl back and forth, mechanized, aimless, bumping against each other, and against the barrier limits which force them back, crowding their backs up on one another. A girl in an airline office, a girl in a bank, have been sheltered; how do they get from their homes to work? Small boys attempt to get their hands in one's pockets. The way back, on the military pavement, leads past the American Embassy. Like a child's castle of the knights of old it stands behind the high walls turreted at each corner; above the gates, barbicans bristling with machine guns, ever-swiveling, a GI calls out "Hi," smiling. A staff car with the eagle insignia enters. All snap to attention. Inside stands an anxious, rather prim building. Here is the true Parliament. Lesser embassies and legations are trivial, unguarded; the Australian one, tree-shaded, open to all, is run by two girls.

Newly arriving at the Saigon airport, the mere opening of the door and placing of the descent steps introduces chaos into the antiseptic mass-convenience atmosphere of the cabin. We file out into a sky buzzing with giant airlift; there is vast confusion, howling, at the entrance wickets. No one can change a check; everyone has black market notes. There is no transport; the lone rentable car approaches, scenting carrion. The hotel, a money-devouring machine, is in league with the rentable car. On the top floor of the hotel some senior US businessmen dine or have breakfast. The thudding continues.

To visit Cambodia one must have an exit permit. Another struggle with a taxi. The passport office swarms with desperate people who, until they arrived there, thought they had enough money to get out of the country. I am the only tourist. The hours pass; the closing bell is about to sound. The eyes are burning through to the pocketbooks of the suppliants. The clerks are decorative and obstructive, dreaming of their own air tickets; their function is to funnel the majority of the money away from the applicants before the squeeze is applied. The higher office waits until only the rind is left, exhausted and penniless, scarcely able to board the plane. But I do not require an escape ticket; merely an exit permit to Cambodia.

I return next day. The passport is lost. If one lives there, and knows the methods, it can all be done by a telephone call, a discreet messenger. They look at me to see what I will offer. I know the answer to this; it is that fortified building, that fairy-tale child's castle, in the center of town, with the US flag on top of it. The inner-office apologizes. The passport appears. It is the only US passport in the office.

But why would anyone want to go to Cambodia, an enemy country? No Vietnamese, no employees of the US Government are allowed in. It has been many weeks since they were asked for an exit permit to Cambodia. Why do you want to go? What is your plan? What is your work? Why do you not want to go to Bangkok?

But I am in no hurry. I have no schedule. I have fallen down another notch in the hotel scale. When they see that I can wait, when I point out that I can actually go to Bangkok, like everyone else, the passport is handed back. I have not had to pay. The stamp is in it. But they still cannot understand why I do not want to go to Bangkok; that is where they want to go; that is where everyone wants to go. What is Cambodia, just more rice fields, without any mortar fire.

Returning to the second-best hotel to eat, I see that it has features; an inner court, with tent awnings, remains of a French-trained staff; carved wooden beams and tinted glass. In cinemas one sits with hands in pockets; fingers are extracting money everywhere: money to get out, money to eat, money to build a bar for the Americans and the whores. The more beautiful, the whiter the woman's face, the more erect her carriage, the more ruthless her nature; they have a gift for business. They are sharp and clutching; these are business-women; they are desperate.

No one can sleep; the women fill up with barbiturates; wake up again, and watch their bars and restaurants and taxi-fleets. The brown and scaling wart throbs and throbs; it cannot stop heaving and moving and breathing in its fumes; it will not sleep ever but watches and waits. The Americans will not lose, they are counting on that; they have their money on it; else there would be no shops or bars or whore-operators; the money would then all be in Switzerland.

But it earns such high returns here; just a little more, just a little more time, while it can earn, only part being siphoned off; besides, the American presidents are both on their side. When a rocket comes in, near the center, no one hears it until the heavy crash; there is a hole in the pavement; gutted trucks and buildings. Badly guided, coming from a distance, they don't seem to hit anything important. Viet Cong creep in and bomb a city street, kill a policeman, a few whores, try to get a general. The Catholics, French-educated, French-protected, are the ruling class; their prudence is to have half their money outside the country; the earning half, inside, gives them their local living, and its profits are drained abroad. Taxes, by a series of stratagems, hit mainly the poor. When the shops and the bars and the whores close their shutters, that will be the time to leave; for they will all know when the Viet Cong is coming, when the corpse has been devoured to the bones. And the regime of Hanoi is one of austerity. No dance of death. No profits. Fade out into the rice fields. Get aboard a junk, if you can't get into one of those last airplanes. But if your destination is indeed Switzerland, you will have no trouble getting a luxury seat.

Saigon booms, under Nixon. For a while, in 1968, when Johnson lost his nerve, it was ready to cash in. Now it knows that it will stay, as long as there is a dome on the Potomac. Abandonment of Saigon or Bangkok would be as unthinkable as abandonment of Las Vegas or Miami; the latter provide recreation; the former provide a purpose which gives each administration a focus for its energies and its worries, gives it a raison d'être. Here Old Glory waves with a defiant thrust, and beats its helicopter rotor vanes, screaming and coursing over jungle and paddies; there *is* an American power; it is valid, it is virile, it is enterprising.

The American intention, that the world shall be free, goes out in the military air traffic over Saigon. Our hopes are centrist and executive and ameliorative. To say that thus and so-and-so can put a stop to Saigon, can be elected and cut out and cauterize, is to ignore the moralistic basis of American power, that white-gowned girl going down the steps of the White House, while her Texas or California daddy beams, to be married to a young lawyer, a young soldier, or businessman. It is fashionable to say that Kennedy was a hero and Johnson a villain, but both were steps in the process. The man swiveling in front of that Executive desk in that Executive office is the heir of all the instinct, the momentum and the rhythms that make the American past mythic and make it necessary for that myth to be projected into the future; as impossible for a McCarthy to put a halt to Saigon as, say, for Truman to have put a halt to World War II. The presidential seed is full of white-clad daughters, and it is these whom we are protecting in Saigon, by subsidizing the whores. The guns boom on, but they are purifying. The American suburbs, where presidents live, the hippies who parade in the doomed cities and are objects of curiosity, are being cleansed and protected while they are cleansed.

There are rock singers in Saigon; the blast of electronic amplification proclaims the triumph of the West, not its decline; Mao and Ho and Marx would have us do without these things; thus they are the losers; they have miscalculated the future. The girl going down the White House steps knows what the future is, it is freedom, it is Las Vegas. All the books, and all the dialectic, all the little red volumes of *Thoughts*, all the useful, durable, padded-cotton blue uniforms are not equal to the blast of the electronic guitar or the growing of hair long over the shoulders. The heroic mortar and rocket fire, the grenades of the teams of the heroes of the Revolution, stepping out of political posters, bear the date of 1917 or 1935; they are no match for the chance of owning a Honda or having a transistor radio, rock-blaring, of your own. The wild, Western, corrupted avant-garde wears the beards of Marx, but the revolutionaries are expected by their regimes to be clean-shaven; they must be totalitarians, living austere lives, adhering to military disciplines; they must be Puritans.

There is an airport bus for passengers departing from Saigon. One gets to a central point in the city; then it lumbers toward the airport, passing the barriers. The desk at the hotel is enraged that I have found this out. At the airport I move in a file of US military and civilian workers.

In the waiting bar, a Bangkok-bound, recreation-aiming civilian worker tells the usual tale of huge salary, barbiturates and alcohol, the dwindling of sexual energy. All is lost, he says, in Saigon; it is a matter of months before the Viet Cong take over the city, the higher officials have prepared cushions for themselves (brothers in Hanoi, transmission of war plans) with the Viet Cong, or have planes warmed up ready for exit. But there are still guns sounding at the airport as we leave. American power is pounding away, as real as the assembly lines of the River Rouge or the blast furnaces of the Alleghenies. Washington is not giving up. The Dome is gleaming. It is only money, and there is plenty of that.

Now we lift off, and the thick brown coating of this last circle in the city of Dis fades into a jumble and a blur, not to be seen again until we encounter Minos at the gates of the underworld. It will be familiar to us, when we see that the black-coated judge has a wisp-bearded Chinese face, for we have been here before. And just as each GI takes his appointed cell in his appointed ring of that Dry Tortugas Fort Jefferson hostelry of the damned, to spend his virility into the rubber sac of a softly urinating Chinese whore, we will take our final places, without appeal. But why devise this on earth, before our time? The rotor vanes of the helicopters are like the wings of the lazy, slowly rotating monsters which hover over the pits and fires, and flaming bogs, and hot quicksands of Doré's hell; pterodactyls, these dinosaurian birds come not to lift us higher and higher into the empyrean where the president's daughter, a white-clad Beatrice, awaits, but into a hospital full of flasks of plasma, flowing through the gravity tubes, where a course of drugs unhinges the mind and undoes the brain.

We will not be dropped by US power back into Phnom-Penh or the flowers or the temple ruins, for we are warned against going there; the Prince is evil, and his is an enchanted garden designed to pervert and numb our sense of what is right, corrupt our sense of mission, so that we will never become worthy of the girl. She must be won by blood and suffering, by the vanes of slowly rotating pterodactyls above bogs and burning lakes, not by sniffing blossoms and sipping wines, savoring moonlight on barges propelled by an evil Prince, who would seduce her while she sleeps. The hero must be covered with blood; he must, in part, look like that concrete statue in front of the Saigon Parliament.

But I, having seen and met and talked with Minos before my time, prefer to browse on the poisoned flowers of the Prince, eschewing my chance to raise my sweat-stained helmet and, putting down my bayonet, to awaken with my bloodstained lips the sleeping Beauty. It is in another forest, that of Angkor, I would wander, and by another castle, that of Avalokiteshvara, that I would dream, my life away if possible.

And so I drop to earth, rescued, not by rotor vanes or a pterodactyl, but by a simple transport. And I come to the small airport, and its small buildings, and gentle, idling, courteous, helpful people. The nightmare has ended. The Beauty, unawakened, goes on to be married. I have not awakened her, and it is she, like her spouse, who walks in a trance. For I have awakened, and it is the Prince who is real, and they who are false. How can they let him exist? How can Phnom-Penh, forbidden to any American personnel, civil or military, be allowed to bloom and flourish between the Dis of Saigon, the Acheron of Bangkok?

It is monsoon time, and down at the Prince's port, reached through the US-financed highway, the wind and rain soak the sand continuously. I walk along the white strand, among the trees of the jungle. From the hill of the town bazaars I watch the British-flag freighters, four at a time, unloading war supplies bought in the world markets, for the Viet Cong, with which to attack unawakened Beauty on the very day of her White House wedding. Can this be allowed to continue? Will not someone press a button, black or red, on a giant, shining mahogany desk below the great eagle insignia? But another four freighters, and another and another, lie waiting. The railway, the highway, are fully utilized, speeding war supplies to the Viet Cong. The ornamental pile of downed US military aircraft grows on the avenue beside the river in Phnom-Penh; fuselage tails brightly numbered are in greatest demand; downed pterodactyls with their giant rotors.

Phnom-Penh is much dryer than the port; its rhythm goes on in the showers. Angkor is beginning to be wet. The great lake is filling. The villages leading down to it along the Siem Reap River are idyllic. Pigs, ducks, and chickens; babies appearing, fat, at every door, every year; the population blends with the paddies and the canals; there is a great rice surplus. We dance at night; I watch sunsets from the three main Phnoms (hills).

The peasants haunt the green underneath the trees, like slender surprised Avalokiteshvaras. Many die young, especially the men; there is not much effort made to preserve life. There is the hospital, free clinics, all that, at Siem Reap, which is a provincial capital. The peasants are not greatly concerned about longevity. Procreation is not a world-shaking event, merely a routine occurrence. The sex act is not of great importance. Dancing is greatly enjoyed.

Mostly these people are contemplative. They know, and have learned, for many years, how to pass the time. They walk and sit and look. Descendants of the last artisans and caretakers left to guard the cities, they belong to the ruins; know where to find individual stones far out in the tangle. They don't want to sell the stones. The flying horse of Avalokiteshvara raises the merchants, trapped by vampires on a desert island, high above the demons; its wings, pieced together, beat from a stone lotus in a dried pool, slowly filling as the rains begin.

Delicate small ruins, of earlier, discriminating dynasties, lie far out, with roseate, pillaged sculptures. In the wet season, all is softer, blurred. Sras Srang mills about, impervious to the slowly increasing rain. The cart sludges along the wet ruts; the bullocks have been feeding. We move in a private cloud of rain, passing the misty trees and streams. The odor of the animals, straining at the shafts, is pungent and piercing; a compound of digested grass, and stomach linings, and saliva, dripping mouths; intestines and bowel. As they strain harder, their aroma becomes all-powerful, the perfume and fuel of our moving cloud.

Because the light is failing, the cart halts at the village of Pradak, and the animals are turned to feeding. Beyond the village lie ruins of Banteay Samré. They know every stone, leaping ahead. We stumble across moats, up steps, into galleries and halls. Through carved balusters inner courts are seen; we go deeper into the ruin; here coconut oil lights up in a shell.

Above, the gods and demons appear, pulling at the serpent which churns Vishnu's sea of milk; the liquor of immortality streams down the walls. Inside the shrine, the square-browed, flat-cheeked, flat-nosed broad faces look out, perfectly composed, ready to stay till dawn. A carved naga serpent, with upraised heads, winds around the galleries outside, its mouths washed with rain.

They do not move. Here flesh, brown-yellow, immortalizes as stone. I have heavy breathing, vibrate and twist and quiver. Their only movement is that of the pupils of the whites of their eyes which must alter direction to take in my eccentricities.

We are awaiting the Bodhisattva of the current cycle, perhaps as a flying horse, perhaps as a woman with four arms, the naked doctrine itself; perhaps as a being with four faces. We await release from the current cycle, through the agency of these divine beings.

Back to Phnom-Penh, then up the Mekong, past Kompong Cham, to Kratie, on the steamer. I go with a Chinese (Vietnamese), not a merchant; the family lives in Kratie; they are peasants. Here is nothing but rice and rubber; temple after temple; Avalokiteshvara, slender-headed, in yellow plaster, with ten heads, in three tiers, four, four, and two, overseeing the world from the gates. His wife is a Khmer: we go down the opposite direction, south toward the coast, to Kampot Province, on the railway that brings up munitions for the Viet Cong from the Prince's port.

Here in the village I meet not so much the wife but the all-important "Sa mère Yen," who owns the stilt-house and the strip of paddy field. All the men are dead; only Chhea Kan, the Vietnamese-Chinese peasant from Kratie, is available to help the women in the paddy field at the working times. He is delicate and shy. He drops everything at Phnom-Penh, where he earns money in the port, when it is time for planting, Sa mère Yen making the decision.

Why did the women select such a slender, refined worker (headaches, dizziness, stomachaches) for their paddy field? An attack of everything combined assails him next morning in the rain. Sa mère applies the universal remedy (even for fractured limbs)—silver coins are rubbed and rubbed, painfully, into the area of the afflicted spot, until raw angry weals, exactly round, exactly the shape of the coins, appear, and begin, gratifyingly, to throb with pain.

At least partially redeemed, Kan sets out for the fields, admonished by the stern Sa mère; he may have been saved by his marriage to a Khmer, by the fact he was not a merchant; he may have been driven back into Vietnam with the mass; his body may have floated down the Mekong with thousands of Phnom-Penh Chinese when the button was pressed in Washington. I feel that this must be a requiem for Kan; too fragile and sickly and delicate a creature for the responsibilities even to Sa mère and the paddy field; ill at ease in Phnom-Penh and not aware or informed enough to get out of that river port, focus of the town, in the dry season when he was normally on the barge. They swept down the steps at the port, cutting down the Chinese concessionaires, for which I cannot blame the Khmers. But a pogrom of race claims the innocent as well as the guilty, and I wonder if Sa mère Yen is back again at the undignified (for one of her august age) task of working her own paddy field.

Conversely, there can be no question that the Oeur Sam Bath family has survived at Sras Srang; the villagers live inside the temple of Angkor Wat, and the Viet Cong keep them supplied with rice. Naturally they must worship their Prince (they did that anyway), and unnaturally they must let their mouths water over the enticing prospect of Mao Tse-tung; like any American hippie, a portrait of Ho Chi Minh (this last, one of the Khmer-hated Annamites, successors of the Chams of the water-battles on their reliefs) must adorn their living space in the galleries, but it is a service they perform, adoring or at least tolerating this icon, in return for rice—even today they lead you at once to the reliefs showing the victories of the Khmers over the Chams on the Lake; though they hate the Siamese more, their memory is long, and the Chams are as real, the Annamites are Chams—

The Viet Cong has recruited the peasants of the Angkor villages who are of military age to join their forces, so Croi-Oeur himself is now prowling the jungle, knife and rifle in hand, ready to massacre brother and cousin Khmers from Siem Reap, only three miles to the south, and heavily intermarried, who have been recruited into the American forces. The line between the Viet Cong and the US-supported forces lies exactly halfway between Siem Reap and Angkor Wat, where the family is now living. Croi-Oeur, at Angkor Wat, is learning the martial arts as practiced by the Viet Cong in Hanoi; his cousins Posoman and Khou-Chea, who lived in Siem Reap and were my friends, are learning those practiced by the United States in distant Saigon.

Both sides, north and south of that line one and a half miles from Angkor Wat, are running training camps to instruct peasants how to kill, since each accuses the other of doing so—"pre-dawn rifle training in Angkor Wat." And of necessity, how to kill each other, since each other is the enemy. Croi-Oeur is learning bayoneting and eviscerating, and Posoman and Khou-Chea, children of his mother's sister, are learning rifle-shooting and grenade-tossing. On alternate days they shift classes. It is too much to say that perhaps they have the same instructors, adepts who slip back and forth between the lines to garner fees. But if the instructors are Chinese, I would say it is not impossible.

If they are the best instructors, if the supply of field-trainers is limited, why should they not change uniforms each day and go back and forth (so easy for countrymen in this jungle), teaching Croi-Oeur how to hurl grenades at Posoman and Khou-Chea one day, and Posoman and Khou-Chea how to bayonet Croi-Oeur the following day? The important thing is to teach killing, as quickly and efficiently as possible, to peasants who have never had a punch in the nose before. Both Hanoi and Washington would have it so. To Ho Chi Minh's successors in Hanoi, Croi-Oeur's cousins are ideologically inferior; they can be butchered. To Johnson's successors in Washington, Croi-Oeur is a communist; he is shooting for the Viet Cong; one more vermin to be gotten rid of. For all the world must be free; Marine generals can relax in Bangkok, it is a free country; Saigon itself is more for the recreation of enlisted men. . . .

Get the cement up and get it carved. Phnom-Penh, according to its generals, lacks the inspiration of a martial spirit. Siem Reap may plead in vain for a statue of Avalokiteshvara. Perhaps it will get a replica of the Saigon Statue, reduced in size for its tiny population. Perhaps a Las Vegas entertainment celebrity, such as are provided to Saigon, may come through.

What was there in Johnson that caused him to hold off? What caused him to refrain from taking the obvious step in those dark days of February 1968, when the defeat of his policies faced him with the necessity of abdication? He did not clutch at this last straw, as the generals would have had him do. It was so easy: cut off the port, shut off the supplies, make the Viet Cong divert troops to confront the Khmers. The chance of success was there, and Texans like to succeed. Johnson refused to destroy this fragile, lotus-eating, defenseless, incapable nation, with an army made up only of generals from royal families, an army of epaulets and medals and dummy rifles, ivory-handled ceremonial pistols. There was the chance of gazing down on the record as final victor of an insoluble war.

Now that we know how easy it was to seize Cambodia, Johnson's refusal to comply is perplexing. The drowning man did not clutch at the lotus blossom. He preferred to sink himself and let the lotus float for a while in the jungle pool, below the walls of Angkor, with the winged horse rising and succoring from amid the pink and blue blossoms.

Avalokiteshvara had a friend in LBJ; or, in theologically more accurate terms, LBJ was pulled up on the back of that horse from the desert island of the vampires, eager to suck at his jugular; he fell under the protection of the all-seeing, four-sided gaze.

Thus the bodhisattva, all-powerful in the current cycle, who renounced his own divinity to suffer in our midst, had a facet in the presidential forehead; LBJ acted in accordance with the wishes of the god; for a while longer the maidens danced on the terraces of Angkor.

Autumn 1971

The Night of Alcibiades

John Finlay

1

Alcibiades was the child of the democracy. I say this aware at the same time of the irony involved in the assertion. He belonged to one of the most aristocratic families in Athens. Through his father's side he traced his ancestors to Telamonian Ajax; through his mother's side he was connected to the Alcmaeonidae, perhaps the most influential of the Athenian tribes. He was brought up in the household of his cousin Pericles, who ruled Athens not as a democrat, but, so Thucydides implies, as an enlightened tyrant. Alcibiades himself insisted, often arrogantly and explosively, on all the privileges and immunities of his high station. He likewise possessed in his character that peculiar combination of forbidding insolence and ingratiating charm which we associate with the aristocratic temperament. But nevertheless underneath this solidly formed aristocratic exterior there swarmed all the fluidity and pluralism of democracy.[1] And

1. Some might argue that instead of being fragmented by democracy, the interiors of Alcibiades's soul were firmed up enough by the Greek aristocratic concept of honor. They would see him, like Achilles of the epic, as being part of that "shame-culture" which E. R. Dodds discusses in *The Greeks and the Irrational.* For someone in such a culture, the most important thing, what gives meaning to his life, is the respect, honor, and glory he obtains from his fellows for performing noteworthy deeds. This is doubtlessly true to a great extent with Alcibiades. But two considerations immediately intrude themselves and undermine the "honor"

isn't the last test of a true democracy, that is, in the final stages of its self-destructive purity, a toleration of anything, including an aristocratic egoist who once disdainfully told the oligarchic Spartans that of course he knew democracy was a "patent absurdity"?

It was Alcibiades whom Plato most likely had in mind as he delineated the democratic soul in Book VIII of *The Republic*. The philosopher defined democracy as that kind of constitution which has renounced the authoritative guidance of the intellect and embraced a hedonism which by definition is multiple and various—no one pleasure should dominate our soul and deny us the others. The basic animating principle of such a regime is that "all pleasures are equal and must be equally valued." The democratic soul is consequently characterized above all by its versatility, by the presence within it of many styles, attitudes, philosophies, and cults, each one of which frequently contradicts the others. To use the terminology of modern psychology, the democratic soul is ambivalent at its core. It is,

---

thus attributed to him. First of all, his egotism existed, unlike Achilles's, in a philosophical and religious vacuum. If we can say that Achilles believed in himself and in the gods, we must say that Alcibiades believed solely in himself. The difference between the two positions is great indeed. In the older culture, for instance, there was an objective standard provided by the divinity and the society protected by that divinity by which one could determine exactly what "honor" was and on whom and why it should be conferred. But in the newer culture honor was determined by the discrete individual, and there was always the possibility that the private determination might not agree with that of one's fellows. Since honor presupposes some public agreement in fact as to what is honorable and what is not, such relativism undermines its very existence. With Alcibiades it lost its public sanctions and became outrage. The second consideration is concerned with what-gets-done. Shame-cultures will tolerate only successes and care nothing for unrealized interior intention, whether good or bad. Judged by such an uncompromising and severe standard, we are forced to see Alcibiades's life as a failure. He never finished anything. He never was long enough at any one place for him to acquire and keep consolidated political or military power. He showed indeed at all times brilliant promise and actually achieved some considerable military successes at the end, but they were not sustained. Whether this was his fault or not, shame-culture would have dismissed him as unentitled to its honors.

though, when Plato turns from the more theoretical part of his definition to the details of descriptive psychology that we begin to feel the actual historical presence of Alcibiades:

> And does he not, said I, also live out his life in this fashion, day by day indulging the appetite of the day, now winebibbing and abandoning himself to the lascivious pleasing of the flute and again drinking only water and dieting, and at one time exercising his body, and sometimes idling and neglecting all things, and at another time seeming to occupy himself with philosophy. And frequently he goes in for politics and bounces up and says and does whatever enters his head. And if military men excite his emulation, thither he rushes, and if moneyed men, to that he turns, and there is no order or necessity to his existence, but he calls this life of his the life of pleasure and freedom and happiness and cleaves to it to the end.

All these illustrative marks of a democracy are derived from a decadent aristocracy. There is not a trace of vulgarity in the refined but corrupting list. Consequently, Plato's composite figure cannot be referred to any of those popular leaders, a Cleon or a Hyperbolus, for example, who rose to power from the lower ranks, all of whom had the reputation for a kind of crude violence. It would be quite hard to conceive of Cleon as applying himself, even superficially, to the study of philosophy, or to the lascivious charms of flute-music. Alcibiades is the only one of the more important of the Athenian democratic leaders whom Plato's illustration fits in its details. Besides, since Plato believed that democracy originates out of a decaying aristocracy which has lost its mind, Alcibiades would have been for him the more appropriate example. In his biography of Alcibiades, Plutarch gives the most essential characteristics of his nature as being its open-endedness and diversity, the multiplicity and inconsistency of its passions, and, above all, its adaptability to different foreign cultures and influences. He could "submit himself," Plutarch says, "to more startling transformations than a chameleon." All of these features we see are prominent in Plato's portrait of the democratic soul in Book VIII of *The Republic*.

Alcibiades drank the black broth and ate the stale bread of the Spartan mess hall when he lived there in exile from an Athens which had sentenced him in absentia to death—"I'll show them I'm still alive," he is related to have then said. He wore his hair long and untrimmed in the Spartan way, took cold baths and then robed himself in the coarse, homespun cloak of a Spartan aristocrat. He sweated through all the manly exercises. For someone so much a victim of a multitude of passions this ascetical regimen must have been the last novelty. But he adapted himself with equal facility and abandonment to the manners of other cultures. In Thrace he outdrank them all in the drunk place. In "horse-breeding" Thessaly he was more of a centaur than the natives. While he lived in Asia Minor he was luxuriant and indulged in the pomps and the ostentations of an Eastern satrap. With cunning skill he moved through all the oily and vicious intricacies of the Oriental diplomatic game in which the least false step would have put a dagger in his back. His entire life seemed only a succession of brilliantly maintained but quickly discarded exteriors, a series of costumes and cosmetics such as figure in the haunting transvestite dream he had just before he died, which Plutarch relates and which is emblematic of the man's whole life:

> One night he had a dream that he was wearing his mistress's clothes while she was holding his head in her arms and painting his face with pigments and white lead like a woman's.

We see the same versatility in Alcibiades's political and his sexual lives. It seems that he was pathologically incapable of an impersonal loyalty; consequently, he could be whatever he wished under the impulse of the time and the place. He successively fitted into the democracy of Athens, the aristocracy of Sparta, and the despotism of Persia. He became a participant in whatever political philosophy he could use for his own machinations. He believed in anything that would further himself. As to his sexual life, he began in the homosexuality of his age, that is, one involving a youth and an older man. He was extraordinarily beautiful. The strange combination in him of a feline elusiveness and a masculine toughness many Greeks found overwhelming. He was effeminate in his dress at Athens, trailing long purple cloaks behind him as he paraded through the marketplace; he carried pet quail about his person; yet he could explode in a second and strike a man down for the least affront to his manly honor. But he had no respect for his admirers and treated them cruelly and contemptuously. He collected lovers as a part of a power game. Their flattery and importunity confirmed the irresistibility of his attraction and the finality of his hold over their minds. When he was older he shifted to heterosexuality. But the same ruthless egotism is seen in his heterosexuality as it is in his homosexuality. He married but was never long faithful to his wife, indulging in countless affairs with courtesans. When he was at Sparta he seduced the wife of King Agis and so violated one of the most sacred bonds of the Greeks, that between host and guest. Plutarch cites ancient sources that attributed his death to his apparently uncontrollable sexuality:

> They say that he had seduced a girl belonging to a well-known family in Phrygia and had her living with him. It was this girl's brothers who were enraged at her dishonor, set fire by night to the house where Alcibiades was living, and shot him down, as has been described, when he dashed through the flames.

Some have explained this egotistic versatility in Alcibiades as an inevitability of the sophistic culture in which he lived. Moral law had lost its absoluteness in the minds of many of the intellectuals and their followers, among whom Alcibiades was included. It was revalued as custom, which changes from time to time and from place to place; its violations involve no supernatural visitation; it actually exists only on leave and for the convenience of powerful individuals who naturally manipulate, dominate, and exploit the weak and the helpless. In those demagogic circles of power that received Alcibiades this philosophical relativism taught by the Sophists became translated into a brutal, amoral imperialism according to which Athens considered herself released from all morality in her treatment of the subject states composing her empire. She could be whatever she wished in the maintenance of her power. Her variousness extended through the entire political spectrum. In Sicily she presented herself to the smaller cities as their maternalistic liberator from Syracusan and Dorian oppression; in Melos, a small island in the Cyclades which pathetically tried to maintain neutrality in the Peloponnesian War, she was the inhuman dictator who massacred the entire male population of the island in order to teach the would-be rebels in her own empire a lesson impressed in blood. A democracy at home, she elsewhere encouraged oligarchic tyrannies whenever it suited her self-interest and sought alliances of friendship with dictatorial rulers of the Persian Empire. Translate this relativistic imperialism into psychological terms and we have Alcibiades.

This public culture was reinforced by private loss. Alcibiades was fatherless. During his earliest years his father, a famous general of the time, was killed in the Battle of Coronea, and Alcibiades was raised as the ward of Pericles. The ancient Greeks placed the highest value on the father-son relationship. For a Greek boy to grow up deprived of it, as many a Greek doubtlessly did, must have made him a kind of freak in the eyes of other more fortunate boys. There is, as Nietzsche tells us, a streak of cruelty in the Greeks. Alcibiades as a child must have had his fatherlessness rubbed into his soul. Older boys must have made him the butt of their jokes. He would have been forced to feel his unnaturalness. Furthermore, what could have prevented the boy's unformed and irrational mind from interpreting his father's early death as abandonment and the abandonment as a verdict against his own existence? So attacked, all the forces of Alcibiades's proud and aristocratic nature would have aroused and mobilized themselves. But in his sophistic culture and without the rational discipline which a good father would have given him, he had nothing by which to assert himself but his naked ego. And in the unphilosophical depths of that ego to which he descended he released the compulsion and multiplicity that drove him through all the roles of his versatility.

If this last insight contains validity, we can now understand the nature of Alcibiades's attachment to Socrates. He was seeking his father. And I do not mean the word in a crudely specific sense but in a symbolic one which involves the *logos* of reason that brings an order to the soul, calms its passions, and feeds it on truth. How bafflingly opposite the two must have seemed, the glittering beautiful youth with his perfectly formed body and the ugly older man who had the wisest and most ordered soul any human being ever possessed. Instinctively Alcibiades desired the contagion of wisdom to affect him too and resolve his conflicts so that in the presence of his master he could achieve philosophical peace. We know, of course, that this vision was not realized and that Alcibiades ended in tragedy. No matter how beautiful his body, his soul was finally too infected, distorted, and maimed for it to acquire philosophical form. But while it lasted, in the years before the war—in the brilliant light of Athens, as Euripides says—the attachment of Alcibiades to Socrates is one of the most compelling examples we have of the human desire for wholeness.

Without such philosophical form Alcibiades never had peace. He was of the essence of those Athenians whom the Corinthian ambassador warned the Spartans of in the first part of Thucydides's *History of the Peloponnesian War.* The Athenians, the ambassador emphasized, are addicted to innovation. They are never at home. *They were born into the world to take no rest themselves and to give none to others.* It was Alcibiades, with the earlier help of the demagogue Cleon whom Thucydides terms "the most violent of men," who caused Athens to break with the Periclean policy of defensive containment, which had guided her during the first years of the Peloponnesian War, and to embark on the new one of expansion and aggression. The Sicilian expedition of 415 was the turning point. In the debate before the Athenian Assembly convened to decide on the expedition, the radical restlessness of Alcibiades was pitted against the conservative caution of Nicias. We should consolidate the empire we now enjoy, Nicias pleaded, not risk everything we have in uncertain and dangerous ventures in western waters. But Thucydides tells us that a madness for the exotic land of Sicily, its conquest and exploitation, possessed the Athenian soul, and reason was hopeless against the intensity of its passion. Alcibiades countered Nicias's argument with a policy of imperial limitlessness, a strategy of kill-or-be-killed which would make peace impossible. Under the influence of his brilliant rhetoric the Assembly voted for an expedition which resulted in the annihilation of the entire fleet sent out and the slaughter of thirty thousand men. We cannot fix the limits of our empire, Alcibiades argued; we must be constantly expanding it; and in the presence of our enemies we shall always be making, we must be continuously aggressive or we shall be destroyed. He told the Athenians:

> Remember, too, that the city, like everything else, will wear out of its own accord if it remains at rest, and its skill in everything will grow out of date; but in conflict it will constantly be gaining new experience and growing more used to defend itself not by speeches, but in action.

For the religious among the Greeks such a policy of pure process which has eliminated achievable purpose and which has refused the restraint of meaningful limits was not only impious but also insane. According to legend, the daemon of Socrates warned him against the evil recklessness of the Sicilian expedition. The whole of Nicias's speech was informed by his belief that the Athenians should leave Sicily within its own limits and that if the Athenians invaded the western island they would be transgressing divine sanctions. It would be an act of mindless hubris that would incur the wrath of the god. We should always remember too that the western part of the sea was associated with death in the Greek mind. It was on Sicily that Odysseus found the entrance to the Underworld in which he spoke with his bloodless ghosts. Monsters infected the Straits and devoured the ships that tried to navigate the narrow passageway. Without those countless islands which are found in the Aegean and which enabled Greek ships to hug to shores and always to keep land in view, the western sea was open, pure, and treacherous. Sicily to the untraveled Athenian was as strange as the moon. Thucydides's account, in fact, of one of the last night battles on Sicily, in which the minds of the Athenians were confused by the lunar light so that they often ended up turning against and killing themselves, imagistically summarizes the whole death and insanity of the Sicilian expedition. Alcibiades himself was relieved of his command during the very first part of the campaign because of his involvement in the profanation of the Mysteries, but the expedition was always tied to him by the Athenians. It was to his own mind. He was the one who fomented their passion for the tragic venture. We can then understand the justice of that one single attribution that the ancient writers all agree in giving to him: the *fatality* of his charm. His Egyptian soil, as Plutarch has it, produced some good drugs, to be sure, but intermingled with those drugs were found poisons. Aristophanes in *The Frogs* compared Alcibiades to a lion. You shouldn't raise up such a beast in the city, he warned the Athenians, but if you do, then humor every one of his moods. They love him and they hate him, he said in the same play about the Athenian people's ambivalent fixation on Alcibiades, and they cannot live without him. According to Plutarch, Timon the misanthrope told Alcibiades when he was young, and just after he had won a victory in the Assembly, "You are doing well, my boy! Keep it up and you will destroy them all."

The war dragged on for eight years or so after the defeat of Athens in Sicily. By the time it was finished Alcibiades had shifted to every position he could have. He betrayed Athenian strategy to the Spartans. In the mysterious shadow-theater of the court of the satrap Tissaphernes, as F. E. Adcock calls it, he sought the aid of the Persians for the Spartans against the Athenians and, finally, for the Athenians against the Spartans. He cared no more for oligarchy than he did for democracy. The one motive which united him through that shifting and elusive world was self-interest, for him a solipsistic pride and safety of the self in imposing his irrational will upon others. Ironically and tragically that self-interest caused the destruction of the self. He created so many enemies that he lost himself in a crepuscular world of assassins and paranoia. When he returned to Athens for the last time, after his recall and pardon, he waited some time on the deck of his ship, not trusting in the apparent friendliness of the people gathered to greet him, his eyes darting nervously through the crowd for murderers. Can it be that the ethic of self-interest is not at all motivated by an actual love of the self and the sources of the self's true power in the soul? Might it not instead be motivated by a fear of an impoverishment and inadequacy of the self, a fear that then drives the self through all the self-destructive strategies of power politics and forces it continually and futilely to prove itself?

He must have exhausted himself. Plutarch tells of an incident involving Alcibiades during the last days of the war that contains a great deal of pathos. He was living at the time not far from where the Athenians massed their ships at Aegospotami. He had played every card in his hand and now lived in isolation, scorned and rejected by all three of the powers involved in the Asiatic theater of the Peloponnesian War. But he was a man obsessed by action to the end, and so he observed the Athenian navy, knowing that the Spartans immediately across the narrow waters were preparing the deathblow. Alcibiades saw with alarm the general lack of discipline to which the Athenian fleet had degenerated, in contrast to the cool scientific precision and the deadly efficiency of former times. At some risk to his own safety, he was moved to warn his fellow countrymen of the dangers to which their carelessness was exposing them. But after riding over to the Athenian camp and giving his opinion, he was insulted and rudely dismissed by the Athenians. Every bit of his expert advice was disregarded as coming from an untrustworthy traitor. One of their generals superciliously informed him that "it is we who are in command now, not you."

How are we to explain this final public act of Alcibiades? We cannot do so by asserting it to be an example of his egotism. He gained nothing by it and actually exposed himself to considerable danger by going alone and defenseless to the camp of his enemies, even if they also were his fellow countrymen. We must then conclude that it was a disinterested act motivated by charity toward the Athenians, who had so far lost their minds as to become utterly vulnerable to their enemies. If so, Alcibiades must then have been groping his way out of the fluidity of egotism toward an objective and impersonal notion of the good such as Socrates would have approved of. But history can be brutal. It was too late for both the Athenians and for Alcibiades. The Athenians were destroyed at Aegospotami. Alcibiades himself was soon assassinated, not most likely by the brothers of the ravaged girl whom Plutarch cites, but more probably, as the same writer further states, by agents of the Persian satrap acting at the request of the Spartan King Agis, the man whose wife Alcibiades had earlier seduced and violated.

2

Why did Socrates become intimate with Alcibiades? Why did the philosopher leave the cool serenity and comedy of his thought, descend into the cave which Plato would later describe, and contaminate himself with the man of tragic action? It is some such question as this that I would now like to try to answer.

We will begin with a fact about Socrates's body. He was physically an ugly man. With him it was as if the creative force had totally spent itself on the construction of his powerful intellect and had nothing left for his body, which then fell off as something unformed and gross. His huge nose was flattened against his face, the nostrils at the base abnormally distended. His eyes were set wide apart, and they bulged out from their sockets. For that man caught under their spell, the effect would have been unnerving and frightening, especially if he were also being cut to pieces by the Socratic *elenchus*. Socrates's mouth was thick and fleshy. His bodily ugliness was accented by the oddity of his dress and his habits. He wore the same ragged cloak throughout the year and went barefoot even in winter and, so Plato informs us, even during the Potidaean campaign in the freezing Chalcidice when he fought there as a soldier. Aristophanes tells us that when he walked he waddled like a waterfowl. He had the power to withdraw from his surroundings, to stand so motionless in a trance that his face suggested someone dead. But his ugliness wasn't the ugliness of sickness and emaciation. There was something in fact perennially green and tough about the man. His powers of brute endurance were enormous. He sired a child in his late sixties. It was, I think, his physical strength combined with his ugliness which made him grotesque in the eyes of some Greeks and which prompted Alcibiades once to compare him to a satyr. Seized by the intensities of the philosophical quest, he must have indeed seemed like a weird primal creature who had wandered into a disturbed Athens from some savage country of the naked mind. No wonder, some might be led to conclude, that the Athenians got rid of him.

Plato teaches us in the *Symposium* that when a man desires and loves, he is suffering from the absence and from the deprivation of whoever or whatever is being loved. Love then is that force by which the human being moves outside himself and seeks to acquire what he does not have but what he needs for the completion and perfection of his being. When this movement is consummated, the emotion of love becomes transformed into the delight of actually possessing the desired object. Now if Socrates was grotesque in his ugliness, Alcibiades was pleasing in his beauty to a degree that the Greeks found astounding. Plutarch states that Alcibiades throughout all the seasons of his life, from his youth to his maturity, possessed in turn the beauties peculiar to each season, going from the vernal to the autumnal, so that he was a continual living embodiment of beauty in all its forms and aspects. Socrates then would have loved Alcibiades because both when young and when mature Alcibiades had what Socrates found that his own life was deprived of. In the presence of the younger man Socrates could enjoy that physical beauty which, added to the proportions of his own soul, would make him complete in all aspects. Since the human response to beauty is the least susceptible of all the emotions to rational analysis—we cannot readily see what beauty is good for and so lack a reason for its effect on us—we then have to say that there is an element of the irrational in Socrates's attachment to Alcibiades. Following the Greek habit of attributing anything in human nature for which no rational cause can be given to the operations of an intrusive deity, Socrates himself would have said that his love of Alcibiades was the work in him of the god Eros.

Allied to this is Socrates's bisexuality. I do not wish to be held to something binding in a clinical sense when I use this word. By it I only mean to express a fact which is clear in the historical testimony of Plato and Xenophon, namely, that while Socrates was a sexually adequate husband, he also at the same time was peculiarly attracted to male beauty and that his attraction contained sexual elements that actually affected him in the physiology of his person. I do not mean to imply that Socrates indulged in homosexual acts. In fact, the evidence from Plato and Xenophon overwhelmingly suggests that he did not, that he instead channeled the admittedly fierce energy of his eroticism into nonsexual areas and subsumed it under his philosophical mission to educate the minds of the youths committed to him. We have here the origin of Platonic love, the doctrine which our Victorian grandparents emasculated in their great desire to spiritualize everything they could grasp. But neither Socrates nor Plato, no matter how far they sublimated the erotic, ever forgot or disregarded the fact that the basis of the sublimation was human blood. Consider this passage from the *Charmides*, one of the earliest of the dialogues, written when the memory of Socrates was still fresh in Plato's mind. Socrates has just been introduced to Charmides, a youth who, like Alcibiades, is noted for his extraordinary beauty. The boy is now suffering from a headache Socrates is said to be able to cure:

> And he came and sat down between Critias and me. But I, my friend, was beginning to feel awkward. My former bold belief in my powers of conversing naturally with him vanished. And when Critias told him that I was the person who had the cure, he looked at me in an indescribable manner and made as though to ask me a question. And all the people in the palaestra crowded about us, and at that moment, my good friend, I caught a sight of the inwards of his garment and took the flame . . . I could no longer contain myself. I thought how well Cydias realized the nature of love, when, in speaking of a fair youth he warns someone "not to bring the fawn in the sight of the lion to be devoured by him," for I felt . . . I had been overcome by a sort of wild-beast appetite.

It is inconceivable that Plato should have made this up to the extent that his contemporary readers, many of whom had known Socrates personally, would have been unable to recognize in it the historical reality of the older philosopher. Everything in Plato's own philosophical and moral temperament, which some have described as puritanical, would have caused him instead to suppress the scene. Its evidence of a strong sexuality barely held in check by Socrates we may then accept as truthful. We should also remember a fact which, as with another great moralist, Samuel Johnson, we habitually forget about Socrates, namely, that he was not always an old man. He was only about twenty years older than Alcibiades. He was in his thirties when he first met the boy. Their friendship was carried on when Socrates was in his prime, not in his old age when the debilities of the blood weaken or extinguish the sexual drive. He would still have been susceptible physically to the sexual appeal of Alcibiades if, that is, such a tendency existed in him. Both Plato and Xenophon inform us that it did. We conclude that one reason Socrates became intimate with Alcibiades was the sexual attraction he must have felt for the younger man. Again we encounter an irrationalism in Socrates, one that exists in all other human beings as well. Human sexual identity is rooted in the dark region of instinct. While there is something inherent and automatic about it, the psychologists also tell us that the specific form it takes in us is derived from uncontrollable accidents of our earliest history. By the time our rational minds have formed themselves, these events have been either repressed or obliterated, so that in sexual matters we become governed by the unknowable in us.

But Socrates turned away from such obscurities. He was a philosopher, not a victim of his psychology. As we have noted, he sublimated the powerful erotic force he discovered in himself and disciplined it so that he was able to direct it to philosophical ends. The testimony of Plato and Xenophon unambiguously asserts this. But exactly what philosophical form did this sublimation take, and how was Alcibiades related to it?

Socrates began his intellectual life as a student of that kind of non-experimental and excessively theoretical physical science which was what philosophy consisted of in the earliest stage of its development. Such philosophy sought to discover the one basic element that underneath the diversity and multiplicity apparent to the senses composed the stuff of the physical world. But with neither the right instruments of investigation nor a properly thought-out scientific method to guide them, the philosophers lost themselves in what we can call systematic and theoretical unrealities. At some decisive but now indeterminable point in his life Socrates became dissatisfied with this kind of knowledge. He might have felt instinctively what Plato would later believe consciously, that no science in the real sense of the word is possible of anything so subjected to change as atomic matter. We do know that he thought the physicists neglected important and immediate realities for those Socrates considered remote, problematical, and practically useless. Why go off into fine-spun problems, he must have asked, and disregard essentials at hand and at home? But he meant no disparagement of such knowledge, as he said in the *Apology*, thus disassociating himself from anti-intellectualism and from the popular superstition which judged such science as subversive to religious authority. It was just finally irrelevant to what had become the main preoccupation of his life, the knowledge of what is necessary to live a good life here and now. In so placing this moral knowledge of the good as the central concern of his mind Socrates initiated a revolution in Greek systematic thought. He shifted it away from the detached, morally disengaged contemplation of what we would now call pure science and introduced it to the conduct of this life. As Cicero said, Socrates brought philosophy down from the sky and set it up in the streets and in the houses of men.

It is the nature of the good that it seeks to diffuse itself into all areas where it may possibly proceed. If it decided to hold itself aloof from those areas and so deprive them of its benefits, it would then be wishing them evil since evil is not some positive force of its own, but merely an absence of the good. But this is impossible. It would defy the law of contradiction. Nothing can be both good and evil at the same time and under the same aspect. Therefore, the good seeks by its nature to diffuse itself. This doctrine receives its fullest articulation in the Christian doctrine of creation. The divine goodness created a universe that contains all conceivable degrees of participation in the good, beginning with the angels closest to God, descending to the mediocrity of man, and plunging, if you will, into creatures which seem the slime of the universe but which yet, through at least the pure fact of their existence, are able to receive the last degree of the good. As we have seen, the controlling passion in Socrates's life was for the good. He thought of his philosophical mission as the attempt to define the good so that others of the city might understand it and live a good life according to the knowledge. If he had not been born and reared in Athens, the intellectual capital of his world, he would have had to go there as Jesus finally went up to Jerusalem where the benefits of his sacrifice would be most extensively felt. It is, in fact, inconceivable that Jesus or Socrates should have spent his life in some obscure village. Both required the great city, the capital of each man's world where the greatest concentration of power, the greatest diffusion of good were possible.

And what better agent of moral and intellectual diffusion could there have been for Socrates than Alcibiades, that is, the Alcibiades the boy promised to be; the one who existed in Socrates's hopeful mind before the poisons grew in Alcibiades and destroyed him? The Greeks never envisioned the moral life as being transacted by some isolated conscience in its privacy, the etymology of which in Greek means idiocy. One's moral life and one's public life were for them the same. "We alone," Pericles said of the Athenians in the great funeral speech as related by Thucydides, "regard the man who takes no part in public affairs not as a harmless but as a useless person." Alcibiades as a youth must have struck all who could understand and who came into contact with him, not only Socrates, as being potentially the man who could acquire complete political control of the city—so that if he were good, the city would likewise be good. He came from one of the great families; he possessed the keenest of minds and was receiving the best education Athens provided; from his earliest years he instinctively knew the ways of power and, besides, exuded the magnetism that captivates, sways, and compels the intoxicated multitude. We are now in possession of the sublimated reason for Socrates's love of Alcibiades. He became intimate with the youth because he hoped, tragically it turned out, that through him ethics could be fused with politics, knowledge with power, so that the greatest degree of the good could be effected in the city. It was in the service of accomplishing this end that Socrates consigned the raw energy of his eroticism and so baptized it in philosophy. He did so undogmatically, not by virtue of some positive knowledge he enjoyed, but by the nature of the good he sought but always said he himself never possessed. But Alcibiades died even before his older friend, assassinated among barbarians in Asia. His whole life had turned out to be one violation after another of the good Socrates had lived for. The memory of what the boy could have been but the man never became must have given Socrates some of his bitterest moments in prison as he awaited his own execution.

3

To understand Alcibiades's connection with the execution of Socrates, we must go back to the last stages of the Peloponnesian War and to two oligarchical revolutions which occurred in Athens, one in 411, the other in 404. The central purpose of the first of these, called the Revolution of the Four Hundred, was to procure the financial and military aid of the Persian satrap Tissaphernes, which the Athenians desperately needed in their war against Sparta. But they would never secure the aid, Alcibiades informed them, as long as democracy existed at Athens to offend the despotic sensibilities of the rich Easterners. Abolish the democracy, Alcibiades promised his alienated countrymen whose favor he wished to regain, and he would get for them the friendship of the Persians in their death-struggle with Sparta. The last of the two revolutions was brought about at the very end of the war by the so-called Thirty. Again, a small band of aristocrats seized power in the city, demolished the democratic constitution, ruled briefly as a self-destructive tyranny, and subjected the state to terror.

Though the two revolutions each lasted for only a short time, the memory of them persisted with full strength in the collective mind of Athens. The experience had been bitter. The revolutions had been infected with that systemic disease of all Greek political life.

I mean the unwillingness, even the stubborn refusal, of the ancient Greeks to form impersonal political loyalties, and the consequent fragmentation of their polity into sects formed to gratify personal grudges and to carry out endless vendettas. Fratricide marked the revolutions, and judicial murders were a matter of course. The same paranoia of paralysis occurred in both. No one could trust his neighbor not to betray him to the government. Everyone lied for fear that the truth would have fatal consequences for him. The whole spirit of the people was extinguished in the silence and inactivity which the tyrants murderously imposed. And so it is understandable that after the fall of the Thirty the restored democracy would have wanted its revenge, especially after the city had also suffered the annihilation of her entire navy, the consequent surrender to Sparta, and the final humiliation of having the very walls of the proud city torn down by the victorious Spartans, so that she now lay exposed to anyone.

It was the leadership of these two revolutions which related most directly to the execution of Socrates. Nearly all the plotters belonged to aristocratic and intellectual circles at the highest levels of Athenian society. These circles had always accepted Socrates as their own. Some of the revolutionaries had been his closest friends. He himself had been an unrelenting critic of the democracy. It is true that he also opposed the injustices of the oligarchical Thirty, but the popular mind chooses what it wishes to believe and emphasize, and the Socratic gibes against popular rule stuck in the sensitive democratic mind and festered. Above all Alcibiades cast the longest and deepest shadow. He wasn't involved in the last revolution—by then he had been assassinated—but it was his promise of Persian aid that had brought the first revolution to life and had given it its reason to exist. He did indeed later shift sides and embraced the very democracy he had earlier tried to subvert, but what was that but more evidence of his elusiveness and changeability? The democracy held Socrates responsible for the corruptions of Alcibiades. Xenophon in the *Memorabilia* refers to a contemporary writer named Polycrates who wrote a violent attack on Socrates. According to Xenophon, Polycrates in justifying the people's execution of Socrates pointed to the philosopher's "friendship" with the "unprincipled and licentious" Alcibiades and to the great injuries the latter had done the Athenian state under the influence of the philosopher. G. C. Field in his *Plato and His Contemporaries* summarizes the controversies which arose out of the attacks of Polycrates:

> For there is evidence that Socrates' relation to Alcibiades was a subject that excited great interest in the Socratic controversies of the time. It was an important element in the accusation of Polycrates that Socrates was responsible for Alcibiades and all the evil he had done. And it is quite likely that a similar accusation was also brought at the actual trial.

The friends of Socrates who defended him after his death constantly and single-mindedly assert that the degeneration of Alcibiades occurred not because of but in spite of Socrates. A fragment of Antisthenes survives in which that minor Socratic philosopher, exculpating his friend, criticizes the character of Alcibiades as vitiated by such terrible passions that even the influence of Socrates was unable to subjugate them. And in a fragment of Aeschines, an orator who had been another friend of Socrates, we find the following dramatic passage in which Socrates himself speaks to defend himself against the implied accusation of corrupting the youth:

> For my part, the love I bore to Alcibiades brought me an experience just like that of the Bacchae. They, when they are inspired, draw honey and milk in places where others cannot even draw water from wells. Similarly I, though I have learned nothing that I could impart to a man to do him good, nevertheless thought that, because I loved him, my company could make him a better man.

That all these writers felt compelled to answer the same charge proves that Alcibiades was central in the Athenian mind as it tried and executed Socrates, then justified itself afterwards. The bill of complaint against Alcibiades would have indeed been a detailed one. It stretched back for more than fifteen years and included the profanation of the Mysteries immediately before the Sicilian expedition, an act which the mass of Athenians would have thought polluted the very existence of the state. The rest of his betrayals and treasons we have already noted, as well as the mad passion he constantly fomented in the Athenian soul for a bitter war that finally ended in the tragedy of Aegospotami. The democracy had always both loved and hated the man, fatally drawn to him and repelled at the same time—he had been the spoiled child of the democracy—and in the irresolution of its contradictory emotions Alcibiades had eluded its justice and escaped punishment for his outrages. Besides, he was now dead. But who was that old man who had been ceaselessly at his side during all his youth, the one who had insultingly pitted aristocratic skill and knowledge against democratic incompetence and mere belief?

Others connected with Socrates were implicated. Critias, a first cousin of Plato's mother and a familiar of the Socratic circle, was a ringleader of the Thirty, as was also Charmides, Plato's uncle and that same beautiful youth whom we met earlier in the wrestling-school, the one in the insides of whose cloak Socrates spied the boy's cock and had thereby been inflamed. Xenophon quotes Polycrates as calling Critias "the most rapacious and violent figure of the oligarchy." Xenophon also tells us that "it was Socrates himself who first encouraged Charmides to overcome his bashfulness and take part in politics," without realizing the tragic consequences it would have for the youth, who with Critias was killed in the last battle of the Thirty. The popular mind which condemned Socrates would quite deliberately have deceived itself, misjudging Socrates's involvement with these men as all the evidence it needed for his own treason. The popular mind was not in any mood to distinguish fairly and justly between Socrates's mere friendship with the oligarchical revolutionaries and an actually criminal complicity with their thefts and murders. As we have noted, the people had just been defeated in a war that had lasted for more than a quarter of a century. They were exhausted, disillusioned, angry, and bitter. The Alcibiadeses of their politics had all but annihilated them. They needed a scapegoat, and what better candidate for the job was there than Socrates, the eternal babbler and questioner, the prying and irritating gadfly who had disturbed social peace for too long with his search after imaginary wisdom and imaginary virtue, the very one who loved, schooled and groomed those scintillating youths who had proved to be the bane of Athens? Let him collect on his ugly body the fears and sins of the people so they could be done with them and return to the proper business of this world. And so Socrates was put to death, and the democracy got its revenge.

At the end of Plato's *Symposium* Alcibiades abruptly and unexpectedly intrudes on the party. It is one of the great scenes. He stands there framed intoxicated on the threshold, his head crowned with ivy and violets, among which brilliant ribbons are meandering over his hair. All eyes are directed to him. A flute-girl helps the drunk youth into the room. Later he gives a speech about Socrates to the guests, of whom Socrates is one. Socrates is the only man, he says, who can make him ashamed of himself. Socrates has wounded and stung him in his soul "by philosophical talk which clings more fiercely than a snake when it gets hold of a not ill-endowed young man." Socrates compels Alcibiades "to realize that I am still a mass of imperfections and yet persistently neglect my own true interests by meddling with the affairs of the state before my time." He further tells the guests of that night he once spent with the man. He was deliberately trying to seduce him sexually. He wished to tear through the philosophical facade and to discover in the hidden parts of Socrates the same blinding sensuality which would make the man just as compulsive and messy as everybody else. But Alcibiades discovered in the interior of Socrates's soul, instead, self-control and an imperturbable calm:

> But in spite of all my efforts he proved completely superior to my charms and triumphed over them and put them to scorn, insulting me in the very point on which I piqued myself . . . I swear by all the gods in heaven that for anything that had happened between us when I got up after sleeping with Socrates, I might have been sleeping with my father or elder brother.
>
> What do you suppose to have been my state of mind after that? On the one hand I realized that I had been slighted, but on the other I felt reverence for Socrates' character, his self-control and

> courage; I had met a man whose like for wisdom and bravery I could never have expected to encounter. The result was that I could neither bring myself to be angry with him and tear myself away from his society, nor find a way of subduing him to my will. It was clear . . . that he was more completely proof against bribes than Ajax against sword-wounds, and in the one point in which I had expected him to be vulnerable he had eluded me. I was utterly disconcerted, and wandered about in a state of enslavement to the man the like of which has never been experienced.

I could not bring myself to be angry with him. So Alcibiades did feel some anger against Socrates, of the kind which disordered persons experience in the presence of those whose ordered lives are a standing reproof to their own. They love the ordered man since he has that which will save them from themselves and which they desire. They hate him to the extent that a despair has seized them that finally they cannot be saved, that the irrational principle in them has been fed like a beast with too much and is now too strong to resist and overcome. The pain of denying the beast is far greater than the pleasure of the incipient good only beginning to be formed. Disordered persons suffer a contradiction in their inner being. And their actions will reflect the contradiction. At the same time they will cleave to the ordered man and seek to destroy him, each impulse checked by the other. Some sort of resolution will eventually be found by the victim, but one not worked out by his conscious will. Our actions often contain consequences uncontrollable by us which oppose all our conscious intentions and act out some of our most buried and suppressed impulses and desires. It is this uncontrollability and compulsion which frequently make history a tragedy that can only be redeemed by the freedom of philosophic thought. It was the ghost of the dead Alcibiades, the one who existed as an inevitable historical consequence in the imagination of the democracy, who finally reached out of Hades and removed the disturbing philosopher by death from Athens. The political actions of Alcibiades, all proceeding from a ruthless egotism and a bewildering versatility and fluidity, indirectly seized and polluted Socrates and brought him down too. Thus Socrates paid an enormous price for that sexually uneventful night he spent with Alcibiades. Did he have something like this in mind when he made his last statement? As the mortal chill was spreading up from his legs to his waist, he pulled back from his face the sheet that he had placed there and told his friend Crito that he owed a cock to Asclepius. Did he mean by this debt of gratitude to the god of health and medicine that he believed human existence was fundamentally diseased by passion and that death alone could heal us, as it was then about to heal him? And yet the mind of Socrates had remained unpolluted by Alcibiades, no matter what the restored democracy might think, and his whole life was a comedy in the old sense of the word, not a tragedy. The democracy had simply made a blind error. Its immorality, as Socrates himself would have said, was the result of ignorance alone. It was resolving its own ambivalent fixation on Alcibiades by executing the lover and teacher of the unforgettable young man.

I referred earlier to Socrates's ugliness, his unconventionality and uncouthness. But such is only one-half of the truth. The other half is an amazing courtesy in the man, a fluidity of ease in human encounters, a mordant wit perfectly balanced with a natural kindness. He has to be the most social of the philosophers. He could engage in the smoothest and most meaningless banter of the symposia, fight it out verbally with the thugs and bullies of the street, and philosophize with logical precision and emotional intensity on the graver problems of human life and death with closer friends. His severe intellectualism was furthermore balanced by religious faith. He revered the powers of the conscious intellect and saw in the clarities of the rational the natural source of virtue. "A man is good insofar as he is wise," he was reported to have once said, "evil insofar as he is stupid." At the same time he respected and obeyed the *daemon* that spoke to him out of his irrational unconsciousness. Above all, it is the courtesy of wholeness that most impresses us about this complex and endlessly fascinating man who holds us more than any other person except Jesus. "Be always to thy gathered self the same," Ben Jonson commands us in one of his epigrams. And Aristotle speaks of the internal friendship of the mind with itself in which no faculty of our mental being is in conflict with another, but all powers exist together in peace, the emotions and desires in subordination to their own good under the rule of reason—an aristocracy of the psyche. Multiple difference and variance at the very core of our being indicate a traumatic fragmentation of the mind against itself that soon will cause extreme anguish. Socrates possessed this wholeness and self-control to a preeminent degree, and without a trace of puritanical self-hatred or ascetical desolation—his morals are happily unembarrassed by pleasure. Through his wholeness he was able to withstand the seduction of Alcibiades and to face his executioners with a courtesy which must have infuriated them.

What is the ultimate source of Socrates's inner strength? It was his belief that he himself was not his body but his mind. When he came to make the philosophically most exact definition of human identity, he turned away from the body with its multiple, different, and decomposing parts—that which we cannot *know* since it constantly suffers change in its sublunar vagueness—and went instead to the immaterial intellect. There in the mind he located who we really are. The body, Socrates believed, is merely the tool or vestment of the soul. He would not take the body for the self any more than he would take any instrument for its agent or user. The soul contains our essence; the body is its accident. He furthermore believed that since the intellect possesses unity and is immaterial, it also is deathless. Death means the dissolution of those material parts which just happen to have a temporary but unessential cohesion. But if something is not composed of material parts but instead is a unity, it cannot suffer their dispersion and will never die. And if the mind is deathless, it is also for Socrates divine, since the deathless and the divine mean the same for him, as they do in all of Greek thought and culture. From his belief in this immortal and godlike intellectual principle in him Socrates derived his inner strength, his self-control, his courtesy of wholeness. It explains the actual meaning of his pregnant sentence that no evil can happen to a good man in this life or in the next. For how could it if the man is such a soul? And so the inexpert and tragically blind and misguided democracy could poison and kill his body—Plato in scathing disgust would call his trial that of a doctor indicted and prosecuted by cookie-makers in front of a jury of children—but the executioners couldn't reach the man. Even as the hemlock was coursing through his blood, Socrates was already somewhere else in the indestructible cohesion of the undivided intellect. He maintained the enigmatic and baffling smile of the archaic Ionians, the refined and electric comedy of philosophy up until and beyond the very end.

Spring 1994

Aborigine in the Citadel

Marilyn Nelson

Because of the confluence of many forces—among them a Contemplative Practices Fellowship offered under the auspices of the American Council of Learned Societies for the design of a new course to be taught in spring 2000—I find myself—a fat, inexorably aging, California laid-back, funky, left-leaning, dreadlocked Aframerican woman poet—teaching this semester at the US Military Academy at West Point. I have two sections of an upper-division course on poetry and meditation. This is the weirdest thing I've ever done. West Point is integrated and, since 1976, coeducational, but it still seems to me to be the antithesis of the cultures suggested by my physical and intellectual presence. Surrounded by uniformed young people in tiptop physical condition, I feel as visible and as out of my element as a cockatoo in a flock of ravens, an aborigine in the citadel. Most of the other courses at West Point are taught by Army officers. Their classes begin with the section leader calling the cadets to attention and reporting absentees, then the teacher salutes and tells them to take their seats. My classes begin with five minutes of silent meditation in a dark room. Then we embark on the hour's discussion of poetry. My cadets struggle to fit the required fifteen minutes of daily meditation into their overpacked schedules, while I struggle to hold on to the belief that I'm teaching them something meaningful and relevant to their lives, and to accept and understand the multiple contradictions of their world.

I grew up in a military family. My father spent sixteen years in the Air Force as a B-52 navigator. As a protected and proud child, a nomad among nomads, my status in elementary and junior high schools was determined more by my dad's rank than by our race or my character. My father was an officer, always one of a handful of black officers on any base, and he was thus treated with official respect. Subordinates, black and white, saluted him and called him "Sir." While we could not ignore the hellish response to the Civil Rights Movement unleashed on the civilian world of the 1950s, we lived on Air Force bases and were effectively insulated from explicit discrimination. Our car was saluted every time we drove through the gates. The military world, my father's world, was the orderly cocoon in which I grew a poet's wings. I expected, since I grew up around men in uniform, that my transition to West Point would be smooth and painless, a return to my father's world. Instead, West Point has shown me how firmly my mother rejected military values, and the lengths to which she went to keep her children from being too much indoctrinated with the authoritarian ethos of military life.

Sitting with the principal of the West Point Middle School on the morning I enrolled my daughter as an eighth grader, I remembered that military children are trained to respect adults. Each of the children who came into the office that morning ma'amed the school secretary and sirred the principal. My daughter, of course, did not. Nor did my sister and I, when we were children. Mama insisted we *not* do so. Indiscriminately applied honorifics were for her a symbol of slavery and the South. She was born and raised out West, in the all-black town of Boley, Oklahoma, and her life was imbued with Boley's radical pride. We were under her strict orders never to call anyone sir or ma'am, unless we felt they deserved our respect. I've raised my own children with that habit of intentional respect, so I've noticed with some embarrassment that at West Point, adults look at my daughter with slightly raised eyebrows when she responds to their questions with a teenagerly "yeah." My mother would have been proud of her. She was an artist, a gifted musician. She raised my siblings and me in the counterculture, to be artists (my sister an actress/director; our brother a jazz musician), rather than soldiers. Mama taught us to question authority—even our father's authority. We straddled two value systems in our household, between Daddy's Saturday morning white-glove inspections of our rooms and Mama's lighthearted refusal to take rules seriously. While he checked one corner of the room for lingering traces of disorder, she might wink and slide an overlooked dust bunny under the rug. If she ever called anyone sir, she did so with the same twinkle of merriment with which she sometimes saluted our father.

I am ma'amed by my West Point students and find that fact both amusing and curious. At first I took the cadets' addressing me as ma'am to be a sign of respect. However, I soon realized that it is a rote response, like their saluting the eagles on a colonel's shoulders. Under this habit of verbal respect, my cadets, most of them white males, many of them Southerners, can be less respectful than students I've taught elsewhere. There is, for instance, their palpable contempt for civilians. West Point cadets are accustomed to being taught by Army officers. During my first weeks at the academy there was a teacup tempest in the department about a cadet's attempt to transfer out of a civilian professor's class because the cadet wanted to be taught by an officer. I understood from conversations with colleagues that this attitude is not unusual, though few cadets express their preference openly. While I am not the only civilian professor in the English department, nor the only Aframerican, I am the only professor there this year who is both civilian and black—and I'm the only professor at West Point wearing dreadlocks. I have noticed cadets attempting to assess my status: "Ma'am, do you have a PhD?"

I love my cadets, though, and am touched by their sense that poetry is important to them. There have been days when I've gone into class filled with near-despair at the apparent meaninglessness of what I'm doing; when I feel I can almost see through those uniformed young people to the officers they will become, and I wonder why in the world the commander of, for example, a battalion of tanks would need to know how to recognize a metrical substitution in an iambic pentameter line. On these days I've sometimes stopped my headlong recitation of information, or my enthusiastic demonstration of a given poem's merits, to ask whether the cadets really *care* about these things. Yes, ma'am, they respond; they do care; they're interested; they want to know. They are in the course, they say, because they want to learn as much about poetry as they can. One or two have gone so far as to list for me the names of soldier-poets in various cultures, wanting me to see the models they have inwardly set for themselves. Their regimen of academic, military, and physical training makes it very difficult for them to find the downtime necessary for the reading and writing of poetry. They cannot study poetry as they say they do other subjects, by the "spec and dump" method: cramming for exams, then forgetting most of the material immediately after the exam. What I am teaching is not a body of information, but a way of thinking, a way of feeling. It is goal-less, open-ended.

Mine is not the only poetry course available to West Point cadets. For the past ten years the plebe (freshman) year English course has focused on contemporary poetry. Each spring the entire plebe class has read books by four poets, who then appeared on campus to read their poems and to answer questions. This is the last year of this exciting experiment; next year's plebe English course will more predictably focus on a martial theme. The poetry-focused plebe course tried to make cadets sensitive to the nuances of language. Their writing assignments asked them to distill a poem by selecting one small phrase from which to extrapolate a reading of the poem as a whole. While this approach has its rewards, it runs the risk of reducing the pleasures of poetry reading to a task, a search for the key word or phrase which will unlock the poem's meaning. The method I am trying to teach requires time and quiet. And these are in short supply at West Point.

My cadets often ask how they compare to "normal" university students; whether I have modified my "normal" teaching to accommodate them. I haven't been sure how to answer their question. I could say that, knowing how little discretionary time they are allowed in a day which begins at 5:30 and ends with taps at 11:30, I am more careful making their assignments than I am when making assignments to my "normal" students, much of whose time is their own. I know that I'm less likely to be annoyed, and certainly less likely to express my annoyance, when they inform me that they will miss classes. Receiving email messages in which I am addressed as "ma'am" and respectfully informed that a cadet has guard duty, or must be away for a "trip-section," or field trip, evokes a different emotional response from noticing that a student is missing from class, or has come to class unprepared, or is completing work for another class as I lecture. And, given the nature of human history, given unforeseen natural disasters, given our failure to learn from our mistakes, these young people are liable to be in a situation of turmoil or armed conflict someday. I teach them both more gently and more urgently than I do my other students.

We've been studying prosody, writing and reading poems. A few days ago, when one of the cadets exclaimed, "Wow! This is cool!" as I pointed out the fact that Frost's poem, "Acquainted with the Night," is a terza rima sonnet, everyone laughed, but then they agreed that knowing something about the sonnet enhances their enjoyment of one. I'm pretty certain that I can teach them enough about technique to enhance their appreciation of poetry. I've been delighted by the progress I've seen in the exercises they hand in or bring to my office. They are learning to use sophisticated tools: metrical substitution, slant rhyme, caesura, enjambment. I like to imagine them twenty years from now, Army officers who read poetry and write poems. Officers like my dad, in whose briefing notebooks pages of acronym studded militarese and doodles are punctuated by pages of his original sonnets.

Possibly more valuable than prosody or even poetry, however, is the contemplative practice I'm requiring of them. I've been telling them that poetry is a slow art; that poetry readers must stop to savor words, phrases, sentences; that they can't read a poem with the same minds that read novels or engineering texts. I've been arguing that meditation practice teaches skills essential to the enjoyment of poetry. Yet, though I really believe this, and have regularly listened to inner silence for many years, I am only a dabbler, a dilettante, a daydreamer, most of the time a backslider feeling slightly guilty about not meditating. But the Contemplative Practices Fellowship enabled me to work with several serious practitioners and students of meditation, from whom I've learned a great deal. One, a solitary priest who was a Benedictine monk for many years, said he thought meditation might offer something very important to West Point cadets, that it will teach them the gifts of interiorization and humanization, and that learning to confront their vulnerabilities and weaknesses through trying to meditate will teach them compassion. He said the best leaders are compassionate, and that military history shows the worst leaders to have been more macho than compassionate. Meditation, he said, will teach them to see beyond surface appearance, to recognize what real strength is.

One of my high school classmates, who was graduated from West Point in the class of 1968, also reassured me, writing that:

> I spent almost 25 years in the Army and think I have a pretty good handle on the character traits and values that are both needed and present in the best leaders. We have a unique profession and it requires almost an oxymoronic type of individual to do it well. A good leader in times of stress, whether combat or peacetime, must not only know the men he leads, but also himself. He must know his limits and theirs, when to push and when to back off. He must have compassion yet be ruthless in imposing and enforcing standards. He must be able to go days at a time without rest, demand it of others, yet find a way inside himself to relax whenever he can. Do we call that repose? If so, who else needs it more?

Armed with their advice, as well as that of several other friends, among them a poet who practices Zen, an Episcopal priest who holds a Yale PhD in mysticism, and two other scholars of the mystical tradition, I planned a course we put online.

The plan has, of course, changed as I have worked with the cadets during the semester. As in any other course, the semester develops out of the interplay between the syllabus, the instructor, and the students. And, as in many of my courses, I have been plagued by self-doubt, never sure I'm teaching well, never sure the students are learning what I am trying to teach them. That self-doubt has, this semester, been exacerbated by the clash of our very different cultures. Sometimes I feel like an aborigine lecturer at Oxford. These ramrod kids in their gray uniforms, their shiny shoes, their "yes, ma'ams" and "no, ma'ams"? I'm teaching these people to meditate? Sometimes it feels absurd. Yet, when I've asked them whether they would like to abbreviate our communal meditation, or dispense with it altogether, the cadets have unanimously elected to maintain those five minutes of silence at the beginning of class. "Ma'am, those are the best minutes of my day," they say. "I look forward to those five minutes, ma'am." Several have suggested we meditate for *more* than five minutes. They turn off the lights, loosen their ties; some of them take off their shoes and sit cross-legged on the floor. I set the timer. We close our eyes; we enter silence.

I'm having them practice several different techniques during the semester: We've done two weeks of breath-awareness meditation, two weeks of mantra meditation, two weeks of meditating on small pebbles, two of meditating on the gift of forgiveness, a walking meditation during Spring Leave, two weeks of awareness meditation, two of koan meditation, a final week of simple silence. In the last week of the semester we will lay out a labyrinth, inviting the entire Corps of Cadets into its meditative space. Sitting there in the dark room, surrounded by intelligent, strong, healthy, dedicated young people in uniform, I sometimes cheat, open my eyes, and look around. They sit with closed eyes: so young, so full of future.

I've asked them to keep meditation journals. Sometimes a cadet will ask for a minute or two of silence after our classroom meditation, so he or she can jot down a thought that occurred. They bring their journals to class; occasionally one will open his or her journal as we converse and read to me a fragment of verse or an observation. They write of the trivial frustrations of meditation practice: "I did 15 minutes right before I went to bed. Bad idea. I didn't go to bed until 3 the night before and ended up going to sleep until this morning." "I quit tonight after 5 minutes. It was useless to even try b/c all I see are Fluids equations. I have a test tomorrow & I have a big fat F in the class." One wrote a little poem:

Meditation

(with bubble gum in my mouth)

chomp
I forgot. Hard to focus on

smack
clearing my mind
chomp chomp.

Now the
BUBBLE
YUM
has lost its flavor.

no smack
So I wait until the
no chomp
alarm sounds.

Another cadet wrote:

> Today's meditation was so great for me, although perhaps it stepped away from the intentions of our meditations. There were so many thoughts in my head and angry, frustrated, stressed-out, mad, sad feelings inside I was having trouble with a focus and keeping my mind "blank" and open minded. So, along with breath awareness, I felt my breath pull all of my negative emotions and feelings from the bottom of my feet to the top of my head and out with my exhale. Then, I followed that breath a little. I saw the clean air enter my mouth and travel through from the bottom to the top and through my lungs and back out all over again. I am disappointed in the way that I am explaining/describing this, but it really helped me relax and feel calm and refreshed and hopeful that things will get better or that a new day will come.

Later in the semester, as, slowly, our practice deepened, she wrote:

> In class, we had to pick a couple of verbs from poems that we wrote and make sentences. Kevin made one that I loved: "Swim through a heartbeat of clouds." Anyway, while I meditated, I thought about swimming through clouds. It was incredible. And over & over in my head, I said the sentence. I don't know if that was meditation or not, but I got up and felt so wonderfully relaxed. It was like I had been swimming in clouds.

Another cadet wrote midway in the semester:

> **The Cry of the Seagull**
>
> I meditated today down by the river. I watched the ripples in the river and felt the wind in the trees. I did not have much success counting my breaths and keeping my focus, but I felt relaxed afterwards. I was inspired by what I saw and felt. I have recently had trouble understanding the purpose behind human suffering and its relation to the Christian idea of God. However, I enjoyed stepping away, sitting down and focusing on my breathing. Oh yeah, I entitled this entry "The Cry of the Seagull" cause a seagull cried and shook me out of my meditation.

Another cadet wrote:

> I have been wanting to focus more on the present than I have been; the predominant West Point attitude is to look a hundred years into the future, deciding everything short of which wallpaper you are going to put in your house. I need to remember, in this gray winter paradise, that we exist for today; if I were to die tonight, would I be pleased to know that the last thing I did was Engineering homework? I doubt it. So, I used "here, now" and it seemed to pretty much focus me on the present.

He later made up his own mantra: "Become the virtue of all that is true."

Of the twenty-eight students, only two or three found the meditation practice unsatisfying, and those were the ones whose first few journal entries demonstrated a great deal of resistance to the very idea of meditation. Yet even these, while writing that meditation was doing nothing for them, often betrayed something else:

> I noticed the way West Point smells today. It has a distinct odor to it all its own. I can't actually identify what it smells like other than perhaps wet stone . . . but that doesn't sound right because what does wet stone smell like, right? Unless, of course, you have smelled wet stone.

I am tempted to quote insights from each of the journals which I find deeply interesting:

> Today a lot of things happened with me and the rock. It told me that imperfections are what make us interesting and beautiful; if we were all perfect and flawless, there would be no satisfaction in differences, no wonder, no awe. It also asked me to channel my negative energy into its cracks, much like we channel our energy into the cracks of other people's souls. When we channel it into other people's "cracks," it usually ends up being offensive or confrontational; the rock has no feelings, so there is no need to worry about pissing it off.

Another:

> I became preternaturally aware of the *silence.* Even the roar of the blood was silence, for I alone could hear it. And I think I hear something beyond the silence, the voices in my head which this meditation spiel is so interested in. They weren't saying anything to me; they were babbling, murmuring amongst themselves. And they sounded happy. The silence in the air and in my head seemed like a clog in the toilet. Or a great big bite of peanut butter stuck in your throat. It was in the way. It obstructed reality. Poets are always so gloomy, but I think it's only the dead silence that's really dark and sorrowful. The unintelligible voices behind it sounded like songs; they sounded like green grassy hilltops in the sun.

Reading these meditation journals, I feel like a parent watching her child learn to ride a bike.

So here I am, a fat, old, dreadlocked blacklady poet, in a world in which everyone is young, everyone is jogging around, perpetually in training. A world in which students and faculty are told which uniform they must wear, and what they must teach and learn. An academic world in which many of the teachers have seen combat. A world in which cooperation and camaraderie are literally lifesaving values. A world in which people seriously, without irony, refer to the "art" of war. A world of individuals dedicated to serving our nation. Sometimes I have to pinch myself, remembering how I fell out of my patriotic dream in high school when we studied the history of the Panama Canal, remembering my participation in marches against the war in Vietnam, my regular donations to the Fellowship of Reconciliation. I grew up believing in this country, in its dream. Yet the older I grow, the firmer my conviction that the American Dream has devolved into the planet-eating nightmare of multinational corporations. Would I be willing to kill or to die for Microsoft?

Yet I hold the conviction that peacekeeping is a noble calling. Of the twenty-eight cadets in my classes this semester, several have jumped from airplanes; two plan to fly helicopters. One wants to be an astronaut. But most of them say they're not sure why they have stayed at West Point beyond the two-year point of no return. They are third- and fourth-year students, now, and are therefore committed to at least five years in the Army after graduation. Most of them say they don't necessarily plan to have military careers; they are English majors; what they really want to do is read and write. Yet, apparently lacking the cynicism of my "normal" students, they seem more idealistic; ironically, more innocent. They are as willing to put themselves on the line in their poems as they are to try new meditative techniques. Some of them are writing pretty good sonnets, experimenting with slant-rhyme and split-rhyme. I read their poems delighting in the growing facility with which they are learning to use the tools and respecting the emotional risks they are willing to take in order to speak their truths. I hope that by teaching these twenty-eight cadets how to find and hold interior quiet, I am giving them the wherewithal of wise conflict resolution. Perhaps poetry will help them to lead others toward peace. There are, after all, precedents: warrior-poets. The great general George S. Patton, a West

Point graduate, though no Wilfred Owen, was nevertheless a serious amateur poet. In 1945, in a poem which described the moon looking down on a battlefield, he wrote:

> Yet not with regret she mourned them,
> Fair slain on the field of strife,
> Fools only lament the hero
> Who gives for faith his life.
> She sighed for the lives extinguished,
> She wept for the loves that grieve,
> But she glowed with pride on seeing
> That manhood still doth live.
> The moon sailed on contented,
> Above the heaps of slain,
> For she saw that manhood liveth,
> And honor breathes again.
>
> The Moon and the Dead

Heroes, faith, pride, honor: values the majority American culture has not believed in since the Lost Generation got lost. No one believes in those values anymore, we say, except rightwing religious fanatics and fools. But who distributes food in famine? Who delivers disaster relief? Who goes when we need to send someone into strife? Although it has not altered my congenital pacifism, working with West Point cadets has allowed me to see our military almost as I did when I was a child proud of my father's uniform. To see soldiers not as uniformed, musclebound GI Joe skinheads, but as volunteer firefighters willing to enter a heat-blinding inferno to rescue a terrified child still clutching the burnt match. I hope meditation will help my cadets recognize, even disobey, stupid and unjust orders, and to give wise and well-considered ones. I hope they will be soldiers who live the all-but-lost values of a nation conceived in the absurd concept of liberty and dedicated to the ridiculous proposition that we are all created equal. I hope they will be soldiers who live the humanist values kept alive by the poets, aborigines, and fools who refuse to close the door on our inner wilderness, with its echoing silence. We, after all, are crazy. We bring that verdant underworld jungle of absurd and necessary values into the marketplace, into the classroom, into this white man's world, even—as crazy as it seems—into the citadel.

Winter 2001

Don't Forget the Butterfly Effect

Brooke Allen

The best thing about reading lively narrative histories is the realization that we do not, in fact, live in uniquely strange times. The last few years have been unsettling, to say the least; but as Matthew Lockwood reminds us in his new book *To Begin the World Over Again*, so were the 1770s, '80s, and '90s.[1] In his lengthy, leisurely study, he takes his readers from the eye of the storm in North America and London to the myriad lands that were affected by the American War of Independence, demonstrating that "a local protest over taxes in a remote corner of North America would end on the streets of Dublin, the mountains of Peru, the beaches of Australia, and the jungles of India." Lockwood draws a moral from this spectacle and lays it out in his introduction:

> Examining the revolution from a truly global perspective, both geographically and thematically, forcefully reveals the often tragic interconnectedness of the world, compelling us to contemplate ourselves in an entangled world rather than as an isolated, exceptional chosen people. Removing the blinkers of a narrowly national political point of view opens new horizons of understanding, allowing us to realize the most urgent lesson taught by America's founding moment: American actions have, and have always had, unforeseen, unimagined global consequences.

1. Matthew Lockwood, *To Begin the World over Again: How the American Revolution Devastated the Globe* (New Haven: Yale University Press, 2019).

Well, this should come as a surprise to no one; any reader with the educational level and attention span to peruse this hefty tome will probably not imagine that events on the North American continent have ever occurred in a vacuum. Reflective Americans are in a self-hating mood right now, with some justification; nevertheless, it is more than a stretch for us to conclude that "the American Revolution Devastated the Globe," as Lockwood claims in the title of his book. More correctly, one might say that the American Revolution had certain ripple effects that caused certain portions of the globe to be devastated, or at any rate radically altered; but the same could be said for any major historical crisis. One is immediately reminded of the so-called butterfly effect, according to which the tiniest action, let's say the flapping of a butterfly's wing, can set in motion a series of actions that might result in a typhoon. But then of course the American Revolution and the global war it engendered were themselves the result of earlier butterfly wings flapping, most notably between 1756 and 1763 when the Seven Years' War roiled the world and reset the European balance of power strongly in Britain's favor, creating a spirit of bitter revanchism in France and Spain. In fact the American Revolution can best be seen as part of a series of political, social and economic changes that began in the mid-eighteenth century and continued well into the nineteenth, causing a wave of revolution, creative rebuilding and, yes, devastation across the globe. Some historians have dubbed this period the second Hundred Years' War between France and Britain.

While not an elegant writer, Lockwood can certainly spin a yarn, and he provides fascinating accounts of individuals whose lives were dramatically uprooted by the effects of the Revolution. Boston King, for example: born a slave in South Carolina, he joined the Loyalist army during the Revolution, since the British had promised slaves their freedom should they fight on their side; after the war he was settled with other ex-slaves in Nova Scotia; finding that his situation there was hardly better than it had been in slavery south of the border, he immigrated to Sierra Leone, where he helped found Freetown and became a Methodist missionary. Or the unlucky Eliza Fay, a young Englishwoman who arrived in India with her barrister husband after extraordinary travel adventures only to be captured and imprisoned by Haidar Ali, raja of Mysore. Or Bennelong, a native Australian captured by the British in the new settlement of Sydney Cove who eventually traveled to London and became something of a cultural link between the Aborigines and the conquering British. Or Micaela Bastidas, the Peruvian woman who masterminded the great rebellion against the Spanish and helped her husband establish himself as Tupac Amaru II, the last Inca, before they and their family were executed by the Spanish in a barbaric act of revenge and example. These people indeed lived in turbulent times—even more turbulent than our own—and Lockwood's narrative gifts do their stories justice.

It's one of the great ironies of history that Britain, apparently the ignominious loser in the American War of Independence, proved ultimately to be the global winner. Lockwood demonstrates how this happens. France was still smarting over her defeat to Britain in the Seven Years' War, in which she lost most of her possessions in North America and India. The American colonists' struggle for independence provided her with an opportunity to redress the balance, and the Comte de Vergennes, Louis XVI's foreign minister, apparently acted on the principle that "my enemy's enemy is my friend" when he agreed generously to subsidize the rebelling colonists. Silas Deane, who preceded Benjamin Franklin as American minister to France, sweetened the pill by assuring Vergennes that after an American victory "a great part of our commerce will naturally fall to France," and France entered the fray with high hopes. She was soon joined by Spain, which also desired to see Britain humiliated and stripped of her American spoils. France and Spain, both ruled by the house of Bourbon since 1714, were joined in a "family pact," and in 1779 they signed the so-called Convention of Aranjuez, pledging cooperation against Great Britain.

With the cessation of hostilities in 1783, it appeared that France and Spain had made the right bet. But appearances were very deceptive. France, which had spent the equivalent of two years' annual revenue on the war, was now effectively bankrupt, and the hollowness of Silas Deane's promises was revealed when the new United States turned back to its natural trading partner, Britain, at the expense of her one-time ally France. France's empty coffers would result in revolution and the fall of the French monarchy only a few years later. Spain, in 1783, seemed triumphant, but her military victories would prove costly and unsustainable. For example, the Spanish had successfully fought off a British attack in Nicaragua and had managed to seize Florida, but Britain ultimately benefited from her own failures: "The expenditure necessary to protect and govern such unproductive colonies from the inevitable Spanish and American attacks would be better spent elsewhere. Both were Spain's problem now . . . By securing its empire Spain was now set on a collision course with the new United States." The Count of Aranda, Spain's ambassador to France at the time, could already foresee the disaster that would ensue in the long run: the new American republic, he wrote,

> has been born a pygmy . . . and it needed the support and power of two states as powerful as Spain and France to win its independence. The day will come in which it grows and turns into a giant, even a frightening colossus, in that region. It will then forget the benefits it has received from the two powers, and it will only think of its own expansion . . . And within a few years we will see with real dismay the tyrannical existence of this colossus of which I am speaking. The first step for this power . . . will be to take over Florida, in order to dominate the Gulf of Mexico. After harassing us and our relations with New Spain in this way, it will aspire to conquer this vast empire, which we will not be able to defend against a formidable power established in that very continent and a neighbor of it.

All of his predictions, of course, came true. Spain would learn the hard way, as Britain did a bit earlier—with the loss of her American empire, in fact—that land empires were expensive and difficult to maintain.

It is instructive to look (though Lockwood does not do so) at Adam Smith's attack, written exactly at the beginning of the

American uprising, against the inefficiency and waste of the imperial system as exemplified by the thirteen colonies, and of the mercantilist system in general. Smith is often seen as advocating a particular system, and to a certain extent he does, but his *Wealth of Nations* is for the most part a *description* of a process that was taking place as he wrote: the birth of modern capitalism. Smith was brutal in his assessment of the imperial, mercantile project as it stood in 1776:

> [C]ountries which contribute neither revenue nor military force towards the support of the empire, cannot be considered as provinces. They may perhaps be considered as appendages, as a sort of splendid and showy equipage of the empire. But if the empire can no longer support the expense of keeping up this equipage, it ought certainly to lay it down . . . The rulers of Great Britain have, for more than a century past, amused the people with the imagination that they possessed a great empire on the west side of the Atlantic. This empire, however, has hitherto existed in imagination only. It has hitherto been, not an empire, but the project of an empire; not a gold mine, but the project of a gold mine; a project which has cost, and which, if pursued in the same way as it has been hitherto, is likely to cost, immense expense, without being likely to bring any profit; for the effects of the monopoly of the colony trade, it has been shewn, are, to the great body of the people, mere loss instead of profit.

Britain, he snidely concluded, should "endeavor to accommodate her future views and designs to the real mediocrity of her circumstances."

Britain did learn some lessons from the American disaster, if not precisely the one Smith had endeavored to teach. One of them was authoritarianism, which increased in her manner of government both at home and in the colonies. While Britain had initially been "arrogantly sure that an easy victory over America was foreordained," she quickly became "suffused with fear, paranoia, and panic. The mood of the country changed. Attitudes toward dissent and disloyalty, crime and disorder hardened, precipitating the worst violence in London's history." Here Lockwood refers to the Gordon Riots of

1780. The need for more and more soldiers to fight in America had made Ireland a prime recruiting ground for the British, who realized the need to ease up on the discriminatory penal laws against Catholics in Ireland, their oldest colony. The subsequent Catholic Relief Act of 1778 raised a panicky bigotry among Protestants throughout the British Isles, culminating in the terrifying Gordon Riots, during which anti-Catholic mobs looted and pillaged London in a weeklong spree; several hundred people were killed. Both ideologically (with its assertion that all men are created equal) and politically (with Britain compelled for practical reasons to offer a few rights to the oppressed Irish Catholics) the American war offered "a clear, if fleeting, opportunity for [Irish] independence." Leaders of the so-called Volunteer movement, allied with the English Whigs, pushed for legislative reform and the lifting of trade restrictions, and to some extent they succeeded. But a period of reaction set in in England with the end of the American war, and greater reaction upon the beginning of hostilities with revolutionary France a decade later. "The lesson [the British government] took from the American Revolution was not that British rule had been overly strict and selfish, but that it had in fact been too weak. In the years after the war, Britain became more conservative and authoritarian." The 1798 Irish rebellion was brutally quashed, and two years later the Act of Union with Great Britain was passed and the Irish parliament ceased to exist. The new conservatism and authoritarianism had, it goes without saying, at least as much to do—more—with the French Revolution as it did with the American. But of course the French Revolution was enabled by the American. Which was enabled by the Seven Years' War. Which was enabled by the War of the Spanish Succession . . . Oh dear! Once we start thinking about the butterfly effect, we can establish no point of origin. Again, Lockwood's purported thesis—"How the American Revolution Devastated the Globe"—is thin, to say the least.

Lockwood devotes a good deal of attention to India, where British control had become as unsustainable, by the 1770s, as it had in America. At that time, as Lockwood points out,

> India was a geographical expression, not a focus of common identity or national cohesion. The British were not seen as imperial oppressors of some nascent united India, but rather as simply one in a long line of overlords that had ruled parts of the subcontinent for centuries. Indeed, before the reforms of the late eighteenth century, the British had consciously modeled their rule on indigenous precedents, adopting native law, finance, and administration . . . It should come as no surprise that many people in the Hindu majority of India thus saw little practical difference between the British ruling class and the Persianate ruling classes that had held sway in Bengal or Benares, or still ruled in Mysore, or Hyderabad.

The parts of India under British control were ruled not by the crown but by the British East India Company, a monopoly trading company that had over the years taken on most governmental functions, including its own army. In an attempt to bring the activities of the Company under a bit of government scrutiny, Parliament passed a Regulating Act in 1773, appointing a governor-general of Bengal, Warren Hastings, and beginning the process of centralization. But these measures didn't begin to fix administrative confusion on the subcontinent. As the American Revolution progressed, it became evident that the British Empire in India, like that in America, was overstretched and underfunded. Indian states were taxed at punitive rates and often quite openly robbed to foot the bill for Britain's trading shortfalls and insatiable demand for armies and manpower. In Whitehall, there was little agreement on how the Indian possessions were to be governed and what role the East India Company should play in that government, though William Pitt's 1784 India Bill made a more extensive attempt at untangling affairs.

Eventually Hastings was impeached for mismanagement and corruption and made the fall guy for all the skullduggery perpetrated by the East India Company administration. His trial, which began in 1788 and lasted a full seven years, could justly be said to be the trial of the century, and as well as judging Hastings the man it judged the entire system of exploitation that had developed over the course of nearly two centuries. Edmund Burke gave a lurid description of

Company officials in one of the many famous speeches he made before the tribunal:

> animated with all the avarice of age, and all the impetuosity of youth, they roll in one after another; wave upon wave; and there is nothing before the eyes of the natives but an endless, hopeless, prospect of new flights of birds of prey and passage, with appetites continually renewing for a food that is continually wasting.

Lockwood describes the trial, probably with some justice, as "a spectacle of histrionic oratory, vicious invective, and a stubborn refusal to conciliate or bend." But the rhetorical heights struck during the trial by the leaders of the prosecution—Burke, Charles James Fox, and Richard Brinsley Sheridan—were of unexampled brilliance and would set the political and emotional stage for reformist zeal throughout the nineteenth century. Perhaps inevitably, though, Hastings was acquitted. By that time Britain was hard at war with revolutionary France, and political reaction had set in; chaos could not be allowed to rule in India lest the subcontinent go the way of the American colonies. Lord Cornwallis, fresh from his drubbing at Yorktown, was appointed governor-general. Having witnessed "the disastrous consequences of American separatism first-hand," Cornwallis "feared that British India was well on its way to repeating the mistakes of British America. To prevent the growth of a distinct political class in India, Cornwallis passed measures intended to divide British officials from India and Indians," laying the legal foundations, with his Cornwallis Code, for what would become the rigidly hierarchical, race- and caste-based British India of the nineteenth century.

The most fascinating part of Lockwood's narrative, for me, was the section on the haphazard, tragic settlement of Australia. This settlement did indeed occur as a direct result of the American War, since with the loss of her American colonies, Britain found herself lacking sufficient dumping grounds for the many convicts and prostitutes who were overflowing England's inadequate prisons and prison hulks. The east coast of Australia, explored by Captain Cook in 1770, was deemed a suitable spot, and the first convict ships arrived at Botany Bay in 1788 under the command of Arthur Phillip, the colony's first governor. The anecdotes Lockwood provides about first contact with the Aborigines are unbearably poignant, for Phillip came with good intentions. King George III had urged him to "endeavor by every means possible to open an intercourse with the natives, and to conciliate their affections," and Phillip tried his best: "The authorities in Britain, and Phillip himself, had been concerned to learn from the mistakes of North America, and had taken steps to ensure that the violence that consumed the Atlantic colonies was not repeated in the Pacific." Attempts were certainly made to establish warm relations, and many of the new arrivals took to the natives: "They laugh when they see us laugh," noted one settler, "and they appear to be of a peaceable Disposition, and have a Generosity about them, in offering You a share of their Food. If you meet with any of them, they will readily offer You Fish, Fire, & Water." There were numerous attempts to gain knowledge about the land and how to survive on it from the Aborigines, but there were frustratingly few opportunities to do so, so eventually Phillip simply kidnapped a few. And some of the more thuggish convicts inevitably committed violence against the Eora settlements. But as in America, the great killer was smallpox; just a year after the colonists' arrival, 70 percent of the local population had died.

The settlement of Sierra Leone, too, was a result of the American War, which gave birth in Britain to a new awareness of the plight of the former slaves, quite a few of whom showed up in Britain, rootless and desperate, after the Revolution. The nation's conscience had already been shocked by the horrific fate, in 1781, of the slave ship *Zong* (subject of the famous *Slave Ship* painting of J. M. W. Turner): finding themselves in mid-ocean with insufficient supplies, crew members pushed the less valuable women and children slaves out through the portholes to die—as many as 150 of them. This tale might not have been publicly known had the slaving syndicate not tried to make an insurance claim on the murdered slaves! The outrage that ensued did much to shift the social conscience of Britain.

> Many began to see a link between slavery and a corrupt political system, between the act of denying the liberty of slaves, and the trampling of the liberties of British subjects. The American War, and its discourse of imperial critique, provided room to debate and reimagine the British Empire on a new moral foundation of free labor and free trade.

The Sierra Leone Company, an attempt to resettle former slaves in West Africa, was one result: "In the years after the American War, familiar criticisms of an immoral empire were replaced by a more supportive public sentiment as the empire was portrayed as a force for good around the world." Of course, public sentiment and the new portrayal of empire hardly matched the reality of what we nowadays would call the colonized peoples' "lived experience," and Lockwood's descriptions of life in Sierra Leone are, like life in many other British colonies, quite appalling. In the end the Company failed, and Sierra Leone became a crown colony, part of Britain's quickly expanding African empire.

In 1792, the first official embassy from the King of Great Britain to the Emperor of China set out on its mission. This, too, was a result of the American Revolution: with the loss of its previous "triangle trade"—England to Africa, Africa to the Americas, the Americas back to England—British merchants began to conceive of a new triangle trade, England-India-China. China produced lots of things that England wanted, but there appeared to be only one Chinese demand that England could fulfill—opium, from its vast poppy fields in India.

> In the wake of Britain's American debacle, [the China mission] was nothing less than a mission to save Britain's soul. The expansion of British trade in Asia provided the possibility of resetting the terms and conditions of British imperialism. In the place of territorial Atlantic empires built on the backs of slaves, a new empire of free labor could be constructed in the east . . . That it sought to do so on the back of an expanded opium trade seems not to have troubled them overmuch.

Thus began the policy that would eventually lead to the terrible Opium Wars.

Here, abruptly, Lockwood's narrative comes to a close: without any sort of conclusion or attempt to restate and assert his central thesis. It's a long book; one gets the feeling he might simply have become exhausted by his task. In the end, he's left us with a great deal of information, a lot of loose ends, and an inconclusive and incoherent thesis he does not trouble to summarize. Plenty of readers who enjoy narrative history will get pleasure from this book, but whether it really advances our understanding of historical causation is dubious.

Autumn 2020

Part Four

Memoirs

“The Impossible Real”

Abraham Pais

I have heard it said that a witness to past disasters often finds it impossible to make clear to others what he or she is talking about. I am no exception. When I hear myself talk to others about World War II experiences of mine, I invariably have a peculiar sensation. I hear my own words, know that I speak the truth as honestly as I can, yet cannot believe what I hear myself saying. In other words, the me of those past days has become totally estranged from the me of today. Dissociative reactions like these are fairly common among survivors of suffering and sorrow, as recorded case histories demonstrate. Maurice Blanchot has coined an elegant expression for this sort of experience: “The impossible real.”

I have observed that the norms of human conduct do not apply in the stressful times of war. I should now add that—as my own case illustrates—the same appears to be true of some aspects of the behavior of survivors. Only twice in the years since World War II have I been able to get in touch with the enormously strong pain and hurt that lie hidden within me.

The first occasion was during one of my several stays in Jerusalem when I visited for the first time the memorial Yad Vashem. The name means “a monument and a name,” a superbly chosen quotation from Isaiah 56:5: “I will give in my house a monument and a name better than sons and daughters. I will give them an everlasting name that shall not be cut off.” The memorial is built on a hilltop near Mount Herzl in Jerusalem.

The most impressive and moving part of Yad Vashem is its Memorial Hall (Ohel Yizkor). The interior, with its granite dome and floor, gives a sinister impression, meant to convey aspects of concentration camps. It is sparsely lit to bring into focus the eternal flame burning in the center of the floor, in front of which ashes of murdered Jews are interred.

After entering the Memorial Hall, I was given a *keppel*, a head covering male Jews, and also Gentiles, are obliged to wear when entering a Jewish sanctuary or place of worship. I walked up to a balustrade, behind which lies the message of the memorial, chiseled into the floor's granite. It is a stark and extraordinarily powerful one. Just the names of twenty-two camps: Auschwitz, Belźec, Bergen-Belsen, Buchenwald, Chelmno, Dachau, Draney, Flossenbürg, Kaiserwald, Majdanek, Mauthausen, Natzweiler, Neuengamme, Ravensbrück, Sachsenhausen, Sobibor, Stutthof, Szebnie, Theresienstadt, Treblinka, Westerbork, Zemun.

When I stood there, reading those names, something completely unexpected happened to me that has never occurred before or since. I started yelling loudly. No tears. These were the wounded cries of an animal. Even as I was doing so, I could simultaneously understand what was happening to me. After many years I had finally come in touch with pain, deep inside, which could not be expressed in ordinary words in everyday settings.

I have visited Yad Vashem on two later occasions. On the second visit I only wept quietly. On the third I did not even do that, just stood there in a solemn, somber mood. Which only corroborates the well-known fact that repeated exposure to events or their images diminishes the impact. That was also evident to me as I walked through Yad Vashem's exhibit of photographs (I believe they are mostly from Bergen-Belsen), showing emaciated human beings, barely alive, and piles of corpses. While these pictures never fail to make an impression, they affected me much less strongly than the starkness of the Memorial Hall. I had seen the pictures too often, there and elsewhere.

It seems to me that the total absence of death camp photographs only serves to enhance the Frenchman Claude Lanzmann's *Shoah*, his monumental documentary film about the extermination of the European Jews, to my taste the most powerful and moving account of those events. Seeing the film on television, in 1991, provided the second occasion on which I experienced my old pain.

The film consists of a series of interviews with survivors and with people who lived near the camps, interspersed with pictures of those camps, not as they were then but as they look now, and with shots of trains moving toward one campsite or another. For hours I sat transfixed, watching the stories unfold.

One interview that particularly affected me was with a Jew who had been a barber before being deported and who in camp had been assigned to cutting off the hair of women, for reasons of "hygiene." Actually, they were about to be gassed; their hair was subsequently sent on for industrial purposes. The barbershop was situated right next to the gas chambers. He and his fellow workers were strictly forbidden to talk to the women, who were all naked by then, on pain of being gassed themselves. At one point our man sees the wife and sister of his best friend enter, both of whom he knows very well. He cannot say a word to them. Then he sees them march off to their doom.

Up to that moment the barber had spoken casually, almost businesslike, about his experiences, as he had also done in earlier parts of the documentary. When, however, he came to the point of describing how he saw those two women walk to the gas chambers, he fell apart completely, overwhelmed by the pain of memory. The very same thing happened to me as I sat there by myself watching him. For a long time I sobbed uncontrollably. It was not because of the scene he was describing—I was never in a camp myself—but because the sequence—first talking casually, then breaking down—resonated with my own pain, likewise hidden most of the time.

I feel that common language is inadequate to those events, which were too singular to be described by such terms as horror, tragedy, disaster. Those words sound too worn to serve their well-meant purposes. For the same reason I refuse to use the H-word, in writing as well as in speech. I have a visceral dislike of people like Eli Wiesel, professional *shewa* sitters,[1] who make a living from H-word tales.

If I am not clear as to whether this past contains lessons, and if I am not sure that my language has been adequate, then why do I write of these memories at all? My purpose, I think, is to show how one may find it possible to emerge from catastrophe into a fulfilling life.

I was born in Holland, and there I was, in the autumn of 1941, with my PhD from the University of Utrecht in my pocket but without a job. I had only a small amount of money at my disposal. I had, however, ideas on how to continue the line of physics research I had begun in preparation for my doctorate and went to work on these. Sometime between then and June 1942 (I don't remember precisely when), when Jews were forbidden to use trains, I moved back from my room near Utrecht to my parents' home in Amsterdam. During that period, I traveled regularly to Utrecht to discuss my research with Professor Rosenfeld, my adviser. He and his wife graciously offered me a place to sleep in their home, so that I could spend an extra day or two talking about my work. They are both gone now. My memories of them are affectionate and respectful.

In the autumn of 1941, Jewish children were barred from public schools; the Jewish community now provided schooling for them. Teachers for these schools were in demand. I felt I should participate; I could also use the few extra guilders. I still have a yellowed letter dated May 3, 1942, confirming that I teach mathematics in the youth center at Plantage Franschelaan 13, as well as at a center for adult education at Nicolaas Witsenkade 14. I also have an identity card dated October 13, 1942, issued by the JR (*Joodse Raad*, or Jewish Council) and signed by presidents Abraham Asscher and David Cohen, which states, in Dutch and German, that I am an *Oberlehrer*

1. *Shewa*, meaning seven, refers to the number of days Orthodox Jews sit in mourning for the death of a next-of-kin.

(secondary school teacher) who is *unentbehrlich* (indispensable) to the education of Jewish pupils.

Almost from the start I had to walk to get to my place of work. In June public transportation was forbidden to Jews. In addition I had to hand in my bike at that time.

The really bad times had started. Since May I'd worn a star. In July deportations were initiated. In September the stamp drama began. The first in my family to get a stamp was my father. Between June and September he had received four different bilingual legitimization cards, two issued by the Office of Social Affairs of the city of Amsterdam, two by the JR, stating that he was *Religionshauptlehrer* (headmaster for religious education). Then, on September 30, he received a stamp on his ID card stating that until further notice the holder was exempt from mobilization for labor. The stamp was numbered 82.226. It was one of the so-called 80.000 series, issued to those connected with the JR. If my father counted among these, it was not because of any involvement with deportation measures, but simply because he taught at a Jewish school.

For that same reason an 80.000 stamp, no. 85.303, was issued to me as well, on October 6. On February 11, 1943, mine, however, was upgraded to a 40.000 stamp, no. 40.874, one of the 640 stamps in that most coveted category of all, Jews enjoying various forms of German protection.

The institution of that classification had been the result of initiatives by the Dutch Secretaries General of the Interior and especially of Education, Science, and the Protection of Culture. These men had been able to convince the Germans that there was a small group of Jews who had contributed so much to advancing Holland's cultural life that they deserved preferential treatment. What had brought me into such company? I had been a university assistant, an appointment which in its time had gone to the Minister of Education in The Hague for approval, so that I was registered as a Jew who had lost a nationally recognized position. My assistantship in physics may actually have added very little to the culture of the Netherlands, yet this official registration sufficed to make me a candidate for a 40.000 exemption.

I turn now to my sister Annie, who was nearly twenty when the war came to Holland. Already earlier, in October 1939, she had become engaged to Herman de Leeuw, a young Jewish businessman. I believe that he too had managed to obtain an 80.000 stamp. People used to pull strings in those days. They married in May 1942. I recall how my family first went to Amsterdam's City Hall for the civil wedding, then to the Sephardic synagogue for the religious ceremony. There she sat, my pretty little sister, under the chuppah,[2] wearing a lovely white dress—with a star attached. Afterward we had a fine dinner. I do not remember where that took place, but can recall the main course: sweetbreads, hard to get in those days, with peas in the pod.

Annie's marriage abruptly transformed her personality. From a rather indolent girl she turned into a young woman who took charge. How well I recall looking at her with new respect and increased affection. Because of her marriage, she shared the protection of her young husband's stamp.

One late evening around the end of 1942, I was in my upstairs room in my parents' home when suddenly I heard yelling and shrieking in the room next to mine, in the house next door. It was the bedroom of an old man in his eighties, a Jew. I knew at once what was happening: Germans had come in to take him away. There I stood, one ear glued to the wall, listening to those terrible and frightening noises that went on for some twenty minutes. Then all became silent. The next morning I learned that my guess had been correct. My old neighbor, in his nightclothes, had been clinging to his bed, refusing to move and yelling for mercy. He was gone. The Germans had struck meters away from me.

My father had three brothers and three sisters, all married. My mother had one brother and one sister, both unmarried, and another

2. Literally baldachin, under which the betrothed sit during the ceremony. The word has come to mean the marriage ritual as a whole.

sister who was a widow. My mother's father, well into his seventies, was my only grandparent then still alive. I had five cousins in all. Of these, only one sister of my father and her two children survived (she had been married to a non-Jew), as well as one cousin from my mother's side who went into hiding. The other seventeen family members were deported and never returned. How could these gentle people possibly have harmed Germany? It is the kind of question every survivor keeps mulling over when thinking of lost dear ones . . .

When I began courting Tineke Buchter in the days before the war, it was my custom on Saturday afternoons to go to her home at Nieuwe Zyds Voorburgwal 282 and stay over until Sunday. Tineke, a non-Jew strongly involved with Jewish issues, lived there with Marie, her mother (who was divorced), of whom I also became very fond. Marie's mother would also often be there, a spry, corpulent, determined little lady. After the summer of 1940, when my parents had accepted her, Tineke would come to our home Friday nights for the weekly festive Sabbath dinner and would stay over.

By 1941 Tineke and I had begun to drift apart a little. That nothing ever came of our relationship was entirely due to my own immaturity. Yet we remained close, and her most important role in my life was yet to come, as will soon be seen. We stayed close until in the beginning of 1946 I left Holland, to return only for short visits. Now Tineke is an esteemed psychiatrist living near New York City. We continue to see each other occasionally, have tea or dinner together, and, of course, talk of old times. Our bonds remain strong. She was and still is one of the most important persons in my life.

Tineke and Marie's home became a haven for hunted people almost from the day of Holland's capitulation. In the first days of the occupation, those who sought refuge were not so much Jews as persons who feared incarceration because of their political convictions. As the situation grew more and more threatening for Jews, they began to be hospitably taken in, not so much for prolonged stays as in transit to safe premises. Tineke chiefly, but also Marie, became increasingly active in helping to find hiding places.

When deportations started in the summer of 1942, I began to think seriously of going into hiding myself. I had sworn to myself that I would never respond to any order to move to a place where Germans would have direct control over my movements. My exemption stamps gave me some respite, but I never for a moment believed that their guarantees would last. I first discussed my hiding plan with Tineke, who fully agreed and pledged her help. Sometime thereafter I talked it over with my parents, urging them to make similar plans. I vividly recall their response. My father said he felt he had to go to a labor camp when called up because of his intense feelings of solidarity with his fellow Jews. Whereupon my mother said, "Go if you want to—but I won't." In the event, she prevailed. I did not have such discussions with my sister because after her marriage she and her husband had moved to an apartment of their own. I have happy memories of visits there, in particular of a nice lunch Annie prepared for Herman, me, and herself.

In the fall of 1942, I was unofficially informed that I was under consideration for a high class 40.000 stamp. That would give me extra respite, but my mind was nevertheless made up. At an appropriate moment I would go into hiding. Tineke had meanwhile arranged a place for me. I began to make preparations. Little by little I would bring clothes of mine to Tineke's house, for temporary storage. Next came my better books—with my name on the flyleaf cut out. I left behind books of my youth, the adventures of Pietje Bel, of Dik Trom, of Prikkebeen, as well as my schoolbooks. All of these are lost. In later years I have wished off and on to hold them in my hands again. This is one of the ways—by no means the worst—in which I feel cut off from my childhood.

Then I began to take from a Jewish acquaintance some lessons in indoor physical exercise, since I wished to be prepared for keeping physically fit during a period of confinement which might well be prolonged. A student friend of mine gave me a pair of lightweight dumbbells to be used for exercise purposes; these too were duly stored with Tineke.

At that juncture an unforeseen alternative came my way. My early Zionist friends Síeg Gitter and Leah Neubauer, now married, had begun planning their own escape from Holland via Belgium and France to Spain. They asked me whether I would like to join them—at their own rather substantial expense. I asked for one day's time to think this over.

I decided to decline their truly generous offer. At that time I was deeply immersed in theoretical physics research. I could not imagine abandoning that work nor see how I could concentrate on it while I was in flight. That, much more than the obvious risks of the enterprise, held me back. So there came a day when I embraced the two of them and from the bottom of my heart wished them bon voyage. They did make it to Spain, and from there to Argentina.

In 1943 I made my own move—inside Holland. On January 13, the Secretary General of Education, Science and Cultural Affairs signed a letter addressed to me, written in German. At the heading stood: *Betrifft Arbeitseinsatz* (concerns mobilization of labor). The text read: "I hereby inform you that I have called the attention of the [German] General Commissioner for Special Affairs to your situation. He has agreed to give the matter special consideration." It was the formal announcement that I would get a 40.000 stamp which, as mentioned, I indeed received in February. While I was of course pleased, I did not change my plans.

On March 12 I received a form letter signed by the Secretary General for the Interior, this one in Dutch. It said: "I have the honor to inform you that you will neither be transported to Amsterdam nor put to work in a work camp abroad." The mention of transport did not apply to me but to Jews living outside the capital. The reference to no deportation had to do with the decision made meanwhile to move all holders of 40.000 stamps to De Schaffelaar, a small chateau in Barneveld, a little town in the province of Utrecht, this to prevent their accidental capture in razzias (roundups). Some had moved there the previous December; the rest had to move now. That, I decided, was the ideal moment for me to go to the hiding place Tineke had arranged for me. If people wondered where I was, my parents could simply say that I had gone to Barneveld. On March 19, I arrived at my hideout.[3]

My new home was a patrician house on one of Amsterdam's famous old canals, Keizersgracht 499—not far from Anne Frank's place of hiding. My host, Mr. Koehorst—I called him "Pa"—was a gentleman tailor who had his workshop downstairs. The rest of the family consisted of his wife, Ma, two sons, Lou, a few years younger than I, and his younger brother Rob, and one daughter, about my age, Alwien, a very pretty young woman. The family quarters were in the building's top two floors. I had a pleasant room on the top floor to myself. It was on the whole a cheery family, though I could feel some tension between the parents (who divorced after the War). We took our meals together; otherwise I spent my time in my own room.

I had a false identity card, under the name Arthur Meerwaldt, MD, with of course my own picture inserted. The card, provided by Tineke, was most probably a real card voluntarily "lost" by its owner, who could apply for a new one. From now on I was called Ad or Adje. On arrival I still had my own valid ration card. Later I would get one stolen from a card distribution office. A financial arrangement with my hosts had been agreed upon, whereby I paid them a reasonable monthly sum for room and board. The money came from the sale of my father's stamp collection. He had been a collector since his youth, though spending only modest sums of money on his hobby. He had

3. A few words about the fate of the Barnevelders, as those who went there came to be called. They lived in an island of tranquility, cut off from the rest of the world. Life was not unpleasant. Schooling for children and evening lectures for adults were organized by the participants themselves. Food was tolerable. So it remained until September 29, 1943, the day on which the JR in Amsterdam was dissolved. On that same day, Germans arrived in Barneveld and gave the inmates thirty minutes to pack for transport to Westerbork. In September 1944 they were transported from there to Theresienstadt, the better-class concentration camp. From there, some were brought to Switzerland in the spring of 1945; the others were liberated by Soviet armed forces and returned safely to Holland. Had I gone to Barneveld, I would therefore most probably have survived.

a very presentable set of albums. For example, he had a complete set of Dutch stamps from the first issue on (dating, I seem to remember, from the 1850s). In those war days there was great demand among the well-to-do for diamonds and for stamps, since both these items take up very little space and could be stored in tiny containers that were fire- and bombproof—and could easily be hidden. At that time the value of my father's collection must have risen to many thousands of dollars, which provided for the material security of our family.

And so I settled in for a life that may be called carefree—given the circumstances. I developed a regular routine. Every day, all through my years in hiding, I did forty-five minutes of physical exercise before breakfast, in front of an open window with curtains closed, and another forty-five minutes in the late afternoon before dinner. I gave hours of each day to research, helped by the few books I had with me. These included one I had specially bought in preparation for my isolation: Volume 24, part 1, of the *Handbuch der Physik*, an 800-page tome that contained the best summaries of what was known about quantum physics to date. It is by far the most expensive book I have ever bought; it still graces my shelves in my present university office. If I had need for books not in my possession—that happened only infrequently—Tineke would fetch them for me from the university library. I would interrupt my studies once in a while for a chat with Lou, who worked at home as a tailor in his father's business. I would also spend long hours reading belles-lettres.

I of course keenly felt—especially in the beginning—the restrictions imposed on my movements: I could never be out on the streets or enjoy casual encounters with friends and acquaintances. This lack of stimulus caused me to do something I had never done before: keep a diary, in which I wrote regularly during the remaining war years, noting events, unbosoming feelings, recording thoughts and ideas. It was shortly after the war that, in a fit of melancholy, I burned those diaries. It was an irrational and in fact futile attempt to rid myself of very painful memories. Now I find the act both understandable and regrettable. Had I not done so, I would now have documents about the daily life of one who lived practically next door to Anne

Frank—but who survived. Those lost diaries would certainly have been a valuable help in the present undertaking.

On May 19, exactly two months after vanishing from the surface of the earth, I reached my twenty-fifth birthday. My hosts made it a pleasant day for me, but there were of course no family or friends dropping in, nor even letters in the mail. Not one person of my past life knew where I was, except for Tineke. That was one of the crucial precautionary rules of the times. The less you knew the better, in case you got caught. Not even torture can make you confess what you do not know.

Dear Tineke saw to it, however, that I would get an occasional letter that she would pick up for me. I still have one of these, birthday greetings from my sister Annie, written the week after. She began by congratulating me on the "two birthdays"—Tineke, two years younger, and I were born on the same day. She further wrote that the following week she would be celebrating her first wedding anniversary with family and friends, and that she would miss me greatly on that day. Her letter went on to describe a visit to our father at his school for Jewish children. Just after she arrived the air-raid siren sounded. A war plane went right over the school; a few machine gun bullets hit the playground. Many children became hysterical; one fainted. The letter continues: "Jews who had been baptized Christian have to leave next Friday. They received a call-up at their home address, just like we did." It ends: "Perhaps we shall soon be together again." This letter is the last memento I have of my dear sister. Two weeks after having written it, she was killed.

The German letter of call-up to Annie and Herman is lost, but I still have an accompanying printed notice in Dutch, dated May 23, signed by the two JR presidents. It says: "On the strength of the accompanying call-up, the German authorities order you to appear on Tuesday, May 25, between eight and eighteen hours, at the constabulary barracks, Polderweg, to be put to work in Germany . . . You should note that the sharpest possible measures will be taken against you if you do not appear."

As soon as I learned of Annie's call-up, I made plans to meet with her. I do not recall the specific arrangements. In any event, one day very soon afterward I went to my parents' home, on a borrowed bike and without a star. There I found Annie waiting for me. I took her to my old room upstairs, where we sat down and talked. The gist of what I said was to urge her most strongly not to go to the camps but rather to go into hiding with her husband. I was in a position to suggest that because Tineke and I had discussed their hiding option some time earlier, whereupon Tineke had come up with a concrete proposal for a hiding place.

Annie said no, she could not do that, because Herman had refused to entertain the idea on grounds I had heard earlier from others: Being cooped up would drive him crazy. What could I say? Even though information on gas chambers awaiting Dutch Jews had not yet reached us, all my instincts had told me: Don't go. But what arguments could I marshal against a young woman's desire to stick it out with her husband? I simply did not know what more to say to her. So we sat and talked a little more about this and that. Then I took her in my arms and hugged her. For the last time. Then I said good-bye to my parents and left forever the home of my teenage years and returned to my hiding place.

Just a few days later Alwien came into my room to tell me that Annie and Herman had departed. My reaction was what I believe amounted to hysterics. For minutes on end I cried but also laughed and felt completely irrational. Then, exhausted, I calmed down.

A few days later, my parents received a postcard from barracks 64, Westerbork, written by Herman. It read:

> Dear parents, just back from a soccer match which we lost, 4-3, at the last moment. It was a great match. Annie looks well and is a wonderful and dear woman . . . We laugh a lot . . . Westerbork agrees much better with us than we anticipated . . . Food is good. Do not worry about us. Now I say farewell and hope to see you soon. Annie is *very well.* Kisses.

It is the last sign of life we ever had from them. When the war was over, I did everything possible to find out what had happened to them, but could nowhere obtain any information. Fifty years later, in the fall of 1991, I found out.

With typical thoroughness, the Germans had classified the *Lager*, camps where Jews and others were confined, into a variety of categories—from places to stay, to concentration camps, to *Vernichtungslager*, extermination camps, the principal settings for the *Endlösung der Judenfrage*, the Final Solution. There were six of the latter. The oldest, Chelmno, sixty miles west of Warsaw, went into operation in late 1941. The other five were (distances always counted from Warsaw): Auschwitz Birkenau, 120 miles to the southwest, also in part a concentration camp, according to Raul Hilberg, "the largest death center the world had ever seen"; Treblinka, 30 miles to the northeast; Sobibor, 80 miles to the southeast, 5 miles from the town of Wlodawa; Majdanek, near Lublin, 60 miles to the southeast; and Belźec, near Lemberg, 125 miles to the southeast.

When on January 26, 1945, Russian forces first entered Auschwitz, they found only 2,800 invalid survivors. In 1946, *Obersturmbannführer* (lieutenant-colonel) Rudolf Hoess, the camp commander, earlier a convicted murderer, would boast at the Nuremberg trials that he had overseen at Auschwitz the extermination of two and a half million persons, not counting the half million who had been allowed to succumb to starvation.[4] Present estimates, varying to within twenty percent, put the number of people killed in Auschwitz at about one million.[5]

The capacity for death at Auschwitz far exceeded that of the other killing centers. The method used was to drop crystallized prussic acid, known as Zyklon B, through an opening in the death chambers.

4. William L. Shirer, *The Rise and Fall of the Third Reich: A History of Nazi Germany* (New York: Simon and Schuster, 1960), 664.

5. G. Reitlinger, *The Final Solution: The Attempt to Exterminate the Jews of Europe, 1939–1945* (London: Vallentine, Mitchell, 1953), 460, 461.

"When the Soviets moved in, twenty-nine of the thirty-five store rooms had been burned down. In the six remaining ones, the liberators found part of the camp's legacy: 368,820 men's suits, 836,255 women's coats and dresses, large quantities of children's clothes."[6]

The first camp to be liberated by the Western Allies was Bergen-Belsen at Celle, near Hanover, in western Germany. When on April 15, 1945, British troops entered the German camp, administration had already broken down completely. Food supplies had been shut off, the starving inmates were left to their own devices, spotted typhus and diarrhea raged unchecked, tens of thousands of corpses rotted in barracks and on dung heaps, rats attacked living inmates (dead ones were eaten by starving prisoners). The British troops found 2,800 women, 12,000 men, and 13,000 unburied corpses. Another 13,000 died within a few days of liberation. After the camp was freed, every rag and stick had to be destroyed by fire.

Holland had to make its contribution. 3,722 Jews were transported from there to Belsen. Of these, 2,184 survived, the highest percentage of Jews from Holland as compared with those sent to any of the other camps. Of the 62,000 Dutch Jews sent to Auschwitz, only 1,000 survived.[7]

Of the camps mentioned, Auschwitz has become the lasting symbol of the Final Solution. It was there that the Russians found survivors who could testify to what had happened. It was also there that they found the killing machinery largely intact, as well as materials that give silent testimony to the plunder of the dead. It was about Auschwitz that Rudolf Hoess, its commander, testified freely in Nuremberg about the killings. Moreover, the ex-Auschwitzers have established a number of national committees that, every year on January 26, organize memorial meetings, events that are fittingly mentioned in the press.

6. Cf. Raul Hilberg, *The Destruction of the European Jews* (London: W. H. Allen and Co., 1961), 632.

7. E. A. Cohen, *De negentien treinen naar Sobibor* (Amsterdam: Elsevier, 1979), 22.

By comparison, the other killing centers have caught much less public attention. Perhaps the least known of all is camp Sobibor on the river Bug, even though several hundred thousand Jews were killed there. One can understand why not much has been heard of Sobibor. First of all, when the Russians reached it, they found no signs of survivors nor, in fact, of a camp. Already in the fall of 1943, orders had come from above to destroy the camp without leaving a trace. The same happened in Treblinka and Bełżec. This was done because by that time the German armies were already retreating from Russia. On the preceding July 15, Soviet forces had launched their first summer offensive and had since retaken Smolensk and Charkov. The area of the three death camps in eastern Poland was therefore increasingly exposed to recapture, and the German authorities were determined to keep their annihilation operations a deep secret.

After *Vernichtungslager* Sobibor had been razed, the entire terrain was planted over with saplings by thirty Jewish forced laborers, who were all shot in November 1943. It was as if the Final Solution had never taken place there. "Sobibor was Himmler's best kept secret."[8]

On the campsite now one can only find a commemorative plaque which reads: "Sobibor. A Nazi death camp stood here from May 1942 to October 1943. In it were killed 250,000 Russian POWs, Jews, Poles, and Gypsies." This is a lie since no Poles or Russians were exterminated there. The Poles, a notoriously anti-Semitic nation, would not even see fit to record who were the only sufferers.

A second reason for history's comparative silence about Sobibor is that among the millions of pages of German documents captured by the Allies in 1945, there are only three short documents referring to it. Finally, there were very few who, after the war, could tell what happened. The best estimate of Sobibor survivors is forty-six. As a result of all these circumstances, only a small fraction of the voluminous literature on camps is devoted to Sobibor. From these books and articles I was able to compose the following picture.

8. R. Rashke, *Escape from Sobibor* (Boston: Houghton Mifflin, 1982), vii.

The building of the camp began in March 1942. *Obersturmbannführer* Christian Wirth was in charge of this construction project as well as of those in Bełżec and Treblinka. The camp covered an area of some 170 acres and was surrounded by three seven-foot-high electrified fences. Between the middle and the outer fence lay a path that was constantly patrolled.

Extermination started in May 1942 and lasted till October 1943. The camp's commanders were first *Hauptsturmführer* (Captain) Franz Stangle, then *Hauptsturmführer* Frank Reichleitner. The camp staff consisted of thirty SS men and about one hundred Ukrainians. Many tasks were performed by Jewish inmates never numbering more than one thousand; two hundred of these worked near the gas chambers, on the disposal of corpses and on the sorting of their clothes. An unknown number of Gypsies and of people declared insane or incurable (such as sufferers from tuberculosis) were also killed in Sobibor.

In these and related activities, German officialdom systematically aimed to leave as few traces as possible. In their documents, there is never mention of *Endlösung* but rather of *Sonderbehandlung* (special treatment). Incurables were sent to "clinics." Transports to camps were labeled "labor mobilization." Such camouflage reached its extremes in the camps, where it had a further purpose: to keep the Jews calm and as long as possible unaware of what was in store for them, so that they would not revolt or warn the next arrivals of what was about to happen to them. For example, the arrival platform—transports came by train, most often in cattle cars—at Treblinka was disguised as a normal railway station with signs like *To Warsaw* and *To Bialystok.*

These precautions were especially elaborate in Sobibor. The arrival platform was situated in the *Vorlager* (front camp), the only section visible upon detraining. The rest of the camp was hidden by wooden fences. The various buildings in the *Vorlager* bore such signs as *Die Heimat Gottes* (God's Fatherland), *Das Schwalbennest* (The Swallow's Nest), *Zum lustigen Floh* (The Merry Flea). Various crossings were marked with wooden signposts reading: to the bath, to the casino, to the bowling alley.

> The newly arrived would be addressed via loudspeaker by an official who told them that they would be transferred to work camps in nearby Wlodawa. Families would be kept together. Those who worked hard would be awarded certificates of good conduct. Meanwhile, they had all come a long way and would no doubt welcome a good wash in the bathhouse.[9]

From the *Vorlager* the victims walked along the Himmelfahrtallee (Ascension Boulevard), passed *Lager* I, where the sorters and other Jews working as shoemakers, dressmakers, electricians, bakers, etc., were housed, to come to *Lager* 2, where inmate *Kommandos* deposited the luggage which the newcomers had brought with them and sorted their contents. Here also room was provided for tables and benches to write letters—never sent off.

For almost all comers, their day of arrival in Sobibor was also their day of death. The assembly-line procedure went like this. In *Lager* 2 there were barracks in which one had to strip. From there one walked to the strictly isolated *Lager* 3, which bore the sign *Lazarett* (infirmary) over the entrance gate. Women's hair was now cut. Then everyone entered the *Badehaus* (bathhouse), a single building surrounded by flowerbeds that contained the six gas chambers, each one—camouflage to the end—equipped with dummy shower fittings, each one with a capacity for exterminating five hundred to six hundred people at a time. Jews were driven into the chambers by Ukrainians wielding truncheons and whips and holding dogs. Those who had been unable to walk, the sick, the old, the little children, were shot separately behind the gas chambers.

After the chambers had been loaded, doors were shut and gassing began. Carbon monoxide from engine fumes was fed into the chambers, causing death in fifteen to thirty minutes, unless an engine broke down. An SS man would look through a spyhole in the roof to make sure that everyone had suffocated. That done, doors were opened and Jewish special *Kommandos* entered, wearing gas masks

9. L. de Jong, "Sobibor," *Encounter*, Vol. 52, no. 12, December 1978, 20.

and gumboots and carrying hoses to remove blood and defecation. "The twenty or so Jews who were made to clear the gas chambers were shot every few weeks and made up again by a selection from among the sorters."[10] Some *Kommando* members were ordered to check teeth for gold fillings and crowns; these teeth were ripped out with pliers. The corpses were transported to open pits where they were cremated. "Those selected for these tasks knew they had just another 4 to 6 weeks of life left to them. Quite a number, it would seem, lost their minds or committed suicide."[11]

These gassings, this hell on earth, came to an end when on October 14, 1943, several hundred Jews staged a revolt, described in the following "Report of the Security Police in the Lublin district—October 15, 1943 (City of Lublin)":

> On October 14, 1943, at about 5 P.M., a revolt of Jews in the SS camp Sobibor, twenty-five miles north of Chelm. They overpowered the guards, seized the armory, and after an exchange of shots with the camp garrisons, fled in unknown directions. Nine SS men murdered, one SS man missing, two foreign guards shot to death.
>
> Approximately 300 Jews escaped. The remainder were shot to death or are now in camp.[12]

Many of the three hundred escapees were subsequently murdered or betrayed by Polish and Ukrainian anti-Semites. Only forty-six survived.

Between March 2 and July 20, 1943, nineteen trains, carrying in all 34,294 Jews, left Westerbork for a voyage lasting three days and three nights, making the 1,100 mile trek eastward to Sobibor. According to a man who was in Westerbork through this March–July period:

> Not only after the war was the name Sobibor virtually unknown; the same was true in Westerbork during the war. The name was

10. de Jong, "Sobibor," 20.

11. de Jong, "Sobibor," 20.

12. Report reproduced in English in M. Novitch, *Sobibor, Martyrdom and Revolt* (New York: Holocaust Library, 1980).

> never mentioned in relation to the nineteen trains to Sobibor. There was reference to Auschwitz, even occasionally to Riga, but never to Sobibor. I can state this so firmly since I had transport duty in Westerbork on departure of all these nineteen deportation trains.[13]

As far as I have been able to ascertain, the only Jews from Western Europe to end their trip and their lives in Sobibor were those on the nineteen trains from Westerbork.

A Polish-born survivor who saw the Jews from Holland arrive in Sobibor has said: "The Dutch bounced off the trains in furs and silk dresses or woollen suits, carrying their valuables. Unlike the Polish Jews, they were, for the most part, well educated, not Orthodox, and totally western . . . They had not been prepared for Sobibor by ghettos, typhus, starvation, fear and hatred, slow death, bullets, whips . . ."[14] Of those more than 30,000 Jews from Holland, only two survived,[15] both women: Ursula Stern, German-born, and Saartje Wÿnberg. They had been in the group of three hundred escapees.

Already before V-E Day, the Dutch government-in-exile had discussed the need for setting up an institution that would gather and analyze information on war events in Holland. As a result the *Rÿksinstituut voor Oorlogsdocumentatie* (Netherlands State Institute for War Documentation) was officially founded on May 8, 1945, within the week following the end of the War in Europe. It has since obtained and catalogued documents that can fill a mile and a half of stacking space. The institute is now housed in Herengracht 474, Amsterdam.[16]

I remained in Holland for most of the eight months following the end of the war. As mentioned earlier, during that time I had tried without success to find out about the fate of Annie and her husband after their departure from Westerbork. I do not remember whether

13. Cohen, De negentien treinen naar Sobibor, 23.

14. Rashke, *Escape from Sobibor*, 108, 109.

15. de Jong, "Sobibor," 20.

16. For a history of the Institute, see Max Pam, *De onderzoekers van de oorlog* (The Hague: SDU, 1989).

or not I contacted the *Rÿksinstituut* at that time. In any event, it was a new venture then, not yet well organized. In later years I heard the Institute mentioned several times. As I started preparations for writing this memoir, it struck me that I ought to make a last try at finding out about my sister. Accordingly I wrote to Amsterdam (in Dutch, of course), asking whether they had the information I so much wanted. On September 25, 1991, I received an answer. The relevant sentence follows:

"Your sister Anna de Leeuw-Pais and her husband Herman de Leeuw were deported from Westerbork to Sobibor, where they died on June 4, 1943."

How could this date be fixed with such precision? Because it must have been known at Westerbork that they were among the 3,006 Jews who left Westerbork on June 1, and because Jews were gassed on the very day of arrival at Sobibor. I had heard of Sobibor by the time I received the letter but did not know much more about it than its name. Since then, I have read all I could lay my hands on about that camp, so that I now have an inkling of the environment in which Annie and Herman spent their final hours.

By the time I received that letter, I could no longer weep. I have in fact often wondered through the years why, after the day the news of Annie's departure had caused me to respond hysterically, I have never felt again the acute pain of her loss. It was as if her earlier existence had become a sealed-off part of my soul. Subsequent reading about the reactions of other survivors has made clear to me that my own was not unusual. By the time the information about Annie's death reached me, she would have been seventy-one years old had she still been alive—and my last memory of her is as a young woman of twenty-three. I was therefore not surprised at my own calm when the news reached me. After reading the letter, a copy of which I immediately sent to Tineke, I became silent and withdrawn for days on end remembering especially about my last talk with Annie. Once again I asked myself, as I had so often done during the past half century: Should I have insisted more emphatically that she must go into hiding?

Since the receipt of that letter, I have tried numerous times to imagine what it must have been like for them. In thought I have tried to walk with them to those gas chambers in *Lager* 3, holding Annie by the hand and talking softly to her. My powers of imagination fail me, however. For me, a survivor, the reality is too impossible.

I come next to how my parents managed to survive the war. I have before me two documents addressed to my father. The first, dated July 4, 1943, was signed by the secretary of the Portuguese-Israelitic parish in Amsterdam. It states that both my parents appear on the list, presented to the Portuguese government, of persons being considered for possible immigration to Portugal. It is a bit of a puzzle to me how my mother, who was Ashkenazi, made her appearance on that list.

The second document, dated July 10, 1943, and signed by an official of the JR, states: "It is with pleasure that we can inform you that the Department of Education of the municipality of Amsterdam has informed us that you will receive an *Ausnahmebescheinigung* (Certificate of Exemption)." I do not remember what that exemption meant. However, by September 1943 the deportation of Dutch Jews was virtually complete, and already in July the situation had become extremely critical. I had continued to urge my parents by letter to go into hiding, informing them that Tineke had a place waiting for them. My sister's departure in late May had finally convinced them. In the summer of 1943, they went.

Their home was on a farm in the neighborhood of the village of Hillegom, near Haarlem. They now assumed new identities; I have their false IDs at hand. My father became Fredericus Leonardus Groenewege, born in The Hague, *Stucadoor*, whitewasher, by profession. My mother was now Elisabeth Elerie, born in Usquert, in the province of Groningen. I also still have in my possession her *Stamkaart*, a document needed for obtaining new ration cards when the old ones had expired. By the strict rules of the game, I of course did not know where they were, except that it was somewhere outside the city. Knowledge of hiders' whereabouts could in fact be exceedingly dangerous. If someone did know, and that person was caught by the Germans, then the person hiding had at once to move elsewhere, since no one, however trustworthy, should be expected to remain silent under torture.

The following true story will illustrate that in those days knowledge could have mortal consequences. One day *lange* Jan (tall John), as he was known, was walking along an Amsterdam street. This man, whom I had once met, was an important figure in the resistance movement in our city. At one point on his walk he noted that he was being followed by two men whom he knew to belong to the Gestapo. He started to run. They started to run. *Lange* Jan ran into a house, up the stairs. The Gestapo men followed him inside. Jan climbed all the way to the roof, the other two still on his heels. Since he could not risk being captured, as he knew a lot, he took his own life by jumping off the roof. The ending of the story is even more bitter. Sometime later it became known that the Gestapo people had not been after him, did in fact not know who he was, but had started pursuit after they saw him beginning to run.

All through the rest of the war, my mother walked freely outside; her appearance was not markedly Jewish. Since the farmer's family was Catholic, so was my mother, who passed for a cousin of the farmer's wife. She was supposed to be an evacuee from a region the Germans had requisitioned for military purposes. My father, on the other hand, had to stay hidden indoors during the day but could come out on dark evenings, when he would walk around on the farmer's land.

My mother could therefore do her share of the shopping. She also regularly visited a village store where she could borrow books at a modest rate. This led to one of her more hilarious war experiences. One day she asked the store owner if he knew a certain book she had heard of. I do, the man said, but must warn you that this one is on the Catholic Index of forbidden books. In that case, my mother replied, I shall of course not take it along.

Reading became my parents' main diversion. In addition, I had undertaken to teach my father English. He and I each had a copy of the same textbook, which contained many exercises. My father would study a chapter and write out the assignments. These reached me by courier. I would check these and on the next occasion return them with corrections.

My father, an inveterate smoker, also developed the hobby of planting tobacco, which he would tend himself during evening hours. When the leaves were mature, they were brought inside and hung in the attic to dry. When that was done, my father had plenty for his pipe. I too got a share, finely cut, to roll cigarettes. These tasted awful, but it was the only tobacco I could lay my hands on.

Their life at the farm continued in peace and quiet until sometime in the spring of 1944, when German Army personnel came into their area to begin construction of launching sites for the V2 rockets which in September of that year began hitting London. It now became far too dangerous for people in hiding to stay in that area, since residences would most likely be thoroughly searched for hidden weapons and unauthorized persons. Once again, Tineke went into action, finding them this time a flat in the town of Heemstede. There they stayed safely till the end of the war. It was there that I saw them again for the first time after the war, having come on a borrowed bicycle.

By the time I went into hiding, it was already clear that Germany would lose the war, but nobody in his right mind could have foreseen how long our misery would last. The Germans had been driven out of Africa and out of Stalingrad. On a July evening in 1943, Pa Koehorst and I got seriously drunk celebrating the fall of Mussolini.

Soon after I had arrived on the Keizersgracht, a special place had been constructed where I could hide in case of a German raid on the house. In an attic next to my room, a wooden wall panel had been cut loose, behind which was a tiny space into which I could crawl if necessary. A lock had been attached to the panel's inside so that I myself could close off the wall once I was installed. I regularly trained myself to go rapidly through the necessary motions.

Life during the following months was a period of calm and routine. I had one wonderful diversion throughout that period. I have said that only Tineke knew where I was. This is not quite the whole story. One other person knew: Hans Kramers, the physics professor with whom I had become on increasingly good terms since my first visits to him in Leiden in the autumn of 1939. Ever since his university had been closed down by the occupying powers, he had been forced to seek income elsewhere. That is why he had become a consultant for the Bataafsche Petroleum Maatschappij, one of Holland's major corporations. This position brought him once a week to the company offices in Amsterdam. By contacting Tineke he had learned of my whereabouts. After consultation with my host, it was arranged that he would come and visit me once a week, on Mondays, after having finished his consultant's duties. He and the Koehorst family took to each other, and Hans—as I now called Kramers—was invited to stay for dinner on the days he visited me.

Kramers and I would of course talk physics. In particular we had intense debates on questions having to do with the theory of the electron. Other subjects came up as well. Naturally we argued about the war situation. One day the discussion turned to music. Kramers said that my hiding period would be a good time for me to learn to play an instrument and offered to give me instruction on the cello, his own favorite. I said that sounded great, except that I had no cello. That was not a problem, he replied; he knew a music store in Amsterdam where one could be rented. Shortly thereafter Rob, the younger Koehorst son, was delegated to visit that store and rent an instrument. Now I had a wonderful new pastime. The noises I produced caused no problems. My hosts told neighbors in passing that Rob had taken up the study of the cello. And so my life went on, by no means unpleasantly, until one Monday in November 1943, when disaster struck.

It was about six o'clock in the evening. We were at dinner, Kramers included, when the bell rang. Whenever that happened, at an unusual hour like this, one of the Koehorst children would go down to open the door in person. This time it was the Gestapo. There was a special button near the front door which on being pressed sounded an alarm upstairs. When it rang, I ran from the table (someone at once took my plate away) to my hiding place. On my way upstairs I heard German spoken below, so I knew enough. I opened the panel in the attic wall and crept inside behind it. Then, dammit, I was so nervous that I could not work the inside lock. I therefore held the panel in position by hand. That way it did not fit perfectly; a narrow open crack remained.

The Gestapo people came upstairs and went into the attic. One man carried a strong torchlight which at one point he shone straight at my panel. I could see the light through the crack—I can still see that light even as I write these lines. He played the light around for a while. Then they left. For the moment at least, I had escaped the most dangerous situation in my entire life.

I kept on sitting in the tiny space, practically bent double, holding onto the panel. Then I heard the door to my room, across from my hiding place, open softly. Someone entered, I did not at first know who. Then that person sat down on a small bench that stood right at the wall behind which I was folded up. The person began to read, not loud but quite softly. It was Kramers. Earlier he had lent me a volume of Bradley's *Lectures on Shakespeare*. What this good man was doing now was reading to me from that book, in order to calm my nerves. Sometime between ten and eleven one of the sons came to the attic to tell me that the coast was clear and I could come out. I vividly remember that I believed I had been cooped up for some fifteen minutes. In actual fact it was for four hours.

It was obvious that I had to leave the Koehorst home, but I could not depart at once. It was late at night now, and a person on the virtually deserted streets could attract too much attention. So I rested, remaining fully dressed, until the next morning. Tineke and Marie had been alerted meanwhile. Shortly after eight I went by bike to their home.

Either that night or the next day (my memory is understandably hazy), the Gestapo ripped off the floor of Pa Koehorst's workshop downstairs. There they found hidden a quantity of fine ladies' fur coats and other valuables that well-to-do Jewish clients of Mr. K. had asked him to hide for them. As a result of that discovery, Pa was sent to prison, where he was kept for about a year.

After only a very brief stay in Tineke's home, I went to my next hiding place, an apartment on Admiraal de Ruÿterweg. I deeply regret having forgotten the names of my hosts. I now lived with a couple and their two daughters. The husband had an office job. The younger girl was about fourteen, the older about seventeen. It was a quite modest-sized flat in which, however, I had a small room to myself, all I needed.

It was a friendly family with whom I had very pleasant relations. A shadow hung over their life because the older daughter was epileptic. Her attacks were fairly frequent, at times several per week. It occasionally happened that I was all alone with her in the house when one of these attacks occurred. I had seen what one should do: Pillow under the head; place something between her teeth to prevent her from biting her tongue; hold on firmly to both arms; sit on the lower legs if necessary—all this to prevent the poor girl from hurting herself. When it was over, see to it that she rested quietly on top of her bed. I had a curious feeling of inadequacy, being unable to do more for her while she was in her epileptic state.

During my stay in my second hiding place, I continued my regime of physical exercise. I also listened to the BBC—including Churchill's occasional addresses—lying on my host's bed, a blanket over me and the small radio set. What I remember most particularly about that period is an enormous amount of reading. Tineke knew a man who lived nearby who had quite a decent private library, and who had been kind enough to make a list of his books, at Tineke's request. That list was for me; I would select books, Tineke would fetch them for me. My recollection of what books I read in those days is poor. All I remember are wonderful hours with Tolstoi's *War and Peace* and with many of the writings of Dostoevsky. The library also contained a four-volume German edition of the complete plays of Ibsen. In one week I read all of them. In spite of all the ways I kept my mind occupied, I could of course not quite escape feelings of monotony. By way of mild diversion I decided to grow a moustache, just to look different. I nurtured this growth for a month or so, then shaved it off.

From that period dates one of the most important discoveries I ever made, and which forever changed my life. It concerned new insight into the process called thinking. Since my earlier years at the university and especially in preparing my doctoral thesis, thinking had taken on ever-increasing importance in my life. In those years, I had to tell myself: Now sit down, young man, forget everything else and concentrate on your thoughts. Diversions could not only easily deflect me but would also cost time and effort afterward as I reverted to the thinking mode.

Now, in hiding, it all worked differently. I would get up, exercise, have breakfast, then sit down at my little worktable and presto, thoughts came totally unforced, by themselves, you might say. It was as if it was not I who did the thinking but as if thinking took place independently of my willing to think. It was, in other words, as if the self became the passive receptacle of thoughts that came independently of any doing by me. That was the most important positive experience of my years in hiding.

The influence of isolation on the creative thought process has been experienced frequently. Isolation is intimately related to the emergence of religious visions. It has been written that Moses wrote the words of the Covenant, the Ten Commandments, during his solitary stay of forty days and forty nights on Mount Sinai, in the presence of only the Lord (Exodus 34:28). And that Jesus stayed in the wilderness for forty days (Mark 1:13). According to orthodox Buddhist belief, the Buddha Gotama remained in deep meditation under the Bo tree for seven times seven days and nights.

The most famous example of the positive influence of isolation on progress in science may well be the case of Isaac Newton, who in the 1660s was forced to live in seclusion on his mother's estate at Woolsthorpe for the larger part of two years, after the great plague closed Cambridge University. "That a youth should immediately after graduation retire to a lonely village and there, unaided, make three capital discoveries[17] in science, is nothing short of miraculous."[18]

One also finds the isolated state of the individual described in stories and novels. In several books by Charles Morgan, one finds a poignant term for the resulting state of grace: singleness of mind, in particular in *The Fountain.* Here the author describes the experiences of a British officer who, during World War I, spends a number of years interned in a small chateau in Holland. That novel, which I read for the first time in the 1950s and have reread several times since, has made a deep and lasting impression on me. I find it puzzling that Morgan's novels are now so little known. Those days of untrammeled thinking have taught me to appreciate quiet evenings spent later by myself at home.

My absorption in my own thinking led at one time to an embarrassment. Normally I had the freedom of walking around in the whole apartment. I was confined to my own room when my hosts had guests and had to take off my shoes to minimize noise. That was the situation when, one day, deep in thought and oblivious to my surroundings, I stepped out of my room and, in stockinged feet, entered the living room where my hosts were having tea with a couple of visitors. Everyone in the room, including myself, was quite startled. My hosts simply had to explain the situation. Fortunately, their guests, very decent people, understood at once. Nor did my stupidity have any further consequences. Afterward, I offered my apologies and pledged that never again would I cause similar embarrassment.

The sixth of June 1944 came, D-day. On the BBC a name was mentioned which I had never heard before: Eisenhower. I still have an old notebook filled with calculations with a marking in the margin

17. These were the mathematical method of fluxions; the law of composition of light and the law of universal gravitation—not bad for a graduate student in his early twenties. It was during those Woolsthorpe years that, as alleged, he hit upon his fundamental idea of gravity after having seen an apple fall from a tree.

18. L. T. More, *Isaac Newton* (New York: Dover Publications, 1962), 41.

of one page: D-day. All over Holland rules of curfew were tightened. That meant nothing to me, of course. In fact my focus on work, thinking and reading was not interrupted.

On July 20, a German attempt was made to assassinate Hitler while he was in his headquarters at the *Wolfsschanze* (Wolves' Entrenchment) in East Prussia. In the course of the day, the BBC broadcast the news which, however, was still quite vague. We kept the German radio going that day. Just after midnight, Hitler himself came on the air. In a curiously hoarse voice he told the world that a bomb had exploded two meters away from him, that he was unhurt, and that the criminal elements responsible would be destroyed without mercy. It was the last time I would hear that hated voice.

That event did not interrupt my concentration either.

Then came *Dolle Dinsdag* (Crazy Tuesday), September the fifth, 1944. Antwerp fell to the Allies. An erroneous Radio London report that the southern Dutch city of Breda had been freed led to an epidemic of rumors all over Holland suggesting that liberation was near at hand. Gone was my focus and singleness of mind, never to return for the remainder of the war. Like practically all Dutchmen, I was in a state of turmoil. At that time there was no doubt that Germany was well on its way to defeat. On that day it seemed as if we would be free within hours. Imagine my feelings. After having been cooped up for a year and a half, I would be free to walk the streets again! All of a sudden every additional minute of waiting became an agony.

Years later I was reminded of those explosive feelings when I read the account of slavery in the United States by Alexis de Tocqueville in his book *Democracy in America*. What Tocqueville pointed out is that people can endure being enslaved for an unlimited time. When, however, they become aware of the possibility that this condition may not endure, their lives become all at once unbearable. This was exactly my experience on that Tuesday in September. But I had another very hard eight months to live through before it was all over.

Later that September I received an unexpected piece of news. My mother was coming to Amsterdam for a brief visit and hoped to see me. A meeting was arranged through the kindness of the Schönitzer family, friends of Tineke and Marie, who lived on the same street where I was hiding. My mother was to arrive there at an appointed hour. I was to join her there shortly afterward. (It was of course out of the question that she would come to the place where I was staying.) It was impressed on me that I must walk leisurely to that house, so as to avoid attracting attention.

And so, for the first time in I no longer remember how many months, I walked on a street. On arrival I thanked the hosts—whom I also knew—and embraced my mother, who looked well. We sat and talked for about an hour. Then she left. I was supposed to wait for a while longer before returning home.

Then the doorbell rang. The wife peeked out the window, looking scared, turned to me and said, "Quick, to the basement, there are two men at the door I have never seen before." It was the Gestapo. I ran into the basement, unprepared for the situation, looked around and saw a large vertical box of the kind used for storing clothes. I opened its lid, wormed myself inside, pulled some women's dresses over me and waited.

Minutes later the cellar door opened, and the men came in. What I experienced next is unique in my life. I had the intense sensation of leaving my body and becoming a spectator of what was happening. The men puttered around in the cellar, never opening the box in which I was hiding, then left. I do not recall how long I stayed in the box, but after some time someone came down, called me, then told me I could come out. The coast was clear.

I went upstairs and had to sit down. My strange mental state had disappeared meanwhile, to be replaced by limpness and exhaustion. I was given a shot of brandy, waited a while longer, then returned to my own residence. No one ever found out what brought the Gestapo there at that time—minutes after my mother had gone. She too returned safely to her home.

Not long after, for reasons I cannot recall, I left the house on the de Rüyterweg, where I had spent nearly a year of my life in the company of good and kind people. I stayed next in the home of a psychiatrist and his family in the Lairessestraat. After a brief sojourn I moved again, this time to a house on the Herengracht.

That was an altogether different type of hiding place. The house was in the hands of the resistance movement. It was situated opposite Amsterdam's central telephone offices and was intended to serve as the basis for occupying that vital communications center when orders came. The basement of the house was a storage place for weapons to be used on that occasion. The inhabitants included a number of people in hiding like myself.

It was there that the hunger winter of 1944-45 hit all of us hard. It was cold; we often spent daytime hours huddled in blankets. It was dark—gas and electricity services had been suspended. Fortunately, the resistance people had provided us with a lot of candles, which enabled us to light one room. I have memories of our evenings together, cheery in spite of everything. It was a time during which I, like nearly all the Dutch, could think of only one thing: food. There was not much energy left for my beloved physics or for reading.

Early in 1945 I changed hiding places again—for the last time. Once again, the style was different. Together with three friends from my old Zionist days, I rented an apartment on the Hobbemakade in Amsterdam. The three were: Lion Nordheim, my admired friend from prewar days, the leader of the young radical Zionists, who on May 9, 1940, the evening before the German invasion of Holland, celebrated his engagement to Jeanne van Amerongen, whom he married later that year; Jeanne herself; and her youngest sister, Truusje. We had the apartment all to ourselves. Jeanne and Truusje went out freely on the streets. They had of course false identity documents and, blonde-haired and blue-eyed as they were, could easily pass for Gentiles. Lion, who had a very pronounced Jewish physiognomy, and I stayed indoors.

I should explain the layout of our domicile. First of all, the place was a trap; there was no possibility of hiding anywhere in case of unwelcome visits. We had a living room, kitchen, bath, and three bedrooms, one for Jeanne and Lion, one for Truusje, and one for me.

It should be noted for what follows that there were no intimate relations between Truusje and myself.

The lifestyle differed from that of my earlier sanctuaries in that we had occasional friendly visitors. One of these was Bert Broer, a Gentile friend of mine from my undergraduate years in Amsterdam. He would turn up once in a while to discuss problems in physics. Another was a young Jewish woman whom I shall call Miriam. She had been engaged to a Gentile who was active in the resistance. They were both caught; her fiancé was executed. She had been in prison until a German official proposed that she become his mistress, to be installed in an Amsterdam apartment. She accepted and escaped soon afterward. Now she was at risk but nonetheless went freely outside. (I seem to remember that she had dyed her hair blonde.)

Life was on the whole uneventful. I spent much of the daytime in my room with my physics calculations, which I copied in notebooks, and with my diverse reading. So it went on until one day in March, I believe it was the fifteenth.

That morning we had a visit from Miriam, who stayed for a while and then left. A bit later Johan van de Kieft came to see Lion and me. He was an important figure in the resistance movement, in contact with London. (Right after the war he became chairman of the socialist faction of the upper house of the Dutch parliament, and from 1952 to 1956 was Minister of Finance in the so-called third cabinet Drees.) The purpose of his visit was to discuss a draft bill, under consideration by the Dutch government-in-exile, which dealt with the fate of Jewish children who had been hidden during the war but whose parents had been deported and would probably not return. The issue was who should be responsible for them after the war: the natural parents if they returned, the foster parents if they so desired, or the Jewish community at large? This complex and delicate problem had been discussed among resistance leaders since early 1944. On February 14, 1945, they had sent a proposal to London providing for the establishment of the *Voogdÿraad OPK* (Guardian Commission for Wartime Foster Children).

Van de Kieft wished to discuss the issue with us because we had been assigned (I do not remember by whom) to represent the Zionist youth movement with the resistance. That was my closest involvement with the resistance. I never participated in sabotage or use of arms. There were Jews who did so, however. One of them, Philip de Leeuw, was a friend of mine also from the prewar period. I was at his religious marriage in an Amsterdam synagogue early in the war, where he appeared in the uniform of a reserve first lieutenant. He was a brave man. In November 1944 he participated in an attack on a Dutch railway line, was caught, and was executed that same month.

After Van de Kieft had departed, Lion and I talked things over and decided that a memorandum should be prepared for use by the resistance. Lion said he would write it, and started at once, while I repaired to my own room. Shortly afterward lunch was ready. As we sat down to our frugal meal, Lion put his unfinished writing in his jacket pocket—instead of storing it in a cache we had prepared for sensitive material.

After lunch Bert Broer came to see me. That day we discussed a paper recently published by the great German physicist Werner Heisenberg and a coworker on the theory of superconductivity.

When the bell rang, I did not pay attention. Only the ladies were permitted to open the door. Moments later the door to my room opened. There stood a tall man in SS uniform, the skull and bones symbol on his cap, a drawn revolver in his hand. My first reaction was a quick look at the window. Could I jump out? Impossible. Not saying a word, the SS man moved his revolver to indicate that Bert and I should go to the hallway. The women and Lion were herded in there as well, rounded up by another German.

My strongest recollection of the next moments is the total collapse of Lion. I was of course frightened out of my wits, but that was as nothing compared to his behavior. He was visibly in total panic, had lost all semblance of composure, and moved erratically, causing one of the Germans to hit him in the face, sending his glasses flying. I heard Jeanne pleading with one of the men, offering diamonds to let us go, an offer that enraged them.

Next we were led down the stairs. Two cars were waiting. We three men were shoved in one, the women in the other. As we drove off, I experienced fears more intense than I have ever felt in my life. It was a degree of fear that caused physical pain. My body ached all over.

As I heard later, the women were driven to the women's prison. I did not see them again until May, when it was all over. We were taken to Gestapo headquarters (I believe it was on the Apollolaan), where the three of us were shoved into separate rooms.

As I was waiting for what was to happen next, I remembered advice given me by resistance members on how to behave in such situations. First, and most important, try not to show fear. Behave politely. Ask for an interpreter who could translate spoken German into Dutch, the purpose being to gain time for replies. I actually never asked for that favor.

A man in mufti came in. I jumped to attention. As he paced slowly back and forth in the room, he began to interrogate me, speaking in conversational tones, never raising his voice. First he asked me if I was a Jew. I said no, I was not. Whereupon he ordered me to let down my pants. In Holland in those days circumcision was a procedure applied to Jews only. So I said, "All right, I am a Jew. But I am also a physicist, and all I did in that apartment was to pursue my researches, as you can verify from the papers and books in my room." The questioning went on, the man keeping up his slow pacing. At one point, when he came quite close to where I was standing, he slapped me hard in the face, then continued his movements as if nothing had happened.

It was a shattering moment. The pain was only minor. But there was the shock effect of experiencing an abrupt and unexpected interruption of a basically conventional situation, two men talking, by an act of very brief but violent aggression. Its purpose was obvious: not so much to cause physical pain as to make me lose my mental equilibrium. Even though the man had succeeded in doing so, it did not interrupt the continuing interrogation, the questions now turning to my possible dealings with the resistance. I denied any such involvement.

The man left. I waited again. After a while I was ordered out of the room, whereupon I met Bert and Lion again, the latter looking ashen. Once again we were shoved into a car which brought us to the Weteringsschans, where we entered a building that before the war used to be the city's House of Detention but had since become a Gestapo prison. We three were pushed into a cell, and the door was banged shut and locked. I had arrived in my next residence, cell IB4.

It would no longer have been possible to transport me to one of the camps in the East. On March 9 tanks of the US 9th Armored Division had crossed the Rhine over a still intact bridge at Remagen, southeast of Bonn, near the Dutch border. On March 24 General Patton and his troops had occupied another bridgehead, at Oppenheim, and his tanks were already moving to Frankfurt. The night before, General Montgomery's armies had crossed the lower Rhine and were headed into the North German plain. *Festung* Holland was cut off.

When we arrived in our cell, another man was already there. He at once began to tell us of his capture earlier that day. When he had finished, he started the same story all over again. This went on for a while. It was not, you might say, an ideal ambiance for us who had just gone through the most wrenching experience of our lives. After a time, we simply told the chap to shut up, which, to our relief, he did.

We got nothing to eat that night; the first food we received came twenty-four hours later. When it came I was surprised to note that, in spite of a normally strong appetite, I had not noticed earlier the absence of anything to eat. The small cell contained four cots, a portable latrine, and a washbasin. I fell into an exhausted sleep that night, to be awakened by banging on the cell door, which then was opened. Like the others, I kept lying on my cot, awaiting developments. Moments later a prison guard came in and started yelling at us. Didn't we know that we had to get up on the double when the cell was opened, quickly get dressed, place the latrine outside the door, then stand at attention to await cell inspection? No, we didn't know, but of course learned quickly.

It had weighed heavily on my conscience that I had dragged Bert Broer into this predicament. It came as a relief when, two days later, a guard came in and told him that he was to be released forthwith. Bert was good enough to visit Tineke to tell her where we were.

The days took on a regular routine. Meals were miserably small. In the late mornings we were let out of our cell for airing and walked around for a short while with other prisoners in a small yard surrounded by high walls. It was beautiful spring weather. We could observe a triangular piece of pure blue sky through our small barred window. As I looked out one day, I saw a gull flying in my field of vision. I stood hypnotized, watching the gull glide effortlessly back and forth. What harmony, what freedom that single gull represented in my little patch of sky. Never have I had a more beautiful view of nature than was given me by that solitary bird.

Days in prison were mostly quiet, but nights were bad. We would hear heavy metal doors clanging, shouts, shrieks. We knew that some poor bastard was being taken away but had only grim forebodings as to where. The monotony of the days was broken by periodic interrogations that took place inside the prison building. Sometimes Lion, sometimes I, was taken out of our cell. I was brought to a small room and remember one setting in particular.

As I came in, I saw a man sitting behind a desk, leaning back, relaxed, with hands clasped behind his neck. The room was otherwise bare, as was the desktop, except for a revolver lying in the middle. I stood in front of his desk, at attention as always. The man began to speak. "You will now tell me all you know about the resistance," he said calmly, "and you will speak the truth. If you do, it will help your situation considerably; if you don't, I shall shoot you right here in this room." My instincts told me: this is intimidation, stay calm, look the man in the eye, firmly but not aggressively. I remember how the thought came to me: he is the animal in this circus, you are the tamer; look at him in the way the animal trainer stares steadily at his beast. I replied to his question as I had done before: "I had nothing to do with the resistance. It is true that I am a Jew. But I am just a young scientist absorbed in my work, as can be seen from the papers found in my room. I am just a *weltfremd*, unworldly, young man." That worked.

Another day, when it was Lion's turn, he came back stumbling into our cell, quite pale and deeply shaken. "What has happened?" I asked. He said: "I have been condemned to death." My immediate reaction was and still is astounding to me. It was as if, inside my head, a blinding light shone and a voice spoke: I SHALL LIVE. I had not been condemned.

Lion had fallen on his cot. I picked him up and cradled him in my arms, as one does a young child. I spoke calming words to him; I do not recall what I said. Lion quieted down somewhat but remained deeply withdrawn and hard to reach during those next days, staring out of our little window, unseeing.

A few days later the cell door opened at an unusual hour. We jumped to attention. There stood the guard and next to him a man in SS uniform who, I later found out, was the prison commandant. The SS man looked us over, head to toe, one after the other. Then, silently, he pointed to me, indicating that I was to step out. Oh my God, I thought, now it is my turn.

Never saying a word, the commandant indicated that I was to follow him. We walked through a corridor, cells on both sides, until we came to a metal door. He opened it, I stepped through, he locked it behind me. Next a second door, same procedure. Then we came to an ordinary wooden door. He opened it, shoved me through, then said only: "*Fahrräder reparieren*" ("Repair bicycles"), and walked away.

I looked around me in amazement. I was in a good-sized hall; bicycles were standing along the wall. In the center about half a dozen men were at work on some of them. They were obviously prisoners since, like myself, they looked disheveled and were unshaven. Two *Grüne Polizei* (Green Police)[19] were sitting at ease, rifles on their shoulders, smoking cigarettes.

19. German units, wearing green uniforms, whose task it was to maintain civil order in occupied territories.

I went up to one of the prisoners and asked what I should do. He said, "Talk to Jan, who is in charge," pointing to a tall, thin man who was busily occupied. I walked up to Jan and said, "I am supposed to work here but don't know from shit about bicycle repairs." Jan turned out to be an amiable fellow from the Jordaan (derived from the French *jardin*, garden), a workers' quarter in Amsterdam renowned for its special kind of slang and for the tough customers living there. Jan gave me some pointers, and soon I was busy. I felt happy to have something to do and to have so much company. Some hours later I was brought back to my cell.

About happiness while in prison. From that period I have learned that even in times of misery there are good days and bad days. The next morning I was returned to the bike hall. It was then that I learned of Jan's brilliant idea of how to smuggle messages out. He had been put in charge because in real life he had his own bike shop. Every once in a while he would walk up to the guards and inform them that such and such a bike needed work that demanded special tools not available. But if someone would ride the bike to his shop and tell them that Jan had said to repair the bike free of charge, then it would be taken care of. Meanwhile, messages were written on scraps of paper with a pencil stub someone had swiped. These were inserted between the inner and outer tube.

Some days later—we were now well into April—I found upon returning to the cell that Lion was gone. "Where is he?" I asked the man who had been with us from the beginning. He told me that two guards had come in and had ordered Lion to take his things along and come with them. He did not know anything more. I sat down on my cot, in despair. What else could I expect but the worst?

A day or so later the bike repair adventure came to an end when an SS officer marched in, walked up to Jan, smacked him over the head and told him that our courier service had been found out. Everyone was ordered back to his cell, and that was the end of that.

Another diversion came along shortly afterward. One day my cellmate and I were both ordered out of our cell and together with more prisoners were marched to the exit door. Outside stood a horse-drawn truck. All of us were ordered to get in, a tarpaulin was thrown over us, and off we went, ending up at a house somewhere in Amsterdam South. We got out, were ushered inside, and instructed in our tasks: there were cellars full of potatoes that had started to sprout. These had to be put in bags, carried up some stairs, then emptied into a courtyard. There we had to remove the runners, bag them again, and return them to the cellars.

I remember sitting outside, a pleasure in itself. It was a balmy spring evening. The fellow sitting next to me turned out to be Hermann Schey, a Jew and well-known basso, whom I had heard sing a number of times in the Concertgebouw. We were talking of music when suddenly another prisoner moved over and whispered that he had just heard bad news—President Roosevelt had died. It must have been about April 13 when we heard.

One last time I was taken out for a chore. A number of us were marched through Amsterdam to the port area, under guard by the *Grüne Polizei.* I engaged in an amiable chat with one of them, who was walking alongside me. Our job was to unload freight from a small German ship. In the course of the day the captain gave each of us a big slice of brown bread, saying, "*Wer arbeitet soll auch essen*" ("He who labors should also eat").

On May 13, 1988, friends and colleagues of mine organized a one-day symposium in honor of my seventieth birthday. In the evening a festive dinner had been arranged for well over one hundred guests. In the course of that event, a number of people spoke. None touched me more than Tineke. When she had finished, several guests were crying. My heart was full and my voice quavered as I spoke to thank her. From the text of her speech, combined with conversations we had in later years, the following picture emerges.

She had one funny story about me. One morning, while she was still in bed, the bell rang. "Who is there?" "Open up, police," a man said in Dutch. Tineke and Marie, her mother, were scared to death that this had to do with hiding Jews. The man came in and said he was from the morals squad. Complaints had been received that

Tineke was visible in the nude as she was making her morning toilet. She solemnly promised never to do that again. I was there at the time and, curious as always, stood near a door to listen. The door had an opaque glass panel through which my silhouette was clearly visible. I removed myself when the man came near but was properly read the riot act afterward.

After the war Tineke and Marie drew up a list of people who at one time or another had been hidden in their home. Their count ran up to about one hundred names. I never knew more than maybe half a dozen of these, since, quite properly, the others' identities were not revealed to me. One I knew, Hans de Jong, a wealthy industrialist, had been betrayed by his bookkeeper. This led to a house search by the Gestapo, during which Tineke was thrown against a wall, headfirst. Marie was hiding elsewhere at that time. Tineke asked and was permitted to call her grandmother to tell her that she could not come for dinner that evening. The person answering said, with great presence of mind, "But you were not supposed to have dinner. Do you have visitors? Shall I call your mother?" "Yes," Tineke said. At that point the Gestapo man broke off the conversation.

The Gestapo left, but a week later Tineke and Marie were ordered to appear at their headquarters in The Hague for a long interrogation concerning Hans and to be instructed on how to recognize Jews and report them. They were shown photographs of eye shapes as true criteria of Jewish physiognomy. Then they were let go. Apparently the Gestapo had swallowed whatever Tineke had told them earlier.

Right after my three friends and I were captured, Tineke went to the house on the Hobbemakade where we had been living. When she rang the bell, the door was opened by a Gestapo agent. She was arrested on the spot, then interrogated at length. They had found men's socks and women's underwear in the same room and said that Lion must have been sleeping with Jeanne (whose story that she was Aryan had been believed by the Gestapo). So the tragic situation developed that the Germans believed that Lion, properly married to a Jewish woman, was considered guilty of *Rassenschande* (racial disgrace). This is why I earlier made the point that Truusje and I were not intimate.

That, I am sure, is why the Germans had it in for Lion rather than for me. There may well have been the following additional reasons. It was Lion rather than I who had in his pocket when we were caught the draft reply to the resistance about the Jewish war orphans. It was Lion who fell apart in the presence of the Gestapo who, animals as they were, could smell fear. Finally, it was he who looked so very Jewish.

After hours of interrogation, they let Tineke go with the warning that she would be watched, that she probably was Jewish herself or hid Jews, or had a Jewish husband.

At this point I should note that Kramers, advised by Tineke of my capture, had written (in German) to Heisenberg, probably stressing that I was a talented apolitical young physicist, or words to that effect. Kramers had sent a copy of the letter to Tineke. As he later told me, he did receive a reply. Heisenberg wrote back that he understood, was very sorry, but could do nothing.

It was Tineke who got me out. She had gotten hold of the name and address of a high Nazi official in Amsterdam and decided to call on him. She was received in his office. On his desk stood a photo of Goering, with a dedication *Für meinen Freund* (To my friend). Tineke was afraid that the man would ask for sexual favors but was prepared to grant them if necessary. Fortunately, he did not. She showed him her copy of Kramers's letter to Heisenberg and asked for his help. After reading the letter, the man did not say a word to Tineke but picked up the phone to call the Weteringsschans. "*Hast du ein Jude Pais dort?*" ("Do you have a Jew Pais there?") Yes, they did. "*Lass ihn gehen*" ("Let him go").

So it came about that I gained my freedom thanks to physics, the devotion of Kramers and, above all, Tineke.

On one of the last days of April I was taken out of my cell, IB4, and brought to the office of the prison commandant. He told me I was free but would at once be picked up and shot if I committed any act against Germany. I stepped out of his office and was brought to a small window near the exit, behind which sat a scribe who must, I knew, be a prisoner. He had to register my departure. I whispered to him, "Where is Lion?" He replied, also in a whisper, "He was shot several days ago." Then the small outer gate was opened. I stepped out onto the street. For me the war was over.

For maybe ten minutes I stood motionless in front of the prison on that sunny spring day. I felt no joy, I did not feel sad. I felt nothing. It is a state, called anhedonia by William James, in which one is incapable of experiencing emotions of any kind. In my case it was due to exhaustion, hunger (I never was thinner than at that time), feelings held back for too long to be readily reachable, and the shock I had just had of the news of Lion's death.

Then I started walking, to Tineke's home—where else? No longer wearing a star, I went through the Leidsestraat, crossed the Koningsplein. When I rang the bell, there was pandemonium, laughing, crying. I was embraced by Tineke and by Marie and hugged them both.

In the living room, there was a familiar sight. It was a woodburning furnace, on top of which rested a tiny woodburning stove with a big simmering pan of diced sugar beets. I was given a cup of the brownish, intensely sweet beet liquid and drank it. It tasted like ambrosia. I washed myself (with cold water, of course), then sat down. The first thing I had to tell them was about Lion. They already knew; when Tineke had gone to the German official to plead my case, she had also tried to help Lion and had been told of his execution.

Across the street from the house, there was a newspaper office with a barbershop on the ground floor. I said I would go there to be shaved. I went into the shop, told the barber that I had just come out of prison, and asked if I could have a shave. The man's response can only be called loving. He led me to the barber chair, made me sit down, and said he still had one bar of shaving soap, which he only used on special occasions. Feeling ever so much more cheerful now that my dirty beard was gone, I got up and asked how much I owed him. This one is on the house, was the barber's reply. We warmly shook hands, and I left.

I spent the next few weeks in Tineke and Marie's house. We no longer feared raids. I could come and go freely. First I had to catch up on the news; I was told that Allied troops had already penetrated *Festung* Holland. No Allied forces had yet reached Amsterdam.

Negotiations between the opposing powers had begun. As a result the Germans gave permission for Allied planes to fly over Holland in order to drop crates of food by parachute. This relief came none too early. By late April the food available per capita in the cities of Western Holland averaged 225 calories per day, which means a loaf of bread a week and two potatoes per day. Only later did we learn that on April 28 the last kilograms of potatoes were distributed. By May 5, the final slender reserve would have been gone.[20]

Sunday, the 29th of April, 1945, is an unforgettable day for all who were then living in Amsterdam. Everyone was on the rooftops, waiting for the planes to come. There they were, large, low-flying bombers. Everybody wept. By early May, 1,400 Flying Fortresses and 180 British Lancasters had dropped 1,200 tons of food in Western Holland.[21]

On the afternoon of April 30, Hitler took his own life. On May 7 German military leaders arrived in a little schoolhouse in Reims, France, where they signed the document of unconditional surrender of all German forces.

On that same day Tineke and I left the house, intending to walk to the nearby Central Square, the Dam, which is flanked along one side by the Royal Palace, and which is the traditional gathering place for momentous events. We never got there. We had barely started on our way when shots rang out. Marie had opened a window and was yelling to us, "Come back, come back." As we were running back a man (whom we knew) fell, shot to death. What had happened was that drunken German marines, barricaded on and near the Dam, had opened fire with hidden machine guns.[22] Crossfire began as armed

20. David Anderson, "Hollanders Press Demands on Reich," *New York Times*, July 23, 1945.

21. *New York Times*, May 6, 1945.

22. "Germans Kill Many in Amsterdam Rally," *New York Times*, May 10, 1945.

members of the underground fired back. We later heard that several people were killed on the Dam. So it came to pass that I saw my first war casualty after the war itself was over.

On May 8, V-E Day, Canadian tanks of the *Régiment de la Chaudière* entered Amsterdam. That midnight the guns of Europe fell silent. After twelve years, four months and eight days, the Third Reich had ceased to exist.

On September 12, 1988, I sent off a letter to the Director, Department of the Righteous, Yad Vashem. Part of the letter follows:

> The purpose of this letter is to propose a person as most worthy to be recognized by the Designation of the Righteous and to suggest that a tree be planted in her name at Yad Vashem. She is Tina Buchter Strobos, MD . . . I owe her my life. We have ties that will never break . . . It would be silly to make comparisons with other rescuers, of whom I have known several. But I have never known anyone with Tineke's moral nobility.

I have a copy of the letter, dated January 22, 1990, sent by the Director to Tineke. Part of it reads:

> I have the pleasure to inform you that the Special Commission for the Designation of the Righteous, at its session of November 28, 1989, decided to confer upon you and your mother Marie [who had died in the meantime] its highest expression of gratitude: the title of Righteous among the nations . . . Your name [will be] inserted in the Garden of the Righteous, Yad Vashem, Jerusalem.

Spring 1993

Soldier's Heart

Louis Simpson

It begins in France in June of '44. Men are lying face down on the earth. The air is filled with sounds, shrieks that come out of the sky and terminate with an explosion. This may be a matter of seconds. If the sounds continue, the men will be seen scraping the surface of the earth with shovels and burying themselves in it until, like a species of animal, they vanish from sight. A head emerges now and looks around cautiously before disappearing again.

Or the men are walking up a road in two parallel lines, with an interval between every man and the one in front of him and the one behind. They are heavily burdened, with a pack on their back, and they are carrying rifles, machine guns, and mortars. If the shrieking from the sky begins they will turn quickly out of the road and lie face down. Or they have spread out and are walking in an open field. An embankment runs across it . . . the railroad. There is a brief purring sound, then a rhythmic drumming. If you should happen to be with these men it would sound as though the air were being torn. One of them falls. The others run forward and crouch in the shelter of the embankment.

Such is the life or death of an infantry soldier in France in the summer of 1944. These actions will be repeated many times . . . the scenery will change, from small fields separated by hedgerows to a flat landscape with windmills, to a forest covered with snow. The soldiers will pass through villages. Now they are on the banks of a river and rowing across in rubber boats. Finally they are among mountains.

I was discharged from the US Army in 1945 and went home. I returned to the University. I have a vague recollection of sitting with other students in a room—only a few around a long table. Some great book was being discussed . . . it was the course for upper-division students known as the Colloquium. I was reading furiously about . . . everything. When I was not reading I was writing stories, essays, poems. From what I have been told I would hardly stop to eat. The man with whom I shared an apartment on Morningside Heights told me that he would be making dinner and would ask me if I wanted some, and I'd say no.

I had some success with all this typing—a short story was published in *Esquire*. I cannot bear to think of it—I do not recognize the young man who wrote it. It must have been the manic humor with which this tale about a man who ran a beauty salon was told that appealed to the editors.

What followed I do not know. One person had it that I lost my key to the apartment I was sharing and was found lying unconscious outside the door. A friend would inform me in a letter that I had been wandering in the streets and picked up by the police, and that I resisted violently. Both versions cannot be true—or were they referring to different episodes? Perhaps each of my informants brought to my "breakdown," as such things were called, his own idea of my character.

Shadows were moving around me. The blind man in the Bible said, "I see men as trees walking." So did I. The darkness cleared, and I was in a large room with barred windows and saw men as they were.

I was in a hospital ward. It wasn't an army hospital, but Kings Park on Long Island. Why wasn't I in a veterans' hospital? I suppose that after the war they were too crowded, and the rest had to be put in other places. Or perhaps the members of my family did not know that there were such things as hospitals for veterans. The war had passed them by. My father died when I was a boy, and my mother was traveling in Latin America. She sold cosmetics and advised women how to make themselves beautiful—like the owner of the beauty salon in my story. The only other relatives I had were some aunts and an uncle. They did as they were told, signed the necessary papers, and I was sent to Kings Park.

What name have they given it now . . . the illness I had as a result of being shot at and shelled for months on end? I don't suppose many of our soldiers in the Gulf War have suffered from it . . . they were spared a long engagement. After Vietnam it was called "post-traumatic stress disorder." In World War II it was called "combat fatigue." In the Great War (I prefer that name, for the Great War was what people at the time thought it was) it was called "shell shock." In the Civil War it was "soldier's heart." This name strikes me as the best, for it describes an illness that involved my heart as much as my head. My heart would beat faster, I would tremble and sweat and, on occasion, pass out.

The patients in Kings Park Hospital saw very little of the doctors. There was one who came into the ward now and then, but I don't recall any conversation I had with him. None, surely, that lasted more than a minute. There were two women—one was a nurse, the other seemed to have had some training in psychology. Their main duty was to see that the patients were quiet or harmlessly busy playing cards or board games or reading a magazine. The female psychologist was intelligent and kind. There were also three guards. They were the ones who kept order. Much of the time, especially during the evening and night hours, they ran the ward.

Two of the guards were the kind Chekhov describes in "Ward No. 6." One was a scrawny man with a vacuous face. He showed me his right hand—the trigger finger was missing. He waggled the stump under my face with a sly smile. This, he gave me to understand, was why he had been excused from military service. The other guard was an older man, stocky and muscular, with a bullet head. He was dangerous—he liked to beat up the patients. He informed me that he was the one who had knocked out my front teeth when I was first brought to the ward. He seemed to think it was a joke I would like to share. The third guard was a black man.

One of the patients was a young black man—I don't think he was more than eighteen or nineteen years old. There may have been other black patients in the ward, but I don't remember any. This one, however, I remember very well. He came toward me one day carrying a newspaper. "You can read it," he said. "Read it for me." The stocky, bullet-headed guard was standing nearby. The young man turned toward him and hit him lightly on the chest. It wasn't a blow . . . scarcely more than a tap. The guard knocked him down. The other guard, the one with the missing trigger finger, came over, and the two of them stood over the boy and kicked him repeatedly in his sides and belly.

The next day the black guard told me that the young man had died. He asked me if I had seen what happened. I said I had—it was right in front of me. "Will you testify?" he asked. I said that I would. That evening the guard who had knocked the boy down and kicked him to death spoke to me. If there was an enquiry, and if I was called as a witness, and if I said anything about what happened, I would never leave the hospital.

I was not called, and I did not bear witness. If I had I would surely have been killed, or these murderers would have seen to it that I spent the rest of my life in a hospital ward. Such was the treatment of patients at Kings Park Hospital in 1946. I have no doubt that such incidents are still occurring in hospitals, though not as frequently as they did at that time. I can imagine what being in prison must be like.

I received shock treatments, and later I was assigned to help the doctor, lifting each patient onto the table. I watched as the current passed through and the body convulsed. There has been much controversy over shock treatments—whether or not they did irremediable harm. Speaking only for myself, I think they brought me out of the fog in which I had been walking. They may also have destroyed areas of memory. It took me some years to remember episodes of my early life, and I have never been able to recall the months leading to my collapse.

The war itself I have recovered in bright patches. The areas immediately surrounding these remain dark. Perhaps they would have been so in any case—life in barracks and between battles can be dreary. In fact, by writing about the war I may have recalled it more clearly than most of my fellow soldiers. Writers are different—they don't forget.

One of the symptoms of my illness had been hearing voices. But one day—and this was after I came out of the fog and was quite calm and rational—looking out of the cage, the barred windows behind which we lived, at grass and trees and clouds, I heard a voice say, "Praise God, they resist, they resist!" I could say, I *thought* I heard a voice, but am not willing to hand over the victory to those who believe that they know what is real and what is not. Most doctors are of this mind. It is a rare psychoanalyst who, like Freud and Jung, reads works of imagination. They don't take such things seriously—they cannot afford to take them seriously—it would be disastrous in the line of work they have chosen.

Who was it who was resisting? Others like myself I suppose. I believe with Shakespeare and Blake and Rimbaud that there are more things in heaven and earth than are dreamed of in the philosophy of those who serve the world, and who administer its institutions, and, by a fortunate concatenation, grow rich.

Being pronounced whole, more or less, and discharged from Kings Park, but with instructions to report to a government-appointed doctor at regular times, is not the end of this history. The more evident symptoms of my illness would disappear so that I was thought of by most people as a reasonable and level-headed man. But the cure would take time.

For some years after leaving the hospital I was subject to the sudden onsets I have mentioned: a heart that beat faster, and shaking, and sweating. I would imagine shells falling and hear the sound of guns. I could not stand being confined. I went to the theater to see the first run of *I Am a Camera* and had to walk out during the first act to breathe the air of Broadway. I was having dinner in a restaurant with a woman who supported the arts. I began eating swordfish, a thing I had never eaten, and just as she was saying something I thought foolish I was overtaken by the palpitations and nausea, and had to rise and, without a word, walk out of the restaurant. I looked back once and saw her staring in astonishment.

Such was my social life. And I had the habits that remain with soldiers. One in particular . . . when I went walking I would keep an eye peeled for an enemy position. If there were an open field I would think, "How are we going to get across that?" I imagined lying again on a railroad embankment in Normandy, waiting to be told to go over it in spite of the bullets that were sweeping to and fro directly above me. That day I was sure I would be killed. Or I was in a graveyard in Holland with shells falling and the living getting mixed in with the dead. I was in the Ardennes, standing in a foxhole among trees covered with snow, and stamping my feet. They were freezing.

The University informed me that before I could return I had to be cleared by their doctor. He picked up a folder and said, "You aren't going to be so taken up with your music, are you?" The question was probably one of their tricks, to test my sanity. He spoke again, saying that I ought to go out in the world and "meet the common man." I was silent. I had seen the common man . . . his guts spilled in a road, his limbs strewn in a field. The doctor told me that he could not recommend my returning to the College. It was only on the way home that I realized he had been looking at the wrong folder. What would the musician, whose file it was, say when he was advised to give up writing poems and stories?

So I looked for work and found it . . . as a copyboy on a newspaper. If I stayed with it I might someday be a reporter. But this didn't appeal to me. I didn't have the fascination with gossip that a reporter needs to have—whether it is about a quarrel between nations or a politician and his mistress. Then I worked for an import-export firm as a packer, shipping "seconds," damaged stockings or ballpoint pens with some small imperfection, not visible to the eye, to Brussels where such things were in demand. But this too did not appeal to me—to succeed in this kind of business you have to think about the money you can make, and I preferred to think about other things.

I went back to the University, but not by the front entrance. I slipped in by a side door, the School of General Studies that wasn't so particular about whom they let in. I took courses that met in the evening and on Saturday, and I worked at writing. I was no longer intent on writing prose and becoming a novelist . . . all that typing. I was unable to imagine someone who had a life different from my own, to feel intensely about such a person, sustain an interest in his fate for days, weeks, months . . . even years! That was what novelists had to do. I lacked consistency—my mind went shooting off in all directions—and I lacked patience. I couldn't take any pleasure in writing about furniture, or lighting a cigarette, the kind of stuffing of which fiction consisted.

Unless it were written by a great author, fiction had a fairly common plot, spun out for three or four hundred pages. But you could put everything that you felt and thought in the space of a poem. You could get it out of your system and put it behind you.

I had been granted a pension for my disability, and the checks for several months started coming all at once. I also had the GI Bill. I would be able to go to Paris. In the winter of '44 I had been hospitalized briefly in Paris. After Germany surrendered the regiment was stationed at Sens, and I was appointed managing editor of the regimental newspaper. The staff would take a truck to Paris to fetch the big rolls. I saw enough of the city to want to see more of it after the war.

I traveled to France on the *Queen Mary* and registered as a student at the Sorbonne. There were other Americans taking the course in "French Civilization and Culture," but we had our own agenda, writing or painting. In any case, frequenting the cafes between St.-Germain-des-Près and Boul' Mich.

I have told this story before, but artists may make several paintings of the same subject. Why shouldn't a writer tell a story again, seen in a different light? One night while I was in Paris I dreamed that I was walking with G Company along a strip of land with trees. There was water on each side. Suddenly shells began falling and I was lying prone. Bullets were sweeping the trees—a trunk a few inches above my head was slashed white. Someone close by was calling for his mother in Italian.

The next morning I wrote out the dream in ballad stanzas:

This was the shining green canal
Where we came two by two
Walking at combat interval.
Such trees we never knew . . .

As I wrote I realized that it wasn't a dream but a memory . . . our first contact with the enemy. With this dream, other memories of the war began to return.

"Carentan O Carentan," is well known, insofar as poetry is known in our time. It was set to music by a French composer, Aubert Lemeland, and played over the radio on the fiftieth anniversary of the landing of the Allied armies in Normandy . . . at the moment of the landing. This poem has also been set to music by the American composer Benjamin Lees. The strangest things come together if you live long enough. One moment, you are lying prone with bullets flying around you, mortar shells falling, and a man a few feet away dying and calling, "Mamma mia!" Blood is running down your back. The next moment you are writing about it. And half a century has gone by.

I am both the man there and then and the one who is writing this. Buddhists speak of seeing your life as part of a pattern. I do not have to practice Buddhism in order to do this—it happens when I write.

The process of regaining my memory began with the dream about Carentan. And there were other passages of my life that had been lost—I had forgotten much of my life before the war. I pushed into memory as into some cloudy stuff. So I recovered the house in Jamaica where I lived when I was a child. I recovered the veranda with its climbing vine on which lizards crawled and croaked. The drawing room with the piano, the closet with Chinese and Russian objects, the Victrola with a handle that you wound, and the goldfish bowl on a stand. I was listening to a record on the gramophone and moved back and knocked over the goldfish bowl. There were fragments of glass on the floor, and goldfish gasping and dying. I remembered how I wept.

Such events came back at a great distance, like a story that was read to me as a child. I pushed into the cloud of memory, and people and incidents reappeared, and were connected, and made sense.

Those who have had a break such as I have been describing live in fear of a relapse. You can never be sure . . . The fear affects your behavior in all sorts of ways. You are afraid of the stranger inside you, the one who emerged . . . murderous Mr. Hyde to your good-natured, sociable Doctor Jekyll. You are afraid of yourself . . . you don't know what he may do. As a result you keep your feelings under lock and key.

An episode like this could destroy an artist—a composer of music, a painter, or writer. For the essence of art is self-expression. The poet Rimbaud stopped writing when he was only nineteen and at the height of his powers. People wonder at this . . . I do not. I think he saw shades of the madhouse in front of him and preferred to be a trader and gunrunner in Africa.

There are artists—Van Gogh comes to mind—who have psychotic episodes but don't let this hold them back. They just let themselves go. The end in such cases may very well be self-destruction, but they get themselves expressed. Which would one prefer to be, the man who kept his emotions under strict control, gave up writing, painting, or composing, and lived on as a "well-adjusted" man, or the one who blazed out and spent the rest of his life in darkness?

But isn't there an alternative to either of these ways? The more you pay attention to the world outside the self and think about individuals and the things they do, the more interesting they become. It seems that they need to be expressed, and in expressing them you express the best part of yourself.

But it may take years to arrive at this. Those who have had the kind of break I have described fear a recurrence. A chance remark by a stranger strikes you to the heart . . . it is clear that he knows your weakness. The fear is accompanied by a feeling of shame. For it is a shameful thing to have been weak and at the mercy of others. I am reminded of what I have read about some of the prisoners in concentration camps. They felt ashamed. Of what? Of their suffering. It is a shameful thing to be weak. Their tormentors played upon this feeling . . . they deserved what was coming to them.

Some people after the war argued that the Jews were to blame for not defending themselves—they conspired with their executioners! Hannah Arendt spoke for this point of view. The Nazis would have been pleased . . . wasn't it just what they had been saying, that Jews were an inferior race? The fact is that some Jews defended themselves as well as they could. But if you are standing with your parents, and your wife and children, under the eyes of men armed with machine guns, what are you to do? What would Hannah Arendt have done? Torn a gun from the hands of the guards? And what if you believed as those Jews did that it was a sin to shed blood?

I relived the war almost every night in my dreams. This continued for years. When Miriam and I married she woke one night to sounds that were coming from different parts of the room: sounds of battle, shelling and gunfire. They were coming from me! I was projecting them like a ventriloquist.

I dreamed of encounters with the Germans that I never had. But I had anticipated such meetings as—this was my job—I walked alone among trees or over fields, carrying a message from G Company to Battalion. Or I dreamed about horrors . . . the field in Holland I had to walk through night after night. It was strewn with the dead bodies of German infantry and American paratroopers who had shot each other at close range. The bodies changed, putrefying and swelling. I had to walk around arms and legs and faces shining with corruption.

I used to think that having such dreams was a thing to be ashamed of. For what had I suffered in comparison with others? When I thought of them, the dead, and those who were in wheelchairs, or blinded, or insane, had I really known war at all? What have we to complain of who have only known "soldier's heart"? Nothing, sir, nothing at all.

Some years ago a man from Czechoslovakia came to interview me. He said he was conducting interviews with writers who had seen combat during the Second World War. I told him about the dreams I had about the war—at first almost every night. In recent years they had been tapering off. "Yes," he said. He had been interviewing Russian soldiers, combat veterans. They had the same dreams. It was to be expected.

Why write about such things? Are they not better forgotten? After a war the millions who have been through it want to forget. It was terrible, and sordid, and boring. Besides, everyone knows the things you do. But time passes, and the number of those who remember is suddenly diminished. Who remembers the Great War?

When I was a teacher and the subject of war came up, I would write a name on the blackboard: Somme. Who, I would ask, had heard of it? None of the students would answer. Only one or two knew anything at all about the Great War. I would tell them that the Somme was a battle in that war, a terrible battle in which thousands were killed or wounded . . . 60,000 casualties in the British army on the first morning alone. It was Hell on earth, but the men who went through it consoled themselves with a thought: "Generations will remember what we did here. It will never be forgotten." Yet not one of the young people in front of me had ever heard of it.

I have not forgotten the men I knew in the 101st Airborne Division. The men and women I worked with in universities were pale and unreal in comparison. They were hollow and filled with words. For the essential human virtue, courage, without which there is no other, I give you "point," the man walking up the road ahead of the company, his rifle held across his body at port arms.

What was I to think of the new breed of university professors, structuralists, poststructuralists, deconstructionists, who taught that experience had no meaning, that the only reality was language, one word referring to another, one "sign" to another, with no stop in any kind of truth? Who put the word "truth" in quotes?

It is right to remember such things as I have described—in the first place, because those who have lived and died before us should be remembered, insofar as it is possible. Otherwise our own lives seem worthless. In the second place, war is a permanent human condition, and men and women will have to face it. It may help them to know how people no stronger physically or mentally than they have faced it. In any case, everything that human beings do is interesting, when you think about it.

The war and its aftermath changed me. It gave me a respect and affection for the so-called "common man" that I have never lost. As if any life were common! The men I knew in the 101st, most of them, had no education beyond high school. And they weren't stunning physical specimens either, though they could carry a pack, trench tool, rifle or carbine, machine gun, tripod or ammunition boxes, for miles at a good pace.

> Most clearly of that battle I remember
> The tiredness in eyes, how hands looked thin
> Around a cigarette, and the bright ember
> Would pulse with all the life there was within.

They complained about it, of course. Then why were they willing to go through it? They were not indoctrinated like the Germans and Japanese and Italians with a belief in their racial superiority and a right to enslave other peoples. What most of them wanted was to get the fighting over with and go home . . . to the good life. The life of every day.

I was different from the men around me in one respect . . . the war gave me poetry. I had had what some would call a troubled childhood, though at the time, with the sea and sky of the Caribbean, I wasn't aware of being troubled. My parents were divorced when I was seven years old, and my mother left Jamaica and returned to the States. She disappeared, and no one told me why. So I grew up as a rather lonely boy, though I had friends at school. My father died when I was sixteen. There was no place for me, so I left the island

and came to New York, an entirely different world. There must have been a great deal of trouble in my mind, and no doubt this surfaced as rage when, after the war, I had my break.

But I shall leave the cause to professional explainers of the psyche. What the war and its aftermath gave me was the feeling that, since I had managed to survive, I owed no one anything for my existence—neither my parents nor the government. By moving my body some inches to the left or right, on more than one occasion I had saved my life. From now on it was my own, to do with as I liked.

I liked reading novels and poems. I could lose myself for hours, days even, in a story. And I had a driving need to write . . . a few lines for a poem, a paragraph of prose . . . anything! Even at the University there were very few who felt about such things as I did.

What did that matter? What if the only thing I could do was held in contempt by others . . . or just indifference? Most people cared nothing about the kind of writing that mattered to me more than anything else. They were deaf to the music. So what! I was alive and doing what I liked.

Winter 1997

Part Five

Poetry

Yugoslavia in Ruins

Nina Bogin

As if we could hear dark thunder
across the snowfields, across the battle-green
hills. As if the hawk circled
with a message in its grip, scrawled
in rust. If we put on our boots,
fill our pockets with warm chestnuts, we can start
before morning. We'll follow their voices, the lost
notes ringing from the screes. We'll sing
the echoes ourselves. We'll climb through
the forest with its gongs of silence. This is all
we'll have to give them—fistfuls
of autumn and smoke, words
broken on every crag of these forsaken outposts.

Summer 1994

The Miracle of Camp 60

Anne Stevenson

(The speaker is a fictive Italian ex-POW revisiting the Italian Chapel on the Orkney Island of Lamb Holm in 1992.)

Amici d'arti, amici dei fiori, amici d'amore,
when in our towns they told us *go fight for Il Duce*
we Dolomiti had to go. We were . . . coscritti, we
had no choice. I wept when I departed from Trento,
my poor mother, my so sad new young wife.
Credi in Dio, we embraced each other as the train
stretched us apart. But then in the deeps of misery
I had some luck. My seat-partner, how do you say,
was Chiocchetti. L'artista Domenico Chiocchetti
of Moena, a man very sensitive . . . you understand?
And so he saw my tears. With him he kept always—
like this, around his neck—a spiritual picture,
Madonna dell'Ulivo—Our Lady of the Olives—
of our great Italian painter, Nicolò Barabino.
This medallion Domenico let me hold, for hope,
as the train transported us human meats to Roma,
then to Tunis, to Egitto, to fight the war.
See over the altar, the Madonna of Chioccetti,
Regina Pacis, Ora Pro Nobis. As we prayed many many times
in that desert of death under the stars.
Our prayers were answered when Tommy beat us.
No more did we have to fear the brute Tedeschi.
So we were glad. Not to be prisoners, you understand,
but to be not any longer soldiers, while we were sad
not to go home. We did not know what was happening
in our country, to our families. When we came to Orkney,
we did not know where we were, so far, so . . . smorta
this terrible island, not one tree, not one flower.
Only polvere, calcina, cemento . . . everywhere

filo barbato—all sunshine strangled in it—and huts
we would use for pigs in Italy, to share.

Only Chiocchetti saw . . . a holy place.
Look, he pointed through the wires, the azure water,
isole, islands, emerald in the sea. He was painting them
already in his head while we worked through rain and wind
to build the barriers. Labour we did not mind.
Better to work than to despair. Even so,
there was too much time to think of home.
Before the war my occupation was giardinere.
I made gardens for the city of Merano.
(After I went back, I was the capo.) One day on Lamb Holm
I spied among the rocks a small flower, an iris rare
in Italy, and I thought, here we could grow plants,
make little beds, walkways, sentieri.

So with some men I went to the Commandante. "Please
may we have some seeds." Seeds? he was surprised.
He found us seeds and bulbs, in some months we had iris,
geranio, calendula, lupini, giglio—you say lily?
We made your desert bloom. Now, why not a piazza with a
  statue?
"OK," says Chiocchetti, "without marble, I carve cemento;
without bronze, I twist barbed wire." Eccola,
the marvel he created! St. George spearing the Dragon.
To show the wish of us Italians to exterminate evil.
Into the base we put our names and coins we saved
from home. Our padre, Gioachino Giacobazzi, swung his
  censer.
We wept for sadness and joy because from memory
we had made in our ugly camp a dream of Italy.

Allora, came winter and the long nights. We found
some space for a teatro; talented men among us played
harmonica, mandolin; always we prisoners had the spirit

to make beauty, but up to that time we had no church,
no place of God to celebrate mass. Yet once again
il padre, Chiocchetti and myself were called to Major
    Buckland,
"Signori, you are Catholics. Do not you need a chapel?"
That English Major was, I think, exceptional. Under his
traditional reserve beat surely the Italian heart.
A short time and two new huts appeared, placed end to end
—like so—to make one bigger one.
And now the talent of Chiocchetti became genius.
He picked skilled helpers and they, too, caught fire.
Palumbo, who studied metal-working in America, contrived
from scrap—gracile, delicate—the screen of iron.
And Bruttapasta whose speciality was concrete.
Regard his altar, made out of just cemento; the same for
la facciata, colonne, campanile, pinnacoli, vetri—
painted in all colori, l'arco, i pedimenti. Also, in sandstone,
la testa di Cristo crocefisso that was moulded by Pinesi.
It was as if, on this far island, by the mercy of God,
we few had been chosen to prepare in a world destroyed
a home for the immortal dove who alone brings peace
to men and women. Regard—on the vault of the sanctuary
in the fresco of Chiocchetti—white dove among angels.

Mi scusate. Excuse me. I am incapable of beholding this place
without tears. War was good to us. We were prisoners
but we were happy, making our chapel beautiful.
Happier than ever again. When the war finished
we had to depart. I sobbed because we had not finished.
I wept again in Merano. La mia madre, morta . . . my poor
    wife,
you know what i bruti soldati did to beautiful women,
we could not have children. To forgive myself for joy
while my loved ones suffered—so many suffered—
it was not easy. Chiocchetti did not come home with us.

He stayed to complete his font, and when I met him in Moena—
many many years later—he told me he, too, felt guilty.
But guilt is not right, he said, for art is joy.
Short is our suffering in this life, joy is forever.
Now, an old man, I visit again our joyful chapel
to read, in your language, a prayer of blessed Francis.
"Lord make me an instrument of peace.
Where there is hatred, let me sow love,
where there is injury, pardon,
where there is darkness, light,
where there is sadness . . . gioia, la gioia."

Note: Domenico Chiocchetti died at Moena on 7 May 1999.

Summer 1999

On First Looking into Lattimore's Homer

Daniel Hoffman

With smaller Latin and less Greek
Than Keats, I had to roam
With those who rowed on perfumed seas.
My trireme was launched in the Eighteen Nineties,
The wrath of Achilles but a tinted scene
On tapestries
Embroidered, unreal,
In a language none could feel or speak.

Now the seas snarl where an arrogant keel
Supple through swell and spume
Dares tread the god-infested Mediterranean.
See doom-bound Hektor, eager to assuage
Blood-maddened rage—
How we are torn,
Whether to exult or mourn,
Swept on the surge of lines we speak and feel.

Summer 2000

Sir Gawain and the Green Knight, Part IV

Anonymous Fourteenth-Century Poet,
Translated by John Ridland

Synopsis: *The four seasons, brilliantly sketched, had passed, and Sir Gawain had begun his search for the Green Chapel and its "half-giant" Green Knight, whose head he had chopped off at Camelot during the previous Christmas festivities. By agreement made then, the green man will be waiting at his "chapel" to return the favor on New Year's Day the following year. After battling wild beasts and wild men, and the rigors of a long journey in frigid weather, Gawain had realized it was Christmas Eve, and he was anxious, for his soul's sake, to take Mass the next day. He was therefore much relieved to come upon a gleaming, up-to-date castle with its own priests and a proper chapel, where he was heartily welcomed by its lord, a huge man with a bushy red beard, and a wife more beautiful than Queen Guenevere. The Christmas festivities in the castle concluded with the lord setting up a "game" between himself and Gawain: for his three remaining days, while the lord goes out hunting early, Gawain will rest up at the castle for his coming ordeal, and each evening they will exchange whatever they have gained that day.*

Like a skilled film editor, the unknown author cuts between outdoor scenes, where the lord leads his men in hunting, on successive days, herds of deer (which must be culled), a dangerous wild boar, and a measly but crafty fox, and, back at the castle, an indoor hunt with Sir Gawain as the quarry. Early each morning the lord's beautiful wife sneaks into Gawain's room and slips inside his bed curtains to sit by him and assail his knightly virtue, her manner rapidly accelerating from the merely courteous to the openly seductive. Each evening, in accordance with their pact, Gawain passes on to the lord all he has received that day: one kiss, then two, then three. The lord presents him with the corpses of the animals he has killed.

However, on that third morning, the day before he must go and get his head chopped off, besides the three kisses, the lady had offered Gawain a woven belt which, she said, would protect its wearer from being killed—but if he takes it, he must not tell her husband. He accepted it with calculated reluctance, and that night, in the final exchange of winnings, he gave the lord the requisite kisses but concealed the belt in his room. Next morning he sets off for the Green Chapel, which, conveniently and most coincidentally, lies only two miles from the castle. As they all say their final good nights and tearful goodbyes, the lord assigns a servant to guide Sir Gawain to his place of doom in the morning. Translator's Note

Part IV: The Meeting

Now as the New Year was drawing nigh, and the night before it
passed,
Daylight was driving the dark away, as the Lord above commands.
But a wild weather was working up in the world outside their doors:
The clouds emptied their cold contents keenly down on the earth,
With cruelty enough from the north to torment the naked flesh.
The snow fell snittering sharply, nipping the wild creatures;
The whistling wind whipped down upon them shrilly from the
heights,
And filled the hollows of every dale up full with heavy drifts.
The knight was listening closely to this as he lay awake in his bed,
And though he locked his eyelids shut, he got very little sleep:
From each cock crow throughout the night he could tell what hour it
was.
Hurriedly he got out of bed before the break of day,
For there was light enough from a lamp that was glowing in his room.
He called out to his chamberlain, who promptly answered him;
He bade him bring his chain-mail shirt, and saddle up his horse.
The man obediently got up, and fetched the garments for him,
And began to get Sir Gawain dressed, in most resplendent style.
First he put on his warmest clothes, which would ward off the cold,
And next he brought the armor out that had been carefully stored:
Both the belly piece and all the plate polished bright and clean,
The rust on the rings of his costly chain-mail shirt had been rubbed
off,

And all gleamed fresh as when first forged, for which he was keen to thank
Them all.
When he had donned each piece—
All had been polished well;
Unmatched from here to Greece,
He said, "Bring my steed from his stall."

While the noble knight was being arrayed in his most handsome clothes—
The surcoat draping over his armor adorned with the pentangle badge
Stitched onto velvet, framed around with precious, potent stones
Inlaid along the embroidered seams, setting it off so well;
And on the inside the coat was beautifully lined with the finest fur—
Yet he did not leave the lace behind that had been the lady's gift;
That present Gawain did not forget, for the good of his own self.
After he had belted the sword above his powerful hips,
He wrapped the love-token carefully two times around his waist;
Quickly that knight, and delightedly, wound it about his middle.
The girdle woven of green silk well suited that splendid man,
Against the royal red of the cloth, which looked so rich in itself.
But he wasn't putting this girdle on because of its costliness,
Nor out of pride in its shiny pendants, however polished they were,
Nor even for the glittering gold that glinted upon the fringe,
But in order that he might save his life when he was obliged to submit,
To face, without dispute, what he would take from the sword's or knife's
Sharp stroke.
Once the brave man was set,
He hurried out and spoke
His thanks to all he met,
To all the noble folk.

Then Gringolet was made ready to ride, that was an enormous horse
That had been stabled comfortably and in a secure fashion:
That proud horse, due to his fit condition, wanted to gallop now.

The knight walked out to where he stood, and gazed on his glistening coat,
And soberly he said to himself, swearing it on his oath,
"Here inside this moat is a company setting their minds on honor:
May joy come to the lord who maintains and manages them all;
And as for the delightful lady, may she have love in her life!
If out of charity they can receive and cherish a guest so kindly,
And offer such hospitality, may the Good Lord reward them
Who holds the heavens up on high—and also all of you!
And if I should stay alive on earth, for any length of time,
I would quickly pay you some recompense, if I were able to."
Then the knight stepped into the stirrup, and swung astride the horse;
His servant offered him his shield, which he settled on his shoulder,
And he dug his spurs into Gringolet, kicking his gilded heels,
And the horse started forward over the stones, no longer standing still,

To prance.
His man was mounted then
Who bore his spear and lance.
"This castle I commend
To Christ against mischance!"

The bridge was let down for him to pass, and the broad gates in the wall
Were unbarred, swung open without delay, all the way back on both halves.
The knight rapidly blessed himself and passed across the planks,
Thanking the porter who kept the gates, who knelt before the prince—
He wished the knight "Good day" and prayed that God would save Gawain—
And he went on his way accompanied by a single guide
To teach him the turns by which to reach at last that perilous place
Where he was destined to receive the grievous, terrible stroke.

They bent and stooped beneath bare boughs along the hillside slopes;
They clambered along below the cliffs where the cold was clinging close.
The heavens were holding high above, but were threatening underneath;
The mist was mizzling on the moor and melting on the mountains;
Each of the hilltops had a hat, a huge mantle of mist.
The brooks were boiling and foaming, bursting over their banks,
White water shattered against the sides, as they made their way downhill.
The route was wild and meandering that they followed through the woods,
Until it would soon be time, in that season, for the sun to break
From night.
They were on a high hilltop;
On all sides snow lay white;
The guide with him called, "Stop!"
Abruptly, to the knight.

"For I have brought you here, sir, at the appointed time,
And now you are not far at all from that noteworthy place
That you have sought and asked about so very particularly.
But I shall tell you the truth, my lord, since now I know you well,
And you are one man on this earth whom I regard most highly:
If only you'd act on my advice, it would be much better for you.
The place you are pressing forward to is held to be perilous;
A man lives in that wasteland, the worst man in the world,
For he is strong and stern and grim and above all loves striking blows,
And in his massiveness more of a man than any other on earth;
His body is bigger than four of the best and biggest knights to be found
In Arthur's house—he is bigger even than Hector or any other—
And he is in charge of all mischance that happens at the Green Chapel,
For nobody passes by that place, however proud in arms,

But he will batter him to death with a blow from his strong hand,
For he is a man without restraint, and has no use for mercy:
Whether it be a churl or a chaplain that's riding by the chapel,
Whether a monk, or a priest who says Mass, or anybody else,
He thinks it as fine to murder a man as to stay alive himself.
Therefore I have to say to you, as sure as you sit in your saddle,
If you go there, you will be killed, if that knight has his way—
Trust me, I'm telling you the truth—even if you had twenty lives
To spend.
He has lived a long time in this land,
And stirred up strife no end;
Against his deadly hand
There's no way to defend.

"Therefore, good Sir Gawain, please leave the man alone
And ride away by some other road, for God's sake and your own.
Take yourself off to another land, where Christ may give you speed!
And I shall hurry home again; and further, I promise you
That I shall swear on oath, 'By God and all his hallowed saints,
So help me God and the holy relics,' and other oaths enough—
That I shall loyally keep your secret, and never let drop a word
That ever you tried to run away from any man I know of."
"Thank you so much," Gawain replied, though he said it with irritation.
"I should, I suppose, wish you good luck for caring about my welfare,
And you say you will loyally keep my secret, as I believe you would;
But, though you kept it ever so close, if I hurried past this place,
Fleeing away from him out of fear, in the fashion you propose,
I would be called a cowardly knight and could not be excused.
So I will go on to the Green Chapel, to whatever challenge I meet,
And talk there to that knight himself, and tell him whatever I think;
Whether it brings me well or woe, it will only be what Fate
Decrees.
He may be a fearsome knave
Who could club me to my knees,

But God shapes things to save
His servants, should He please."

"By Mary!" said the other man. "Since now you have spelled it out
That you are bringing your own destruction down upon yourself,
And it pleases you to lose your life, I will say nothing against it.
Here, put your helmet on your head, and take your spear in hand,
And ride this rough path downstream by the side of that rock yonder,
Till it brings you to the bottom of the broad and rugged valley.
Then look to the glade not far away, a little off to the left,
And you shall see, set in that dale, the very chapel you're after,
And on its grounds the burly brute who keeps it in his care.
Now farewell, noble Gawain, in God's name, fare thee well!
For all the gold there is in the earth I would not go with you,
Nor travel in your company through this forest one foot farther."
With that, in the middle of the wood, the fellow yanked his bridle,
Kicked his horse's flanks with his heels as hard as he could spur,
Galloped him off across the glade, and left the knight there, all
Alone.
"By God's own Self," he said,
"I will not weep or groan.
God's will must be obeyed,
His wishes are my own."

Then he struck his spurs into Gringolet, and followed the stream path down:
He pushed his way on past the rock, at the edge of a small thicket,
And rode along the ragged bank to the bottom of the dale.
Then he looked around on every side, and it seemed a wilderness.
Nowhere could he see a sign of a place where he might shelter,
Only high banks rising steeply, on both halves of the dale,
And rough and knobby rocky knolls, with sharp and craggy outcrops;
It seemed to him that the lowering clouds were grazed by the jutting rocks.

Then he drew his horse to a halt, checked for a little while
As he sat him, turning this way and that, to seek the chapel out.
He saw no such thing on any side—and that seemed strange to
    him—
Except that a little off to the left in the glade was a sort of mound,
Or a smooth and rounded barrow on a bank-side above the brim
Of the channel of a watercourse that was flowing freely through;
The brook was bubbling within, as if it had come to a boil.
The knight then urged his horse along, bringing him up to the
    knoll,
Alighted from him gracefully, and at a linden tree
Attached the reins of his noble steed to one of the rough branches.
And then he walked across to the mound and he strode all around it,
Turning over in his mind what this strange thing might be.
It had a hole on one end, and the same on either side,
And it was overgrown with grass in patches everywhere,
And all was hollow on the inside—nothing but an old cave
Or a crevice in an old crag, but which it was he could not
                                        Be sure.
                "Ah, Lord!" sighed the noble knight,
                "Can the Green Chapel be here,
                Where the Devil, around midnight,
                Might say his morning prayer?

"Now indeed," said Gawain, "without doubt this is a wasteland;
This chapel is horrifying, overgrown with greenery—
A very fitting place for that man who dresses himself in green
To do his devotions dutifully—in the Devil's fashion.
Now I feel in my five senses that in fact it is the Fiend
Who has imposed this tryst on me, and will destroy me here.
This is a chapel of mischance—may it be checkmated!—
It is the cursedest kind of church that ever I came into!"
With his helmet high up on his head and his lance held in his hand
He climbed up to the top of the roof above the rough abode
Then, farther up on the high hill, he heard, by a hard rock,

Beyond the brook, above the bank, a wondrously loud noise.
What! It clattered against the cliff as if it would cleave it in two,
Like someone at a grindstone who was sharpening a scythe.
What! It whirred and whetted, like water at a mill!
What! It made a rushing, and a ringing, harsh to hear.
Then, "By God!" Sir Gawain said, "that weapon is being prepared
To welcome me as a knight of my rank ought to be greeted, it would
Appear.
God's will be done. To moan
Will never help me here.
Though my life may soon be gone,
A noise won't make me fear."

With that the knight cried boldly out, as loudly as he could,
"Who is the master in this place, who holds this tryst with me?
For right now, good Gawain is walking all around, right here.
If any man wants anything, let him appear at once,
It's now or never, if he intends to get this business done."
"Wait!" shouted somebody on the bank up above his head,
"And you will quickly have it all, that I once promised you."
He kept on making that rushing sound, for a while more rapidly,
As he turned back to finish his whetting before he would come down.
And then he picked his way past a crag and emerged out of a hole,
Whirling from a nook nearby, armed with a dreadful weapon:
A Danish axe that was freshly forged to pay the return blow,
With a mighty blade curving back on itself until it touched the helve;
It had been honed on a whetstone, and it was four feet wide—
No less than that if measured by the brightly shining belt!
And the man came out arrayed in green, as he had been at first,
His face and cheeks, his flowing locks of hair, and his broad beard,
Except that now he went on foot, grandly over the ground,
Setting the haft on the stony earth and stalking along beside it.
When he came to the stream, he wouldn't pause at the water's edge to wade,

But hopped across it on his axe, and hurriedly strode on,
Fiercely grim, on a broad and grassy patch of ground that was cloaked
In snow.
Gawain greeted the seigneur,
Bowing, but not too low.
The other said, "Monsieur,
So—one can trust your vow."

"Gawain," the Green Knight went on, "may God protect you now!
I bid you welcome, sir, to my place, my chapel and domain,
And you have timed your travels well to reach it when you ought;
And you understand the covenant that was agreed between us:
At this time just twelve months ago, you took what was your lot,
And I, at this New Year, should promptly pay you in return.
And here we are in this valley, which is verily ours alone;
Here are no knights to part us; we may dance our dance as we please.
Take your helmet off your head, and receive your payment now.
Do not resist me any more than I resisted you
When you whipped my head off with a single whack of your battleaxe."
"No," said Sir Gawain, "by the God who granted me a soul,
I will not begrudge you a bit for any hurt that happens;
Only hold yourself to a single stroke, and I will stay stock still
And offer no objection at all, whatever you want to do—
Not one."
He bent his neck and bowed,
Exposing the bare white skin;
Acting as if uncowed,
Unafraid for him to begin.

Then all in a rush the man in green prepared himself to strike:
He grappled and lifted the grim tool to give Gawain the blow;
With all the force in his massive frame he bore it up aloft

And aimed his swing as mightily as if he meant to destroy him.
If he had driven that stroke down as staunchly as he began,
He would have died from the dreadful blow, the one who was always brave.
But from the corner of his eye Gawain caught a glimpse of the axe
As it came gliding down at him to demolish him in a flash,
And he flinched a little with his shoulders, shrank from the sharp iron.
The other man suddenly checked his swing, held back the shining blade,
And then how he reproved the prince with many disdainful words:
"You are not Gawain," the Green Knight scoffed, "who is held to be so good,
Who never quailed on hill or dale before an enemy horde,
And now you flinch from me for fear before you are even harmed!
I never knew such cowardice on the part of that knight before.
I neither winced nor shied away, friend, when you swung at me,
Nor came up with some caviling argument in King Arthur's court.
My head flew off and fell to my feet, and yet I never fled;
But you, before you take any hurt, are terrified in your heart.
So I deserve, without a doubt, to be called the better man,
Therefore."
Said Gawain, "I flinched once,
But I will not any more,
Though if my head falls on the stones,
It cannot be restored.

"But hurry up, man, by your faith, and come to the point with me—
Deal me the destiny that is mine, and do it out of hand.
For I shall wait to take your stroke and startle at it no more,
Until your axe has hewn into me: you have my plighted oath."
"Have at you then!" the other shouted, heaving it up aloft,
And grimacing as furiously as if he were out of his mind.
Ferociously he swung at him, but did not touch the man,
For in an instant he checked his swing before it might do him harm.

Gawain awaited the blow as he ought, and not a limb of his flinched,
But he stayed as still as any stone, or rather, like a stump
That is anchored into the rocky ground, locked by a hundred roots.
Then once again the man in green harangued him playfully:
"So, now you have your courage back, it's time to strike the blow.
May that high knighthood Arthur dubbed you with preserve you now,
And save your neck from this next stroke, if it can manage to."
Gawain's fury grew more and more, and fiercely he lashed out,
"Why, thrash away, you fearsome fellow, you waste time flinging threats!
I suspect that in your heart of hearts you have terrified yourself."
"Indeed," replied the other knight, "you speak so defiantly,
I will no longer delay about it and hinder you on your mission—
Right now."
He took his stance to strike,
Puckered both lip and brow.
Sir Gawain didn't like
His chance of rescue now.

The knight lifted his weapon up, easily, letting it down,
With the sharp blade of the cutting edge onto the bare neck.
Though he hammered with his full force, it harmed him barely enough
To nick his neck on the one side, severing the skin.
The sharp edge sank into the flesh and through the shining fat
So the bright blood shot over his shoulders and out onto the earth.
And when Gawain glimpsed his own blood there, gleaming on the snow,
He sprang forth more than a spear's length with his feet planted together:
He grasped his helmet hurriedly and clapped it onto his head;
With a shake of his shoulders then he jerked his shield down into place,

And drew his bright sword from his belt and challenged fierily.
Never since he had been a newborn babe in his mother's arms
Had he ever felt himself in this world to be half so happy a man.
"You can put a stop to your bold strokes, sir! Give me no more of
them!
For I have taken one blow in this place, without resisting it,
But if you offer me any more, I will pay you back at once,
I will repay you to the full, rely on it—and be
Your foe.
Only one stroke must fall—
Thus did we make our vow
Which we pledged in Arthur's hall—
And therefore, man, stop now!"

The great lord turned away from him and rested on his axe—
He set the shaft on the riverbank and leaned on the sharp blade
And took a good long look at the knight who had taken a fighting
stance,
How that doughty hero stood up to him, so fearless and undaunted,
Fully armed and free of dread: it warmed his heart to watch.
Then he addressed him cheerfully in his resounding voice
And with a ringing resonance he spoke thus to the man:
"Bold knight, don't be so fierce and grim, here on this grassy
ground.
Nobody has used you ill, or in unmannerly fashion,
Nor acted against the covenant that we shaped at the King's court.
I pledged you a stroke, and you have it—you may hold yourself well
paid;
I release you from the rest of it, from any other claims.
If I had not been nimble, perhaps I'd have dealt you a blow
More out of anger, one that might indeed have provoked your wrath.
The first stroke, though, I threatened you for fun, with only a feint,
Not slicing you open with a slash. In this I gave you justice
According to the agreement we crafted your first night in my castle,
When you faithfully fulfilled our pact and were a man of your word:

All of your winnings you gave to me, as an honest man should do.
The other feint I gave you, sir, because on the following morning
You kissed my lovely wife and gave me back the kisses taken.
For those two days you took from me those merely feigning blows
At your nape.
If a true man keeps his word,
Then he meets no mishap.
You fell short on the third,
And thus you took that tap.

"For that is my garment you are wearing, that selfsame woven girdle.
It was my own wife gave it to you, I know it very well.
And I know all about your kisses, and all the things you did;
And as for your wooing by my wife, it was I who set it up.
For I sent her to test your worth, and to tell the truth, I think
You are one of the most faultless men who ever went on foot:
As a pearl beside a white pea is so much more to be prized,
So is Sir Gawain, for good faith, beside all other knights.
You were lacking only a little here, and your fidelity failed,
Though not from greed for this craftsmanship, nor for making love,
But only because you loved your life, so I blame you all the less."
The other, valiant as he was, stood silent a long while,
So overcome with mortification he shuddered inside himself;
And all the blood in his breast flushed up and mingled in his face;
So that he winced and shied for shame at what the knight had said.
There at that moment the first words bursting out of him were these:
"A curse upon such cowardice and also covetousness!
In the pair of you are villainy and vice, that destroy virtue."
The good knight then caught hold of the knot, unloosed the fastening,
And roughly flinging the whole belt to the lord who owned it, said,
"Look at it! There the false thing is, may the Fiend take it away!
Because I was anxious about your stroke, cowardice instructed me

To accord myself with covetousness and forsake my character;
The largesse and the loyalty which truly belong to knighthood,
Now I am found faulty in them, and false, who have been afraid
Always of treachery and untruth—both of which lead to sorrow
And care!
I confess before you, knight,
My faults in private here.
Your good will, if I might
Regain, will make me wary."

At that the other lord stood laughing, and answered amiably,
"I hold it to be wholly healed, the injury that I had.
You have confessed yourself so cleanly, acknowledging your faults,
And you had your penance put to you at the sharp edge of my blade,
That I hold you cleansed of that offense, and purified as clean
As if you had never sinned at all since the day that you were born.
And I will give you this girdle, sir, with the gold along its hems;
For it is as green as my gown, Sir Gawain, and wearing it you may
Think back upon this selfsame game, when you are pressing forward
Among other princes of excellence; this will be a noble token
Of the feat you performed at the Green Chapel, when you're among chivalrous knights.
And now you shall, in this New Year, come back with me to my house,
And we shall revel away the rest of this glorious festival
Most happily."
He pressed him hard, that lord:
"I think that with my lady
We shall bring you to accord—
Who was your bitter enemy."

"Indeed I cannot," said the knight, and seizing hold of his helmet,
He doffed it out of courtesy, and offered the lord his thanks.

"I have lingered here quite long enough. Good luck to you and yours,
And may He who determines all rewards repay you generously!
Commend me to that courteous lady, your gracious, lovely wife,
Both to her and that other one, my honored noble ladies,
Who so adroitly have beguiled their knight with their trickery.
But it is not an unusual thing for a fool to act foolishly,
Or for a man, through the wiles of women, to be brought down to grief.
For in the same style Adam once was beguiled by one on earth,
And Solomon by many women, and Samson was another—
Delilah dealt him his destiny—and David afterwards
Was blinded by Bathsheba and endured much misery.
Now, since these were ruined by women's wiles, it would be an enormous gain
To love them well, but not believe them—if any man could do that!
For these were the favored ones of old whom fortune followed after,
Yet they all went astray, although they were the most excellent men
Under heaven!
All of them had the wool
Pulled over their eyes by women;
If I'm an equal fool,
Might I not be forgiven?

"But as for your girdle," Gawain said, "may God reward you for it!
That I will wear with all good will, though not for gain of gold,
Nor for the cincture, nor the silk, nor for the long pendants,
Nor for its costliness and prestige, nor the wonderful workmanship;
But as a token of my transgression, I shall see it often
When I am riding out to renown, and remember with remorse
The faultiness and the frailty that cling to the obstinate flesh,
How it tends to be easily enticed to the spots and stains of sin.
And thus, when my prowess in battle shall prick me on to pride,
One look at this love-lace will remind me, and humble me in my heart.

But one thing I would like to know, so long as it won't offend you:
Since you are the lord of yonder lands which I have been staying in,
So honorably received by you—may He repay you for it
Who holds the heavens above the earth and sits enthroned on high—
What are you called by your rightful name?—and then I will ask no more!"
"I will tell you that without deceit," the other man replied.
"Bertilak of Hautdesert is how I am known in this land.
Through the mighty force of Morgan le Fay, who is living in my castle,
And her skill in the magical lore and crafts that she once learned so well
Through the masterful arts of Merlin himself, many of which she acquired,
For she had pleasant love-dealings over a long while
With that wise and excellent wizard—as is known to the knights from whence
You came.
Morgan le Fay the goddess
Therefore is her name.
Whatever his haughtiness
There's no man she can't tame.

"She sent me out in this disguise to assail your handsome hall,
To put your vaunted pride to the test, to see if it held true,
The great renown of the Round Table, that is vaunted everywhere.
She sent me out as this marvel you see, to drive you out of your minds,
And to so distress Queen Guinevere that she would be startled to death
From horror at seeing that selfsame knight, that ghastly phantom speaker
Talk from his head that he held in his hand, facing the high table.
She is the one who lives at my home, that ancient, agèd lady;

Even more than that, she is your aunt, half-sister to King Arthur,
She is the Duchess of Tintagel's daughter, whom noble Uther later
Fathered Arthur himself upon, who is now your sovereign King.
Therefore, my lord, I now beseech you, come and visit your aunt,
Make merry once again in my house, where my people love you so,
And I, my fine fellow, bear you as much good will, by my faith, as any
Man living under God on earth, for your great integrity."
Gawain said nothing except that he could not stay, by any means.
The two knights then embraced and kissed, commended one another
To the high Prince of Paradise, and they separated right there
In the cold.
Gawain on his fair steed
Made haste to the King's stronghold,
And the knight in brightest green
Wherever he wanted to go.

Gawain now went riding over many wild ways in the world
On Gringolet, since, through the grace of God, he had gotten away with his life.
Often he lodged inside a house, and often out of doors,
And met with many adventures in valleys and won many victories
Which I, at this time, do not intend to tell you all about.
The hurt had healed and was whole again that he'd taken in his neck,
And he wore the gleaming belt about his body all the time,
But slantwise as a baldric that is fastened at the side,
The lace locked under his left arm, and tied there with a knot
As a token of the spot of sin—the fault—he'd been taken in.
And thus that knight, all safe and sound, came to the King's court.
Delight was wakened in that house when the noble folk were told
That good Gawain had come again: they thought it amazing luck.
The King walked out and kissed the knight, and the Queen kissed him too,

And after them many a trusty knight who came to hail him there
Asked him about his travels; he told them fantastic tales,
Describing all the tribulations he'd met with since he left—
His adventure at the Green Chapel, the deportment of its Knight,
The amorous actions of the lady, and then at last, the lace.
He bared the scar of the nick on his neck in order to show them all
What he had taken at that lord's hands for his unfaithfulness,
His blame.
It tormented him to tell;
He groaned for grief, and pain—
The blood in his face upwelled
When he showed the cut, for shame.

"Look at this, lords!" the knight cried out, handling the lace.
"This is the ribbon of the blame that I also bear on my neck.
This is the sign of the injury and damage I have deserved—
From cowardice and covetousness that both caught hold of me.
This is the token of the untruth that I was taken in,
And I must keep on wearing it as long as my life may last,
For though a man may hide his offense, he cannot be rid of it,
For once it is attached to him, it never will come loose."
The King then sought to comfort the knight, as all the court did, too,
Laughing out loud at what he confessed, and they amiably agreed—
The lords who belonged to the Round Table and all their ladies as well—
That each bold knight of that brotherhood should obtain a similar baldric,
A cross-belt slantwise from the shoulder, colored a bright green,
Which for the sake of that good man they would follow suit and wear.
For that was agreed to be the highest glory of the Round Table,
And whoever wore it thus was honored, forever afterwards,
As is recorded, written down in the best book of romance.
Thus it came about in Arthur's day that this adventure happened,

And the books of British history bear witness to it as well,
Ever since Brutus, the bold knight, first landed on these shores,
After the siege and the assault had been exhausted at Troy:

Finis.

Many strange things have been found
In Britain before this:
Now He that once was crowned
With Thorns bring us to bliss.

AMEN

HONI SOIT QUI MAL PENCE

Translated from Middle English by John Ridland[1]

Winter 2010

1. The translator wishes to acknowledge his enormous debt of gratitude to the late Mary Veazey for her subtle, collaborative editing.

Knives

Maria Terrone

> "In most kitchens all over Jerusalem or Tel Aviv, there are Palestinians and Israelis cooking together, shoulder to shoulder, with long knives."
>
> —A Chef for Peace, quoted in the *New York Times*

Sulphured air, the fire
beneath convulsing pots,
sudden roar of jets
igniting. Sweat of bodies
whirling in chaotic space,
blunt impact, flying shards.
Orders shouted through tents
of steam.

But the only blood here
is the lamb's as it pools
on a scarred plank.

The knives,
crossed daily against
ancient stone,
keep to themselves.

Autumn 2010

Three Poems

Maxine Kumin

Red Tape and Kangaroo Courts I[1]

On this tropical refrigerated paved-over island
where banana rats are rampant

endangered species iguanas dine on
McDonald's and Subway discards

and the list of things that are prohibited
in the camps is itself prohibited

—not Kafka but George Clarke, a tax lawyer
working pro bono at Guantánamo

where special clearance and special papers
required to reach this "theater" are months in coming

where Arabic-speaking inmates are pressed to serve
with no skilled translators available

and capital cases are heard with no
capital defense attorneys allowed

Red Tape and Kangaroo Courts II

Soundproof glass between
the accused and observers in the courtroom

shields what cannot be said
what must be interrupted if the detainees

speak of the dark acts at the dark
heart of what took place during their confinement:

1. The titles and key phrases embedded in these two sonnets are excerpted from *The Guantánamo Lawyers: Inside a Prison Outside the Law*, ed. by Mark P. Denbeaux and Jonathan Hafetz (New York: NYU Press, 2009).

for interrogation they held his head in
the toilet and flushed it over and over

for hunger strike they forcefed him until he vomited, then
fed him again until he vomited again

and when he passed out, they doused him awake in a cell
with a steel bunk, no mattress, no blanket

if we don't talk about the torture
it never happened.

Old News

The *New York Times*: 5.4.10, 7.11.08

Medic Recalls Detainee Chained to Cage
like laundry, draped in neat pentameter.

He tended bullet wounds in the teenager's
Back twice daily in a five-foot square

Crate at a US lockup at Bagram.
The Pentagon defended what was done

To the chained and hooded prisoner
As sactioned punishment of young Khadr.

The medic didn't object; chaining was approved.
He borrowed him to translate for other captives.

He didn't inquire how long they let him hang.
Shackled, the boy soiled himself. Beatings.

Threats of rape. Solitary. Prolonged cold.
It only makes page 6. The news is old.

Winter 2012

Préface en Prose

Benjamin Fondane,
Translated by John Balaban and Donka Farkas

I am talking to you, my opposite Others.
I am talking man to man
with that bit of myself which remains a man
that bit of my voice still stuck in my throat.
My blood is on the streets, may it—oh, may it not—
cry out for vengeance.
The hunter's horn is sounded. The hounds are on the track.
So let me now speak to you in words we once shared,
though few still make sense.

A day will come, for sure, when thirst quenched,
we will have gone beyond memory, and death
will have finished hatred's work, and I
will have become a bunch of nettles under your feet.
But, look, you need to know I had a face like you.
A mouth that prayed, like you.

When a speck of dust or a dream
entered my eyes, they wept a little salt.
And when a nasty thorn pricked my skin,
it bled red blood, just like yours.
And, yeah, like you, I was cruel, and hungered
for tenderness, for power, money, pleasure, and pain.
Just like you I was mean, filled with anguish,
reliable enough at peace, drunk in victory,
and staggering and worn in times of failure.

And, sure, I was a man like other men
nourished by bread, by dreams, and by despair,
and sure, I loved, wept, hated, and suffered.
I bought flowers and sometimes I skipped on my rent.
On Sundays, I might go to the countryside and fish,

to catch, under God's eye, his fish of irreality
and bathe in the river that sang in the bulrushes
and eat fries in the evening. Later, I'd go back
and sleep, my heart worn out and lonely,
full of pity for myself, full of pity for mankind,
searching, searching in vain on a woman's body
for that impossible peace we lost once in a great orchard
with the tree of life flowering at its heart.

Like you I read all the newspapers, the books,
and understood nothing of the world,
understood nothing about men,
though often I may have claimed to.
When death, when death came, perhaps
I pretended to understand but, really
(I can tell you now),
when all of death entered my astonished eyes
I was stunned by how little I had understood.
Did you understand it any better?

And, yet, NO!
I wasn't a man like you.
You were not born on the road.
No one ever dropped your children into a sewer
like blind kittens, you never had to wander
from city to city, tracked by cops.
You never knew calamity at dawn,
or cattle cars, or bitter sobs of humiliation
when accused of a crime you never committed,
a murder without a body, or had to change your name
and face, not to have an abused name or a face that served
as a spittoon.

But a day will come, for sure, when this poem
will lie before you, asking nothing.
Leave it. Leave it. It's just an outcry.

You can't turn that into a poem.
(Will I have time to polish this?)
But when you tread on this clutch of nettles
that was once me, reading this in some other century
like an outdated story, remember that I was innocent
and that like you, mortals of your day, I too
had a face marked by anger, and by pity, and by joy.

A man's face, quite simply.

Translated from the French by John Balaban and Donka Farkas

Winter 2018

Part Six

Fiction

In Spain There Was Revolution

Tennessee Williams

From where he lay on the end of the dock, the river was like fluctuant diamond-paned glass of two colors, olive green and steel blue, leaded together by wavering white stitches of sun. The summer was dry. There had been a long succession of these flawless, brilliant days. It was now the middle of August, but already the trees along the opposite hills were turning color. Reds and oranges and yellows stood like a motionless and smokeless fire above the intense, burning green of the river willows. Things were drying up in the earth. But it was a death that wore bright colors. It looked like a flaming opulence of life. Only the desiccated patches of pale yellow corn glimpsed between folds of the Ozark hills seemed willing to admit without any bright evasion the solemn fact of things dying.

Steve heard the rasp of oarlocks and the faint plash of a leisurely moving boat. The black blades lifted and caught the white reflection of sky and dripped a thin sheet of silvery water on each side. The girl rowed perfectly. Her approach had an air of quiet inevitability unhurried as time itself. There was no swerving, no unnecessary motion. There was perfect timing and absolute poise. It was herself graceful and shining and entirely at ease and not the clumsy wooden boat that moved toward him.

He breathed in deeply and felt his body expand against the warm, moist boards he was lying on. He raised an arm in casual salute. She didn't return it, but the white gleam of her teeth became more distinct, and the oars rasped with a quicker rhythm. The boat curved in slightly toward the shore.

The girl was a counsellor at the Idle Wild Camp a mile up on the other side of the river from the resort where the boy was lifeguard. Every morning or afternoon she rowed or paddled down to see him. At night they met sometimes on the middle span of the new white concrete bridge, which was a lovely, unearthly place suspended between the dark water and the sky in both of which the stars were clearly visible. Being a long bridge, it was reasonably safe. When headlights curved out of the highway on either side of the river and wrinkled the dark with fiery prismatic radiations there was always time enough for the boy and girl to draw discreetly apart and meet the passing glare with blinking, unabashed eyes, and there were many long intervals between when the darkness was loud with cicadas and the flow of water and the silky, rippling soliloquies of owls. At about ten-thirty the double engined Red Ball freight thundered its forty or fifty car chain over the railroad bridge down the river. They waited until the red and green lamps at the end of the caboose winked finally out among the swallowing hills and then the girl raced breathlessly away to reach her camp before the bell rang for "lights out."

"How many lives have you saved this morning?" she called up to him.

"Nobody's been in yet. Wait a minute. I'll swim out."

He looked quickly around to see that the beach was still empty, then dove off the dock and reached the boat in a few easy strokes. He clung to the end of it and expelled a jet of water between his teeth. It trickled down her smooth brown legs.

"I've got the blues," she said. "I looked at the calendar this morning."

"You shouldn't look at calendars."

"I couldn't help it. It stared me right in the eye."

"What did it say?"

"Only two more weeks of this."

"Sorry?"

"Of course."

"So'm I."

"It's been so perfect here."

His eyes dropped from her face and traveled leisurely down the wet blue suit. His voice softened.

"It'll go on being that way."

"I don't know."

Her voice had lowered also, and he could feel her awareness of his eyes on her body.

"That suit's a humdinger! Silk, isn't it? I can even see your belly button!"

"Shut up! Don't be disgusting!" she laughed.

He looked up and smiled.

"*Sure* it will be just the same."

"What?" she asked, her voice still shaking and her eyes not able to meet his.

"At school. The way it is here."

"I don't know," she repeated gloomily. "School isn't like here." "I know it isn't," he admitted. "Here it's just perfect."

He pulled himself lightly from the river and into the boat. He stood over her, dripping water, and she frowned at him without conviction.

"I've got to get back."

"Not right now."

"I'm late. They'll ring the bell in about twenty minutes."

"What's the diff?"

"Both of us are holding jobs, you know."

"We don't care if we get fired."

"Yes, we do."

"That's right," he admitted mournfully. "I wouldn't see you for about three weeks."

She smiled and met his eyes. His face was beaded with water that gathered on the stubbles of his chin and looked as though he had grown a bubbly golden beard.

"You forgot to shave."

"I know. I was too lazy. I had a strenuous night."

"What doing?"

"Dreaming about you."

"Was that necessary?"

"It is sometimes."

She looked slowly across the brilliant water.

"That suit of yours takes the cake," he murmured. "You might as well be completely nude."

"You're terribly vulgar sometimes."

"But you like it."

"I certainly don't like scratchy chins."

"Yes, you do."

"How do you know?"

"I can just tell."

"Get out now, Steve. I've got to row back."

"Not right now. Let's go under the willows a moment."

"No, not this morning," she said almost sharply.

"Yes, right now."

He looked around once more, very quickly, then seized an oar and turned them in toward the bank. She leaned against his shoulder and closed her eyes, feeling the warmth of the sun and of his body. He looked down at her as he rowed. She had tanned very deeply and smoothly. There were no visible pores in the skin, and the fine hairs of the lower legs were bleached white. Rowing had pulled up the lower edges of her trunks and exposed half-moons of untanned flesh. He loved to see the white parts of her body between shoulder and thigh that were supposed to be kept unseen. Their more private quality seemed to be expressed in that contrasting whiteness.

As soon as the willow shade had closed over them he caught the shoulder strap nearest him and jerked it down. His hand cupped her breast. She looked up at him with eyes half frightened and lips falling apart. It was always that way. She let things go until they had gone too far to be stopped. Then she felt herself absolved of the responsibility.

"Steve, it will be your fault."

"I don't care."

"Just suppose."

"What?"

"Something happened sometime."

"I wouldn't care. Would you?"

The wet shoulder straps dangled coldly over her legs. With a long fretful sigh, like a person twisting in fever, she arched her body and pulled them slowly away.

"Would you care?" he repeated softly. His words arched over her like the rook of a tunnel. They shut out daylight and the sky and the incandescent willows. The tunnel bored down without effort into the darkness below them. The day was left a long way behind. The sun was glittering on the other side of the world. The boat and the lake and the humming dragonflies had slid away with one complete, lubricious gesture from under and around them, and in that cavernous darkness their bodies grew larger and larger till they had outgrown everything but each other.

"Would you care?"

"Not much if you didn't," she answered without hearing her own voice. He laughed softly. Their bodies stirred a little to make a closer embrace. All the while her eyes peered dreamily through the interstices of their green-gold-curtained alcove. He laughed at her whispered protestations which she herself did not listen to and felt her breath coming faster.

From up the river he heard very faintly the tolling of the camp bell. But it was she this time who was altogether lost to the world outside. Her eyes were closed, and he knew that she didn't hear. For a moment he selfishly planned not to warn her. Then he remembered what the loss of her job would mean. The sacrifice of two more weeks together . . .

He tightened his arm.

"Darling, it's ringing."

"I know," she smiled.

"I thought you didn't hear."

"I did. I just couldn't move."

Now she sat up and straightened her blue silk suit. The lovely white parts of her body disappeared.

"I never would have thought things like this could happen to me a few months ago."

"Neither would I."

"Hmm. I bet you're an old hand at seductions."

"I learned about women from you."

"I'm just the first lesson, am I?"

"First and last."

"Get out, you liar!"

He dove off the end of the boat, and she made a wide arc from the hidden bank.

Sun and water widened between them. He clambered up the ladder and resumed his place at the end of the Bide-A-Wee dock. A fat man with an inner tube was waddling down from the shore. It was the morning swimming hour. Resorters descended behind the fat man in little clusters. Family groups and weekend parties. He knew some of them. Some of them were strangers.

He sat up alertly on the folding chair, expanded his naked chest and adjusted his sun goggles.

The girl was nearly around the bend of the river. He could still see her body rhythmically bending to the oars and sunlight flashing on the wet blue suit. Out there in the glittering distance was the girl shadowed by willows. Then the curving bank intervened, and he could see only the rippling forked trajectory of the boat.

The man with the inner tube had waddled onto the end of the dock and was seated beside Steve, waiting to be given some notice. That was mostly what they came down for, men of his sort, to be looked at and listened to. At work they were stooges. White collar nonentities. But on their vacations, at their play, they wanted to be vital and specific personalities. They wanted to disentangle themselves from the soft, spongy webs that had grown around them, and the way they went about it was very silly. They overexercised frenziedly the first two or three days, exposing their moist white skins immoderately to the sun's indifferent burning, and then they slumped helplessly into exhaustion, smearing themselves with creams and lotions and complaining about the mineral taste of the water and the weak coffee and the uncomfortable beds. Steve looked at them with contemptuous pity, these men who lived narrow, slavish lives in cooped-up places, men caught in ruts, graves with both ends kicked out . . .

He avoided the fat man's searching squint, kept his eyes fixed stonily on the water. He wanted to think of the girl. Nothing else.

The man was not to be snubbed. He cleared his throat.

"What do you think of this trouble in Spain?"

The lifeguard shrugged his coffee-brown shoulders.

"Trouble in Spain? Didn't know there was any."

"My God, man, what's the matter with you? Don't you read the newspapers?"

Again Steve shrugged.

"Not lately. What's going on?"

"*Revolution*," said the man. "*Next it will be the whole world!*"

He gave Steve a disgusted glance and then climbed awkwardly down the ladder and plopped into the shallow water. He waded carefully out with the inner tube girdling his middle. Water rose to his armpits. Then he pushed himself gently forward and moved out with the sidewise paddling motions of a fat turtle.

Steve looked down at him and shook with noiseless laughter.

Spring 2003

War and Peace

Leo Tolstoy, Translated by Richard Pevear and Larissa Volokhonsky

Volume One, Part Three: The battle of Austerlitz

XIV

At five o'clock in the morning it was still quite dark. The troops of the center, the reserves, and Bagration's right flank still stood motionless, but on the left flank the columns of infantry, cavalry, and artillery which were to be the first to descend from the heights in order to attack the French right flank and drive them back to the Bohemian Mountains, according to the disposition, had already begun to stir and get up from their night camp. The smoke of the bonfires, onto which everything superfluous was thrown, stung the eyes. It was cold and dark. Officers hastily drank tea and ate breakfast, soldiers chewed on biscuits, beat their feet to warm them up, and streamed towards the bonfires, throwing onto them the remains of their lean-tos, chairs, tables, wheels, barrels, everything superfluous which it was impossible to take with them. Austrian column leaders shuttled among the Russian troops and served as heralds of the departure. As soon as an Austrian officer appeared at a regimental commander's camp, the regiment began to stir: soldiers ran from the bonfires, stuffed pipes into boot tops, bags into wagons, took their muskets and fell in. Officers buttoned their coats, buckled on their swords and pouches, and strode along the ranks, calling out; carters and orderlies harnessed, packed, and tied down the wagons. Adjutants, battalion and regimental commanders mounted up, crossed themselves, gave final orders, instructions, and commissions to those who were staying with the train, and the monotonous tramp of thousands of feet began. Columns started to move, not knowing where and, owing to the surrounding people, the smoke, and the thickening fog, seeing neither the place they were leaving nor the place they were going to.

A soldier in movement is as hemmed in, limited, and borne along by his regiment as a sailor by his ship. However far he may go, whatever strange, unknown, and dangerous latitudes he gets into, around him—as for the sailor always and everywhere there are the same decks, masts, and rigging of his ship—always and everywhere there are the same comrades, the same ranks, the same sergeant major Ivan Mitrich, the same company dog Zhuchka, the same superiors. A soldier rarely wishes to know what latitudes his whole ship has gotten to; but on the day of battle, God knows how and from where, a stern note is heard in the moral world of the troops, the same for everyone, which sounds the approach of something decisive and solemn and arouses in them an unaccustomed curiosity. On days of battle, soldiers excitedly try to get beyond the interests of their regiment, listen intently, look about, and greedily inquire into what is going on around them.

The fog was so thick that, though day was breaking, one could not see ten paces ahead. Bushes looked like enormous trees, level places like cliffs and slopes. Everywhere, on all sides, one might run into an enemy invisible ten paces away. But the columns marched for a long time through the same fog, going down and up hills, past gardens and fences, over new, incomprehensible terrain, without coming across the enemy anywhere. On the contrary, the soldiers realized that ahead, behind, on all sides, our Russian columns were moving in the same direction. Every soldier felt pleased at heart, knowing that many, many more Russian soldiers were going where he was going, that is, no one knew where.

"See there, the Kursky lads just marched by," came from one of the ranks.

"It's scary, brother, the troops we've gathered! Last night I looked, when they lit the fires, there was no end of them. Moscow—in short!"

Though none of the column leaders rode up to the ranks and spoke to the soldiers (the column leaders, as we saw at the council of war, were ill-humored and displeased with the action undertaken and therefore were only following orders and did not bother cheering up the soldiers), despite that, the soldiers marched on cheerily, as always when going into action, especially on the offensive. But, having gone for about an hour in the thick fog, the major part of the troops were forced to halt, and an unpleasant awareness of disorder and muddleheadedness passed through the ranks. How such awareness is conveyed is quite difficult to define; but it is unquestionable that it is conveyed with extraordinary sureness, and flows swiftly, imperceptibly and irresistibly, like water through a glen. If the Russian army had been alone, without allies, much time might still have passed before this awareness of disorder became a general conviction; but now, ascribing the cause of the disorder with particular pleasure and naturalness to the muddleheaded Germans, everyone became convinced that the harmful confusion taking place was the doing of the sausage-makers.

"What's the holdup? Is the way blocked? Or have we already run into the French?"

"No, doesn't sound like it. Otherwise they'd have started shooting."

"So they were in a hurry to get started, but once they got started—here we stand witless in the middle of a field—it's all these cursed Germans confusing things. What muddleheaded devils!"

"So I'd have let them take the lead. But no, they huddle in the rear. And now we stand here on empty stomachs."

"Well, how long will it be? They say the cavalry's blocked the road," said an officer.

"Eh, the cursed Germans, they don't know their own country!" said another.

"What division are you?" an adjutant shouted, riding up.

"The eighteenth."

"Then what are you doing here? You should have gone ahead long ago; now you won't get through till evening. Such stupid orders; they don't know what they're doing themselves," the officer said and rode off.

Then a general rode by and angrily shouted something not in Russian.

"Tafa-lafa, and there's no telling what he's mumbling," a soldier said, mimicking the general as he rode off. "I'd shoot the scoundrels!"

"We were ordered to be in place before nine, but we're not halfway there. What orders!" was repeated from different sides.

And the feeling of energy with which the troops had set out for action began to turn into vexation and anger at the muddleheaded orders and the Germans.

The reason for the confusion was that, while the Austrian cavalry was moving on the left flank, the superior officers decided that our center was too far from the right flank, and the entire cavalry was ordered to cross over to the right. Several thousand cavalry were advancing ahead of the infantry, and the infantry was forced to wait.

At the head, a confrontation took place between an Austrian column leader and a Russian general. The Russian general shouted, demanding that the cavalry be stopped; the Austrian insisted that the fault lay not with him but with the superior officers. The troops meanwhile stood there, bored and losing heart. After an hour's delay, the troops finally moved on and began to descend the hill. The fog, which was lifting on the hilltop, only grew thicker in the bottom where the troops were descending. At the head, in the fog, a shot rang out, then another, at first irregularly, at various intervals: trata . . . tat, then more regularly and rapidly, and the action at the Goldbach stream began.

Not counting on meeting the enemy below, by the stream, and coming upon them by chance in the fog, hearing not a word of encouragement from the superior officers, with the awareness spread among the troops that they were late and, above all, seeing nothing ahead or around them in the thick fog, the Russians lazily and slowly exchanged fire with the enemy, moved forward and again halted, not receiving timely orders from the officers and adjutants, who wandered through the fog over the unfamiliar terrain, unable to find their units. Thus the action began for the first, second, and third columns, which had descended the hill. The fourth column, with which Kutuzov himself was, occupied the Pratzen heights.

In the bottom, where the action began, the fog was still thick; up above it had cleared, but nothing of what was happening ahead could be seen. Whether all the enemy forces were six miles away from us, as we supposed, or were there in that fog, no one knew until past eight o'clock.

It was nine o'clock in the morning. An unbroken sea of fog spread below, but at the village of Schlapanitz, on the heights, where Napoleon stood, surrounded by his marshals, it was perfectly light. Over him was the clear blue sky, and the enormous ball of the sun, like an enormous, hollow, crimson float, bobbed on the surface of the milky sea of fog. The whole French army, including Napoleon himself and his staff, not only were not on the far side of the streams and bottomland of the villages of Sokolnitz and Schlapanitz, where we intended to take up a position and begin the action, but were on the near side, so close to our troops that Napoleon with his naked eye could distinguish between our troops on horseback and on foot. Napoleon sat a little in front of his marshals on a small gray Arabian horse, in his dark blue greatcoat, the same in which he had made the Italian campaign. He peered silently at the hills, which seemed to rise up from the sea of fog, and over which Russian troops were moving in the distance, and he listened to the sounds of gunfire in the hollow. On his face, still lean at that time, not a muscle stirred; his glistening eyes were fixed motionlessly on one place. His conjectures turned out to be correct. Part of the Russian army had already descended into the hollow towards the ponds and lakes, part was still clearing off from the Pratzen heights, which he intended to attack and considered the key to the position. He saw amidst the fog, in the depression between two hills near the village of Pratz, Russian columns, their bayonets glittering, moving all in one direction towards the hollows, and disappearing one after another into the sea of fog. From the information he had received in the evening, from the sounds of wheels and footsteps heard during the night at the outposts, from the disorderly movement of the Russian columns, from all his conjectures, he saw clearly that the allies considered him to be far ahead of them, that the columns moving near Pratz constituted the center of the Russian army, and that the center was already sufficiently weakened for him to attack it successfully. But he still did not begin the action.

That day was a solemn day for him—the anniversary of his coronation. Before morning he had dozed off for a few hours and, healthy, cheerful, fresh, in that happy state of mind in which everything seems possible and everything succeeds, he mounted his horse and rode out into the field. He stood motionless, gazing at the heights appearing from the fog, and on his cold face there was that particular tinge of self-confident, well-deserved happiness that can be seen on the face of a boy who has happily fallen in love. His marshals stood behind him, not daring to distract his attention. He looked now at the Pratzen heights, now at the sun floating out of the fog.

When the sun had fully emerged from the fog and its dazzling brilliance sprayed over the fields and the fog (it was as if he had only been waiting for that to begin the action), he took the glove from his beautiful white hand, made a sign to the marshals, and gave the order for the action to begin. The marshals, accompanied by adjutants, galloped off in various directions, and a few minutes later the main forces of the French army were moving swiftly towards those same Pratzen heights from which the Russian troops had cleared off more and more, descending to the left into the hollow.

XV

At eight o'clock Kutuzov rode to Pratz at the head of Miloradovich's fourth column, the one which was to take the place of the columns of Przebyszewski and Langeron, which had already gone down. He greeted the men of the head regiment and gave the order to move, thus showing that he intended to lead the column himself. Having ridden to the village of Pratz, he halted. Prince Andrei, one of the enormous number of persons constituting the commander-in-chief's suite, stood behind him. Prince Andrei felt excited, irritated, and at the same time restrainedly calm, as a man usually is when a long-desired moment comes. He was firmly convinced that this was the day of his Toulon or his bridge of Arcole. How it would happen, he did not know, but he was firmly convinced that it would be so. The locality and position of our troops were known to him, as far as they could be known to anyone in our army. His own strategic plan, which there obviously could be no thought of carrying out now, was forgotten. Now, entering into Weyrother's plan, Prince Andrei pondered the possible happenstances and came up with new considerations, such as might call for his swiftness of reflection and decisiveness.

To the left below, in the fog, exchanges of fire between unseen troops could be heard. There, it seemed to Prince Andrei, the battle would concentrate, there an obstacle would be encountered, and "it's there that I'll be sent with a brigade or division, and there, with a standard in my hand, I'll go forward and crush everything ahead of me."

Prince Andrei could not look with indifference at the standards of the battalions going past him. Looking at a standard, he thought: maybe it is that very standard with which I'll have to march at the head of the troops.

By morning the night's fog had left only hoarfrost turning into dew on the heights, but in the hollows the fog still spread its milk-white sea. Nothing could be seen in that hollow to the left, into which our troops had descended and from which came the sounds of gunfire. Over the heights was a dark, clear sky, and to the right—the enormous ball of the sun. Far ahead, on the other shore of the sea of fog, one could make out the jutting, wooded hills on which the enemy army was supposed to be, and something was discernible. To the right the guards were entering the region of the fog, with a sound of tramping and wheels and an occasional gleam of bayonets; to the left, beyond the village, similar masses of cavalry approached and disappeared into the sea of fog. In front and behind moved the infantry. The commander-in-chief stood on the road out of the village, letting the troops pass by him. Kutuzov seemed exhausted and irritable that morning. The infantry going past him halted without any command, apparently because something ahead held them up.

"But tell them, finally, to form into battalions and go around the village," Kutuzov said angrily to a general who rode up. "Don't you understand, Your Excellency, my dear sir, that to stretch out in a defile through village streets is impossible when we're marching against an enemy?"

"I intended to form them up outside the village, Your Excellency," said the general.

Kutuzov laughed biliously.

"A fine sight you'd be, lining up in view of the enemy, a very fine sight!"

"The enemy's still far off, Your Excellency. According to the disposition . . ."

"The disposition!" Kutuzov exclaimed biliously. "Who told you that? . . . Kindly do as you're ordered."

"Yes, sir!"

"*Mon cher,*" Nesvitsky said to Prince Andrei in a whisper, "*le vieux est d'une humeur de chien.*"[1]

An Austrian officer in a white uniform with green plumes on his hat rode up to Kutuzov and asked on behalf of the emperor whether the fourth column had started into action.

Kutuzov turned away without answering him, and his gaze chanced to rest on Prince Andrei, who was standing close by. Seeing Bolkonsky, Kutuzov softened the angry and caustic expression of his gaze, as if aware that his adjutant was not to blame for what was going on. And, without answering the Austrian adjutant, he addressed Bolkonsky:

"*Allez voir, mon cher, si la troisième division a dépassé le village. Diteslui de s'arrêter et d'attendre mes ordres.*"[2]

1. My dear . . . the old man's in a foul humor.

2. Go and see, my dear, if the third division has passed the village. Tell him to stop and wait for my orders.

Prince Andrei had only just started when he stopped him.

"*Et demandez-lui si les tirailleurs sont postés,*" he added. "*Ce qu'ils font, ce qu'ils font!*"[3] he said to himself, still not answering the Austrian.

Prince Andrei galloped off to carry out his mission.

Overtaking all the advancing battalions, he stopped the third division and ascertained that there was in fact no line of riflemen in front of our columns. The regimental commander of the front regiment was very surprised by the order conveyed to him from the commander-in-chief to send out riflemen. The regimental commander stood there in the full conviction that there were more troops ahead of him, and that the enemy was no less than six miles away. In fact, nothing could be seen ahead but empty terrain sloping away and covered with thick fog. Having ordered on behalf of the commander-in-chief that the omission be rectified, Prince Andrei galloped back. Kutuzov still stood in the same place and, his corpulent body sagging over the saddle in old man's fashion, yawned deeply, closing his eyes. The troops were no longer moving, but stood at parade rest.

"Very good, very good," he said to Prince Andrei and turned to a general who stood there with a watch in his hand, saying it was time to move on, because all the columns of the left flank had already descended.

"We still have time, Your Excellency," Kutuzov said through a yawn. "We have time!" he repeated.

Just then, from well behind Kutuzov, came shouts of regimental greetings, and these voices began to approach quickly along the whole extended line of the advancing Russian columns. It was clear that the one being greeted was riding quickly. When the soldiers of the regiment Kutuzov was standing in front of began to shout, he rode slightly to one side and, wincing, turned to look. Down the road from Pratz galloped what looked like a squadron of varicolored horsemen. Two of them rode side by side at a great gallop ahead of the rest.

3. And ask him if the riflemen are posted. . . . What they're doing, what they're doing!

One, in a black uniform with white plumes, rode a bobtailed chestnut horse, the other, in a white uniform, rode a black horse. These were the two emperors with their suite. Kutuzov, with the affectation of a frontline veteran, ordered his standing troops to "attention" and, saluting, rode up to the emperor. His whole figure and manner suddenly changed. He acquired the look of a subordinate, unthinking man. With affected deference, which obviously struck the emperor Alexander unpleasantly, he rode up and saluted him.

The unpleasant impression, like the remains of fog in a clear sky, passed over the emperor's young and happy face and disappeared. He was somewhat thinner that day, after his illness, than on the field of Olmütz, where Bolkonsky had seen him for the first time abroad, but there was the same enchanting combination of majesty and mildness in his beautiful gray eyes, and the fine lips had the same possibility of various expressions, with a prevalent expression of good-natured, innocent youth.

At the Olmütz review he was more majestic, here he was more cheerful and energetic. He was slightly flushed after galloping two miles and, reining in his horse, gave a sigh of relief and looked around at the faces of his suite, as young, as animated as his own. Czartoryski and Novosiltsev, and Prince Volkonsky and Stroganov, and the others, all richly clad, cheerful young men on splendid, pampered, fresh, only slightly sweaty horses, talking and smiling, stopped behind the sovereign. The emperor Franz, a ruddy, long-faced young man, sat extremely straight on his handsome black stallion and looked around him with a preoccupied, unhurried air. He called up one of his white adjutants and asked something. "Most likely what time they started," thought Prince Andrei, observing his old acquaintance, and recalling his audience with a smile he was unable to repress. In the emperors' suite there were picked, fine young orderly officers, Russian and Austrian, from the guards and infantry regiments. Among them were grooms leading the handsome spare horses of the royalty in embroidered cloths.

As fresh air from the fields suddenly breathes through an open window into a stuffy room, so youth, energy, and certainty of success breathed upon Kutuzov's cheerless staff as these brilliant young men galloped up.

"Why don't you begin, Mikhail Larionovich?" the emperor Alexander hurriedly addressed Kutuzov, at the same time glancing courteously at the emperor Franz.

"I am waiting, Your Majesty," answered Kutuzov, inclining deferentially.

The emperor cupped his ear, frowning slightly and showing that he had not heard properly.

"I'm waiting, Your Majesty," Kutuzov repeated (Prince Andrei noticed that Kutuzov's upper lip twitched unnaturally as he said this "waiting"). "Not all the columns are assembled, Your Majesty."

The sovereign heard, but this reply clearly did not please him; he shrugged his slightly stooping shoulders, glanced at Novosiltsev, who stood nearby, as if complaining of Kutuzov by this glance.

"We're not on the Tsaritsyn Field, Mikhail Larionovich, where you don't start a parade until all the regiments are assembled," said the sovereign, again glancing into the eyes of the emperor Franz, as though inviting him, if not to take part, at least to listen to what he was saying; but the emperor Franz went on looking around and did not listen.

"That is just why I do not begin, Sire," Kutuzov said in a ringing voice, as if to forestall the possibility of not being heard, and again something twitched in his face. "I do not begin, Sire, because we are not on parade and not on the Tsaritsyn Field," he uttered clearly and distinctly.

All the faces in the sovereign's suite instantly exchanged glances with each other, expressing murmur and reproach. "Old as he may be, he should not, he simply should not speak that way," these faces expressed.

The sovereign looked fixedly and attentively into Kutuzov's eyes, waiting to see if he would say something more. But Kutuzov, for his part, bowed his head deferentially and also seemed to be waiting. The silence lasted for about a minute.

"However, if you order it, Your Majesty," said Kutuzov, raising his head and again changing his tone to that of a dull, unthinking, but obedient general.

He touched up his horse and, calling to him the column leader Miloradovich, gave him the order to advance.

The troops stirred again, and two battalions of the Novgorodsky regiment and a battalion of the Apsheronsky regiment moved on past the sovereign.

While this Apsheronsky battalion was marching by, ruddy-faced Miloradovich, with no greatcoat, in his uniform tunic and decorations and a hat with enormous plumes, worn at an angle and brim first, galloped ahead hup-two, and with a dashing salute, reined in his horse before the sovereign.

"God be with you, General," said the sovereign.

"*Ma foi, sire, nous ferons ce que qui sera dans notre possibilité, sire!*"[4] he replied merrily, nevertheless calling up mocking smiles among the gentlemen of the suite with his bad French.

Miloradovich turned his horse sharply and placed himself slightly behind the sovereign. The Apsherontsy, excited by the presence of the sovereign, marched past the emperors and their suite at a dashingly brisk pace, beating their feet.

"Lads!" cried Miloradovich in a loud, self-assured, and merry voice, obviously so excited by the sounds of gunfire, the anticipation of battle, and the sight of his gallant Apsherontsy—his companions from Suvorov's time—marching briskly past the emperors, that he forgot the sovereign's presence. "Lads, it won't be the first village you've taken!" he shouted.

"We do our best, sir!" the soldiers shouted out.

The sovereign's horse shied at the sudden shout. This horse, who had carried the sovereign at reviews while still in Russia, also carried his rider here, on the field of Austerlitz, enduring the distracted

4. By my faith, Sire, we will do that what which will be within our possibility, Sire!

nudges of his left foot, pricked up his ears at the sound of gunshots just as he did on the Field of Mars, understanding neither the meaning of the shots he heard, nor the presence of the emperor Franz's black stallion, nor anything of what his rider said, thought, or felt that day.

The sovereign turned with a smile to one of his retinue, pointing to the gallant Apsherontsy, and said something to him.

XVI

Kutuzov, accompanied by his adjutants, rode at a walk behind the carabineers.

Having gone less than half a mile at the tail of the column, he stopped by a solitary, deserted house (probably a former tavern), where the road forked. Both roads went down the hill, and troops were marching along both.

The fog began to lift, and enemy troops could be dimly seen about a mile and a half away on the heights opposite. To the left below, the gunfire was growing louder. Kutuzov stopped, talking with an Austrian general. Prince Andrei, standing slightly behind him, peered at the enemy and turned to an adjutant, wishing to borrow a field glass from him.

"Look, look," said this adjutant, looking not at the distant troops, but down the hill in front of him. "It's the French!"

The two generals and the adjutants began snatching at the field glass, pulling it away from each other. All their faces suddenly changed, and on all of them horror appeared. The French were supposed to be a mile and a half from us, and they suddenly turned up right in front of us.

"Is it the enemy? . . . No! . . . Yes, look, he's . . . for certain . . . What is this?" voices said.

With his naked eye, Prince Andrei saw below, to the right, a dense column of French coming up to meet the Apsherontsy, no further than five hundred paces from where Kutuzov was standing.

"Here it is, the decisive moment has come! Now it's my turn," thought Prince Andrei, and, spurring his horse, he rode up to Kutuzov.

"The Apsherontsy must be stopped, Your Excellency!" he cried.

But at that same moment everything became covered with smoke, there was the sound of gunfire nearby, and a naïvely frightened voice two steps from Prince Andrei cried: "Well, brothers, that's it for us!" And it was as if this voice was a command. At this voice everyone began to run.

Confused, ever increasing crowds came running back to the place where, five minutes before, the troops had marched past the emperors. Not only was it difficult to stop this crowd, but it was impossible not to yield and move back with it. Bolkonsky tried only not to be separated from Kutuzov and looked around in perplexity, unable to understand what was happening in front of him. Nesvitsky, looking angry, red, and not like himself, shouted to Kutuzov that if he did not leave at once, he would certainly be taken prisoner. Kutuzov stood in the same place and, without responding, took out his handkerchief. Blood was flowing from his cheek. Prince Andrei forced his way to him.

"Are you wounded?" he asked, barely able to control the trembling of his lower jaw.

"The wound isn't here, it's there!" said Kutuzov, pressing the handkerchief to his wounded cheek and pointing to the fleeing men.

"Stop them!" he cried, and at the same time, probably realizing that it was impossible to stop them, spurred his horse and rode to the right.

A fresh crowd of fleeing men streamed past, caught him up, and carried him backwards.

The troops were fleeing in such a dense crowd that, once one landed in the middle of it, it was difficult to get out. Someone shouted, "Keep going, don't drag your feet!" Another, turning around, fired into the air; someone else struck the horse on which Kutuzov himself was riding. Extricating themselves with the greatest effort from the flow of the crowd to the left, Kutuzov and his suite, diminished by more than half, rode towards the sounds of nearby cannon fire. Extricating himself from the crowd of fleeing men, Prince Andrei, trying to keep up with Kutuzov, saw on the slope of the hill, amidst the smoke, a Russian battery still firing, and the French running up to it. Slightly higher stood Russian infantry, neither moving ahead to aid the battery, nor backwards in the direction of the fugitives. A general on horseback separated himself from the infantry and rode up to Kutuzov. There were only four men left in Kutuzov's suite. They were all pale and exchanged glances silently.

"Stop those villains!" Kutuzov said breathlessly to the regimental commander, pointing to the fleeing men; but at the same moment, as if in punishment for those words, bullets, like a flock of birds, flew whistling at the regiment and Kutuzov's suite.

The French had attacked the battery and, seeing Kutuzov, were shooting at him. With this volley, the regimental commander seized his leg; several soldiers fell, and an ensign holding a standard let it drop from his hands; the standard wavered and fell, stopped momentarily by the bayonets of the soldiers around it. The soldiers began firing without any orders.

"Oooh!" Kutuzov moaned with an expression of despair and looked around. "Bolkonsky," he whispered in a voice trembling with awareness of his old man's strengthlessness. "Bolkonsky," he whispered, pointing to the disordered battalion and the enemy, "what's going on?"

But before he finished saying it, Prince Andrei, feeling sobs of shame and anger rising in his throat, was already jumping off his horse and running towards the standard.

"Forward, lads!" he cried in a childishly shrill voice.

"Here it is!" thought Prince Andrei, seizing the staff of the standard and hearing with delight the whistle of bullets, evidently aimed precisely at him. Several soldiers fell.

"Hurrah!" cried Prince Andrei, barely able to hold up the heavy standard, and he ran forward with unquestioning assurance that the entire battalion would run after him.

And indeed he ran only a few steps alone. One soldier started out, another, and the whole battalion, with a shout of "Hurrah!" rushed forward and overtook him. A sergeant of the battalion ran up, took the standard that was wavering in Prince Andrei's hands because of its weight, but was killed at once. Prince Andrei again seized the standard and, dragging it by the staff, ran with the battalion. Ahead of him he saw our artillerists, some of whom were fighting, while others abandoned the cannon and came running in his direction; he also saw French infantrymen, who had seized the artillery horses and were turning the cannon. Prince Andrei and his battalion were now twenty paces from the cannon. Above him he heard the unceasing whistle of bullets, and soldiers ceaselessly gasped and fell to right and left of him. But he did not look at them; he looked fixedly only at what was happening ahead of him—at the battery. He clearly saw the figure of a red-haired gunner, his shako knocked askew, pulling a swab from one side, while a French soldier pulled it towards him from the other side. Prince Andrei saw clearly the bewildered and at the same time angry expression on the faces of the two men, who evidently did not understand what they were doing.

"What are they doing?" Prince Andrei wondered, looking at them. "Why doesn't the red-haired artillerist run away, since he has no weapon? Why doesn't the Frenchman stab him? Before he runs away, the Frenchman will remember his musket and bayonet him."

In fact, another Frenchman with his musket atilt ran up to the fighting men, and the lot of the red-haired artillerist, who still did not understand what awaited him and triumphantly pulled the swab from the French soldier's hands, was about to be decided. But Prince Andrei did not see how it ended. It seemed to him as though one of the nearest soldiers, with the full swing of a stout stick, hit him on the head. It was slightly painful and above all unpleasant, because the pain distracted him and kept him from seeing what he had been looking at.

"What is it? am I falling? are my legs giving way under me?" he thought and fell on his back. He opened his eyes, hoping to see how the fight between the French and the artillerists ended, and wishing to know whether or not the red-haired artillerist had been killed, whether the cannon had been taken or saved. But he did not see anything. There was nothing over him now except the sky—the lofty sky, not clear, but still immeasurably lofty, with gray clouds slowly creeping across it. "How quiet, calm, and solemn, not at all like when I was running," thought Prince Andrei, "not like when we were running, shouting, and fighting; not at all like when the Frenchman and the artillerist, with angry and frightened faces, were pulling at the swab—it's quite different the way the clouds creep across this lofty, infinite sky. How is it I haven't seen this lofty sky before? And how happy I am that I've finally come to know it. Yes! everything is empty, everything is a deception, except this infinite sky. There is nothing, nothing except that. But there is not even that, there is nothing except silence, tranquility. And thank God! . . ."

XVII

At nine o'clock, the action had not yet begun for Bagration on the right flank. Not wishing to agree to Dolgorukov's request to begin action, and wishing to avert responsibility from himself, Prince Bagration suggested to Dolgorukov that he send to ask the commander-in-chief. Bagration knew that, with a stretch of nearly six miles separating one flank from the other, if the messenger was not killed (which was very probable), and even if he found the commander-in-chief, which would be quite difficult, he would not come back before evening.

Bagration looked over his suite with his big, expressionless, sleepy eyes, and Rostov's childlike face, involuntarily transfixed with excitement and hope, was the first thing that struck his eye. He sent him.

"And if I should meet His Majesty before the commander-in-chief, Your Excellency?" asked Rostov, holding his hand to his visor.

"You can give the message to His Majesty," said Dolgorukov, hastily cutting off Bagration.

After being relieved from the picket line, Rostov had managed to sleep for a few hours before morning, and he felt cheerful, bold, resolute, with that suppleness of movement, assurance of his good luck, and in that state of mind in which everything seems easy, cheerful, and possible.

All his wishes were being fulfilled that morning: general battle was to be given, he was to take part in it; moreover, he was an orderly officer of the bravest of generals; moreover, he was going with a message to Kutuzov and maybe to the sovereign himself. The morning was bright, the horse under him was good. He felt joyful and happy. On receiving the order, he started his horse and rode along the line. First he rode along the line of Bagration's troops, who had not yet gone into action and stood motionless; then he rode into the space occupied by Uvarov's cavalry, and here he noticed movement and signs of preparation for action; having passed Uvarov's cavalry, he clearly heard the sounds of cannon and gunfire ahead of him. The fire kept intensifying.

In the fresh morning air, the shooting was no longer as before—at irregular intervals, two or three gunshots, then one or two cannon shots—now on the slopes of the hills before Pratz one could hear rolling salvos of musket fire, interrupted by such rapid cannon fire that at times the separate shots could not be distinguished from each other, but merged into a general roar.

One could see the puffs of gun smoke as if running and chasing each other on the slopes, and the smoke of the cannon swirling, spreading, and merging together. One could see, from the gleam of bayonets amidst the smoke, the moving masses of infantry and the narrow strips of artillery with green caissons.

Rostov stopped his horse for a minute on a knoll, so as to see what was going on; but no matter how he strained his attention, he could neither understand nor make out what was going on: some sort of men were moving about in the smoke; some sort of sheets of troops were moving in front and behind; but why? who? where?—it was impossible to grasp. The sights and sounds not only did not arouse any sort of dejected or timid feelings in him, but, on the contrary, gave him energy and determination.

"More, more, step it up!" he addressed these sounds mentally and again started riding along the line, penetrating further and further into the area of the troops already going into action.

"How it's going to be, I don't know, but all will be well!" thought Rostov.

Having ridden past some Austrian troops, Rostov noticed that the next part of the line (this was the guards) had already gone into action.

"So much the better! I'll see it close up," he thought.

He was riding almost along the front line. Several horsemen came riding in his direction. They were our life uhlans, who were returning from an attack in disorderly ranks. Rostov passed by them, involuntarily noticing that one of them was covered with blood, and rode on.

"It's none of my business!" he thought. He had not managed to go a few hundred paces after that, when to the left of him, cutting across, there appeared along the whole width of the field an enormous mass of cavalrymen on black horses, in white gleaming uniforms, coming straight at him at a canter. Rostov sent his horse into a full gallop to get out of the way of these cavalrymen, and he would have gotten away from them if they had continued at the same speed, but they kept increasing their pace, so that some of the horses were already galloping. Rostov heard their hoofbeats and the clanging of their weapons growing louder and louder, and saw their horses, their figures, and even their faces more and more clearly. These were our horse guards going into attack against the French cavalry, which was coming towards them.

The horse guards galloped, but still holding back their horses. Rostov could now see their faces and heard the command: "Forward, forward!" uttered by an officer, letting his thoroughbred go at full speed. Rostov, afraid of being trampled or swept into the attack on the French, galloped along the front as hard as his horse could go, and still did not manage to avoid them.

The last horse guard, a pockmarked man of enormous height, frowned angrily, seeing Rostov in front of him, where he would inevitably run into him. This horse guard would certainly have knocked Rostov and his Bedouin down (Rostov felt himself so small and weak compared to these enormous men and horses), if it had not occurred to him to swing his whip at the eyes of the guardsman's horse. The heavy, black, twenty-hand horse shied, laying back his ears; but the pockmarked horse guard spurred him as hard as he could with his huge spurs, and the horse, tossing his tail and stretching his neck, raced on still faster. The horse guards had barely gone past Rostov, when he heard their shout of "Hurrah!" and, turning, saw their front ranks mingling with other, probably French, horsemen with red epaulettes. Beyond that nothing could be seen, because just after that cannon began firing from somewhere, and everything was covered in smoke.

At the moment when the horse guards, going past him, disappeared into the smoke, Rostov hesitated whether to gallop after them or ride where he was supposed to. This was that brilliant attack of the horse guards which astonished the French themselves. Rostov was horrified to hear later that, of all that mass of enormous, handsome men, of all those brilliant, rich men, youths, officers, and Junkers, who had ridden past him on thousand-rouble horses, only eighteen were left after the attack.

"Why should I envy them, mine won't go away, and now maybe I'll see the sovereign!" thought Rostov, and he rode on.

Having drawn even with the infantry guards, he noticed that cannonballs were flying over and around them, not so much because he heard the sound of the cannon, but because he saw uneasiness on the soldiers' faces, and on the officers' an unnatural military solemnity.

Riding behind one of the lines of the infantry guard regiments, he heard a voice call him by name.

"Rostov!"

"What?" he replied, not recognizing Boris.

"Imagine, we got into the front line! Our regiment went into an attack!" said Boris, smiling that happy smile which occurs in young men who have been under fire for the first time.

Rostov stopped.

"Really!" he said. "And what then?"

"We beat them back," Boris said animatedly, becoming talkative. "Can you imagine?"

And Boris began telling how the guards, taking up their position and seeing troops in front of them, took them for Austrians, and suddenly, from the cannonballs fired from those troops, realized that they were in the front line and had unexpectedly to go into action. Rostov, not hearing Boris out, touched up his horse.

"Where are you going?" asked Boris.

"To his majesty with a message."

"There he is!" said Boris, who thought he heard Rostov say "his highness" instead of "his majesty."

And he pointed him to the grand duke, who, a hundred paces from them, in a helmet and a horse guard's tunic, with his raised shoulders and frowning brows, was shouting something to a white and pale-faced Austrian officer.

"But that's the grand duke, and I need the commander-in-chief or the sovereign," said Rostov, and he touched up his horse.

"Count, Count!" cried Berg, as animated as Boris, running up to him from the other side. "Count, I'm wounded in the right hand," he said, showing his hand, bloody and bandaged with a handkerchief, "and I stayed in the line. I hold the sword in my left hand, Count: our race, the von Bergs, Count, were all knights."

Berg was still saying something, but Rostov did not listen any further and rode on.

Having gone past the guards and an empty space, Rostov, to avoid getting into the front line again, as he had during the attack of the horse guards, followed the line of the reserves, making a wide circle around the place where the hottest shooting and cannon fire were heard. Suddenly, ahead of him and behind our troops, in a place where he could never have supposed the enemy to be, he heard nearby musket fire.

"What can that be?" thought Rostov. "The enemy in the rear of our troops? It can't be," thought Rostov, and the terror of fear for himself and for the outcome of the whole battle suddenly came over him. "Whatever it may be, however," he thought, "there's no point now in going around. I must look for the commander-in-chief here, and if all is lost, then it's my business to perish along with everybody."

The bad presentiment that suddenly came over Rostov was confirmed more and more the further he rode into the space beyond the village of Pratz, occupied by crowds of different troops.

"What is this? What is this? Who's being shot at? Who's shooting?" asked Rostov, drawing even with Russian and Austrian soldiers running in mixed crowds across his path.

"Devil knows about them! He's beaten everybody! Perish them all!" answers came in Russian, German, and Czech from the crowds of fleeing men who, like himself, did not understand what was going on there.

"Shoot the Germans!" cried one.

"Devil take them—the traitors!"

"*Zum Henker diese Russen!* . . ."[5] a German grumbled.

Several wounded soldiers were walking down the road. Oaths, shouts, groans merged into one general clamor. The shooting died down, and, as Rostov learned later, it had been Russian and Austrian soldiers shooting at each other.

"My God! What is it?" thought Rostov. "Here, where the sovereign may see them at any moment! . . . But no, it must be just a few scoundrels. It will pass, that's not it, it can't be," he thought. "Just ride past them quickly, quickly!"

The thought of defeat and flight could not enter Rostov's head. Though he saw French guns and troops precisely on the Pratzen heights, in the very place where he had been told to look for the commander-in-chief, he could not and would not believe it.

XVIII

Rostov had been told to look for Kutuzov and the sovereign near the village of Pratz. But not only were they not there, but there was not a single superior officer, there were only various crowds of disorderly troops. He urged on his already tired horse so as to get quickly past these crowds, but the further he went, the more disorderly the crowds became. The high road he came out on was crowded with carriages, vehicles of all kinds, Russian and Austrian soldiers of all

5. To the devil with these Russians! . . .

arms, wounded and not wounded. All this droned and swarmed confusedly, under the grim sound of cannonballs flying from the French batteries set up on the Pratzen heights.

"Where is the sovereign? Where is Kutuzov?" Rostov asked everyone he could stop, and he got no answer from any of them.

At last, seizing a soldier by the collar, he made him answer.

"Eh, brother! They all ran off ahead there long ago!" the soldier said to Rostov, laughing at something and trying to free himself.

Abandoning that soldier, who was obviously drunk, Rostov stopped the horse of an orderly or groom of some important person and began questioning him. The orderly announced to Rostov that the sovereign had been driven away at top speed in a carriage an hour earlier and that he was dangerously wounded.

"It can't be," said Rostov, "it must have been somebody else."

"I saw him myself," said the orderly with a self-assured grin. "I ought to know the sovereign by now: seems I saw him lots of times in Petersburg this close. He was sitting in the carriage pale as can be. Four black horses, saints alive, how they went rattling past us: seems I ought to know the tsar's horses and Ilya Ivanych by now; seems Ilya the coachman drives nobody but the tsar."

Rostov let go of his horse and wanted to ride on. Passing by, a wounded officer addressed him.

"Whom do you want?" asked the officer. "The commander-in-chief? He was killed by a cannonball, hit in the chest in front of our regiment."

"Not killed, wounded," another officer corrected.

"Who? Kutuzov?" asked Rostov.

"Not Kutuzov, but what's his name—well, it makes no difference, there weren't many left alive. Go over there, to that village, all the superiors are assembled there," said this officer, pointing to the village of Hostieradek, and he passed by.

Rostov rode at a walk, not knowing why and to whom he was going now. The sovereign was wounded, the battle lost. It was impossible not to believe it now. Rostov rode in the direction indicated to him and in which he could see a tower and a church in the distance.

Why should he hurry? What was he to say now to the sovereign or to Kutuzov, even if they were alive and not wounded?

"Go that way, Your Honor, here you'll get killed straight off," a soldier cried to him. "Killed straight off!"

"Ah! What are you saying!" said another. "Where are you sending him? This way's closer."

Rostov pondered and went precisely in the direction in which he was told he would be killed.

"It makes no difference now! If even the sovereign is wounded, why should I look out for myself?" he thought. He rode into that space in which the most men fleeing from Pratz had been killed. The French had not yet taken this space, but the Russians—those who were alive or wounded—had abandoned it long ago. Over the field, like sheaves on good wheatland, lay dead or wounded men, ten to fifteen to an acre. The wounded crept together by twos and threes, and one could hear their unpleasant cries and moans, sometimes feigned, as it seemed to Rostov. He sent his horse into a canter, so as not to see all these suffering men, and he felt frightened. He was afraid, not for his life, but for the courage he needed and which, he knew, could not bear the sight of these wretches.

The French, who had stopped firing on this field strewn with dead and wounded because there was nothing left alive on it, seeing an adjutant riding across it, aimed a cannon and fired several shots. The sensation of these whistling, fearsome sounds and the surrounding dead merged for Rostov into a single impression of terror and pity for himself. He recalled his mother's last letter. "What would she feel," he wondered, "if she saw me here now, on this field, with cannon aimed at me?"

In the village of Hostieradek, he found Russian troops, confused, but heading away from the battlefield in greater order. The French cannon fire did not carry that far, and the sounds of shooting seemed a long way off. Here everyone already clearly saw and said that the battle was lost. No matter whom Rostov turned to, no one could tell him where the sovereign was, or where Kutuzov was. Some said that the rumor of the sovereign's wound was correct, others said it was not and explained the spread of this false rumor by the fact that the grand marshal of the court, Count Tolstoy, who had ridden to the battlefield with others in the emperor's suite, had indeed galloped away from the battlefield, pale and frightened, in the sovereign's carriage. One officer told Rostov that he had seen someone from the high command to the left beyond the village, and Rostov went there, no longer hoping to find anyone, but only to keep his own conscience clear. Having ridden two miles and left behind the last of the Russian troops, Rostov saw two horsemen standing near a kitchen garden surrounded by a ditch. They were facing this ditch. One, with white plumes on his hat, seemed familiar to Rostov for some reason; the other, an unfamiliar horseman on a beautiful chestnut horse (the horse seemed familiar to Rostov), rode up to the ditch, spurred his horse and, releasing the reins, lightly jumped over the garden ditch. Only a little soil crumbled down the bank from the horse's hind hoofs. Turning his horse sharply, he leaped back over the ditch and courteously addressed the horseman with the white plumage, evidently suggesting that he do the same. The horseman whose figure seemed familiar to Rostov and for some reason involuntarily riveted his attention, made a negative gesture with his head and hand, and by this gesture Rostov instantly recognized his lamented, adored sovereign.

"But that can't be him, alone in the middle of this empty field," thought Rostov. Just then Alexander turned his head, and Rostov saw the beloved features so vividly imprinted on his memory. The sovereign was pale, his cheeks were hollow, his eyes sunken; but there was all the more loveliness and mildness in his features. Rostov was happy now to be assured that the rumor of the sovereign's wound was incorrect. He was happy to see him. He knew that he could, even must, address him directly and convey to him what Dolgorukov had ordered him to convey.

But as a young man in love trembles and thrills, not daring to utter what he dreams of by night, and looks about fearfully, seeking help or the possibility of delay and flight, when the desired moment comes, and he stands alone with her, so now Rostov, having attained what he desired more than anything in the world, did not know how to approach the sovereign and presented thousands of considerations to himself for why it was unsuitable, improper, and impossible.

"What! It's as if I was glad to take advantage of his being alone and dejected. It may be unpleasant and difficult for him to meet an unknown person at this moment of sorrow, and then, what can I say to him now, when at the mere sight of him my heart stops and my mouth goes dry?" Not one of the countless speeches to the sovereign that he had composed in his imagination came to his head now. Those speeches were for the most part held under quite different conditions, they were spoken for the most part in moments of victory and triumph, and predominantly on his deathbed from the wounds he had received, while the sovereign thanked him for his heroic deeds, and he, dying, voiced the love confirmed by his acts.

"And then, what am I to ask the sovereign about his orders for the right flank, when it is now past three in the afternoon and the battle is lost? No, decidedly, I should not approach him, should not disturb his thoughts. Better to die a thousand times than to get a bad look or a bad opinion from him," Rostov decided and rode away with sorrow and despair in his heart, constantly turning to look at the sovereign, still standing in the same attitude of indecision.

While Rostov was making these considerations and sorrowfully riding away from the sovereign, Captain von Toll happened to arrive in the same place and, seeing the sovereign, rode straight up to him, offered him his services, and helped him to cross the ditch on foot. The sovereign, wishing to rest and feeling unwell, sat down under an apple tree, and Toll stopped beside him. Rostov, from a distance, with envy and regret, saw von Toll say something to the sovereign at length and with ardor, and saw the sovereign, probably weeping, cover his eyes with his hand and press Toll's hand.

"And I could be in his place!" Rostov thought to himself and, barely holding back tears of pity over the sovereign's fate, rode on in complete despair, not knowing where he was going now or why.

His despair was the stronger in that he felt his own weakness was the cause of his grief.

He could . . . not only could, but should have ridden up to the sovereign. And that was a unique chance to show the sovereign his devotion. And he had not made use of it . . ."What have I done?" he thought. And he turned his horse and rode back to the place where he had seen the emperor; but there was no one now on the other side of the ditch. Only wagons and carriages drove along. From one cart driver he learned that Kutuzov's staff was in a nearby village, where the train was going. Rostov followed them.

Ahead of him walked Kutuzov's groom, leading horses covered with cloths. Behind the groom came a wagon, and behind the wagon an old house serf in a peaked cap, a short coat, and with bandy legs.

"Titus, hey, Titus!" said the groom.

"What?" the old man asked distractedly.

"Titus! Don't bite us!"

"Eh, you fool! Pah!" the old man said and spat angrily. Some time passed in silent movement, and the same joke was repeated again.

By five o'clock in the afternoon, the battle had been lost at all points. More than a hundred cannon had already been captured by the French.

Przebyszewski and his corps laid down their arms. Other columns, having lost about half their men, were retreating in disorderly, confused crowds.

The remains of Langeron's and Dokhturov's troops, mixed together, crowded around the dams and banks of the ponds near the village of Augesd.

After five o'clock it was only at the dam of Augesd that the hot cannon fire of the French alone could be heard, from numerous batteries lined up on the slopes of the Pratzen heights and firing at our retreating troops.

In the rear guard, Dokhturov and others, drawing up some battalions, fired back at the French cavalry who were pursuing our troops. It was beginning to get dark. On the narrow dam of Augesd, on which for so many years an old miller in a cap used to sit peacefully with his fishing rods, while his grandson, his shirtsleeves rolled up, fingered the silvery, trembling fish in the watering can; on this dam over which, for so many years, Moravians in shaggy hats and blue jackets had peacefully driven in their two-horse carts laden with wheat and had driven back over the same dam all dusty with flour, their carts white—now, on this narrow dam, between wagons and cannon, under horses and between wheels, crowded men disfigured by the fear of death, crushing each other, dying, stepping over the dying, and killing each other, only to go a few steps and be killed themselves just the same.

Every ten seconds, pushing through the air, a cannonball smacked or a shell exploded in the midst of this dense crowd, killing and spattering with blood those who stood near. Dolokhov, wounded in the arm, on foot, with a dozen soldiers of his company (he was already an officer), and his regimental commander, on horseback, represented the remainder of the entire regiment. Drawn by the crowd, they pressed into the entrance to the dam and, hemmed in on all sides, stopped, because ahead of them a horse had fallen under a cannon and the crowd was pulling it out. One cannonball killed someone behind them, another landed in front and spattered Dolokhov with blood. The crowd pushed on desperately, shrank back, went a few steps, and stopped again.

"Get through these hundred steps, and I'm saved for sure; stand here another two minutes, and I'm sure to be dead," each man was thinking.

Dolokhov, who was standing in the middle of the crowd, tore his way to the edge of the dam, knocking two soldiers off their feet, and ran down onto the slippery ice that covered the pond.

"Turn off!" he cried, skipping over the ice, which cracked under him, "turn off!" he cried to the ordnance. "It holds! . . ."

The ice held him, but it sagged and cracked, and it was obvious that it would give way, not only under a cannon or a crowd, but under him alone. People looked at him and pressed to the bank, not yet daring to step onto the ice. The regimental commander, standing on horseback at the entrance, raised his arm and opened his mouth, addressing Dolokhov. Suddenly one of the cannonballs came whistling so low over the crowd that everybody ducked. There was a wet smack, and the general and his horse fell in a pool of blood. No one looked at the general, still less thought of picking him up.

"Go onto the ice! go onto the ice! Go! Turn off! Don't you hear? Go!" cried countless voices after the cannonball hit the general, themselves not knowing what and why they were shouting.

One of the rearmost cannon going onto the dam turned off onto the ice. Crowds of soldiers started running down off the dam onto the frozen pond. The ice cracked under one of the foremost soldiers and one foot went into the water; he tried to right himself and fell through to the waist. The nearest soldiers hesitated, the cannon-driver stopped his horse, but shouts were still heard from behind: "Go onto the ice, don't stop, go! go!" And cries of terror were heard in the crowd. The soldiers around the gun waved at the horses and beat them to make them turn and move on. The horses set out from the bank. The ice that had held the foot soldiers gave way in one huge piece, and about forty of them rushed, some back, some forward, drowning each other.

The cannonballs went on regularly whistling and smacking into the ice, into the water, and most often into the crowd that covered the dam, the ponds, and the bank.

XIX

On the Pratzen hill, in the same place where he fell with the staff of the standard in his hands, Prince Andrei Bolkonsky lay bleeding profusely and, unbeknownst to himself, letting out soft, pitiful, and childlike moans.

Towards evening he stopped moaning and became completely still. He did not know how long he was unconscious. Suddenly he felt himself alive again and suffering from a burning and rending pain in the head.

"Where is it, that lofty sky, which I never knew till now and saw today?" was his first thought. "And I never knew this suffering either," he thought. "Yes, I knew nothing, nothing till now. But where am I?"

He began to listen and heard the sounds of approaching hoofbeats and the sound of voices speaking French. He opened his eyes. Over him again was that same lofty sky with floating clouds rising still higher, through which showed the blue of infinity. He did not turn his head and did not see those who, judging by the sounds of hoofs and voices, had ridden up to him and stopped.

The horsemen who had ridden up were Napoleon accompanied by two adjutants. Bonaparte, riding over the battlefield, had given final orders about the reinforcement of the batteries firing at the dam of Augesd and was looking at the dead and wounded who were left on the battlefield.

"*De beaux hommes!*"[6] said Napoleon, looking at a dead Russian grenadier who, his face buried in the ground and his nape blackened, lay on his stomach, one of his already stiff arms flung far out.

"*Les munitions des pièces de positions sont épuisées, sire!*"[7] an adjutant said just then, having come from the batteries that were firing on Augesd.

"*Faites avancer celles de la réserve*,"[8] said Napoleon, and, riding on a few paces, he stopped over Prince Andrei, who lay on his back, the staff of the standard fallen beside him (the standard had already been taken as a trophy by the French).

"*Voilà une belle mort*,"[9] said Napoleon, looking at Bolkonsky.

Prince Andrei understood that it had been said about him, and that it was Napoleon speaking. He heard the man who had said these words being addressed as *sire*. But he heard these words as if he was hearing the buzzing of a fly. He not only was not interested, he did not even notice, and at once forgot them. He had a burning in his head; he felt that he was losing blood, and he saw above him that distant, lofty, and eternal sky. He knew that it was Napoleon—his hero—but at that moment, Napoleon seemed to him such a small, insignificant

6. Fine men!
7. The ammunition for the guns in position is exhausted, Sire!
8. Bring up more from the reserves.
9. There's a fine death.

man compared with what was now happening between his soul and this lofty, infinite sky with clouds racing across it. To him it was all completely the same at that moment who was standing over him or what he said about him; he was only glad that people had stopped over him and only wished that those people would help him and bring him back to life, which seemed so beautiful to him, because he now understood it so differently. He gathered all his strength in order to stir and produce some sound. He stirred his leg weakly and produced a weak, painful moan that moved even him to pity.

"Ah! he's alive," said Napoleon. "Lift up this young man, *ce jeune homme*, and take him to the first-aid station!"

Having said that, Napoleon rode on further to meet Marshal Lannes, who was riding up to the emperor, taking off his hat and congratulating him on the victory.

Prince Andrei remembered nothing more: he lost consciousness from the terrible pain of being put on the stretcher, the jolting while he was being carried, and the probing of his wound at the first-aid station. He came to only at the end of the day, when he, along with other Russian wounded and captured officers, was taken to the hospital. During this transfer, he felt somewhat fresher and could look around and even speak.

The first words he heard when he came to were the words of the French convoy officer, who was saying hurriedly:

"We must stop here. The emperor will ride by now; it will give him pleasure to see all these gentlemen prisoners."

"There are so many prisoners today, almost the whole Russian army, that he must be bored with it," said another officer.

"Well, really! This, they say, is the commander of all the emperor Alexander's guards," said the first, pointing to a wounded Russian officer in the white uniform of the horse guards.

Bolkonsky recognized Prince Repnin, whom he used to meet in Petersburg society. Next to him stood another wounded officer of the horse guards, a nineteen-year-old boy.

Bonaparte, riding up at a gallop, stopped his horse.

"Who's the senior man?"

They named the colonel, Prince Repnin.

"Are you the commander of the emperor Alexander's regiment of horse guards?" asked Napoleon.

"I commanded a squadron," replied Repnin.

"Your regiment fulfilled its duty honorably," said Napoleon.

"The praise of a great general is a soldier's best reward," said Repnin.

"I bestow it on you with pleasure," said Napoleon. "Who is this young man next to you?"

Prince Repnin named Lieutenant Sukhtelen.

Napoleon looked at him and said, smiling:

"*Il est venu bien jeune se frotter à nous.*"[10]

"Youth is no impediment to bravery," Sukhtelen said in a halting voice.

"A fine answer," said Napoleon. "You'll go far, young man!"

Prince Andrei, who, to complete the trophy of prisoners, was also brought out before the eyes of the emperor, could not fail to attract his attention. Napoleon evidently remembered seeing him on the battlefield and, turning to him, used the same appellation of young man, *jeune homme*, under which Bolkonsky had been imprinted on his memory the first time.

"*Et vous, jeune homme?* And you, young man?" he addressed him. "How do you feel, *mon brave?*"

Though five minutes earlier Prince Andrei had been able to say a few words to the soldiers transporting him, now, with his eyes fixed directly on Napoleon, he was silent . . . To him at that moment all the interests that occupied Napoleon seemed so insignificant, his hero himself seemed so petty to him, with his petty vanity and joy in victory, compared with that lofty, just, and kindly sky, which he had seen and understood, that he was unable to answer him.

Then, too, everything seemed so useless and insignificant compared with that stern and majestic way of thinking called up in him by

10. He's young to go crossing swords with us.

weakness from loss of blood, suffering, and the expectation of imminent death. Looking into Napoleon's eyes, Prince Andrei thought about the insignificance of grandeur, about the insignificance of life, the meaning of which no one could understand, and about the still greater insignificance of death, the meaning of which no one among the living could understand or explain.

The emperor, receiving no answer, turned away and, as he rode off, addressed one of the officers:

"Have these gentlemen looked after and taken to my bivouac; have my doctor Larrey examine their wounds. Good-bye, Prince Repnin." And, touching up his horse, he galloped on.

On his face was the radiance of self-satisfaction and happiness.

The soldiers who had carried Prince Andrei and had taken from him the little golden icon hung on her brother by Princess Marya, seeing the kindness with which the emperor treated the prisoners, hastened to return the icon.

Prince Andrei did not see how or by whom it was put back on him, but suddenly, on his chest over the uniform, a little icon on a fine gold chain turned up.

"It would be good," thought Prince Andrei, looking at this icon which his sister had hung on him with such feeling and reverence, "it would be good if everything was as clear and simple as it seems to Princess Marya. How good it would be to know where to look for help in this life and what to expect after it, there, beyond the grave! How happy and calm I'd be, if I could say now: Lord, have mercy on me! . . . But to whom shall I say it? Either it is an indefinable, unfathomable power, which I not only cannot address, but which I cannot express in words—the great all or nothing," he said to himself, "or it is that God whom Princess Marya has sown in here, in this amulet? Nothing, nothing is certain, except the insignificance of everything I can comprehend and the grandeur of something incomprehensible but most important!"

The stretchers began to move. At every jolt he again felt unbearable pain; his feverish state worsened, and he became delirious. Those reveries of his father, wife, sister, and future son, and the tenderness he had experienced on the night before the battle, the figure of the little, insignificant Napoleon, and the high sky over it all, constituted the main basis for his feverish imaginings.

He imagined a quiet life and peaceful family happiness at Bald Hills. He was already enjoying this happiness, when suddenly little Napoleon appeared with his indifferent, limited gaze, happy in the unhappiness of others, and doubts and torments set in, and only the sky promised tranquility. Towards morning all his reveries became confused and merged into the chaos and darkness of unconsciousness and oblivion, which, in the opinion of Larrey himself, Napoleon's doctor, would most likely end in death rather than recovery.

"*C'est un sujet nerveux et bilieux*," said Larrey, "*il n'en réchappera pas*."[11]

Prince Andrei, among other hopeless wounded, was handed over to the care of the local inhabitants.

11. He's the nervous and bilious sort . . . he won't pull through.

Volume Two, Part Three: Natasha's first grand ball on New Year's Eve

XIV

On December 31, the eve of the new year 1810, for *le réveillon*,[1] a ball was given by a grand dignitary of Catherine's time. The ball was to be attended by the diplomatic corps and the sovereign.

The dignitary's well-known house on the English Embankment shone with countless lights. Police stood by the brightly lit porch laid with red baize, and not merely gendarmes, but a mounted police chief and dozens of police officers. Carriages drove away and new ones drove up with red-liveried footmen and footmen with feathers in their hats. Men in uniforms, stars, and sashes emerged from the carriages; ladies in satin and ermine carefully descended the noisily flipped down footrests and stepped hastily and soundlessly over the baize of the porch.

Almost every time a new carriage drove up, a whisper ran through the crowd and hats were doffed.

"The sovereign? . . . No, a minister . . . prince . . . ambassador . . . Don't you see the feathers? . . ." came from the crowd. One person in the crowd, better dressed than the others, seemed to know everyone and called by name the most distinguished dignitaries of that time.

A third of the guests had already arrived at the ball, but the Rostovs, who were to be there, were still hurriedly preparing to dress.

There had been many discussions and preparations for this ball in the Rostov family, many fears that they would not receive an invitation, the dresses would not be ready, and everything would not be arranged as it ought to be.

1. The New Year's Eve party.

The Rostovs were going to the ball together with Marya Ignatievna Peronsky, the countess's friend and relation, a skinny and yellow lady-in-waiting of the old court, who guided the provincial Rostovs through Petersburg high society.

At ten o'clock in the evening they were to pick up the lady-in-waiting near the Tavrichesky Garden; yet it was five minutes to ten, and the young ladies were still not dressed.

Natasha was going to the first grand ball of her life. She had gotten up that day at eight o'clock in the morning and had spent the whole day in feverish anxiety and activity. Since morning all her powers had been directed towards getting all of them—herself, mama, Sonya—dressed in the best possible way. Sonya and the countess put themselves entirely in her hands. The countess was to wear a damson velvet dress, and the two girls white gauze dresses over pink silk slips, with roses at the bodice. Their hair was to be done *à la grecque*.

All the essentials had already been done: feet, hands, neck, ears had been washed, perfumed, and powdered with special thoroughness for the ball; they already had on their silk lace stockings and white satin booties with bows; their hairdressing was nearly done. Sonya was finishing dressing, as was the countess; but Natasha, who had fussed over everybody, lagged behind. She was still sitting in front of the mirror, a peignoir thrown over her thin shoulders. Sonya, already dressed, stood in the middle of the room and, pressing painfully with her small finger, was pinning on a last ribbon, which squeaked as the pin went through it.

"Not that way, not that way, Sonya!" said Natasha, turning her head and putting both hands to her hair, which the maid who was holding it did not have time to let go of. "The bow's wrong, come here." Sonya crouched down. Natasha pinned the ribbon on another way.

"Please, miss, it's impossible this way," said the maid who was holding Natasha's hair.

"Ah, my God, wait, then! Like that, Sonya."

"Won't you hurry?" the countess's voice was heard. "It's already ten."

"Right away, right away. Are you ready, mama?"

"I only have to pin on my toque."

"Don't do it without me," cried Natasha, "you won't manage!"

"But it's already ten."

It had been decided to appear at the ball at half-past ten, but Natasha still had to dress, and they still had to drive to the Tavrichesky Garden.

Having finished doing her hair, Natasha, in a short petticoat, her ball slippers showing from under it, and wearing her mother's bed jacket, ran up to Sonya, looked her over, and then ran to her mother. She turned her mother's head, pinned on the toque, and, quickly kissing her gray hair, again ran to the maids who were taking up her skirt.

The only thing now was Natasha's skirt, which was too long. Two maids were taking it up, hurriedly biting off the thread. A third, holding pins in her lips and between her teeth, kept running from the countess to Sonya; a fourth held the whole gauze dress on her high-raised arm.

"Mavrusha, darling, be quick!"

"Hand me the thimble there, miss."

"Will you hurry up, finally?" the count said, coming through the door. "Here's your scent. Mme Peronsky must be waiting."

"It's ready, miss," said the maid, lifting the taken-up gauze dress with two fingers, and shaking it and blowing at something, showing by this gesture an awareness of the airiness and purity of what she was holding.

Natasha began to put the dress on.

"One moment, one moment, don't come in, papa!" she cried to her father, who had opened the door, still under the gauze of her skirt, which covered her whole face. Sonya slammed the door. A moment later the count was admitted. He was wearing a dark blue tailcoat, stockings and shoes, was perfumed and pomaded.

"Papa, you look so handsome, it's lovely!" said Natasha, standing in the middle of the room and spreading the folds of the gauze.

"Let me, miss, let me," said the maid, getting on her knees, pulling at the dress, and moving the pins with her tongue from one side of her mouth to the other.

"Say what you like," Sonya cried with despair in her voice, looking at Natasha's dress, "say what you like, it's still too long!"

Natasha stepped back to look at herself in the pier glass. The dress was too long.

"By God, miss, it's not too long at all," said Mavrusha, who was crawling on the floor following her young lady.

"Well, if it's long, we can take it up, we can take it up in a minute," said the resolute Dunyasha, taking a needle out of the fichu on her breast and setting to work again on the floor.

Just then the countess came in bashfully, with quiet steps, in her toque and velvet dress.

"Ohh! my beauty!" cried the count. "Better than any of you! . . ." He was about to embrace her, but she retreated, blushing, so as not to have her dress rumpled.

"Mama, the toque more to one side," said Natasha. "I'll re-pin it," and she rushed forward, and the sewing girls, who had no time to follow her, tore off a piece of gauze.

"My God! What is this? It's not my fault, I swear . . ."

"Never mind, I'll stitch it up, it won't show," said Dunyasha.

"My beauty, my queen!" the nanny said, coming through the door. "And Sonyushka, too, what beauties! . . ."

At a quarter past ten they finally got into carriages and drove off. But they still had to stop by the Tavrichesky Garden.

Mme Peronsky was ready. Despite her old age and unattractiveness, the same things had gone on with her as at the Rostovs', though not as hurriedly (it was a habitual thing for her). Her old, unattractive body had been perfumed, washed, powdered in just the same way, she had been scrubbed behind the ears just as carefully, and, just as at the Rostovs', her old maid had delightedly admired her mistress's outfit, when she came out to the drawing room in a yellow dress with a monogram. Mme Peronsky praised the attire of the Rostovs.

The Rostovs praised her taste and attire and, mindful of their dresses and hair, put themselves into the carriages at eleven o'clock and drove off.

XV

Natasha had not had a free moment since the morning of that day and had never once had time to think about what lay ahead of her.

In the damp, cold air, in the incomplete darkness of the crowded, rocking carriage, she imagined vividly for the first time what awaited her there at the ball, in the brightly lit rooms—music, flowers, dancing, the sovereign, all the brilliant youth of Petersburg. What awaited her was so beautiful that she did not even believe it could happen: so out of keeping it was with the impression of the cold, the crowdedness, the darkness of the carriage. She understood what awaited her only when, having stepped over the red baize of the porch, she entered the front hall, took off her fur coat, and walked beside Sonya in front of her mother between the flowers on the lighted stairway. Only then did she remember how one had to behave at a ball and try to assume the majestic manner she considered necessary for a girl at a ball. But, luckily for her, she felt her eyes looking everywhere at once: she saw nothing clearly, her pulse beat a hundred times a minute, and the blood began to throb in her heart. She was unable to assume that manner, which would have made her ridiculous, and walked on, faint with excitement and only trying as hard as she could to conceal it. And this was the manner that was most becoming to her. Before them, behind them, also talking quietly and also in ball gowns, other guests were entering. The mirrors on the stairway reflected ladies in white, blue, pink dresses, with diamonds and pearls on their bare arms and necks.

Natasha looked in the mirrors and in the reflections could not distinguish herself from the others. Everything mixed into one brilliant procession. At the entrance to the first room, the monotonous noise of voices, footsteps, greetings deafened Natasha, the light and brilliance dazzled her still more. The host and hostess, who had already been standing by the door for half an hour saying the same words to the entering people: "*Charmé de vous voir*"[2]—greeted the Rostovs and Mme Peronsky in the same way.

2. Delighted to see you.

The two girls in white dresses, with identical roses in their dark hair, curtsied identically, but the hostess involuntarily rested her gaze longer on the slender Natasha. She looked at her and smiled at her alone with a special smile, in addition to her hostess smile. Gazing at her, the hostess may have remembered the golden, irretrievable time of her girlhood, and her own first ball. The host also followed Natasha with his eyes and asked the count which one was his daughter.

"*Charmante!*" he said, kissing the tips of his fingers.

The guests stood in the ballroom, crowding by the door, waiting for the sovereign. The countess placed herself in the first rows of this crowd. Natasha heard and felt that several voices were asking about her and looking at her. She realized that she was liked by those who paid attention to her, and this observation reassured her somewhat.

"There are some like us, and some worse than us," she thought.

Mme Peronsky named for the countess the most important persons at the ball.

"That one is the Dutch ambassador, see, the gray-haired one," she said, pointing to a little old man with abundant, curly silver-gray hair, surrounded by ladies whom he made laugh at something.

"And here she is, the queen of Petersburg, Countess Bezukhov," she said, pointing to the entering Hélène.

"How beautiful! She yields nothing to Marya Antonovna. See how the men dangle after her, young and old. Both beautiful and intelligent. They say Prince—— has lost his mind over her. But these two here, though they're not beautiful, are still more surrounded."

She pointed to a lady who was crossing the room with a very unattractive daughter.

"She's a millionaire bride," said Mme Peronsky. "And here come the wooers."

"That's Madame Bezukhov's brother, Anatole Kuragin," she said, pointing to a handsome horse guard who walked past them, looking somewhere above the ladies from the height of his raised head. "Handsome, isn't he? They say he's to marry this rich one. And your cousin, Drubetskoy, is also dangling after her very much.

Millions, they say. Why, but that's the French ambassador himself," she replied to the countess's question about who Caulaincourt was. "Look at him, like some sort of tsar. But all the same the French are nice, very nice. There's nothing nicer for society. Ah, here she is! No, she's the best, our Marya Antonovna! And so simply dressed. Lovely!"

"And that fat one in spectacles is the universal Freemason," said Mme Peronsky, pointing to Bezukhov. "Set him next to his wife: a real tomfool!"

Pierre walked along, rolling his fat body, parting the crowd, nodding to right and left as casually and good-naturedly as if he were walking through a marketplace crowd. He moved through the crowd, evidently searching for someone.

Natasha looked joyfully at the familiar face of Pierre, that tomfool, as Mme Peronsky had called him, and knew that Pierre was looking for them in the crowd, and for her in particular. Pierre had promised to be at the ball and to introduce partners to her.

But before he reached them, Bezukhov stopped beside a very handsome dark-haired man of medium height, in a white uniform, who was standing by a window talking to a tall man with stars and a sash. Natasha immediately recognized the young man of medium height in the white uniform: it was Bolkonsky, who seemed to her to have grown younger, more cheerful, and better looking.

"Here's another acquaintance, Bolkonsky, see, mama?" said Natasha, pointing to Prince Andrei. "Remember, he spent the night with us at Otradnoe."

"Ah, you know him?" said Mme Peronsky. "I can't bear him. *Il fait à présent la pluie et le beau temps.*[3] And such boundless pride! Takes after his papa. Got in with Speransky, drafting some sort of projects. Look how he treats the ladies! She's talking to him, and he turns away," she said, pointing to him. "I'd give it to him, if he behaved with me the way he does with these ladies."

3. He runs the whole show now.

XVI

Suddenly everything stirred, the crowd began to talk, moved together, parted again, and between the two rows of people, to the sounds of the struck-up music, the sovereign came in. Behind him walked the host and hostess. The sovereign walked quickly, nodding to right and left, as if trying to get quickly past this first moment of meeting. The musicians played a polonaise well known then from the words written to it. These words began: "Alexander, Elizaveta, how we all admire you." The sovereign walked into the drawing room; the crowd surged towards the door; several persons with changed expressions hurriedly went there and back. The crowd surged away from the drawing room door again, and the sovereign appeared in it, talking with the hostess. A young man with a perplexed look pressed up to the ladies, asking them to step aside. Some ladies with faces that expressed a total obliviousness of all social conventions pushed forward, ruining their fancy dresses. Men began to approach the ladies and form couples for the polonaise.

Everyone made way, and the sovereign, smiling and out of step with the music, led the hostess through the drawing-room door. After him came the host with Mme M. A. Naryshkin, then ambassadors, ministers, various generals, whom Mme Peronsky kept naming without pause. More than half of the ladies had partners and were joining or preparing to join the polonaise. Natasha sensed that she would be left with her mother and Sonya among the smaller part of the ladies pushed back against the wall and not asked to the polonaise. She stood, her thin arms lowered, her barely defined bosom rising rhythmically, holding her breath, her shining, frightened eyes looking straight ahead with an expression of readiness either for the greatest happiness or for the greatest grief. She was interested neither in the sovereign nor in any of the important persons Mme Peronsky pointed out—she had one thought: "Can it be that no one will come up to me, can it be that I won't dance among the first, can it be that all these men won't notice me, who now don't even seem to see me, and if they look at me, it's with such an expression as if they were saying: 'Ah! it's not her, there's no point in looking!' No, it can't be!" she thought. "They must know how I want to dance, and how well I dance, and what fun it will be for them to dance with me."

The sounds of the polonaise, which had continued for quite a long time, were already beginning to seem sad—a reminiscence in Natasha's ears. She wanted to cry. Mme Peronsky left them. The count was at the other end of the room; the countess, Sonya, and she stood alone, as if in a forest, in this crowd of strangers, of no interest or need to anyone. Prince Andrei walked past them with some lady, obviously not recognizing them. The handsome Anatole, smiling, was saying something to the lady he was leading and glanced at Natasha's face as one would glance at a wall. Boris walked past them twice and turned away each time. Berg and his wife, who were not dancing, came up to them.

For Natasha, this family intimacy here, at a ball, seemed offensive, as if there were no other place for family conversations except at a ball. She did not look at and did not listen to Vera, who was saying something to her about her green dress.

Finally, the sovereign stopped beside his last partner (he had danced with three), and the music ceased. A preoccupied adjutant ran up to the Rostovs, asking them to step aside somewhere, though they were standing at the wall, and from the gallery came the distinct, careful, and engagingly rhythmic sounds of a waltz. The sovereign looked over the room with a smile. A minute passed—no one began yet. The adjutant master of ceremonies went up to Countess Bezukhov and asked her to dance. Smiling, she raised her arm and placed it, without looking at him, on the adjutant's shoulder. The adjutant master of ceremonies, an expert in these matters, confidently, unhurriedly, and rhythmically, keeping firm hold of his partner, set off with her at first in a glissade around the edge of the circle, then, at the corner of the room, took her left arm, turned her, and now, above the ever-quickening sounds of the music, one could hear only the rhythmic jingle of the spurs on the adjutant's quick and nimble feet, and at every third beat, the velvet dress of his partner seemed to flash, flying, as she turned. Natasha looked at them and was ready to weep that it was not she dancing this first turn of the waltz.

Prince Andrei, in his white cavalry colonel's uniform, stockings, and low boots, animated and merry, stood in the first rows of the circle, not far from the Rostovs. Baron Vierhoff was talking to him about the first session of the State Council, planned for the next day. Prince Andrei, being close to Speransky and taking part in the work of the legislative commission, could give accurate information about the next day's meeting, of which various rumors were circulating. But he was not listening to what Vierhoff was telling him and looked now at the sovereign, now at the gentlemen preparing to dance, who had not yet ventured into the circle.

Prince Andrei was observing these gentlemen grown timid in the sovereign's presence and ladies faint with the desire to be invited.

Pierre came over to Prince Andrei and took him by the arm. "You always dance. My protégée, the young Miss Rostov, is here. Ask her," he said.

"Where?" asked Bolkonsky. "I beg your pardon," he said, turning to the baron, "we can finish this conversation elsewhere—at a ball one must dance." He stepped forward, in the direction Pierre had indicated to him. Natasha's desperate, rapt face caught Prince Andrei's eye. He recognized her, guessed her feeling, realized that she was a *débutante*, remembered her conversation on the window ledge, and with a merry expression on his face went up to Countess Rostov.

"Allow me to introduce you to my daughter," the countess said, blushing.

"I have the pleasure of being acquainted, if the countess remembers me," said Prince Andrei, with a courteous and low bow, totally contradicting Mme Peronsky's remark about his rudeness, going up to Natasha and raising his arm to put it around her waist even before he finished asking her to dance. He suggested a turn of the waltz. That rapt expression of Natasha's face, ready for despair and for ecstasy, suddenly lit up with a happy, grateful, childlike smile.

"I've been waiting a long time for you," this frightened and happy girl seemed to say by her smile, shining through ready tears, as she raised her arm to Prince Andrei's shoulder. They were the second couple to enter the circle. Prince Andrei was one of the best dancers of his time. Natasha's dancing was excellent. Her little feet in satin ball slippers did their work quickly, lightly, and independently of herself, and her face shone with the rapture of happiness. Her bared neck and arms were thin and unattractive compared to Hélène's shoulders. Her shoulders were thin, her bosom undefined, her arms slender; but on Hélène there was already a sort of varnish from all the thousands of gazes that had passed over her body, while Natasha looked like a young girl who was bared for the first time and would have been very ashamed of it, if she had not been assured that it had necessarily to be so.

Prince Andrei liked to dance and, wishing to rid himself quickly of the political and intellectual conversations with which everyone addressed him, and wishing to break quickly this vexatious circle of embarrassment caused by the presence of the sovereign, had gone to dance and had asked Natasha because Pierre had pointed her out to him and because she was the first pretty woman his eyes fell on; but as soon as he put his arm around her slender, mobile, quivering waist, and she began to move so close to him and smile so close to him, the wine of her loveliness went to his head: he felt himself revived and rejuvenated when, catching his breath and leaving her, he stopped and began to look at the dancers.

XVII

After Prince Andrei, Boris came up to Natasha and asked her to dance, then also that dancer adjutant who had opened the ball, and other young men, and Natasha, sending her surplus partners to Sonya, happy and flushed, did not stop dancing all evening. She noticed nothing and did not see any of what interested everyone at this ball. Not only did she not notice how the sovereign had a long talk with the French ambassador, how he talked with particular graciousness with a certain lady, how prince so-and-so did and said such-and-such, how Hélène had great success and was granted the special attentions of so-and-so; she did not even see the sovereign and noticed that he had gone only because the ball became more animated after his departure. In one of the merry cotillions before supper, Prince Andrei danced again with Natasha. He reminded her of their first meeting in the Otradnoe avenue, and how she could not fall asleep on that moonlit night, and how he involuntarily overheard her. Natasha blushed at this reminder and tried to justify herself, as if there was something shameful in that feeling which Prince Andrei had involuntarily overheard from her.

Prince Andrei, like all people who have grown up in society, liked to encounter things in society that did not have the general society stamp on them. And Natasha was just that, with her astonishment, joy, and timidity, and even her mistakes in French. He treated her and talked to her with particular tenderness and care. Sitting next to her, talking with her about the simplest and most insignificant subjects, Prince Andrei admired the joyful shining of her eyes and smile, which referred not to what they were saying, but to her inner happiness. At those times when Natasha was chosen, and she got up with a smile and danced through the room, Prince Andrei especially admired her timid grace. In the middle of the cotillion, Natasha, having finished a figure, still breathing hard, was going to her seat. A new partner again asked her to dance. She was tired and out of breath, and obviously wanted to refuse, but then again cheerfully raised her arm to her partner's shoulder and smiled to Prince Andrei.

That smile said: "I'd be glad to rest and sit with you; I'm tired; but you see, I've been asked to dance, and I'm glad of it, and I'm happy, and I love everybody, and you and I understand all that," and much, much more. When her partner left her, Natasha ran across the room to invite two ladies for the figures.

"If she goes to her cousin first and then to another lady, she'll be my wife," Prince Andrei quite unexpectedly said to himself, looking at her. She went to her cousin first.

"What nonsense sometimes comes into one's head!" thought Prince Andrei. "But the one sure thing is that this girl is so sweet, so special, that she won't spend a month dancing here before she gets married . . . It's a rarity here," he thought, as Natasha, straightening a rose that had gone awry on her corsage, was sitting down beside him.

At the end of the cotillion, the old count in his dark blue tailcoat came over to the dancers. He invited Prince Andrei to come and see him, and asked his daughter whether she was having a good time. Natasha did not reply and only smiled a smile which said with reproach: "How can you ask that?"

"I've never enjoyed myself so much in my life!" she said, and Prince Andrei noticed how her thin arms rose quickly to embrace her father and at once dropped again. Natasha was happier than she had ever been before in her life. She was in that highest degree of happiness when a person becomes perfectly kind and good and does not believe in the possibility of evil, unhappiness, and grief.

At this ball Pierre felt insulted for the first time by the position his wife occupied in high spheres. He was sullen and distracted. There was a deep furrow across his brow, and, standing by the window, he looked through his spectacles, seeing no one.

Natasha walked past him on her way to supper. Pierre's gloomy, unhappy face struck her. She stopped in front of him. She wanted to help him, to transfer to him the overflow of her own happiness.

"Such a merry time," she said, "isn't it, Count?"

Pierre smiled distractedly, obviously not understanding what was being said to him.

"Yes, I'm very glad," he said.

"How can they be displeased with anything," thought Natasha, "especially such a nice man as this Bezukhov?" In Natasha's eyes, all who were at the ball were equally kind, nice, wonderful people, and loved each other: no one could offend anyone, and therefore they should all be happy.

XVIII

The next day Prince Andrei remembered yesterday's ball, but his thought did not dwell on it for long. "Yes, it was a very brilliant ball.

And then, too . . . yes, Miss Rostov is very sweet. There's something fresh in her, something special, non-Petersburg, that makes her different." That was all he thought about the ball, and, having had tea, he sat down to work.

But from fatigue or lack of sleep, the day was not good for work, and Prince Andrei could do nothing, kept criticizing his own efforts, as often happened with him, and was glad when he heard someone arrive.

The visitor was Bitsky, who worked on various commissions, frequented all the societies of Petersburg, was a passionate admirer of the new ideas and of Speransky, an anxious Petersburg newsmonger, one of those people who choose a trend as they do their clothes—according to the fashion, but who, because of it, look like the most ardent partisans of the trend. He rushed into Prince Andrei's room and, barely managing to take his hat off, anxiously began talking. He had just learned the details of the session of the State Council that morning, opened by the sovereign, and was recounting it with rapture. The sovereign's speech had been extraordinary. It had been one of those speeches that only constitutional monarchs make. "The sovereign said straight out that the council and the senate were *estates* of the realm; he said that the government should be based not on arbitrariness, but on *firm principles*. The sovereign said that the finances should be reformed and the accounting made public," Bitsky recounted, emphasizing certain words and widening his eyes significantly.

"Yes, today's event marks an epoch, the greatest epoch in our history," he concluded.

Prince Andrei listened to his account of the opening of the State Council, which he had awaited with such impatience and to which he had ascribed such importance, and marveled that this event, now that it had taken place, not only did not move him, but seemed less than insignificant. With quiet mockery he listened to Bitsky's rapturous account. The simplest thought occurred to him: "What do Bitsky and I have to do with what the sovereign was pleased to say in the council? Can any of it make me happier and better?"

And this simple reflection suddenly destroyed for Prince Andrei all his former interest in the reforms being carried out. That same day Prince Andrei was supposed to dine at Speransky's *"en petit comité,"*[4] as the host had said when inviting him. This dinner in the circle of family and friends of the man whom Prince Andrei so admired had formerly interested him very much, the more so as he had not yet seen Speransky in his domestic surroundings; but now he did not want to go.

At the appointed dinner hour, however, Prince Andrei was already entering Speransky's modest private house near the Tavrichesky Garden. In the parqueted dining room of the modest house, distinguished by its extraordinary cleanliness (reminiscent of monastic cleanliness), Prince Andrei, who was slightly late, found that at five o'clock the whole company of that *petit comité* of Speransky's intimate acquaintances had already gathered. There were no ladies, except for Speransky's little daughter (with a long face resembling her father's) and her governess. The guests were Gervais, Magnitsky, and Stolypin. In the front hall Prince Andrei already heard loud voices and ringing, clipped laughter—laughter similar to what one hears on the stage. Some voice similar to Speransky's rapped out a distinct "ha, ha, ha." Prince Andrei had never heard Speransky laugh, and this ringing, high-pitched laughter from a statesman struck him as strange.

Prince Andrei entered the dining room. The whole company was standing between two windows, by a small table with hors d'oeuvres. Speransky, in a gray tailcoat with a star, and evidently in the same white waistcoat and high white necktie he had worn at the famous session of the State Council, stood by the table with a merry face. The guests stood around him. Magnitsky, addressing Mikhail Mikhailovich, was telling an anecdote. Speransky listened, laughing beforehand at what Magnitsky was about to say. Just as Prince Andrei entered the dining room, Magnitsky's words were

4. In an informal meeting.

again drowned by laughter. Stolypin produced a loud bass, chewing a piece of bread and cheese; Gervais hissed out a quiet chuckle; and Speransky laughed his high and clipped laugh.

Speransky, still laughing, gave Prince Andrei his white, tender hand.

"Very glad to see you, Prince," he said. "Just a moment . . ." he turned to Magnitsky, interrupting his story. "We've agreed that tonight will be a dinner for pleasure and not a word about business." He turned back to the speaker and laughed again.

Prince Andrei listened to his laughter and looked at the laughing Speransky with surprise and sad disappointment. This was not Speransky but another man, as it seemed to Prince Andrei. Everything in Speransky that had formerly seemed mysterious and attractive to Prince Andrei suddenly became clear and unattractive to him.

At the table the conversation did not let up for a moment and seemed to consist of a collection of funny anecdotes. Before Magnitsky finished his story, someone else announced his readiness to tell something still funnier. The anecdotes were for the most part concerned, if not with the world of government service, then with persons in the service. It seemed that the insignificance of those persons had been so definitely decided upon in this company that the only possible attitude towards them was a good-naturedly comic one. Speransky told how at the Council that morning a deaf dignitary, when asked his opinion, had replied that he was of the same opinion. Gervais recounted a whole case about an audit, remarkable for the senselessness of all the persons involved. Stolypin, stuttering, mixed into the conversation and began talking vehemently about abuses under the former order of things, threatening to give the conversation a serious character. Magnitsky began to make fun of Stolypin's vehemence. Gervais put in a joke, and the conversation resumed its former merry course.

Obviously, Speransky liked to relax after work and make merry in a friendly circle, and all his guests, understanding his wish, tried to make him merry and be merry themselves. But this merriment seemed heavy and cheerless to Prince Andrei. Speransky's high-pitched voice struck him as unpleasant, and his constant laughter for some reason offended Prince Andrei's feelings by its false note. Prince Andrei did not laugh and feared he would be a dead weight on the company. But no one noticed his lack of harmony with the general mood. They all seemed to be very merry.

He wanted several times to enter the conversation, but each time his word was thrown out, like a cork out of water; and he was unable to joke along with them.

There was nothing bad or inappropriate in what they said, everything was witty and might have been funny; but that something which constitutes the salt of merriment was not only missing, but they did not even know it existed.

After dinner Speransky's daughter and her governess got up. Speransky stroked his daughter with his white hand and kissed her. And this gesture seemed unnatural to Prince Andrei.

The men remained at the table over the port, English-style. In the middle of the conversation that started up about Napoleon's Spanish campaign, of which they all held the same approving opinion, Prince Andrei began to contradict them. Speransky smiled and, obviously trying to divert the conversation from the direction it had taken, told an anecdote that had no relation to it. They all fell silent for several moments.

Having sat at the table for a while, Speransky corked the wine bottle and saying: "Good wine costs a pretty penny these days," handed it to the servant and got up. They all got up and with the same noisy talk went to the drawing room. Speransky was handed two envelopes brought by a courier. He took them and went to his study. As soon as he left, the general merriment died down, and the guests began talking sensibly and quietly with each other.

"Well, now for a declamation!" said Speransky, coming out of his study. "An astonishing talent!" he said to Prince Andrei. Magnitsky at once assumed a pose and began to recite humorous verses he had composed in French about certain persons well known in Petersburg, and was interrupted several times by applause. When the verses were over, Prince Andrei went up to Speransky to take his leave.

"Leaving so early?" said Speransky.

"I promised to be at a soirée . . ."

They fell silent. Prince Andrei looked closely into those mirror-like eyes, which did not let anything in, and felt how ridiculous it was that he could have expected anything from Speransky and from all his activity connected with him, and that he could have ascribed importance to what Speransky was doing. That precise, mirthless laughter went on ringing in Prince Andrei's ears long after he had left Speransky.

On returning home, Prince Andrei began to recall his Petersburg life of those last four months as if it was something new. He recalled his solicitations, his petitioning, the story of his project for military regulations, which had been taken into consideration, but which they had tried to silence, solely because another project, a very bad one, had already been developed and presented to the sovereign; he recalled the sessions of the committee of which Berg was a member; he recalled how, at these sessions, everything to do with the form and procedure of the committee's sessions was discussed carefully and at length, and everything to do with the essence of the matter was carefully and briefly dispensed with. He recalled his work on legislation, the concern with which he had translated the articles of the Roman and French codes into Russian, and he felt ashamed of himself. Then he vividly pictured Bogucharovo, his occupations in the country, his trip to Ryazan, recalled the muzhiks, the headman Dron, and applying to them the personal rights he had classified by paragraphs, he felt astonished that he could have been occupied with such idle work for so long.

XIX

The next day Prince Andrei went to visit certain houses he had not been to yet, among them the house of the Rostovs, with whom he had renewed his acquaintance at the last ball. Besides the rules of courtesy, according to which he ought to call on the Rostovs, Prince Andrei wanted to see at home that special, animated girl who had left him with such a pleasant memory.

Natasha was one of the first to meet him. She was wearing a dark blue everyday dress, in which she seemed still better to Prince Andrei than in a ball gown. She and the whole Rostov family received Prince Andrei like an old friend, simply and cordially. The whole family, whom Prince Andrei used to judge so severely, now seemed to him to consist of wonderful, simple, and kind people. The old count's hospitality and good nature, which struck one especially nicely in Petersburg, was such that Prince Andrei could not refuse to stay for dinner. "Yes, they're kind, nice people," thought Bolkonsky, "who of course don't understand a whit of the treasure they have in Natasha; but kind people, who constitute the best backdrop for setting off this special girl, so poetic, lovely, and overflowing with life."

Prince Andrei sensed in Natasha the presence of a special world, completely foreign to him, filled with joys of a sort as yet unknown to him, that foreign world which even then, in the Otradnoe avenue and at the window on that moonlit night, had enticed him so. Now that world no longer enticed him, it was no longer foreign; but he himself, having entered it, found in it a new delight.

After dinner Natasha, at Prince Andrei's request, went to the clavichord and began to sing. Prince Andrei stood by the window, talking with the ladies, and listened to her. In the middle of a phrase, Prince Andrei fell silent and suddenly felt choked with tears, which he did not know was possible for him. He looked at the singing Natasha, and something new and happy occurred in his soul. He was happy, but at the same time he felt sad. He had decidedly nothing to weep about, but he was ready to weep. About what? His former love? The little princess? His disappointments? . . . His hopes for the future? . . . Yes and no. The main thing he wanted to weep about was a sudden, vivid awareness of the terrible opposition between something infinitely great and indefinable that was in him, and something narrow and fleshly that he himself, and even she, was. This opposition tormented him and gladdened him while she sang.

As soon as Natasha finished singing, she went over to him and asked him how he liked her voice. She asked it and became embarrassed just after she said it, realizing that it was not a question to be asked. He smiled, looking at her, and said that he liked her singing just as he liked everything she did.

Prince Andrei left the Rostovs' late in the evening. He went to bed as was his habit, but soon realized that he could not sleep. Lighting a candle, he would sit on the bed, then get up, then lie down again, not troubled in the least by his insomnia: he felt as joyful and new in his soul as if he had gone from a stuffy room into God's open world. It did not occur to him that he was in love with Miss Rostov; he was not thinking of her; he only pictured her to himself, and owing to that his whole life appeared to him in a new light. "Why do I thrash about, why do I fuss inside this narrow, limited frame, when life, the whole of life, with all its joys, is open to me?" he said to himself. And for the first time in a long while he began making happy plans for the future. He decided that he must occupy himself with the education of his son, by finding a tutor for him and entrusting the boy to the tutor; then he must retire from the service and go abroad, to see England, Switzerland, Italy. "I must use my freedom while I feel so much youth and strength in me," he said to himself. "Pierre was right when he said that one must believe in the possibility of happiness in order to be happy, and I now believe in it. Let the dead bury their dead, but while I'm alive, I must live and be happy," he thought.

Volume Four, Part Three: The brief career of Petya Rostov

IV

It was a warm, rainy autumn day. The sky and the horizon were both the color of muddy water. Now the fog seemed to descend, now a slanting rain would suddenly come down in big drops.

Denisov, in a felt cloak and a papakha streaming with water, rode on a lean, purebred horse with draw-in flanks. Like his horse, who kept moving its head sideways and laying its ears flat, he winced from the slanting rain and peered ahead worriedly. His emaciated face, overgrown with a thick, short, black beard, looked angry.

Beside Denisov, also in a felt cloak and papakha, on a big, well nourished Don stallion, rode a Cossack *esaul*[1]—Denisov's associate.

The *esaul* Lovaisky was a tall, white-faced, fair-haired man, flat as a board, with narrow, pale eyes and a calmly smug expression in his face and bearing. Though it was impossible to say what made for the peculiarity of the horse and rider, from a first glance at the *esaul* and at Denisov, one could see that Denisov felt wet and awkward—that he was a man sitting on a horse; while, looking at the *esaul*, one could see that he felt as comfortable and at ease as ever, and that he was not a man sitting on a horse, but a man who was one with a horse, a being of twice-increased strength.

A little ahead of them walked a soaking wet little peasant—their guide—in a gray kaftan and a white cap.

A little behind them, on a skinny, slender Kirghiz nag, with an enormous mane and tail and lips so torn that they bled, rode a young officer in a dark blue French greatcoat.

Beside him rode a hussar, with a boy in a tattered French uniform and blue cap sitting behind him on his horse's croup. The boy

1. Captain.

held on to the hussar with hands red from the cold, moved his bare feet in an effort to warm them, and, raising his eyebrows, looked around in surprise. This was the French drummer boy captured in the morning.

Behind, by threes, by fours, along the narrow, sodden, and much-traveled forest road, stretched hussars, then Cossacks, some in felt cloaks, some in French greatcoats, some with horse blankets pulled over their heads. The horses, bay and sorrel, all looked black from the rain streaming off them. The horses' necks seemed strangely thin because of their drenched manes. Steam rose from the horses. Clothes, saddles, reins—everything was wet, slippery, and soggy, like the ground and the fallen leaves that covered the road. The men sat looking ruffled up, trying not to stir, so as to keep the water warm that had seeped through to the body and not let in the new, cold water that flowed under their seats, knees, and behind their necks. Between the strung-out Cossacks, the two wagons, hitched to French and saddled Cossack horses, rumbled over stumps and branches and gurgled through the water-filled ruts of the road.

Denisov's horse, swerving around a puddle that was in its way, pulled to the side and bumped its rider's knee against a tree.

"Ah, the devil!" Denisov cried angrily, and, baring his teeth, he gave his horse three strokes of the whip, splashing himself and his comrades with mud. Denisov was in a foul mood because of the rain, and because he was hungry (no one had eaten anything since morning), and above all because there was no word from Dolokhov, and the man sent to take a prisoner had not come back.

"There could hardly be another such occasion as today for attacking the transport. To attack alone is too risky, but put it off to another day and some bigger party will snatch the booty right from under our noses," thought Denisov, constantly glancing ahead, hoping to see the expected messenger from Dolokhov.

Coming out into a clearing, where one could see far to the right, Denisov stopped.

"Somebody's coming," he said.

The *esaul* looked in the direction in which Denisov was pointing.

"There are two coming—an officer and a Cossack. Only it's not *presupposable* that it's the lieutenant colonel himself," said the *esaul*, who liked to use words unknown to the Cossacks.

The riders descended the hill, disappeared from sight, and reappeared in a few minutes. In front, at a weary gallop, applying his whip, rode an officer—disheveled, soaked through, his trousers bunched up above his knees. Behind him, standing in the stirrups, trotted a Cossack. This officer, a very young boy with a broad, red-cheeked face and quick, merry eyes, galloped up to Denisov and handed him a wet envelope.

"From the general," said the officer, "sorry it's not quite dry . . ."

Denisov, frowning, took the envelope and began to open it.

"They keep saying it's dangerous, dangerous," said the officer, turning to the *esaul*, while Denisov read the letter handed to him. "Anyhow, me and Komarov," he pointed to the Cossack, "are ready. Each of us has two pist . . . But what's that?" he asked, seeing the French drummer boy. "A prisoner? You've already been in battle? Can I talk to him?"

"Ghrostov! Petya!" Denisov cried out just then, having looked through the envelope handed to him. "Why didn't you tell me who you were?" And Denisov turned with a smile and gave the officer his hand.

This officer was Petya Rostov.

On the way there, Petya had been preparing the way he, as a grown man and an officer, without hinting at their former acquaintance, would behave with Denisov. But as soon as Denisov smiled at him, Petya at once beamed, blushed for joy, and, forgetting his prepared officialness, began to tell how he had ridden past the French, and how glad he was that he had been given such an errand, and that he had already been in battle at Vyazma, and that a certain hussar had distinguished himself there.

"Well, I'm veghry glad to see you," Denisov interrupted him, and his face again assumed a preoccupied expression.

"Mikhail Feoklitych," he turned to the *esaul*, "this one is from the German again. He's attached to him." And Denisov told the *esaul* that the content of the letter just brought consisted of a repeated request to join him in attacking the transport. "If we don't take it tomoghrrow, they'll snatch it fghrom under our noses," he concluded.

While Denisov was talking with the *esaul*, Petya, abashed by Denisov's cold tone and supposing that the cause of it was the state of his trousers, was straightening them under his greatcoat, so that no one would notice, trying to look as martial as possible.

"Will there be any orders from Your Honor?" he said to Denisov, putting his hand to his visor and returning again to the game of adjutant and general which he had prepared for, "or shall I stay with your honor?"

"Oghrders? . . ." Denisov said pensively. "But can you stay till tomoghrrow?"

"Ah, please . . . May I stay with you?" cried Petya.

"And exactly what did the geneghral tell you—to ghreturn at once?" asked Denisov. Petya blushed.

"He didn't tell me anything. I think I can?" he said questioningly.

"Well, all ghright," said Denisov. And turning to his subordinates, he gave instructions for the party to go to the appointed resting place by the guardhouse in the forest and for the officer on the Kirghiz horse (this officer functioned as an adjutant) to go looking for Dolokhov, to find out where he was and whether he would come in the evening. Denisov himself, with the *esaul* and Petya, intended to ride up to the edge of the forest that came out at Shamshevo, in order to look over the place where the French were camped, at which the next day's attack should be directed.

"Well, ghraybeard," he turned to the muzhik guide, "lead us to Shamshevo."

Denisov, Petya, and the *esaul*, accompanied by several Cossacks and the hussar who was carrying the prisoner, rode left across a ravine to the edge of the forest.

V

The light rain stopped; only mist fell and drops of water from the branches of the trees. Denisov, the *esaul*, and Petya silently rode after the muzhik in the cap, who, stepping lightly and noiselessly over the roots and wet leaves with his splayed feet in bast shoes, led them to the edge of the forest.

Going up a slope, the muzhik paused, looked around, and made for the thinning wall of trees. By a big oak still covered with leaves, he stopped and beckoned mysteriously with his hand.

Denisov and Petya rode up to him. From the place where the muzhik had stopped, the French could be seen. Just beyond the forest, a field of spring wheat descended over a low knoll. To the right, across a steep ravine, a small village and a manor house with broken-down roofs could be seen. In this village, and in the manor house, and all over the knoll, in the garden, by the wells and the pond, and along the road uphill from the bridge to the village, no more than four hundred yards away, crowds of men could be seen through the undulating mist. One could clearly hear their non-Russian shouts at the horses pulling wagons up the hill and their calls to one another.

"Bghring the pghrisoner here," Denisov said in a low voice, without taking his eyes off the French.

The Cossack got off his horse, took the boy down, and went up to Denisov with him. Denisov, pointing to the French, asked what kind of troops these and those were. The boy, putting his chilled hands in his pockets and raising his eyebrows, looked at Denisov in fear and, despite his obvious wish to tell all he knew, became confused in his answers and only confirmed whatever Denisov asked. Denisov frowned, turned away from him, and addressed the *esaul*, telling him his considerations.

Petya, quickly turning his head, looked now at the drummer boy, now at Denisov, now at the *esaul*, now at the French in the village and on the road, trying not to miss anything important.

"Whether Dolokhov comes or not, we've got to take them! . . . Ghright?" said Denisov, with a merry sparkle in his eyes.

"It's a convenient place," said the *esaul*.

"We'll send the infantry from below, through the maghrshes," Denisov went on. "They'll sneak up on the garden. You and the Cossacks will ghride aghround from there," Denisov pointed to the forest behind the village, "and I'll come fghrom here with my hussars. And at the signal shot . . ."

"We can't go through the hollow—it's swampy," said the *esaul.* "The horses will get bogged down; we'll have to go around more to the left."

As they were talking like that in half-whispers, a shot cracked below, in the hollow by the pond; they saw a puff of white smoke, then another, and heard the concerted, merry-sounding shout of hundreds of voices of the French who were on the hillside. At the first moment, Denisov and the *esaul* drew back. They were so close that they thought they were the cause of the shots and shouts. But the shots and shouts had nothing to do with them. Below, across the marsh, ran a man in something red. Obviously, the French were shooting and shouting at him.

"Why, that's our Tikhon," said the *esaul.*

"Him! It's him!"

"What a ghrascal!" said Denisov.

"He'll get away!" the *esaul* said, narrowing his eyes.

The man they called Tikhon ran to the river, plopped into it with a splash, disappeared for a moment, and clambered out on all fours, black from the water, and ran on. The French who were running after him stopped.

"That's nimble," said the *esaul.*

"What a ghrogue!" Denisov said with the same expression of vexation. "What's he been up to all this time?"

"Who is he?" asked Petya.

"Our *plastun.*[2] I sent him to take a 'tongue.'"

"Ah, yes," said Petya, nodding his head at Denisov's first words as if he understood everything, though he decidedly did not understand a single word.

Tikhon Shcherbaty was one of the most necessary men in the party. He was a muzhik from Pokrovskoe, near Gzhat. When, at

2. Scout.

the beginning of his operations, Denisov had come to Pokrovskoe and, as usual, summoned the headman and asked what they knew about the French, the headman had answered as all headmen would, as if defending himself, that he knew nothing, had seen nothing. But when Denisov explained that his aim was to kill the French and asked whether the French had happened to come there, the headman said that, in fact, some "marowders" had been there, but that in their village only Gap-toothed Tishka concerned himself with such doings. Denisov told him to summon Tikhon and, having praised him for his activity, said a few words in front of the headman about loyalty to the tsar and the fatherland, and the hatred for the French that the sons of the fatherland should observe.

"We do no harm to the French," said Tikhon, clearly cowed by these words of Denisov's. "We just went hunting and had some fun with the lads. We did kill some couple of dozen 'marowders,' but otherwise we did no harm . . ." The next day, when Denisov, forgetting entirely about this muzhik, left Pokrovskoe, it was reported to him that Tikhon had attached himself to the party and asked to be allowed to stay with it. Denisov said he could stay.

Tikhon, who at first did the dirty work of making campfires, carrying water, skinning horses, and so on, soon showed great zeal and ability for partisan warfare. At night he went after booty and came back each time bringing some French clothing or weapons and, when told to, also brought in prisoners. Denisov relieved Tikhon from work, began taking him with him on patrol, and enlisted him as a Cossack.

Tikhon did not like riding and always went on foot, never lagging behind the cavalry. His weapons were a musketoon, which he strapped on mainly for amusement, a pike, and an axe, which he used as a wolf does its teeth, with equal ease picking fleas out of its fur or biting through thick bones. Tikhon, with equal precision, would swing his axe to split logs or, taking it by the butt, whittle thin pegs or carved spoons. In Denisov's party, Tikhon occupied his own exceptional place. When there was a need to do something especially difficult and nasty—to haul a cart out of the mud with one's shoulder, to pull a horse out of a swamp by its tail or skin it, to slip right into the middle of the French, to walk thirty miles a day—everyone pointed, chuckling, at Tikhon.

"What harm will it do the devil—he's sturdy as an ox," they said of him.

Once a Frenchman Tikhon was about to capture shot at him with a pistol and hit him in the soft hindquarters. This wound, which Tikhon treated only with vodka, internally and externally, was the object of the merriest jokes in the whole party, jokes to which Tikhon willingly yielded.

"Never again, eh, brother? All doubled up?" the Cossacks laughed at him, and Tikhon, doubling up on purpose and making faces, pretending to be angry, denounced the French with the funniest oaths. The only influence this incident had on Tikhon was that, after his wound, he rarely brought in prisoners.

Tikhon was the bravest and most useful man in the party. Nobody found more chances for attacking than he, no one captured or killed more of the French; and as a result of that, he was a buffoon for all the Cossacks and hussars, and willingly accepted that rank. Now Tikhon had been sent by Denisov to Shamshevo during the night, in order to take a "tongue." But, either because he was not satisfied with one prisoner, or because he had slept through the night, he had slipped by day into some bushes, right in the middle of the French and, as Denisov had seen from the hill, had been discovered by them.

VI

Having talked a while longer with the *esaul* about the next day's attack, which Denisov, seeing the closeness of the French, now seemed to have definitively resolved upon, he turned his horse and rode back.

"Well, bghrother, now let's go and get dghry," he said to Petya.

Riding up to the forest guardhouse, Denisov stopped, peering into the forest. In the forest, among the trees, a man was walking with big, light strides, on long legs, with long, swinging arms, wearing a jacket, bast shoes, and a Kazan hat, with a gun over his shoulder and an axe in his belt. Seeing Denisov, this man hastily flung something into the bushes and, taking off his soaked hat with its drooping brim, went up to his commander. It was Tikhon. His pockmarked and wrinkled face, with its small, narrow eyes, beamed with self-satisfied merriment. Raising his head high, and as if trying to keep from laughing, he fixed his eyes on Denisov.

"Well, where did you disappear to?" said Denisov.

"Disappear to? I went after the French," Tikhon replied boldly and quickly, in a hoarse but melodious bass.

"Why did you slip in there during the day? Bghrute! So you didn't take . . ."

"I took one, I did," said Tikhon.

"Where is he?"

"I took him first thing at dawn," Tikhon went on, moving his flat, splayed feet in their bast shoes further apart, "and I led him into the forest. I saw he wasn't the right sort. I thought, why don't I go and take another more proper one?"

"See, he's a ghrascal, that's what," Denisov said to the *esaul*. "Why didn't you bring that one?"

"Why bring him," Tikhon interrupted crossly and quickly, "if he's no good? Don't I know what kind you need?"

"Sly dog! . . . So? . . ."

"I went after another," Tikhon continued. "I crawled into the forest like this and lay there," Tikhon unexpectedly and nimbly lay on his belly, acting out how he had done it. "One of them came along," he continued. "I grabbed him like this." Tikhon jumped up quickly and lightly. "'Let's go to the colonel,' I said. He started jabbering. Four of them came. Fell on me with their little swords. I swung my axe like this: 'Come on, Christ help you,'" Tikhon cried, swinging his arms, scowling terribly, and thrusting out his chest.

"We saw from the hill how you cut and ran through the puddles," said the *esaul*, narrowing his bright eyes.

Petya wanted very much to laugh, but he saw that they all kept from laughing. He quickly shifted his gaze from Tikhon's face to the *esaul*'s and Denisov's, not understanding what it all meant.

"Don't play the fool," said Denisov, coughing crossly. "Why didn't you bghring the first one?"

Tikhon began to scratch his back with one hand, his head with the other, and suddenly his whole mug stretched into a beaming, foolish smile, revealing the missing tooth (for which he was nicknamed Shcherbaty—"Gap-toothed"). Denisov smiled, and Petya dissolved in merry laughter, in which Tikhon himself joined.

"No, but he was all wrong," said Tikhon. "Such poor clothes on him, there was no point bringing him here. And a crude one, Your Honor. 'It's like this,' he says, 'I'm a ginneral's son, I won't go,' he says."

"What a bghrute!" said Denisov. "I need to question . . ."

"But I did ask him," said Tikhon. "'Things are bad,' he says—in *signs*. 'There's a lot of us,' he says, 'but in poor shape; just in name only,' he says. 'One good whack,' he says, 'and you'll take them all,'" Tikhon concluded, glancing merrily and resolutely into Denisov's eyes.

"When you get a hundghred hot ones fghrom me, that'll teach you to play the fool," Denisov said sternly.

"Why get angry," said Tikhon, "as if I haven't seen your Frenchmen? Wait till it gets dark, I'll bring you any sort you like, even three of them."

"Well, let's go," said Denisov, and he rode on until they came to the guardhouse, silent and frowning angrily.

Tikhon walked behind, and Petya heard the Cossacks laughing with him and at him about some boots he had thrown into the bushes.

When the laughter that had come over him at Tikhon's words and smile passed, and Petya realized for a moment that this Tikhon had killed a man, he felt uneasy. He glanced at the captive drummer boy and something stabbed his heart. But this uneasiness lasted only a moment. He felt a need to raise his head higher, to encourage himself, and to question the *esaul* about the next day's undertaking, assuming a significant air, so as not to be unworthy of the company he was in.

The officer who had been sent met Denisov on the way with the news that Dolokhov himself would come at once and that for his part all was well.

Denisov suddenly cheered up and called Petya to him.

"Well, tell me about yourself," he said.

VII

Petya, having left his family on their departure from Moscow, had joined his regiment, and soon after that was attached as an orderly to a general in command of a large detachment. Since the time of his promotion to officer, and especially since going on active duty, where he had taken part in the battle of Vyazma, Petya had constantly been in a state of happily excited joy that he was grown up, and in constantly rapturous haste not to miss any occasion for real heroism. He was very happy with what he had seen and experienced in the army, but at the same time it seemed to him all the time that he was not where what was most real and heroic was now happening. And he hurried to get where he was not.

When, on the twenty-first of October, his general expressed the wish to send someone to Denisov's detachment, Petya begged so pitifully to be sent that the general could not refuse. But as he was sending him, the general, recalling Petya's mad behavior at the battle of Vyazma, where, instead of taking to the road and going where he had been sent, he had galloped into the line under French fire and there twice shot off his pistol—as he was sending him, the general precisely forbade Petya to take part in any of Denisov's actions whatever. It was this that had made Petya blush and become confused when Denisov asked if he could stay. Until he rode out to the edge of the forest, Petya thought that, in strict fulfillment of his duty, he ought to return at once. But when he saw the French, saw Tikhon, learned that there would certainly be an attack in the night, he, with a young man's quickness in changing his views, decided to himself that his general, whom till then he had respected very much, was trash, a German, that Denisov was a hero, and the *esaul* was a hero, and Tikhon was a hero, and it was shameful to leave them at a difficult moment.

Night was already falling when Denisov, with Petya and the *esaul*, rode up to the guardhouse. In the semidarkness they could see saddled horses, Cossacks, hussars, setting up little lean-tos in the clearing and making a glowing fire in the wooded ravine (so that the French would not see the smoke). In the front hall of the small cottage, a Cossack, his sleeves rolled up, was carving mutton. Inside the cottage itself, three officers from Denisov's party were setting up a table made from a door. Petya took off his wet things, handed them over to be dried, and at once began to assist the officers in setting up the dinner table.

Ten minutes later, the table was ready, covered with a cloth. On the table stood vodka, a flask of rum, white bread, and roast mutton with salt.

Sitting with the officers at the table and tearing at a greasy hunk of fragrant mutton with his hands, which dripped with fat, Petya was in a rapturous, childlike state of tender love for all people, and consequently of certainty that other people had the same love for him.

"So what do you think, Vassily Fyodorovich," he turned to Denisov, "is it all right if I stay with you for one little day?" And, not waiting for an answer, he answered himself: "I was told to find out, so I'll find out . . . Only let me go to the very . . . to the main . . . I don't need any rewards . . . But I'd like . . ." Petya clenched his teeth and looked around, tossing his raised head and swinging his arms.

"To the main . . ." Denisov repeated, smiling.

"Only, please, give me full command, so that I can be in command," Petya went on. "What is it to you? Ah, you need a knife?" he turned to an officer who wanted to cut some mutton. And he gave him his pocketknife.

The officer praised the knife.

"Keep it, please. I've got many like it . . ." Petya said, blushing. "Good heavens! I completely forgot," he suddenly cried. "I've got wonderful raisins, you know, the seedless kind. We have a new sutler—and such excellent things. I bought ten pounds. I'm used to something sweet. Would you like some? . . ." And Petya ran to the front hall, to his Cossack, and brought back bags with some five pounds of raisins. "Eat, gentlemen, eat."

"And don't you need a coffee pot?" he turned to the *esaul*. "I bought one from our sutler, it's wonderful! He has excellent things. And he's very honest. That's the main thing. I'll make sure to send you one. Or maybe you're out of flints—they get used up, you know. I brought some along, I've got them here," he pointed to the bags, "a hundred flints. I bought them very cheap. Please, take as many as you like, or even all of them . . ." And suddenly, afraid that he had let his tongue run away with him, Petya stopped and blushed.

He began to recall whether he had done any other stupid things. And, going through his memories of that day, he stopped at the memory of the French drummer boy. "It's fine for us, but how about him? Where have they put him? Have they fed him? Have they mistreated him?" he thought. But, realizing that he had gotten carried away with the flints, he was now wary.

"I could ask," he thought, "but they'll say: 'He's a boy himself and he feels sorry for a boy.' I'll show them tomorrow what sort of boy I am! Will it be shameful if I ask?" thought Petya. "Well, what difference does it make!"—and at once, blushing and looking fearfully at the officers to see if there was any mockery in their faces, he said:

"And can I call that boy you captured? to give him something to eat . . . maybe . . ."

"Yes, a pitiful lad," said Denisov, obviously finding nothing shameful in this reminder. "Call him here. His name's Vincent Bosse. Call him."

"I'll call him," said Petya.

"Call him, call him. A pitiful lad," Denisov repeated.

Petya was standing by the door when Denisov said that. He squeezed between the officers and went up close to Denisov.

"Allow me to kiss you, dear heart," he said. "Ah, how excellent! how good!" And, having kissed Denisov, he ran outside.

"Bosse! Vincent!" cried Petya, stopping by the door.

"Who do you want, sir?" a voice said from the darkness. Petya replied that it was the French boy who had been captured that day.

"Ah! Vesenny?" said a Cossack.

His name Vincent had already been changed into Vesenny by the Cossacks, into Visenya by the muzhiks and soldiers. Both changes brought together a reminder of springtime with the idea of a young boy.

"He was warming up by the fire. Hey, Visenya! Visenya! Vesenny!" echoing voices and laughter were heard in the darkness.

"He's a sharp little lad," said a hussar who was standing by Petya. "We gave him something to eat earlier. He was dying of hunger!"

Footsteps were heard in the darkness, and the drummer boy, splashing barefoot through the mud, came up to the door.

"*Ah, c'est vous!*" said Petya. "*Voulez-vous manger? N'ayez pas peur, on ne vous fera pas de mal,*" he added, touching his hand timidly and tenderly. "*Entrez, entrez.*"[3]

"*Merci, monsieur,*" the drummer boy replied in a trembling voice, almost a child's, and began wiping his muddy feet on the threshold. Petya would have liked to say many things to the drummer boy, but he did not dare. He stood beside him in the front hall, shifting from foot to foot. Then he took his hand in the darkness and pressed it.

"*Entrez, entrez,*" he only repeated in a tender whisper.

"Ah, what can I do for him?" Petya said to himself and, opening the door, he let the boy go in past him.

When the drummer boy had entered the cottage, Petya sat down at some distance from him, considering that it was humiliating for him to pay attention to him. He only felt the money in his pocket, and wondered whether it would be shameful for him to give it to the drummer boy.

VIII

From the drummer boy, who, on Denisov's instructions, was given vodka and mutton, and whom Denisov ordered dressed in a Russian kaftan, so that he could stay with the party and not be sent away

3. Ah, it's you! . . . Would you like to eat? Don't be afraid, nobody will hurt you . . . Come in, come in.

with the prisoners, Petya's attention was distracted by the arrival of Dolokhov. In the army, Petya had heard many stories of Dolokhov's extraordinary courage and cruelty to the French, and therefore, once Dolokhov entered the cottage, Petya gazed at him without taking his eyes away, and kept encouraging himself by tossing his raised head, so as not to be unworthy even of such company as Dolokhov.

Dolokhov's appearance struck Petya strangely by its simplicity.

Denisov was dressed in a Cossack coat, wore a beard and an icon of St. Nicholas the Wonderworker on his chest, and in his manner of speaking, in all his ways, expressed the singularity of his position. Dolokhov, on the contrary, who formerly in Moscow had worn Persian dress, now had the look of a most prim officer of the guards. His face was cleanshaven, he was dressed in a padded guardsman's jacket with a St. George in the buttonhole and in a simple peaked cap set straight on his head. He took off his wet felt cape in the corner and, going up to Denisov, without greeting anyone, at once began asking him about business. Denisov told him about the designs that the large detachments had on their transport, about the sending of Petya, and about his response to the two generals. Then Denisov told him all he knew about the position of the French.

"That's all very well, but we must know what kind of troops they are and how many," said Dolokhov. "We'll have to go there. We can't go into action without knowing for certain how many they are. I like to do things neatly. So, gentlemen, does anyone want to go with me to their camp? I've got uniforms with me."

"Me, me . . . I'll go with you!" cried Petya.

"There's no need at all for you to go," said Denisov, addressing Dolokhov, "and him I won't let go for anything."

"That's just fine!" cried Petya. "Why can't I go? . . ."

"Because there's no need."

"Well, excuse me, because . . . because . . . I'm going, that's all. Will you take me?" he turned to Dolokhov.

"Why not . . ." Dolokhov answered distractedly, peering into the face of the French drummer boy.

"Have you had this little fellow long?" he asked Denisov.

"We took him today, but he doesn't know anything. I'm keeping him with me."

"And where do the rest disappear to?" asked Dolokhov.

"Meaning what? I send them off and take ghreceipts!" Denisov cried, suddenly turning red. "And I say boldly that I don't have a single man on my conscience. Is it hard for you to send thirty or even thghree hundghred men to town under escort, instead—I'll say it outghright—instead of besmighrching the honor of a soldier?"

"Such niceties would be fitting for the little sixteen-year-old count here," Dolokhov said with a cold smirk, "but it's time you gave them up."

"What, I'm not saying anything, I'm only saying that I'll definitely go with you," Petya said timidly.

"But for you and me, brother, it's time to drop these niceties," Dolokhov went on, as if he found a special pleasure in talking about this subject, which irritated Denisov. "Now, why have you taken this one with you?" he said, shaking his head. "Because you feel sorry for him? We know those receipts of yours. You send off a hundred men, thirty will arrive. The rest will starve to death or be killed. Does it make any difference if you don't take them?"

The *esaul*, narrowing his pale eyes, nodded approvingly.

"That makes no diffeghrence, there's nothing to discuss. I don't want to take it on my soul. You say they'll die. Veghry well. As long as it's not because of me."

Dolokhov laughed.

"Who told them not to capture me twenty times over? But if they do—for me and for you, with all your chivalry, it's the same aspen tree." He paused. "Anyhow, we've got to get down to business. Send for my Cossack with the bundle! I have two French uniforms. Well, are you coming with me?" he asked Petya.

"Me? Yes, yes, definitely," cried Petya, blushing almost to the point of tears and glancing at Denisov.

While Dolokhov was arguing with Denisov about what to do with the prisoners, Petya had again felt uneasy and hurried; but again he had not quite managed to understand what they were talking about.

"If the big, famous ones think like that, it means it must be so, it means it's good," he thought. "And, above all, Denisov mustn't think that I'll obey him, that he can command me. I'll definitely go to the French camp with Dolokhov. If he can, I can!"

To all Denisov's persuasions not to go, Petya replied that he was also used to doing everything neatly and not any old way, and that he never thought about the danger to himself.

"Because—you yourself will agree—if we don't know for certain how many there are, the lives of hundreds may depend on it, and here it's just us, and I also want it very much, and I'll definitely go, I will, you won't hold me back," he said, "that will only be worse . . ."

IX

Having put on French uniforms and shakos, Petya and Dolokhov rode to the clearing from which Denisov had looked at the camp and, riding out of the forest in total darkness, descended into the hollow. On reaching the bottom, Dolokhov told the Cossacks who accompanied them to wait there and rode at a sturdy trot down the road to the bridge. Petya, his heart thrilling with excitement, rode beside him.

"If we're caught, I won't surrender alive, I've got a pistol," Petya whispered.

"Don't speak Russian," Dolokhov said in a quick whisper, and at the same moment they heard a call from the darkness: "*Qui vive?*"[4] and the cocking of a musket.

The blood rushed to Petya's face, and he gripped his pistol.

"*Lanciers du 6e*,"[5] said Dolokhov, without slowing or increasing the pace of his horse. The black figure of the sentry stood on the bridge.

"*Mot d'ordre?*"[6]

Dolokhov reined in his horse and rode slowly.

4. Who goes there?
5. Lancers of the sixth.
6. Password?

"*Dites donc, le colonel Gérard est ici?*"[7] he said.

"*Mot d'ordre!*" the sentry said without replying and barred his way.

"*Quand un officier fait sa ronde, les sentinelles ne demandent pas le mot d'ordre . . .*" cried Dolokhov, suddenly flaring up and riding his horse into the sentry. "*Je vous demande si le colonel est ici?*"[8]

And, not waiting for a reply from the sentry, who stepped aside, Dolokhov rode up the hill at a walk.

Noticing the black shadow of a man crossing the road, Dolokhov stopped him and asked where the commander and the officers were. This man, with a sack on his back, a soldier, stopped, came up close to Dolokhov's horse, touched it with his hand, and told him simply and amicably that the commander and the officers were further up the hill, to the right, in the courtyard of the farmhouse (as he called the manor house).

Riding up the road, from both sides of which came the sounds of French talk around the campfires, Dolokhov turned into the courtyard of the manor house. Riding through the gates, he got off his horse and went up to a big, blazing campfire, around which several men sat talking loudly. In a pot at the edge of the fire something was cooking, and a soldier in a cap and blue uniform, on his knees, brightly lit up by the fire, was stirring it with a ramrod.

"*Oh, c'est un dur à cuire*,"[9] said one of the officers, sitting in the shadow on the opposite side of the fire.

"*Il les fera marcher les lapins . . .*"[10] another said, laughing. They both fell silent, peering into the darkness at the sound of Dolokhov's and Petya's footsteps as they approached the fire with their horses.

"*Bonjour, messieurs!*" Dolokhov said loudly and distinctly.

7. Tell me, is Colonel Gérard here?

8. When an officer is making his rounds, the sentries do not ask for the password . . . I ask you, is the colonel here?

9. Oh, he's a hard nut to crack.

10. He'll make the rabbits scurry . . .

The officers stirred in the shadow of the fire, and one, a tall officer with a long neck, went up to Dolokhov.

"*C'est vous, Clément?*" he said. "*D'où, diable . . .*"[11] but he did not finish, realizing his mistake, and, frowning slightly, greeted Dolokhov as a stranger, asking what he could do for him. Dolokhov told him that he and his comrade were trying to catch up with their regiment, and asked, addressing them all in general, whether the officers knew anything about the sixth regiment. No one knew anything, and Petya thought that the officers were beginning to look at him and Dolokhov with animosity and suspicion. For a few seconds they were all silent.

"*Si vous comptez sur la soupe du soir, vous venez trop tard,*"[12] a voice said from behind the fire with restrained laughter.

Dolokhov replied that they were not hungry and had to be on their way that night.

He handed the horses to the soldier who was stirring the pot and squatted by the fire next to the officer with the long neck. This officer, not taking his eyes off Dolokhov, asked again what regiment he was from. Dolokhov did not reply, as if he had not heard the question and, lighting up a short French pipe that he took from his pocket, asked the officers how far the road ahead was safe from Cossacks.

"*Les brigands sont partout,*"[13] replied the officer from behind the fire.

Dolokhov said that Cossacks were only a fear for stray ones like him and his comrade, but added questioningly that they probably did not dare to attack large detachments. No one made any reply.

"Well, now he'll leave," Petya kept thinking every moment,
standing before the fire and listening to his conversation.

But Dolokhov began the stalled conversation again and started asking directly how many men were in their battalion, how many

11. Is that you, Clément? . . . Where the devil . . .

12. If you're counting on the evening soup, you're too late.

13. The brigands are everywhere.

battalions, how many prisoners. Asking about the Russian prisoners who were with their detachment, Dolokhov said:

"*La vilaine affaire de trainer ces cadavres après soi. Vaudrait mieux fusiller cette canaille*,"[14] and burst loudly into such strange laughter that Petya thought the French would see through the deceit at once, and he involuntarily stepped back from the fire. No one responded to Dolokhov's words and laughter, and the French officer who could not be seen (he was lying wrapped in his greatcoat) rose slightly and whispered something to his comrade. Dolokhov got up and called the soldier with the horses.

"Will they bring the horses or not?" wondered Petya, involuntarily moving close to Dolokhov.

The horses were brought.

"*Bonjour, messieurs*," said Dolokhov.

Petya wanted to say *bonsoir*[15] but could not bring the word out. The officers were whispering something among themselves. Dolokhov took a long time mounting his horse, which would not stand still; then he rode through the gates at a walk. Petya rode beside him, wishing and not daring to turn around to see if the French were running after them or not.

Coming out to the road, Dolokhov did not ride back to the field but went through the village. In one place he stopped, listening.

"You hear?" he said.

Petya recognized the sounds of Russian voices and saw the dark figures of Russian prisoners by the fires. Descending to the bridge, Petya and Dolokhov rode past the sentry, who gloomily paced the bridge without saying a word, and went down into the hollow where the Cossacks were waiting.

"Well, and now good-bye. Tell Denisov it's set for dawn, at the first shot," said Dolokhov, and he was about to leave, but Petya seized him by the sleeve.

14. Nasty business dragging these corpses behind you. Better to shoot the scum.

15. Good night.

"No!" he cried, "you're such a hero! Ah, how good! How excellent! How I love you!"

"All right, all right," said Dolokhov, but Petya would not let go of him, and in the darkness Dolokhov made out that Petya was leaning towards him. He wanted to kiss. Dolokhov kissed him, laughed, and, turning his horse, disappeared into the darkness.

X

On returning to the guardhouse, Petya found Denisov in the front hall. Alarmed, anxious, and vexed with himself for having let Petya go, Denisov was waiting for him.

"Thank God!" he cried. "Well, thank God!" he repeated, listening to Petya's rapturous story. "Devil take you, I haven't slept because of you!" said Denisov. "Well, thank God, now go to bed. We can still get some sleep before morning."

"Yes . . . No," said Petya. "I don't want to sleep yet. And I know myself, if I fall asleep, that's the end. And then I usually don't sleep before a battle."

Petya sat for a while in the cottage, joyfully recalling the details of his ride and vividly imagining how tomorrow would be. Then, noticing that Denisov had fallen asleep, he got up and went outside.

Outside it was still quite dark. The rain had stopped long ago, but drops were still falling from the trees. Close to the guardhouse, he could see the black outlines of the Cossacks' lean-tos and the horses tethered together. Behind the cottage, the two wagons showed black, with horses standing by them, and the dying fire glowed in the ravine. Not all the Cossacks and hussars were asleep: here and there, along with the sound of falling drops and the closer sound of horses munching, he could hear soft, as if whispering voices.

Petya stepped out of the front hall, looked around in the darkness, and went over to the wagons. Someone was snoring under the wagons, and around them stood saddled horses, munching oats. In the darkness, Petya made out his horse, whom he called Karabakh, though it was a Little Russian horse, and went over to it.

"Well, Karabakh, tomorrow we'll do some service," he said, sniffing its nostrils and kissing it.

"What, master, you're not asleep?" said a Cossack who was sitting under a wagon.

"No, but . . . your name is Likhachev, I believe? I've just come back. We took a ride to the French."

And Petya told the Cossack in detail, not only about his ride, but also why he had gone and why he thought it was better to risk his life than to act any old way.

"Why don't you get some sleep?" said the Cossack.

"No, I'm used to it," Petya replied. "Maybe the flints in your pistols are worn out? I brought some with me. Don't you need some? Take them."

The Cossack stuck himself out from under the wagon to have a closer look at Petya.

"Because I like to do everything neatly," said Petya. "Some do things just like that, anyhow, without preparing, and then they're sorry. I don't like that."

"Right you are," said the Cossack.

"And another thing: please sharpen my saber, dear heart; it's gotten bl . . ." (but Petya was afraid to lie)—"it's never been sharpened. Can it be done?"

"Why not?"

Likhachev stood up, rummaged in the packs, and Petya soon heard the martial sound of steel against a whetstone. He clambered onto the wagon and sat on its edge. The Cossack under the wagon was sharpening the saber.

"And what, are the lads asleep?" asked Petya.

"Some are, and some are like us."

"Well, and what about the boy?"

"Vesenny? He's there in the front hall, just dropped off. Fright makes you sleep. He was so glad."

After that Petya was silent for a long time, listening to the sounds. Footsteps came from the darkness, and a black figure appeared.

"What are you sharpening?" asked the man, coming up to the wagon.

"A saber for the master here."

"That's a good thing," said the man, whom Petya took for a hussar. "Did I leave my bowl here?"

"There, by the wheel."

The hussar took the bowl.

"Likely it'll be light soon," he said, yawning, and went off somewhere.

Petya ought to have known that he was in the forest, in Denisov's party, a mile from the road, that he was sitting on a wagon captured from the French with horses tethered by it, and that under him sat the Cossack Likhachev, sharpening his saber, that the big black spot to the right was the guardhouse, and the bright red spot down to the left was the dying campfire, that the man who had come for the bowl was a hussar who wanted a drink; but he knew nothing of that and did not want to know. He was in a magic kingdom, in which there was nothing resembling reality. Maybe the big black spot was indeed the guardhouse, but maybe it was a cave that led into the very depths of the earth. Maybe the red spot was a fire, but maybe it was the eye of a huge monster. Maybe he is indeed sitting on a wagon now, but it very well may be that he is sitting, not on a wagon, but on a terribly tall tower, from which, if you fell, it would take you a whole day, a whole month, to reach the earth—you would keep falling and never get there. Maybe it is simply the Cossack Likhachev sitting under the wagon, but it very well may be that he is the kindest, bravest, most wonderful, most excellent man in the world, whom nobody knows. Maybe it was indeed a hussar who came for water and went back into the hollow, but maybe he just vanished from sight, vanished completely, and never was.

Whatever Petya might have seen now, nothing would have astonished him. He was in a magic kingdom in which everything was possible.

He looked at the sky. The sky was as magical as the earth. The sky was clearing, and clouds raced over the treetops, as if uncovering the stars. Sometimes it seemed that the clouds dispersed and a black, clear sky appeared. Sometimes it seemed that these black patches were clouds. Sometimes it seemed that the sky rose high, high above his head; sometimes the sky came right down, so that he could touch it with his hand.

Petya began to close his eyes and rock.

Drops dripped. Quiet talk went on. Horses neighed and scuffled. Someone snored.

"Ozhik, zhik, ozhik, zhik . . ." whistled the saber being sharpened. And suddenly Petya heard a harmonious chorus of music, playing some unknown, solemnly sweet hymn. Petya was musical, like Natasha, and more so than Nikolai, but he had never studied music or thought about music, and therefore the melodies that unexpectedly came to his head were especially new and attractive to him. The music played more and more audibly. The melody grew, passing from one instrument to another. What is known as a fugue was going on, though Petya had not the slightest idea of what a fugue was. Each instrument, now resembling a violin, now trumpets—but better and clearer than violins and trumpets—each instrument played its own part and, before finishing its motif, merged with another, starting out almost the same, and with a third, and with a fourth, and they all merged into one and scattered again, and merged again, now solemn and churchly, now brightly brilliant and victorious.

"Ah, yes, it's me dreaming," Petya said to himself, rocking forward. "It's in my ears. And maybe it's my music. Well, again. Go on, my music! Now! . . ."

He closed his eyes. And on all sides, as if from far away, sounds trembled, began to harmonize, scattered, merged, and again all joined in the same sweet and solemn hymn. "Ah, how lovely that is! As much as I like and however I like," Petya said to himself. He attempted to conduct this huge chorus of instruments.

"Softer, softer now, fade away." And the sounds obeyed him. "Fuller now, merrier. More, more joyful." And swelling, solemn sounds rose from an unknown depth. "Now, voices, join in!" Petya ordered. And voices, first men's, then women's, came from far away.

The voices grew, grew in a measured, solemn effort. Petya felt frightened and joyful hearkening to their uncommon beauty.

The song merged with the solemn, victorious march, and drops dripped, and bzhik, zhik, zhik . . . whistled the saber, and again the horses scuffled and neighed, not disrupting the chorus, but entering into it.

Petya did not know how long it went on; he enjoyed it, was surprised all the while at his enjoyment and sorry there was no one to share in it. He was awakened by Likhachev's gentle voice.

"It's ready, Your Honor, you'll split a Frenchman right in two." Petya woke up.

"It's getting light already, really getting light!" he cried.

The formerly invisible horses could now be seen down to their tails, and a watery light was coming through the bared branches. Petya shook himself, jumped up, took a rouble from his pocket and gave it to Likhachev, swung the saber to try it out, and put it in the scabbard. The Cossacks were untying the horses and tightening their saddle girths.

"And here's the commander," said Likhachev.

Denisov came out of the guardhouse and, calling Petya, told him to get ready.

XI

In the half-darkness, horses were quickly taken, girths were tightened, and units were formed. Denisov stood by the guardhouse giving last-minute orders. The infantry of the party, splashing with a hundred feet, went ahead on the road and quickly disappeared among the trees in the predawn mist. The *esaul* was giving some orders to the Cossacks. Petya was holding his horse by the bridle, waiting impatiently for the order to mount up. Washed with cold water, his face, especially his eyes, burned with fire, a chill ran down his spine, and something trembled rapidly and regularly all over his body.

"Well, is everything ghready?" asked Denisov. "Bghring the horses."

The horses were brought. Denisov got angry with the Cossack for the slack girth and, having rebuked him, mounted up. Petya took hold of the stirrup. The horse, out of habit, went to nip him in the leg, but Petya, not feeling his own weight, quickly leaped into the saddle and, looking back at the hussars who set out behind him in the darkness, rode up to Denisov.

"Vassily Fyodorovich, will you entrust me with something? Please . . . for God's sake . . ." he said. Denisov seemed to have forgotten about Petya's existence. He looked at him.

"One thing I ask of you," he said sternly, "listen to me and don't poke your nose anywhere."

During the whole traverse, Denisov did not say a word more to Petya and rode silently. When they rode up to the edge of the forest, it was beginning to grow noticeably light in the field. Denisov said something in a whisper to the *esaul*, and the Cossacks began to ride past Petya and Denisov. When they had all ridden past, Denisov touched up his horse and rode down the hill. Sitting back and sliding, the horses and riders descended into the hollow. Petya rode beside Denisov. The trembling in his whole body kept increasing. It was growing brighter and brighter, only the mist hid distant objects. Having ridden down and looked around, Denisov nodded to a Cossack who was standing next to him.

"The signal!" he said.

The Cossack raised his hand; a shot rang out. And at the same moment came the thud of horses galloping ahead, shouts from different sides, and more shots.

At the same moment, as the sound of thudding hoofs and shouts rang out, Petya, lashing his horse and loosing the reins, not listening to Denisov, who was shouting to him, galloped forward. It seemed to Petya that it suddenly became completely bright, like midday, just as the shot rang out. He rode up to the bridge. Ahead of him Cossacks were galloping along the road. On the bridge he ran into a Cossack who lagged behind and galloped on. Ahead of him some people—it must have been the French—were running from the right side of the road to the left. One fell into the mud under the feet of Petya's horse.

By one cottage, Cossacks were crowded, doing something. A terrible cry came from the midst of the crowd. Petya rode up to this crowd, and the first thing he saw was the pale face of a Frenchman with a trembling lower jaw, who was clutching the shaft of a pike pointed at him.

"Hurrah! . . . Lads . . . ours . . ." cried Petya, and, giving free rein to his excited horse, he rode on up the street.

Shooting was heard ahead. Cossacks, hussars, and ragged Russian prisoners were running along both sides of the street, shouting something loudly and incoherently. A dashing Frenchman in a blue greatcoat, hatless, with a red, frowning face, was fighting off some hussars with his bayonet. When Petya galloped up, the Frenchman had already fallen. "Late again," flashed in Petya's head, and he rode to where he heard the sounds of rapid gunfire. The shots were coming from the courtyard of the manor house, where he had been the night before with Dolokhov. The French had ensconced themselves there behind the wattle fence, in a garden densely overgrown with bushes, and were firing at the Cossacks crowding in the gateway. Riding up to the gate, Petya saw Dolokhov amidst the powder smoke, with a pale, greenish face, shouting something to the men. "Go around! Wait for the infantry!" he was shouting just as Petya rode up to him.

"Wait? . . . Hurra-a-ah! . . ." shouted Petya, and, not losing a moment, he galloped towards the place from which the shots were coming and where the powder smoke was thickest. A volley of shots rang out, stray bullets whined and splatted into something. The Cossacks and Dolokhov galloped after Petya through the gates of the house. In the dense, undulating smoke some of the French dropped their weapons and ran out of the bushes towards the Cossacks, others ran down the hill to the pond. Petya galloped on his horse along the manor courtyard, and, instead of holding the reins, waved both arms somehow strangely and quickly, and kept slipping further and further to one side in his saddle. Running into the campfire smoldering in the morning light, the horse balked, and Petya fell heavily onto the wet ground. The Cossacks saw how his arms and legs jerked rapidly, though his head did not move. His head had been pierced by a bullet.

Having parleyed with the senior French officer, who came out to him from behind the house with a handkerchief on his sword and announced that they would surrender, Dolokhov got off his horse and went over to Petya, who lay motionless with outstretched arms.

"Finished," he said, frowning, and walked out of the gates to meet Denisov, who was riding towards him.

"Killed?!" cried Denisov, seeing from far off the familiar, undoubtedly lifeless, position in which Petya's body lay.

"Finished," Dolokhov repeated, as if uttering this word gave him pleasure, and walked quickly to the prisoners surrounded by dismounted Cossacks. "We won't take any!" he cried to Denisov.

Denisov did not reply. He rode up to Petya, got off his horse, and with trembling hands turned Petya's face towards him. It was stained with blood and mud and already turning pale.

"I'm used to something sweet. Excellent raisins, take them all," he recalled. And the Cossacks glanced around in surprise at the sounds, similar to a dog's barking, with which Denisov quickly turned away, went to the wattle fence, and caught hold of it.

Among the Russian prisoners retaken by Denisov and Dolokhov was Pierre Bezukhov.

Summer 2007

A Desirable Woman

Wendell Berry

for Tanya and David Charlton

She was not beautiful according to the standards of the magazines and moving pictures of the time, and she knew it. But by any standard she was a desirable woman, and she also knew that. She knew it from what she had seen in the eyes of certain men, to which from time to time she had felt something like an echo in herself.

That she was desirable was acceptable to her as a part of the liveliness and also the goodness of the world. It was a gift. But that she was desirable and knew it and accepted it unfitted her somewhat for her role as a minister's wife. It was not expected. She had not expected it herself until her own wits told her it was so. Part of her desirability was her look of knowing more than she was saying, and of being amused by the difference. That, and the utter frankness of her presence. There was in her, even in old age, a declarative force of being that was unhesitating and without disguise.

She was born Laura Stafe. She became Laura Milby. She was in love with her husband and would remain so. Another gift. This was not just because she knew she was desirable to him, as he to her—they had settled that soon enough—but from the beginning she had sensed a goodness in him that she knew she could trust. Later it seemed to her that she had not known such trust was in her until he called it from her and she gave it.

They met at a small denominational college where her parents had sent her because they thought it a safe place to send a girl, and where he had come, after an interval of employment in his father's small lumberyard, to prepare for the ministry. His name was Williams Milby. When they were introduced, she laughed. "Oh! Do they call you Bills?"

His reply, the grin subtracted, she thought was elegant, even courtly: "Not yet, ma'am. But if *you* call me that, that's my name."

He was a good-looking young man, regular of feature and curly haired, his countenance so open and unassuming that it might have passed for naïve except for a self-knowing good humor that sometimes lighted it. He attracted her also because the seriousness, even the solemnity, of his vocation already hung about him as a kind of obscurity, and she loved her own power of drawing him forth, in person, out of that shadow.

"What do you want? What do you want for your own self," she asked. "Oh, that! Oh!" She looked straight at him then, and her laugh undisguised them both.

The day after they were graduated they were married. That was 1938.

They went in the fall of the same year, not having known for a whole summer where they would go, to serve a small church known as The Little Flock at a place called Sycamore on the south side of the Ohio River. Sycamore had once been a river port of some note, but was by then merely a ferry landing, two general stores, two churches, a blacksmith shop, a bank, a loose assemblage of houses, and three shantyboats tied up to trees along the river.

The church paid in money "not much more than you could put in your eye," as one of the members forthrightly told them. But it provided also a parsonage of three rooms, with a cistern and pump conveniently at the back door, a garden spot, and at the back of the garden a privy. Thus they were saved the necessity of living out the rest of the Depression on love alone.

They were neither passive nor incapable, neither careless nor low spirited. They made the most of their garden. Their house was cooled by a huge elm that threw its shadow over it on summer afternoons; in winter it was snug. And the little they were paid in money was aboundingly supplemented in kind: a sack of fresh sausage or an old ham, a dressed chicken, jars of fruit or vegetables or pickles or preserves, baked goods or fresh fish or wild honey. These gifts were sometimes brought to them openly for their commendation and their pleased surprise, sometimes left on their back porch when they were not at home.

There was little enough of money at large in Sycamore at that time, but it was rich in the produce of its fields and woods and the river, and to their young preacher and his wife the church members in general were freehearted to a fault.

The town accepted the arrival of the young strangers, "Brother Milby" and "Mrs. Milby," without surprise. It had expected that they would come, as it expected that they would eventually go. It accepted them formally when the congregation of his church sat down on Sunday morning and listened respectfully to Williams Milby's inaugural sermon. It accepted them less formally by helping them to settle into their house and by giving them things they needed. It accepted them in fact by admitting them into the flow of its talk, the unceasing meandering of its story of itself by which it diverted, amused, and consoled itself.

Small as it was, the town seemed to them to be inundated with self-knowledge. This knowledge moved over it in an unresting current, some of it in stories told openly that eddied with variations from teller to teller and place to place, some of it more darkly and quietly in an undertow of caution, sometimes fraught with the unacknowledged pleasure of malice, sometimes bearing a burden merely of anxiety or concern. It was this subsurface current of gossip that Williams Milby learned to listen to with greatest care, for it told him where needs were.

Needs were everywhere. Sycamore had suffered the poor agricultural economy of the 1920s. It had been hit hard by the Depression of the 1930s, by the severe drouths of 1930 and 1936, and by the great flood of January 1937. But it was a community of farm people and of people related to farmers and dependent on farming. They had never expected to live independently of the weather or to be free of hardship and struggle. They suffered as they had to suffer and did as they had to do. They also knew of one another's struggles, and as they could, they helped.

Also, by their own modest standards and by their skills and thrift, they throve. Because none of them had ever been overly prosperous, their losses were never great. It was not the sort of place where people took large economic risks or contracted large debts. It says much for the hardiness of the place that its population increased during the Depression, as young Sycamoreans who had gone to the cities to prosper returned home to survive.

There were the Wallis twins, Goebel and Noble, elderly sons of an ancient mother, bachelors forevermore, good farmers, both independent and neighborly, who did according to their reasons which often were both unexpectable and unobjectionable, and who drove into town every Saturday afternoon in their like-new Model A, in which they sat side by side, dressed in like-new tan work clothes starched and ironed as stiff almost as tin.

And there was Mrs. Etta Mae Berry, an elderly widow for whom the truth was ever too tame. One day, as she was scattering corn for her hens, a big airplane flew over so low that it blew her dress practically over her head, and she could hear the people talking inside. And she was never sick because she always looked for germs in the dipper before she drank; if she saw any she skimmed them out with a spoon.

There was Uncle Lute Wisely, born a slave, who remembered everything, and now, too old to work, he moved, as he said, in winter from fire to fire and in summer from shade to shade. There had never been many of his race around Sycamore, and now, all the younger ones gone north, he was the last.

There was the family of Bernice and Red Callahan who were sitting at dinner when a big snake fell through the ceiling onto the table, causing, but only indirectly, much breakage of chairs and other furniture and some bodily injury.

On one of the shantyboats lived the perhaps married couple, Lizard Eye and Zinnia Creed, joyfully Frenchified by the Sycamoreans as "Mr. and Mrs. Lizzard." Zinnia Creed was widely esteemed for her language, which was purely her own. When she picked blackberries, the chiggers broke her out all over in whelps. Sometimes the summer apples got all swiveled up before they could be eaten. There was a famous day when she had come to town for a gallon of coal oil, and the lecrik went off and every light bug in Jones's Merchandise went out all to-wunst. She had seen two cars meet in a headlong collusion. She loved, moreover, to refine her pronunciation by adding r's to words such as "crush" and "crunch" and "push" so that they came out "crursh" and "crurnch" and "pursh." Virtually everybody in Sycamore had learned Zinnian and spoke it on every appropriate occasion.

Of these and others, as church members or as not members, the Milbys were given knowledge.

You could usefully think of the consciousness of Sycamore as the continual, continually wandering story that in one way or another included everybody, carrying them through time like the current of the river.

Or, usefully also, you could think of it as graduated depths in that flow. At the top was the convivial talk, open and unembarrassed. Below that, quieter and darker and less free, was the talk that issued from fear and envy, cherished grudges and resentments, meannesses, suspicions, unforgiven or unregretted wrongs. This was not so readily heard by newcomers, but the Milbys stayed long enough (they stayed until after the end of World War II) to hear most of it, if not all. It proved itself continually to be present, to be regrettable, and sometimes to be worried about.

Below that, much quieter and darker, and yet to the conscience of the young minister most present of all, was the depth at which the community suffered its mortality, error, pain, and grief. How many among the older wives or widows had buried a child struck down by a winter illness or an epidemic, who now remembered in silence?

As the knowledge of this depth of suffering grew upon her, Laura understood, as she had not before, the gravity of her husband's calling, for she saw that it was to this suffering that he was called. As he sank inevitably into it or as it rose inevitably out of its depth, its quietness and darkness, to meet him, she saw not only the gravity of his calling but its authenticity. For Williams Milby had the gift of comforting. He carried with him, not by his will, it seemed, but by the purest gift, the very presence of comfort. And yet even as it was a comfort to others, it could be a bafflement and a burden to him. His calling, and the respect accorded to it, admitted him into the presence of troubles he could not mend. When old Mr. Jones McKinney, who had been sick for a long time, finally died, and afterwards his old wife, Aunt Ruth, would hear him calling her in the night and would get up and go to his bed and again find it empty, what could any living mortal do for her that would be of any use at all? A living mortal could do only as Williams Milby did: go and sit with her while she mourned, and then leave her in her mourning, for no living mortal could sit with another time without end. It was plain to him—and Laura knew this—that he was always hopelessly in debt to his own ministry, for he could not give all that he wanted and longed to give. He was needed, even so, and what he had to give, and more, was continually asked of him. People were glad to see him coming. They called him to come. They were glad to have him around when they did not need him, just for the assurance that he would be at hand when they did need him.

And as Laura had earlier given him her trust that until then she did not know was hers, now she granted him a sort of honor that was not personal, not hers or his, but honor to his vocation that he had not known was his until he began to fulfill it.

At Sycamore, then, Laura grew with her husband into a life that probably neither of them had expected. She grew also into knowledge of the church's function of iteration. The church house itself, she now saw, was a place consecrated to the proclamation over and over again of things in which most of the members more or less believed but in which they generally were not greatly interested, and which they helped to make uninteresting by their lack of interest. It was a place where nearly all of the women seemed to feel at home, and where many of the men clearly were not at home. In bearable weather the men would stand outside before the service began, holding themselves until the last minute in one another's company and the unconfined light and air of mere day.

For nearly the whole congregation, or for all of them, and especially the men and children, there was a disconnection between the little white clapboard church with its steeple and bell, its observances and forms of worship, and the world's daily life and work. It was as though the building itself, in its emptiness between services, contained along with its smells of old paper and stale perfume a solemnity that the people entered into and departed from, quickening it for a few hours a week with the stirrings and smells of living flesh, but could neither inflect with the tone of their daily preoccupations nor transpose into their actual lives. This was a disconnection perhaps exactly coextensive with the disconnection they felt between Heaven and Sycamore, eternity and time. Laura recognized these disconnections in the people because she felt them, and labored over them, in herself.

Thus she mapped in her mind the cracks and flaws in the lives of the church and the place. She had been a studious girl, and beyond that a thoughtful one. Since before she'd had much to ponder, she'd been in the habit of pondering. She was a conscious, thoughtful believer in the Gospel that her husband had bound himself to offer and defend, even to obey and enact—that is, to suffer. But the things that she struggled with he seemed to accept with a silence that included a measure of resignation. He could be quiet because in some depth of himself he *was* quiet. She recognized this as his strength, his very faith, at the same time that it fretted her.

Of the pair, hers was the mind that was restless and questing, enticed and disturbed by mysteries. That the world was as it was did not save it from her sense that it might in many ways be different. It seemed to her both tentative and final, unshakable and woefully fragile.

Her husband's ministry, as he conceived it, was not only to the church but to the whole community, and this often involved a thanklessness hard for her to bear. Not only did he stand up week after week to say and to offer again what he and generations of ministers before him had said and offered before, with no dramatic amelioration of this world as a result, but also he made himself answerable to any and every sufferer within a radius of five or six miles. Any sufferer who was in need or want of him could summon him, even by the ringing of the telephone in the middle of a stormy or frozen night, and he would go.

And when, having done all he could do to help a family through a quarrel or an illness or a death, performing services he was not paid for and could not have been paid for, he might never hear from them again, let alone see their faces even for the courtesy of one Sunday among his hearers, Laura felt herself wounded with sorrow for him and anger at them for their ingratitude.

"It's not right!" she cried to him once, breaking for that once into his silence about it. "It's *just not right!*"

"No. It's not right," he said quietly, and he gave her his smile with which he sought to quiet her. "But it's all right."

And yet she knew his own need for comfort, for shelter, for her herself, and for the welcome it was her need, in turn, to offer to him. They did not fit together like the two halves of one apple. Sometimes they were flint and steel, and the sparks flew. But they needed to fit together, and they were trying to. Often they did. They were a good couple. Out of the sometimes far estrangement of their differences, their need to fit together would draw them back to each other again. That was their desire. And desire would then freely have its way with them.

And so desire, her own and his, was one of the subjects of her thoughts. She saw the danger of it. She saw the beauty and the preciousness of it. She saw even the necessity of it, for it imparted beauty and motion, life itself, to the whole world: the desire to be at one with another, the desire to be pleased in living together, seemed to her at times to infuse with light the bedrock of the earth.

To know this was a passion with her. She felt herself to be most alive when she felt it alight within herself. It was this light in herself that strangely made her self matter little in comparison. It had the power, in fact, to cause her self entirely to disappear. And so she was mortified, most deeply thwarted in her instinctive tenderness toward the life and light of this world, when she was confronted, as she often was, with the belief, at large among their church people and in Sycamore itself, that desire merely was lust. It was not an adequate mitigation that she knew surely that desire sometimes was lust, and that the dearest, pleasantest desire, especially for the women, sometimes led to suffering.

"But they think desire is no different from lust," she said to her husband. "Think of the loneliness of that. Think of the terrible loneliness of it!"

"Where do they get that idea?" Williams asked, though he knew.

"They think Jesus said so. 'Whosoever looketh on a woman to lust after her hath committed adultery already in his heart.'"

That a great suffering of shame and loneliness did surround that saying and its history they then acknowledged in the look they gave each other.

Williams Milby laughed, and his laughter granted standing to this acknowledgement, and it made room for her dissent that he knew was coming. He said, "If he meant desire, he has caught us all. I speak of course only for us men."

"Speak for us all!" she said. And now to her own surprise, she felt her tears, for suddenly it was to her as if she were lifting from herself a nearly unbearable weight. "Speak for us all! If he meant desire, he has caught every one of us."

When Williams spoke again he spoke quietly, but his voice had changed, borne upward and unsteadied in his throat by an emotion like hers, for now he felt his great love for her, his great desire for her, pressing like a wind at his back. "You don't think then"—he was testing, teasing her, beckoning her forward—"you don't think then that desire is necessarily the same as lust?"

"No! Lust is selfish. It seeketh its own. Desire without selfishness, with self-denial, is only praise. It is even love."

She had more to learn of the cost of self-denying desire.

In those days, in Sycamore as in all the country around, there was an honored practice known as "feeding the preacher." The housewives of the church, or most of them, held it as an unbreakable law, for they had never known it to be broken, that the preacher and his wife, and their children if any, would be fed dinner and supper in some household of the congregation every Sunday. It was as though the preacher's lesson which was never altogether learned and his comforting which could not sufficiently be given were to be compensated by this hospitality in earnest of a tribute never adequately paid. Part of the organization of the church was the order in which the duty of feeding the preacher was passed around from household to household.

This ceremony of feeding the preacher was a dear privilege to Williams and Laura, for it opened the countryside to them as it was opened otherwise only to the veterinarian. And the veterinarian certainly never received anything like the hospitality that was accorded to the Milbys. It was as if they perhaps were angels who appeared perhaps in the guise of a young minister and his wife. Whatever their hostess had that was best was laid before these strangers, who would always be strangers to some extent because set apart by the minister's calling, which required that he and his wife should be sheltered, so far as they could be, from whatever was harshest in the speech and thought and experience of their hosts. The same compunction withheld also knowledge of the extremer pleasures. The list of things the Sycamoreans did not do "in front of the preacher" granted to the preacher a front as wide as a three-horse team. It took the Milbys a long time to learn of the community's music-making and its dancing, from which it was a mark of piety to stand aloof, and about which it was a mark at least of decorum to say nothing to the preacher.

Whatever was set on the table at those Sunday meals thus was offered somewhat in apology, but also with the unspoken confidence and pride that it was the best available, and the Milbys learned to expect with about the same confidence that whatever was set before them would deserve the praise they would give in return. The food was heaped on the table, and they were urged to eat as if they were being fattened for slaughter, or as if it were the known practice of ministers and their wives to eat only on Sundays.

In the hours between the big dinner and the lighter supper after which they would return to church for the evening service, Williams and Laura discovered two difficulties that they had to exert their ingenuity to deal with. The first was the onset of drowsiness after the noon meal. The second was the possibility that in trying to fulfill their hosts' expectation of a proper Sunday conversation, they would run flat out of anything to say.

"I hate to say *anything* to keep from saying nothing," Williams said. "I look at you for help, and you say for the tenth or twentieth time, 'What a wonderful dinner!' and I say for the tenth or twentieth time, 'Oh, yes, it was wonderful!' It's funny now, Miz Milby, and you can laugh, but it wasn't funny then."

Both of these dangers they learned to avoid by the one expedient of asking to be shown something outside the house—and usually, since most of their congregation were farmers, they would ask to be shown something on the farm. For this they learned always to bring their overshoes. And it was this that brought them into the presence of the place, the country itself, and that taught them their people's ways of belonging to it and living upon it. They found that the farmers generally were proud of their farms, whether justifiably or not, and were ready, often eager, to speak of what they knew. Williams and Laura asked questions and learned and remembered, for they realized that they were being taught where they were, and more profoundly than they had expected to know.

They were not city people exactly, but they both had come from big towns. They had never known before a whole community in which everybody knew everybody, and the life of which went all the way to the ground. The community or neighborhood known as "around Sycamore" was a small place divided into many smaller places—farms and fields and woodlands—each of which, if you asked or if you waited to hear, had its unique, inseparable attachment of memories and stories.

And so on those Sunday afternoons in their unending sequence, when the weather was fit and sometimes when it was not, the Milbys followed their guides through barns and lots, fields and woods, and along the wild streamsides. They were shown flower beds, gardens, crops and animals in all the stages of the year. And so within a year or two they came into the intimate geography and life and worklife of the place. On the Kentucky side of the Ohio there at Sycamore the bottomland was rather narrow, and the farms were not large. The primary intent of the farm families they visited was to live from their land. Every farm produced a few acres of tobacco. Almost every farm had a small herd of beef cattle, and many had a flock of sheep as well. But invariably, and primarily for their own use, the farmers had vegetable gardens, milk cows, hogs for meat and lard, and poultry flocks.

The Milbys' interest in the place and its community fed both upon their understanding and upon their failures to understand. Williams's ministry carried him always along the seams of the community where the people were joined to one another and to the place, and he carried his realizations and his mystifications to Laura. There was always much that needed talking about. They began to know the farms they visited not only familiarly but also critically. From the comparisons that were inevitable, from comments overheard or casually made, they saw that some farms were more kindly and thriftily used than others. They learned to recognize bare ground as a danger. They began to see that the best farms were much grassed and little plowed. When Ernest Russet told them one day, finally breaking his rule against speaking critically in front of the preacher, "You can't *plow* your way out of debt," they knew what he meant.

Those Sunday afternoons afforded occasionally a benefit to Laura that she waited for and prized. When the after-dinner talk involved Williams in a way unusually needful or private, she gladly excused herself and went out alone. She was free then to walk at her own pace, following in silence her own direction and the line of her own thoughts. The only requirement was to get back on time, and for that she carried her husband's watch.

Sometimes on these walks her direction would be one she prescribed to herself. Sometimes her direction seemed to be required by the place, and she went where it beckoned her to go. Sometimes she felt complete in herself and separate, walking in the place. Sometimes the place seemed to occupy her and to have its being within her, and she forgot herself.

At the end of a cloudy day in full spring, the sun suddenly came out. In the woods, along the edge of which she was walking, the thrushes began to call. A mockingbird sang from a dead treetop nearby; a cardinal sang and a wren; in the distance a bobwhite whistled and was answered. Laura felt herself carried up into the freshened light where she seemed to have no life except that which now sang all around her.

On a rainy winter day, just at sunset, she saw the sky divided by the leftward stroke of a rainbow, the other side of which was hidden by trees. Within the visible arc the sky glowed with a vibrant pinkish light while outside it night was falling.

Walking one frozen afternoon in a wooded hollow of the valley side, she realized suddenly that her own steps made the only sound in that place. She stopped. And then an absolute silence came over her, an absolute stillness. Every tree, the wooded slope, the world itself, stood as if in the very nothing from which it had been called out.

At such times as these she felt that the great, mute creation was trying to speak to her. This disturbed her, it moved her almost to tears, for it seemed to intimate the nearness of some consolation—forever imminent and unreachable, almost knowable—for everything that was wrong.

As would be bound to happen, there came to be some farms, some couples, that they preferred above others. Paramount among these were Ernest and Naomi Russet.

Ernest Russet was in his late fifties, beginning to speak of growing old, but still straight and hard fleshed. He was, as he said, a trueborn farmer, who loved eagerly his well-husbanded farm. He loved the work and the care of it, and the abundance that by his passion and his skill he drew from it. He was a humorous man with a hearty, emphatic way of talking, a little too loud, as if his hearers were a little farther away than they actually were. He had only one eye, but a bluer, more intense, more seeing eye than that one never looked out of a man's head. He quickly became an indispensable counselor to Williams Milby, for not only did his seniority and humor make his advice easy to hear, but Ernest Russet was a man of sound, practical judgment; he was likely to know what needed doing and how to do it.

Naomi, a famous cook at that time in that country where good cooks were commonplace, was an ample, round-cheeked, cheerful woman of great sweetness, who from the first always greeted Laura with her arms opened. Her energy and industry matched her husband's. Together, they made their farm a place of abundance and generosity. They loved to eat the food they had grown, and they loved feeding it to others. They took delight, when it was their turn to do so, in feeding their young preacher and his wife. Sometimes, as their friendship grew, the Russets would invite the Milbys out for dinner on a weekday when they had something especially good to offer.

"Eat, now," Ernest Russet would say as soon as Brother Milby had offered thanks. "Ask for what you can't reach."

The Russets looked upon the minister's vocation as in a way a hardship, a cross to bear, and they tried to ease the burden. The Milbys rarely left the Russet place without something good to eat stowed away in their old car. Laura came to depend on Naomi much as Williams depended on Ernest. The Russets became, in fact, the parents the young couple needed in a place unlike any other they had known. Sometimes when an extra hand was needed, Williams would work a day or a few days for Ernest Russet.

The Russet place, the Milbys thought, and not just because of their affection for its owners, was the most beautiful farm in all the country around Sycamore. It was in a valley tributary to that of the great river. The house, standing on a shady rise of the ground well back from the road, was white-painted, with steep gingerbreaded gables, a wide front porch, and a second porch of two stories running along the ell that contained the kitchen and a bedroom above.

Behind the house were the garden and henyard, henhouse, and privy. And then, joined by lots and pens for the handling of livestock, were two barns, a corncrib, a granary, and various other outbuildings, all in good repair and painted white like the house.

From this steading the fields spread away on three sides, the bottomland sloping gradually downward to a winding stream bordered with tall, white-limbed sycamores. Beyond the stream the land rose gradually again, steepening to permanent pasture on the valley side, and from there, as it steepened more, wooded to the hilltop. On the pastures were Ernest's four work mules, a small herd of beef cows, a larger flock of sheep, a few pigs, and three Jersey cows whose surplus cream went to the cream station in Sycamore and whose surplus milk went to the pigs. Because it was orderly and well-kept, this farm, even when Ernest was hard at work upon it, seemed somehow to be at rest within itself.

Always, as the Milbys' knowledge grew or as Williams's gift of sympathy apparently summoned it, the underlayer of suffering or sorrow would be revealed. The sorrow of the Russets was that they had had no child. Their expectation of a child had almost gently graduated into a wish for one, and thence into a doubt that there would be one, and later into the certain knowledge that there was never to be one, and then into resignation of a sort and an ever-deepening commiseration with one another, for never had a place been more lovingly made ready for an inheritor, of whose absence it itself was a daily reminder.

To this place in the spring of 1941 came a young man, hardly more than a boy in age, but to all intents and purposes and by reputation a man: Tom Coulter, from the next county down the river. Ernest Russet, as he said, was getting on in years. He and his place were needing a young man. Tom Coulter was available. He and the Russets had worked out a satisfactory "trade," and Tom had come to them, moving with his few belongings into the room over the kitchen. The room opened onto the upper porch from which an outside stairway went down to the lower porch and the kitchen.

"We could have put him in the room over the parlor, and glad to," Ernest said. "But a fellow that age needs to be a little free."

When Tom Coulter came to the Russets, he came with a story and a reputation both of which were well known to Ernest Russet. When he was sixteen years old, Tom had left home after a fight with his father, and he had been on his own ever since. The fight had been over a small thing—a contest of work in a tobacco patch—but it had been a small thing in which everything was at stake. It could not be got over, and Tom had gone away. He had needed to be out from under his daddy's feet.

"I've known Jarrat Coulter all his life, about," Ernest Russet told the Milbys. "He was all right—hell for work, excuse me, but all right—until his wife took sick and died when Tom and his brother were just little, and then he sort of turned in on hisself. He got unreachable, you might say. Jarrat's folks were on the adjoining farm, and they took the boys and raised them up. They and Jarrat's brother, Burley. That Burley, now, he's in a class all by hisself. There's stories about him that nobody's going to tell you, Mrs. Milby, or anyhow I ain't, but I wish you could know him. He done right by them boys, and he's a good man."

After he left home, Tom raised a little crop and worked by the day for some people by the name of Whitlow. He proved satisfactory, and things went well until Mr. Whitlow died in the summer of 1940. Tom stayed on, finishing the crop and his year's work after the farm was sold and Mrs. Whitlow settled with her daughter in town. And then he got word that Ernest Russet, who was looking for a good young man, wanted to talk to him.

Tom had the reputation of a prime hand, and he was respected for his industry and honesty. He had come up under good teachers, his grandfather and father and uncle, who had taught him from before the time when he knew he was learning. By 1941, when he was nineteen, he was not only a good hand but also a good farmer, a young man with initiative and judgment, fully in charge of himself, needing and eager to know what Ernest Russet could teach him, yet needing no boss. To his elders he was a boy who had come to be honored as a man, and was said to be "promising."

He had the benefit of a proper upbringing too, as Naomi Russet soon was pleased to say. He accommodated himself considerately and quietly to the Russets' life and household. He quickly learned their ways and the ways of the farm. He needed less and less to be told what to do. Beyond his instructions and duties, he looked for ways to be useful, doing on his own various jobs the Russets had not yet thought to ask him to do, and some that they would not have asked him to do. He sometimes accompanied them on their trips to Sycamore or the county seat, and he was always with them when they came to church. Sometimes on Saturday nights he would find a ride to Hargrave, which was the seat and commercial center of his home county, and which was widely known as a "Saturday night town." He could be fairly sure of seeing his brother there, and perhaps his uncle too. And though the Russets never asked, they assumed he knew girls whom he would see there. He did not go too often, and he did not stay too late. His handsomeness, which was considerable, involved not just his looks but also an emanation, an almost visible luster, of intelligent, exuberant strength.

There was a day in the late spring when his brother and uncle came to see him. They were invited to dinner on a Sunday when, as it happened, the Russets were feeding the preacher, and so Laura did meet the storied Burley Coulter, who was, as promised, in a class all by himself. He was then in his forty-sixth year. The marks of time and weather were on him and his hair was gray, though he was still a man unusually attractive, which he seemed to know both frankly and modestly. Though he carried a much-abused felt hat in his hand and his blue suit shone with wear at points of stress, he had made himself presentable for what he clearly thought an important occasion. And on this occasion his obvious gift for sociability wore a sort of patina of formality. He was being conscientiously correct for the sake of his nephews, as if for fear that he might embarrass them. And yet when he was introduced to Laura he gave her an openly appraising look, which communicated both a compliment and his amusement that she had caught the compliment and liked it. She offered her hand; with fine discrimination he shook it *almost* too long, and she laughed.

Nathan Coulter, who had driven them over in his father's much-muddied automobile, seemed younger than his brother by more than the two years between them. He was a nice boy, in looks a little dreamy perhaps, and by nature much quieter than Tom, though obviously a product of the same teaching and upbringing. To everybody's relief, the group of them went together fine, as Ernest Russet later said. It was at first a pleasant and then a happy meal, at which much was eaten in verification of the many praises that were passed over the food. And afterward, to the Russets and the Milbys, it seemed that their acquaintance with Tom Coulter had been enlarged and even lengthened. They knew him better, from farther back, than before.

By the fall of that year two changes had come about that, in Laura's mind, had assumed the standing of facts, and facts moreover that she pretty well understood: The Russets had come to love Tom Coulter as the son they had longed for but never had; and Tom Coulter had come to love Laura Milby as a young man loves a woman whom he conceives to be "above him," forever beyond his reach and his hope.

The first of these facts may not yet have come into speech between the two Russets, but Williams and Laura, who had watched it happening, had talked of it, and to them it was merely obvious. On the one hand there was an absence long unfilled, and on the other hand, now, a presence that might exactly fill it. They thought it only a matter of time, another year perhaps, until the beautiful farm would have its designated heir. "That Tom," Ernest Russet said, "he's a born stockman if ever there was one."

The second fact was known only to Laura herself. If it was plain to her, it was in no general way obvious. Tom was not forward. In the presence of women, even of Naomi Russet, he was somewhat shy. But when he looked at Laura and looked away, his face was marked by a thought she recognized. That he wished to be near her she knew, because when it was possible for him to be near her he would be, though then he would hold himself a little apart and look away. And when, at the Russets' or at church, there was something that could be done for her, something such as a load to be carried, he would be first to see it, for he would be watching, and he would do for her what needed to be done. But even without these visible signs, it seemed to Laura that she would have known his feeling for her by the mere force of it passing to her through the air.

And she knew fairly well what to make of it and how seriously to take it. She was then twenty-five years old, and she was in the fourth year of her marriage. In her thoughtful way she had parsed out the kinds of love and its changes. There was love as mere attraction, mere feeling; as a girl she had known enough of the power and the giddiness of that. By now she had seen how such love could gather knowledge to itself and become different; and how it was changed again, profoundly this time, when it made the solemn offer of trust and submitted to vows. Love and trust, that vow "until death," had carried Laura and Williams into an abyss of sorts, lighted only by the light they could find within and between themselves. They were passing on and on into the unknown life of plighted love; behind them, committed and unchangeable, was the history of their love, which was changing it and would change it.

She necessarily regarded this love of Tom's as young, younger by far than any love of hers would ever be again. And yet, though she could not return it in kind, she was moved by it. She granted a certain respect to it. She saw moreover that, as it was unaskingly given, it was a gift to be honored, and she did honor it. She would not withhold from it even the name of love, for all love must begin without knowledge. Perhaps, as she thought, it is itself a kind of knowledge.

At that time there already was war in Europe and war in Asia. Though war had not, so to speak, yet shown itself above the horizon around Sycamore, neither was it any longer ignorable. To the ones who were living there in those days, war had become a thinkable possibility, a premonition, like a distant mutter of thunder on a clear day.

And then after the seventh of December 1941, war was present among them. Around Sycamore it was as if the people had turned away from the distant thunder, distracted from it by their workaday lives, and had turned back again to find a black cloud covering half the sky. As the magnitude of the opposing forces became manifest to her, it seemed to Laura that the whole sky darkened, and an unsourced light illuminated creatures and objects on all sides so that they stood out in sharp relief against the darkness. The young men in particular looked to her that way. Tom Coulter looked that way to her, as if a dark fate was gathering around him, and he was lighted, not by daylight at all, but by his own small life shining within him.

The realization grew upon them all that everything would be changed. No life would be immune. No life now would be changed merely by time and mortality. Now history was outrunning time.

January came. Though the lengthening of the days was hardly apparent so far, it was felt. The year was beginning. On the floor of Ernest Russet's tobacco barn, now partitioned and bedded and furnished with mangers, the lambs of the new year were being born. Now the Russet household never completely slept. To give help to the laboring ewes when help was needed, to save a wet newborn lamb from the cold, Ernest or Tom would be going to the barn by turns all through the nights, sometimes staying for hours, busy with a difficult birth or a weak lamb, or just sitting and waiting, warming their hands over the lighted lantern between their feet.

At that time knowledge, fear, and sorrow were descending also upon the Russets. For them, the great fact of the war was coming to bear with a singular pointedness upon what was now their dearest hope. The war, as they had tried not to know but nonetheless knew, was going to require Tom Coulter. It would take him away. That it would destroy him they did not yet know, but they knew it could destroy him. Knowledge had begun to shudder in their hearts. The change that was coming had already begun to come, and they felt themselves impaired.

On a Sunday near the end of the month, when the Milbys again came for dinner, sorrow was in the air undeniably—partly because of the Russets' palpable need to deny it. The effect of the presence of Williams Milby, the comforter, was to make grief evident. The Russets were smiling and genial as usual, but there came relentlessly a moment when Naomi lifted a corner of her apron to wipe her eyes, and when Ernest, seeing her do that, stopped twice in the midst of a story he was telling to clear his throat.

As soon as the meal was over, according to her custom at such times, Laura excused herself and left the table. She put on her warm overcoat and scarf, her gloves and galoshes, and began one of her solitary walks, leaving the old ones in their sorrow, Tom in his embarrassment, Williams in his helpless standing by that was yet a comfort.

Her departure had its usual excuse of discretion; Williams was the needed one, not she. But today, as she knew and told herself, there was cowardice in it too. She did not want to bear what in that house that day was to be borne. She wanted the comfort of solitude, she thought, or was she only indulging herself? The place, which normally would have seemed to welcome her, today seemed to exclude her. She felt its indifference to whatever might happen in it. Its quietness, as if waiting or expectant, which usually would have comforted her, she now felt as indifference.

Though it did not comfort her, she continued her walk for some distance, going as far as the little stream under the sycamores, which was flowing too full to cross by steppingstones, and then turning back toward the barns.

The tobacco barn, now the lambing barn, opened front and back into two pastures. In the pasture behind it were the ewes whose lambs were now safely born and strong; in the smaller pasture in front were the ewes still to lamb. Laura walked up the long slope among the ewes with their new lambs, and here she felt a kind of pleasure at last. Here was a small success, even a small triumph, of the kind the world most dependably allows. The ewes moved out of her way as she passed, their lambs following. She walked to the wide-open doorway and went into the barn.

When she had blinked away the outdoor brightness, she saw Tom busy by the row of lambing pens along one wall.

"Hello," she said.

He answered, "Hello."

She knew that he also was there by escape. The barn no doubt had needed to be visited, but no doubt also, like her, he had welcomed an excuse to leave the house. She felt then how strongly his life claimed him, how he needed for his place and being the whole outdoors.

She went to the row of pens. In the second one a ewe was nuzzling and muttering to a lamb as it stood unsteadily to nurse. Almost at her feet her suckling lamb's twin lay on the straw, still slimed and bloody from its birth, marvelously formed to live, except that it was dead and now to the ewe a thing of no importance.

"I should have got that out of there," Tom said.

"No," she said. "It's all right."

He had lifted from a nearby pen an orphan lamb and was holding it, its long legs dangling, in one hand, a nippled bottle of cow's milk in the other.

And suddenly she was filled with knowledge of him that was like love, or was love. In him, as he stood before her then, she saw the ancient unthanked care of shepherds. The sheep merely suffered what was to be suffered, living the given life, dying the given death. They did not ask for care or know when they needed it or appreciate it when they received it. And yet the care was given. The flocks throve by no care commensurate with a price, but by an overplus of love, filling a known need in the shepherd, passionate and beyond memory old.

What Laura said then she said as if merely in answer: "You're in love, aren't you?"

He gave back her look. He grinned. She could see the boy in him then—the boy, anyhow, that he had been not long ago.

"I thought you knew it," he said. "I didn't look for you to say so."

She said, “I would like to thank you.”

Their held gaze seemed then to be one thing to which their two beings were for the moment incidental. It was a moment that had to pass. And it did pass. Time carried them from the moment before to the moment after.

She smiled. “I don’t think we’ll talk of this again.”

He nodded, and the boy he had been was nowhere near him now. “No. We won’t again.”

There was in fact no more to say. Because they said no more, for the rest of his life, which would not be long, she shone in his mind as she had been that day: “I would like to thank you.” And to the end of her own long life she was grateful to him because with his young heart, never old, he had loved her.

Summer 2008

Hunting in July

Julián Ríos, Translated by Nick Caistor

His name was Celso Castillo, and he was a tailor in Tamoga. From early that morning he knew what his fate was. There was no doubt that when the journey came to an end—and there couldn't be far to go because the truck had been bumping along a track in the forest for half an hour now—they would blow his head off, exactly as they had done with the seven men and two women who were found dead the previous morning on the outskirts of the town, next to the stone cross opposite the cemetery (the cross that became known from then on as the Bloody Cross) without anyone in Tamoga trying to discover who the killers were.

Still, the fact that they were taking so much trouble, wasting all that time and gasoline—they were a long way from Tamoga, and the sea was already hidden behind the hills which rise up from the coastal highway—began to intrigue Castillo. Perhaps that was why hope struggled with fear inside him, so that he told himself again and again without conviction, feeling increasingly numbed and exhausted: "They're not going to kill me. This is a joke, they're just trying to scare me."

Yet he was sufficiently clearheaded (he only had to remember the lunacy that had been unleashed on Tamoga in the previous days of this bloody, crazy summer) to know that the men hadn't taken him all this way just as a joke.

Standing on the back of the truck, he could feel the cool air on his face. The vehicle was swaying as it went along the narrow dirt road, leaving in its wake a thick cloud of reddish dust that floated in the still July morning. On both sides the pine tree trunks quickly closed into a wall. He stared intently at the way shadows from the branches stained the faces of the men guarding him.

He had a wild look to him, Castillo. He was thin, on the tall side, with strong shoulders. His black curly hair sat like a cap almost down to the dark line of his brow. His unshaven face was angular and dark; his shadowy, moist eyes were close set; his big mouth was framed by deep lines in its corners. He was thirty-three the previous winter but looked ten years older. Like most of the tailors in Tamoga, he was lame. When he walked he did so with grotesque agility, dragging his left foot perpendicular to the right one. He was wearing a dirty, crumpled blue suit, a waistcoat and a collarless white shirt that was undone and showed the blackish fuzz on his chest.

Now he was standing on the back of the truck, guarded by three men. He didn't understand a thing and thought of death with the same sense of disbelief and helplessness that those gunned down outside the cemetery must have felt the previous day. He was so stunned that every so often his stupor managed to anaesthetize him. Fear had drained his face of color. He felt drowsy and weak, so strange that his legs were like a rag doll's. It was as if he were shrinking by the minute. In the few moments when fear did not completely cloud his mind, he was overwhelmed by a sense of impotence when he realized with amazement that these men whom he had known all his life, and with whom he had never had the slightest quarrel, had overnight turned into enemies ready to punish him for sins he did not even know he had committed.

They were standing close to him. He stared at them, but their faces were only impenetrable masks. When he had tried to talk to them at the start of all this, they had smashed him with their rifle butts. They were either nervous or impatient. The least concerned seemed to be Moreira, a thickset man of fifty, the owner of a soft drinks factory and of the truck they were riding on. Alongside him were José Benito Lozano, the priest's nephew, a tall, pale youth who could not have been more than eighteen, and Nieto, the manager of the kiosk on Plaza Nueva. He was a bad-tempered sort, who liked to drink more than anything else in the world. He had worn strict mourning since the death of his brother (who had apparently committed suicide shortly before this, although almost no one in Tamoga believed it was suicide) and looked like an inconsolable widower, despite the fact that he was past forty and still unmarried.

The three men were carrying shotguns, as if this were a cheerful hunting excursion, although the season wouldn't start for another three months.

Celso Castillo could see the backs of the heads of the other two through the truck's rear window: the driver, a broad-shouldered, corpulent man with a huge, barrel-like belly, was called Soto, and was one of the owners of the Tavares sawmills; next to him sat Doctor Emilio Lago, a lively little fellow better known for his political activities and his admiration for the local big shots than for any medical ability.

The truck had gotten a long way into the wood. They were progressing more and more slowly because the track was a steep dry streambed full of potholes. All at once the vehicle came to a halt, with a faint gurgling sound. They were in a hollow full of ferns and gorse, almost completely surrounded by peaks. Pallid and solemn, Celso Castillo looked enquiringly at his companions. There was an expression of fear on his face, but also resignation and a strange dignity.

"Get down," they ordered him.

As he was about to jump from the truck, he felt himself being pushed. He thrashed his feet in midair, then fell flat on his face, just as though his legs had been taken from under him. He lay face down on the ground. Perhaps he had fallen because of the push they had given him, or perhaps his clubfoot had made it impossible for him to keep his balance.

The men stood around him. He looked up from where he was lying, making no attempt to sit up. He saw pant cuffs, the gunmetal blue of shotguns; then, higher still, unbelievably high, their impassive faces—all of them known to him and yet all of them so different, transformed. And higher still, above their heads, the trunks and dark tops of the pine trees, swaying gently in the breeze, the clear blue sky and the fiery splendor of dawn.

"Pick him up," he heard someone say.

Two men grabbed him by the armpits, dragged him along a little way, then pulled him violently upright. Until he was standing erect it was as if his body had no skeleton, as if all his limbs had been crushed in the same way as his misshapen foot. He stared at the men, panting for breath.

The one who stood out was a giant with broad, muscular shoulders, wide as a door. This was Soto. He wasn't carrying a gun. He looked half asleep, with red-rimmed, drooping eyelids. He lumbered across, the others staring at him in silence. When he was a few paces away from Celso Castillo, he halted. He was wearing a pair of corduroy trousers and a suede jacket with resin stains. He took a revolver out of one of the bulky pockets, looked at it for a few moments as though trying to identify what he had in the palm of his hand, weighed it carefully, then wrapped his fingers around it, laughing quietly, the way he did when he told one of his jokes in the sawmill during the lunch break. Slowly raising his right arm, he pushed the gun barrel against Celso Castillo's chest. The tailor stood facing him meekly. He could feel the pressure against his skin and instinctively flinched. Scared, he fixed his gaze on Soto's half-closed eyes in his faintly smiling face. He looked at the others, standing in a semicircle round him. They seemed amused, expectant. He felt a heavy blow to his chest and dug in his heels to stop himself falling over backwards. He waited for the next assault. Soto hit him again with the revolver.

"Run, Castillo," he told him. "You're going to get a chance no Red deserves."

Two hours earlier, Celso Castillo had been having a nightmare. He hadn't had a good night, constantly disturbed by the solemn chimes of the clock in the main square. At five in the morning, just as he was falling asleep, his wife woke him. Celso Castillo opened his eyes, scratched his unshaven chin, then murmured thickly: "I dreamed a seagull was eating my stomach." Relieved, he smiled and turned to face the wall.

"Did you hear that noise?" his wife asked, shaking his shoulders. "Someone's trying to get in."

"No," he replied. "It must be a dog rummaging in the garbage can."

He listened for a while. After several minutes' complete silence, just as he was about to fall asleep again, he heard a noise at the door to the street. He sat upright in bed.

"Switch the light on," he told his wife.

She fumbled clumsily by the bedside until she found the light switch. The bulb, dangling from the ceiling by a fuzzy cable, filled the room with a yellowish glow. It was a poor bedroom, with white-washed walls and planks on the floor that had often been mended. There was an iron double bed, a cupboard, two chairs piled high with clothes, and a small trundle bed where a boy of around seven was sleeping. The room was at the rear of the house and was linked at the back to the kitchen, with a narrow, dank courtyard outside. The tailor's shop was on the far side of the courtyard: it was spacious and had a door and a window looking out onto Plaza Nueva.

His wife got out of bed, terrified. She was blonde, with a broad, beautiful face. Her name was Adoración, and she had been married to the tailor Castillo for eight years. Before that she had been the mistress of Daniel Tavares, one of the main landowners in the region. Following her marriage, she forgot her amatory generosity (to the despair of the males of Tamoga, including the proud Tavares) and substituted strict fidelity for her previous way of life, when she used to dance naked in one of the shacks down by the river, and satisfied one by one the crowd of men who formed anxious, impatient lines to be with her.

Her wedding to the tailor Castillo caused a great commotion among the many men who had taken their turn with her on Saturday nights.

The couple had a child, a thin, dark-skinned boy with the same sad, deep-set eyes as Celso Castillo, although this wasn't sufficient to dispel the widespread rumor that Adoración was already carrying Tavares's baby in her belly when she married the tailor.

He and his wife heard a long cracking sound, as if someone was trying to lever open the front door from outside.

"It must be Adriano," said the woman, looking over at her husband, who was running to the middle of the bedroom in his underwear.

"Don't talk nonsense," he replied, hurriedly pulling on his trousers.

He was frightened. His wife's idea sent a shiver down his spine. Although everyone in the town knew he hadn't been on speaking terms with his brother Adriano for years, Celso Castillo had been anxious ever since—a week earlier—Adriano had tried to blow up the door to the jail where the Republican authorities were locked up. It was a reckless undertaking, poorly executed, but Adriano Castillo had escaped after killing two Civil Guards. The word was that he was in the hills organizing a resistance, planning to come and attack the whole town.

When news of the military rebellion reached Tamoga, two days after it had happened, the peasants from the surrounding area came down to the town in carts or on foot, some of them bringing their wives. A sad kind of pilgrimage. When they reached the Campo de la Feria, they found that all the exits were blocked, and they were mown down by troops. That same night, the fishermen, potters, and workmen from the local potteries barricaded themselves in the Casa del Pueblo. For almost two days they fought off the combined attacks of the soldiers and the Civil Guard. When at last the building was ablaze, they were forced out. After that, the rebels organized punishment patrols. Right up until the end of that month of July, it was common at night to see the glow of fires in the countryside. When the resistance was finally snuffed out, Tamoga's tiny jail had room for only a quarter of those arrested. The town hall and a school on the outskirts of Tamoga (this school—a mansion surrounded by high walls down by the river—was to be a concentration camp for several years) were turned into prisons. Summary executions soon solved the space problem. New bodies appeared every day, flung by the roadside. The women who used to go down to the public washhouses by the port were greeted one morning by the sight of several corpses floating like fish in the soapy waters of the tanks.

For the inhabitants of Tamoga, the war was an excuse to settle many years of resentment.

Like any other small town, it had always been a place for rumors and gossip, but now the ease and fervor with which true or false news was spread reached unheard-of proportions. Everyone was afraid of everyone; nobody felt safe, because individual responsibility could be extended back to their most distant ancestors.

This was why when he heard his wife mention Adriano, Celso Castillo was filled with a sense of dread.

"If it's Adriano, don't let him in," Adoración shouted as he opened the bedroom door.

"There's no way it can be him," he thought apprehensively as he crossed the yard. He paused for a few moments. He could hear a noise in the tailor's shop. A line of light shone beneath the door. When he went in, he pulled up short, alarmed. First he saw all the bolts of cloth scattered across the floor like giant snakes. Then he saw several men ransacking the cabinets.

"Well, I suppose you haven't hidden him in your bed."

He was so stunned that it was only now, when he heard the voice, that he realized who these people were. Doctor Lago stood in front of him, giving orders:

"Search the rooms at the back," he said.

Soto and Moreira opened the door to the yard. The tailor made to follow them, but José Benito blocked his way, then pushed him back with his gun.

"Sit down," he barked.

Celso Castillo turned slowly until his back was to the door. The doctor pushed him gently toward a wicker chair under the circle of light from the lamp. He studied him silently for a moment, blinking nervously, then placed a hand on Castillo as if he was going to listen to his chest.

"You wouldn't by any chance know where Adriano is, would you?" he asked.

Celso Castillo shook his head.

"You know I have nothing to do with him," he said in a low voice.

The alarm had faded from his face; all that was left was a look of defeat. Doctor Lago sat down in silence next to him.

A quarter of an hour later, the doctor got up and strode across the room. He paused for a moment with his hand on the doorknob to listen, then made his way across the yard. From the back of the house there came a murmur of voices and the unmistakable, though muffled, sound of a child crying. Moreira and Soto came into the shop. As they did so, Soto gave a sigh and Moreira began to guffaw, until José Benito raised a finger to his lips.

"Come with us, Castillo," said the doctor. He had just come back in, his face flushed.

A truck was standing outside the front door of the shop. As he climbed on board, Celso Castillo heard screams. He couldn't see where they were coming from because he was pushed down on the floor of the back of the truck. "On the floor, dammit," he heard them order as they kicked him and covered him with a tarpaulin.

When they let him get up, he saw a dusty track and a horizon of trees.

Sometime later, when he heard the order to run, he didn't move. He was bewildered, as though he hadn't really understood, even though the words were perfectly clear: "Run, Castillo. You're going to get a chance no Red deserves."

An explosion rang out close to his head. Lead pellets ricocheted against his legs. He had to jump in the air as he zigzagged to try to avoid the volleys. His feet sometimes got snagged in the undergrowth, but he ran nimbly, pursued by the rattle of gunfire and the men's harsh voices. Whenever he jumped, he could hear their laughter. They even stopped shooting for a while as he performed his grotesque dance steps in midair, still running with all his might.

"If I reach the ravine, maybe I'll get away," he thought, feeling the race would never end, that the distance separating him from the ravine was infinite, that his lungs were about to burst, that the air was choking him. The sun was boiling his brain, its rays blinding him. Sweat ran down his face like scalding tears. He jumped and fell into a gorse bush. He pushed himself forward, sinking his hands and arms in the thorny branches. The sweat from his forehead soaked his shirt, already stuck to his skin. When he started to run again, he felt a burning sensation in his back and something like the lash of a whip behind his knees. He stumbled, took a few more steps, then leaned against the trunk of a pine tree. At the same moment he heard the explosion inside his chest, he saw the ravine. It was a high, steep gully. At the bottom there was a big forest. He slid to the ground with a sense of relief. His body slipped quickly across the soft floor of pine needles. He fell down and down.

The wind brought the sound of distant voices. He stood up and examined his wounds through his torn clothes. They weren't serious. There was a steady flow of blood from his chest, but it wasn't a deep wound. He felt light and strong. He bent his arms and legs and found he could move them with ease. He set off running through the wood. The sunlight filtered down through the green vaults like rays through the stained-glass windows of a church.

The earth was damp and pleasantly soft beneath his foot, battered from all the leaps he had made. As he ran on, the wood grew darker. A sickly-sweet smell rose from the ground and wafted through the air. The dense silence wiped the memory of the explosions and the shouts of his pursuers from his mind.

He ran exuberantly, quickly and agilely, until his ears began to throb. He fell face downwards, feeling his heart thumping against the ground. He pressed his head against the earth, watching an orderly line of ants making for a tree trunk that had fallen across the path. A red, fleshy fungus sticking to the rotten trunk caught his attention. He closed his eyes for a few seconds, until tears began to well up. It was a feeling of relief. His pursuers had lost his trail, and he was all alone, surrounded by silence. With his eyes shut, he was in a darkness that flooded over him like a tide rising up through his body and carrying him off to a deep, warm, sticky cavern.

He did not hear the sound of footsteps when the men came up and saw him slumped underneath a tree at the edge of the ravine. He did not feel the violent kick that turned his body over, or the deafening thunder of the shotguns fired at point-blank range.

Translated from the Spanish by Nick Caistor

Spring 2011

Allegiance

Asako Serizawa

He was a man of principle, Masaharu told himself. After all, he'd kept his head, even in the midst of that nonsense war, which had gone much too far—anyone could've told anyone that by the dismal end of it. Even the Emperor, the coward, sacrificing more lives just to save a good patch of his own skin. And now in this burnt-out clutter of defeat, his head was still screwed on tightly, despite the rationed-out years no one could justify now. Only when the Americans made their appearance, dotting the wasteland with their trucks and jeeps, did he become aware of a coldness at the center of his being, a coldness that nipped the belly of his heart before sliding away like a silver fish, back into the black depths of his soul. Then again, maybe this had always been his flaw: his vulnerability to feelings that jeopardized his principles. Masaharu had to allow that.

That morning, they'd had breakfast as usual, he and his wife: thin barley gruel and half a sweet potato. And, as usual, he'd raised his chopsticks, imagining a magnificent breakfast he'd once considered plain: white rice, salted sanma fish, miso soup. He slurped the gruel, snatching hints of the sweetness of white rice, the bitterness of the sanma, relishing them. But the potato was an emaciated stump, unsalvageable even by imagination. He ate it in one bite.

"Would you like mine too?" his wife asked, finishing her smaller bowl of gruel.

Last night he'd watched her from the window of their rented room, carefully roasting the potato, its purple skin blistering in a nest of flames—just like a boy's leg. He speared her untouched potato and swallowed it whole, choking on it.

"Do you want anything else before I go?" she asked, nesting her bowl in his.

Masaharu grunted and slid his chopsticks toward her. A year older than he, his wife was an elegant woman he'd chosen for himself—and for his parents, who'd been anxious to see him married. Of course, like everybody else, she'd thinned out considerably over these years, but she'd done so evenly, with none of the sinking and hollowing he saw in the flesh of others. Still, she barely filled her clothes now, no matter how often she took them in. Masaharu lay back on the grimy tatami floor, wondering why she still asked after his wants when, clearly, every want had to go unfulfilled. Possibly it was habit, thirteen years of being a wife, although Nishi Masako—as he still thought of her sometimes in her maiden name—had never been the subservient type. She'd always made sure he knew what she minded and what she did not. She was a resolute woman, certainly a match for himself.

Tucking her hair behind her ears, she wiped the counter that contained the sink where they also kept their toiletries. Every Sunday, it was the same: his brain withdrew into its stony vault while his wife prepared for work—a typing job secured by an acquaintance of his. It still got to him that she was the one with a job now—but for her to have picked up an extra day? It was enough to fell any man. But actually, that wasn't true, Masaharu thought; Sunday or not, they'd never been short of talk until, one October evening four weeks earlier, she'd returned from work refusing to speak. Her silence was unprecedented, so when the next morning she still didn't explain herself, he'd decided to respect it.

"Well, if there's nothing else." His wife pulled on her sandals, and this time it was Masaharu who did not look at her, even though he could feel her eyes boring into the side of his face.

She picked up her cloth bundle and closed the door behind her.

Listening to his wife's footsteps clanking down the metal stairs, Masaharu wondered again when the idea had come to him, or rather, when it had taken hold of him, this concrete need to act. It couldn't have been long after that silent October evening. But actually, that wasn't true either, Masaharu thought now. As a journalist, that need had fueled his whole career, though it had never gripped him this way. Except, he thought, one other time. It was March then, eight months ago, the worst night in their thirteen years of marriage.

That night, the sky, for once, had been empty of the planes that had begun to burn the country built mostly of wood and paper. Like many people, they'd been ignorant of the realities of incendiaries, and all they'd done to prepare, he and his wife and their thirteen-year-old son, Seiji, was dig a shelter two meters deep and cover it with corrugated tin. When the sirens went off, his wife had headed to the foyer to gather their evacuation bags while he made his way to Seiji's room. In the time it took to cross the hall, there was a series of whistling sounds, followed by a succession of eerie thuds, then an eruption of footsteps as people flooded the streets. It took a moment for the incendiaries to flare, but when they did there was a new combustion of noise: the crash of splintering wood, the juddering roar of the flames as gales of heat and smoke rushed to engulf them. By the time Masaharu and his wife staggered into a district shelter, the whole neighborhood had been razed, the two safest evacuation sites—the Olympic-sized swimming pool and the concrete high school—gutted. All Masaharu and his wife could say for sure was that Seiji wasn't in the house when the siren went off that March night, and afterwards he never turned up, not at any shelter, or at any school, or among the things scraped and salvaged from the gummed-up pool.

A hollow clomp resounded on the concrete landing. In a minute his wife would pass under the window on her way to the train station. Masaharu stood. All month he'd asked himself why—why that silence?—and a nameless dread had coalesced in his chest. For here was his wife, a survivor of one of the worst horrors to befall a mother—what could possibly have unnerved her now? Yet she'd come home silent, unable to carry on seamlessly with their domestic routine—an unsettling anomaly for his wife, who'd been trained by years of war to evade the patriotic police.

At the crosswalk, his wife paused, and Masaharu drew back from the window, knowing she'd sensed his presence. They were synchronized in this way, even more so than he and Seiji, who'd resembled each other, casting the same determined shadow when they walked or showing the same propensity for irritation when efficiency was thwarted. She'd connected to Seiji this way as well, the two of them orbiting each other as if their umbilical cord had never been cut. It was something Masaharu had cherished: his little family cell, his wife at the fulcrum keeping them in balance. He'd vowed to do everything he could to keep them intact, even if it meant a little personal compromise.

Masaharu reached for his jacket and cap. Patting his pockets for his keys, he closed the door and quietly descended the metal steps.

To account for the unpredictability of the world, his wife had taken to leaving early, and she stood on the platform now, with over a half hour to spare, gazing out at the wooded hill studded with scaffolding twenty-five meters high, the framework for what was to become an enormous bust of the Kannon, the Buddhist goddess of mercy. Sixteen years ago, in 1929, a volunteer group had begun building the structure, only to be interrupted five years later when conflict with China became imminent. Like everything else, the Kannon, ally of the common people, was sacrificed for war. When Seiji was born, they'd taken the train from their home in Tokyo to visit Masaharu's brother, an esteemed surgeon in Shizuoka, and glimpsed the construction from the train window. It seemed anachronistic to build such a monument at a time of such modernization and militarization, and they were moved. It was the reason they'd decided to come here to Ōfuna, this unfamiliar but intact city, three months ago, when they'd fled Tokyo after learning that a second "new type" bomb had razed Nagasaki. If the Americans were willing to obliterate a Christian city, Tokyo's fate seemed sealed.

"I didn't notice it before, but the Kannon was being built with Her back to Tokyo," his wife had observed the day they arrived in

Ōfuna, clutching their few belongings scavenged from the bombed-out ruins of Tokyo. "Pity they stopped Her construction—it's a shame. I'm not surprised we're being obliterated." She gazed up at the abandoned scaffolding. "Our government certainly deserves nothing less than this. This defeat," she said, the word popping like a rogue balloon.

Masaharu glanced about them. Defeat was surely imminent, but even here in this noisy station crowded mostly with refugees like themselves, there was no telling who might be listening. He took her arm and steered them towards an exit. "It's not like you to be superstitious. If I didn't know you, I'd think you were saying that if She'd been completed, if She'd been facing the right way, She wouldn't have forsaken us."

A prickly light gathered in her eyes. "The Kannon would never forsake us. She'll never forsake her people. No matter which way Her back is turned."

Her vehemence surprised him, and he quickly agreed. "The important thing is that we're here—and we're better off here," he added, even though he knew Ōfuna was home to one of the country's most brutal POW interrogation centers. Though he was unaware of any American or other white prisoners there, with defeat hanging around their necks, he didn't want to consider the ramifications of living in proximity to such an institution. "Let's see who we can convince to let us a room," he said. But his wife, inconsolable, refused to brighten, even after they secured a room in a boardinghouse and slumped onto the tatami floor. For there was now no denying they were here. And as Masaharu sat with this thought, it dawned on him that what had upset his wife had perhaps been his word *forsake*. After all, it was she, Nishi Masako, who'd made the final decision to turn their backs on the raining bombs and pitted streets that had refused to yield even the bones of their only son.

Now, watching her wait for the train, Masaharu wondered what she saw in the ugly scaffolding. Did she see hope, the promise of redemption? Or only regret, the guilt of choosing to move on?

But his wife, a mask of serenity, betrayed only that the shade had begun to chill her.

The train rattled to a stop. Masaharu pushed through the crowd to the car he saw his wife board. Would she sit or stand? Even thirteen years of marriage couldn't help him predict that. He lowered his cap and slid into line, composing an explanation in case she happened upon him.

He spotted her right away, sitting at the opposite end of the car, her coat folded neatly on her lap, her cloth bundle perched above it like an oversized mikan. Darting behind a spindly but tall man, he took up his position, only to be jostled by a throng of *katsugiya* smugglers transporting rice on their backs. Cooing and swaying, they eddied around him, their precious bundles, convincingly wrapped in the kind of *obuihimo* his own mother had once used to carry him, pressing him down the aisle. Two more seats, and sure enough, his wife's eyes fastened onto him.

"Are you on your way to Tomita-san's?" she asked, amused by his contortions.

Masaharu grunted. Tomita Yoshiaki was a fellow journalist, a diehard Communist who'd been released from jail after the Allied Forces abolished the Peace Preservation Law once used by the government to suppress "unpatriotic activity." Tomita, initially censured for questioning the legitimacy of the Japanese presence in Manchuria, had been arrested for criticizing Japan's increasingly aggressive foreign policy. He was detained for ten years, a light sentence compared to the hundreds who'd been incarcerated for upwards of twenty. Masaharu took off his sweaty cap. "I forgot we were meeting today. On a Sunday," he mumbled, grateful for the pretext.

"Tomita-san is a zealot. If you weren't so busy brooding, we could've left together," she said, handing him her handkerchief.

Masaharu wiped his face, ignoring her gentle jab. "Tomita needs to be careful. We don't really know how open American-style democracy is."

"I'm sure Tomita-san isn't keen on returning to jail. Besides, he might have some job leads for you," she said, turning to acknowledge a young woman who'd bumped against her while attempting to unscrew a canteen. She had a small child and a sizable bundle on her lap, the verdant fragrance of tea perfuming her. She bowed apologetically, including Masaharu in the gesture.

"Can I help you with that?" A woman facing them gestured at the canteen. She was wearing a Western-style dress and a pair of Western-style shoes, and her nails were painted a garish red. Oddly, she'd left her face bare, perhaps in consideration of this train ride, or perhaps simply to minimize hostility. The elderly woman next to her sniffed. She was clutching her own bundle, possibly some kimonos she hoped to barter on the black market. The tea peddler glanced about uncomfortably but handed over the canteen. Masaharu turned back to his wife.

"One thing Tomita needs to realize is that it's not Japan, but us men, who were defeated."

"You men have certainly made a mess," his wife agreed, suppressing a smirk.

"That's right," a woman standing near them piped up. "All men do is make war."

"And lose it too," another chimed in.

"I heard they're opening the government to women. Pretty soon women will be running this country," a man behind Masaharu said.

"Lucky for you; you'll never lose another war 'cause we won't make any," a third woman cracked to the others' approval.

Masaharu wondered what these women would be saying if Japan had won the war; victors could justify anything, and hadn't they thrown themselves into the war effort just months before? The man behind him clucked but didn't reply.

His wife said, "Didn't we all contribute to this war? I certainly didn't do enough to prevent it."

A silence descended over the car, the train's rhythmic clatter unpleasantly marking their progress. Of course she was right; unlike most, he and his wife had at least done their part, boycotting send-offs, contesting propaganda news, but in the end these were small individual acts with no collective reach. If his wife and son hadn't been a factor, Masaharu would've also kept writing, hand-copying his exposés and distributing them himself; once upon a time, not so long ago, his name had carried weight. Ultimately, though, he'd never been convinced jail was a useful option, and now, knowing Tomita's ordeal, he had to admit he didn't regret this concession.

Surprisingly, it was the *panpan* prostitute in the Western-style dress who broke the silence. "But we were deceived, weren't we? We were tricked by the Emperor."

The elderly woman shrank at the blasphemy, but the others murmured their assent. Even the Occupation authorities pushed this logic: they, the Japanese, were simply misguided children in need of a little reeducation, this time to obey the American Father. A thoroughly colonial attitude, thought Masaharu.

"Well, if we were all deceived, we're one stupid country, aren't we? No wonder we lost the war." This time it was the tea peddler with the small child who spoke, once again attuning them to the train's fitful clatter.

The doors rattled open. Masaharu gripped his wife's seat. A few passengers pushed their way out as more squeezed in, among them two GIs who, despite the Occupation's segregation rules, had apparently decided to experience native life. Unlike those who strutted around like roosters, at least this pair seemed well-meaning, if revved by the thrill of disobedience.

"*Kunichiwa*," they said, their well-fed faces flushed with optimism. "How are you today? My name is Jim," one said, looking at a group of schoolgirls. "What's your name?"

Several women tittered. The men turned away. A ropy silence hung in the air, low grumbles of displeasure rising. "Name?" The soldiers extended their hands. "Nah-meh?"

The schoolgirls giggled nervously. The man behind Masaharu clucked again. "They occupy our country; do they have to occupy our car too?"

"Maybe their car's full," a woman said.

"Ever see more than five or six in their car?" the man retorted.

"They're just kids," someone else snapped.

And that was true, Masaharu thought, turning to his wife. That was the problem with war. "Kids know nothing about consequences—that's what makes them useful in war. Even Seiji—" He swallowed his words; Seiji wasn't a topic they mentioned freely. The last time he'd slipped up they'd ended up pointing fingers at each other with a viciousness that had alarmed them. He glanced at his wife, expecting the doleful smile he found especially withering.

His wife, though, was gazing out the window, the platform beginning to glide; wrapped in sunlight, she didn't appear to have heard him. Masaharu wiped his forehead with the back of his hand. Something about the way she was sitting, inert and strangely vacant, she looked exactly the way she'd looked when she returned from work that October evening four weeks ago, like a marionette on idle strings, and the memory of how close he'd come to shaking her flashed through his brain. He'd been careful to remove himself then, gently sliding the paper doors behind him.

"Let me see that handkerchief again," he said.

She handed it to him. Shortage had brought a new edge to her face, the kind of sharpness he might have mistaken for hardness if he didn't see her hands, white with nervous pressure. She'd long since mastered her body, but here it was betraying her. Years ago, when the first *kenpeitai* underlings raided their home, she'd almost undone the family with her hands. Fortunately the soldiers were too green to notice, but it was the first time Masaharu had understood how much his dissidence was wearing on her. He looked at her hands again. What had they been doing that October night? She'd sat at the table, legs folded on the tattered hassock, her face frozen in a stare. But her hands? He wiped his face with the handkerchief.

At the front of the car, a schoolgirl stepped forward. Fist on her hip, she regarded the soldiers with teacherly impatience. "*Namae. Kon'nichiwa*," she said.

The soldiers exchanged a glance. "*Nahmeh! Kunichiwa!*" they said, grinning.

"*Nah. Mah. Eh. Kon. Nichi. Wah,*" the girl repeated.

"*Nahmeh! Kunichiwa!*" the soldiers cheered.

A loud bang stilled the air; someone had punched the side of the car. "Think this is a game? Think you're welcome here? Go back to where you belong." The words were in Japanese, but the tone was clear, and for a moment the soldiers' faces wavered with teenage panic, but their bodies hardened, their hands gripping their rifles. Masaharu felt his wife tense. She was a small woman, her seat sufficiently hidden in the rear of the car, but he moved to shield her anyway. The soldiers trained their eyes on the crowd. "What'd you say?" the one called Jim shouted. The tea peddler bounced her stirring child. The car swelled with apprehension as the soldiers spoke to each other, their rapid back-and-forth reminding everyone of how decisions were made these days: from on high and in a language as inaccessible as their own Emperor's had been.

"Hey America!" A man stood up. He had the face of someone who, in his youth, had probably carried a little flesh with charm. "*Haro! Monay? Gaaru? Chocoraito? Ingurishu prease!*" He cupped his ear in humorous apology.

The soldiers swiveled to look at him.

"*Ingurishu?*" the man tried again.

The soldiers did not move.

"*Oh-rai*, oh-kay." The man wiped his upper lip. "USA!" He pumped a thumbs-up.

A few women muffled their laughter; the crowd held its breath, fear slowly loosening into a nervous curiosity. Finally, the soldiers' hands slid from their rifle barrels. "Okay." They smiled warily. "*Tomodachi.*" They returned a thumbs-up.

Tomodachi. Friend. What a word to use, Masaharu thought. He turned to his wife. An odd expression was crossing her face, the soft light he knew well skewed by it. He glanced at her hands; they were resting on her bundle as still as polished stones. A chill climbed to the base of his head.

"Will you be late tonight?" she asked, startling him.

"You know Tomita," he grumbled and pulled on his cap.

They parted at the gate. Masaharu took a few steps, then slid into the milling crowd, looping his way back. Spotting her familiar shape, he wondered at himself. Should he visit Tomita after all? He picked his way after her, picturing Tomita's room, trapped in the quiet of a house its widowed owner had begrudgingly let him. There was no way he'd be there, cooped up on a clear Sunday. Which meant, given his own luck these days, there was a chance his wife could run into him. Would Tomita know to cover for him? She disappeared into the day. Masaharu quickened his pace.

Outside, business was in full swing, the sundry peddlers vying to entice the GIs in search of cheap souvenirs. Melted green glass, uniforms looted from military stockpiles, pipes assembled from antiaircraft shells: these days everything sold as defeat curios—even missing limbs, thought Masaharu, dodging an ex-soldier displaying his stump for alms. Beside him, a brassy woman in a Western-style dress lit a cigarette no doubt supplied by one of her American customers. She languidly appraised him as he passed. The unglamorousness of her life was evident on her skin, rough with makeup that did little to mask her plight, but even for Masaharu, who'd never been one to buy his pleasure, the knowledge that he'd been stripped of that privilege rankled him. He looked away, fixing his gaze on his wife's head swinging this way and that as she peered at every sooty orphan. Masaharu thrust his hands into his pockets.

The fact was, no matter how she might feel, they *had* searched for Seiji, scouring the Tokyo streets strewn with dead wires and glowing cinders, clumps of blackened bodies spoiling in the heat. And at first he'd been hopeful too, angling and digging for information, glad for once to be a journalist, which had brought nothing but trouble for his family. But as the days passed, and the damage became clearer, he found himself wavering. True, Seiji's missing body was a hopeful sign in the midst of the dead and dying who continued to fill the school grounds where they'd begun volunteering, stoking the pyres and gathering the bones. But unlike his wife, who seemed bolstered by the task, Masaharu couldn't subsist on hope alone, savoring stories of unlikely reunions perilously sweetened by the words of Seiji's teacher, who'd once come running, claiming to have spotted him blistered but alive.

Spring turned to summer, and the sun, unimpeded by roofs and trees, began hammering down, chipping away at their collective morale already worn by the maddening buzz of the flies, the ripening stench of the corpses, the dips and flares of hope unbearable in the heat. Even his wife sank into a stupor, a prickle of desperation showing in her new, unfocused irritability. And yet, for her, the future continued to hover like an open road; that Seiji could appear on it haunted her. They stayed on, the unadmitted skipping away like a stone.

Then, one night, as he watched the bonfire cremate the latest B-29 carnage, his wife appeared beside him, her face lit by the heat of the dead. "Do you believe Mori-sensei really saw him?"

The question startled him; it was the closest she'd come to expressing any doubt. He picked up his rod and poked at a half-charred body still too waterlogged to burn. Like so many others, this corpse too had gorged on a river or pond, disbelieving that it had roasted to death. "I suppose nothing's impossible," he said carefully. "But in terms of Mori . . ." He didn't rehash the teacher's recent disappearance, her madly shorn hair scattered like a parting gift in front of their makeshift tent.

"And you?" his wife asked. "What about you? Do you think Seiji . . . ?"

Masaharu gazed at the crackling pyres glowing like mystical landing lights. "All I can say for myself is that I'm glad it wasn't you."

Instead of shunning him, she had touched his arm and left to pack their things.

Drawn back by the noisy street, Masaharu noted with a start that the distance between them had shrunk. He slowed and wiped his face with the handkerchief he realized he'd taken from his wife. Should he or should he not seek out Tomita? He felt sheepish slinking after her like a mole.

At an intersection, his wife paused. Looking left and right, she turned onto a narrower street flanked by shuttered businesses, where only one store flushed with prewar colors. His wife stopped and joined the gathered crowd. Masaharu eased into the throng.

Lacquered mirrors and combs, elaborate entertainment kimonos—he couldn't remember the last time he'd seen such luxuries openly displayed. No doubt they were props consigned for resale by high-class geishas and actors, but even with the discount, which was probably considerable, he couldn't imagine who could afford them. Perhaps a popular *yōpan* prostitute catering to foreign servicemen. Why his wife, of all people, had to gawk like every other woman was another matter. Behind him, a camera clicked, and a foreign reporter scribbled in a notepad. Masaharu could already picture the headline—War-Torn Women Seduced by Cosmetics—his wife's face splashed beside it. He pushed into the crowd, craning to see what she was so captivated by. To his shock, his eyes locked with hers in the window's reflection. He jumped back, lunging into an open doorway behind him.

Had she seen him? The bell above the missing door tinkled as he flattened himself against the inside wall of what had obviously been a confectioner's, its broken counter once full of delicate sweets. He peered around the empty window frame. The crowd was shifting, newcomers replacing the old; his wife was gone. He rushed into the blinding street.

Had he known the consequences, would he have pursued her? This was a question Masaharu would find himself asking from time to time until the end of his life. Looking back, he'd retrace these steps, searching for those moments when he might have turned back, behaved differently.

But here was the end of the intact street; beyond it, a vast wasteland, rusty girders grazing in the ruin. Masaharu shook out his wife's handkerchief and wiped the grit that had accumulated around his mouth. Ahead, his wife was negotiating a path someone had cleared in the rubble. She disappeared behind a block of crumbled buildings. He hurried after her.

To his surprise, he found himself emerging onto one of the main thoroughfares bisecting the city's amusement district. Once closed by the government, the district was bustling again, its shuttered storefronts gaudily made over in Western style, the now segregated bars and dancehalls thriving despite postwar shortages. Tawdry gangsters, inebriated GIs, rich businessmen profiteering from the war: the streets were lively, petty spats constantly in the making. Masaharu picked his way through the crowd, avoiding groups of hollering soldiers snatching at passing women. Ahead, his wife picked up her pace. Waving to a pack of street kids clearly familiar to her, she crossed the street and disappeared in front of a rickshaw bearer, deftly avoiding a pair of swaggering soldiers whose height and girth reduced Masaharu, not a small man, to the size of an adolescent. He widened his stride, resisting the urge to run.

At a roadblock—a construction zone?—he thought he'd lost her. Then he spotted her, stopped by two MPs, their skin so dark that for a moment Masaharu froze. He'd never seen a black person before, and in a district he'd assumed off-limits to them, based on what he'd learned of his Occupiers, their presence was startling, drawing the attention of the other soldiers, whose pale skin suddenly looked delicate, pink and peeled, like boiled shrimp. The crowd around him bunched and murmured. The MPs seized her.

What had she done? Even in his panic, he knew the question was unimportant. Whatever she had or hadn't done, there would be no recourse. He squinted at the soldiers. They didn't seem angry, but what did he know about foreigners? He peered at his wife, her small face minuscule now, her tiny expression creased by what he could only guess was fear. The MPs panned the crowd. Taking her arms, they began escorting her down the street. Masaharu plunged into the crowd.

When he saw them again, two white servicemen had staggered into the street. They were shouting at the MPs, their drunken taunts clearing a ring around them. The crowd stiffened. Several weeks ago, a spat like this had escalated into a riot, killing and injuring hundreds of people caught in the melee. The Occupation had since increased patrols, but nobody was reassured. The MPs kept walking. The white servicemen closed in. Masaharu felt his back bloom.

At the first sound of scuffling boots, he began running. The distance was at most fifteen meters, yet he struggled to traverse it; from every doorway, it seemed soldiers were pouring out. He was less than ten meters away when he heard the first exchange of fists, the heavy thwack ricocheting in his chest; the crowd erupted, hooting and jeering. He clawed on, one human wall after another, until he broke into a band of space several meters wide. The MPs were still fighting, their boots corkscrewing the earth, but he couldn't see his wife. He bobbed and wove, searching the spaces that winked between the men, but there was no sign of her. As he expanded his sightline, he caught a movement, her familiar shape listing as she slipped down an alley. He started after her, only to be blocked by four huffing soldiers who had momentarily united to halt him.

Never had Masaharu imagined pacing this alley, slick with vomit and urine, looking for his wife. He exited the alley and rounded the corner for the third time. The same MPs, the same line of jittery GIs, the same closed doors. He glanced up at the grandiose sign. The same cheap brushstrokes coaxed up the same cheap waves, one word ostentatiously scrawled across it: OASIS.

At first he failed to connect the dots, his skittering brain unable to grasp anything. Then he did, and for a moment he stood rooted: the MPs; the line of GIs; the alley into which his wife had disappeared. His body shimmered with a new fear. The front doors swung open. He saw the smiling proprietor; he saw the row of women. Their faces were too far for him to make out, but every one of them had the same short bob he'd enjoyed on his wife. The doors slammed shut. Masaharu rushed forward.

Two pairs of hands clamped down on him: the black MPs. "No Japs." They pointed at the sign. Their faces were neutral, betraying none of the hostilities of a moment ago, but their grip was firm. Masaharu stared at their hands. No doubt the world's advances had produced the miracle of bringing them—men from opposite ends of the map—together; yet it was also the madness of those advances that spared them no time to understand each other. What means did he have to explain? He pictured their hands on his wife moments ago; a dim light expanded in his brain. Did they know her? Could they have been protecting her? He looked up at their faces, his meager collection of English words scattering like beads. Behind him, the doors opened again. He twisted around, the English word for "wife" suddenly coming to his mouth. He repeated it, pointing and struggling. The GIs laughed. The MPs shook their heads. The doors closed. "*Dah-meh*," they told him, emphasizing each syllable, pushing him away.

Back in the street, Masaharu had no idea what to do. If he'd been a different man, he might have risked the back door and stormed the facility, stripping the curtains to all the cubicles until he found her, sweat-smeared and humiliated. But Masaharu was not a hysterical man; even now, a part of him expected her to emerge, her face lifting with surprise before curling, guessing at his fears. He couldn't imagine her spread on the bedding, her thin body mounted and speared like a pig.

Circling the streets, Masaharu returned again and again to check the alley and the doors. The shoulder-length bob, the new Sunday hours—why hadn't he seen it? He pictured the requisitioned building, the barbed-wire fence, the armed checkpoint to which he'd accompanied her on the first day of her typing job. It had angered him then that they'd barred his way; now he was sour with the irony. Unlike Tomita, he'd banked on Japan's defeat. Every year another year closer to Seiji's conscription, he'd wished for a different life. When the bombings began, Masaharu, if briefly, felt a fizz of hope. It seemed possible that his son, too old to be evacuated to the countryside, might still escape the draft. He never imagined Seiji, so close to the war's end, disappearing.

Looking about the squalid glitter, Masaharu marveled at the world, its history of sanctioned violence that insisted on dividing the victorious from the defeated. For centuries, men, first in the name of blood, then in the name of national interest, had done this: plunder and rape, decimating whole continents as if it were their noble right. Now there were planes and bombs rumored to vanish entire cities—how could they go on? He pictured the burning streets, the half-charred bodies, all the pyres he'd lit. In every corner of the world, someone was still doing as he'd done—grieving all that the greed of men, his own country's too, had helped lay waste to—and the thought filled him with remorse. He looked at the facility, the ever-growing line, his wife's body opening to take every inch of it. He couldn't imagine how he could ever get past it.

It was almost midnight by the time he got off the train and walked the fifteen minutes to the intersection from which he could see their boardinghouse, a single square of light illuminating it. Framed there was his wife, arms on the windowsill, face upturned, as if scrying the stars that were abundant here, unlike in Tokyo, whose spoilt sky showed nothing but a dim smear. But Masaharu knew his wife was merely waiting for him, their best dinner of the week covered by a cloth: the rewards of her labor. Despite himself, his stomach gurgled, and he marveled bitterly at the body's animal will to survive.

Behind him the Kannon's hill loomed unrealized in a dark that hovered there as if held by a new curfew. It occurred to him that he could run away and vanish as many were doing, but after everything, disappearing, he knew, would be nothing short of an apostasy.

Passing under their window, he looked up and met his wife's eyes. There was nothing in them to betray her feelings, but he could feel her agitation, the ripple of worry and perhaps anger competing with her will to spare him the inquisition. He rounded the corner and climbed the metal stairs, his footsteps loud in the chilly air. In less than a month, winter would once again dust these steps, freezing off thousands of the sick and starving, but they would not need to worry.

Loosing his keys from his pocket, he stepped into the shadowy corridor and was again assailed by images of her—her slick mouth and wet thighs, opening for the pleasure of others. For a moment he stood still. How could he do this? He gripped his keys, struggling to recall the person he knew was on the other side of the door, readying his meal, unbegrudgingly. Of course, this was what she'd tried to spare him—he saw that now. And just as she'd tried, he had to try to spare her the knowledge that he knew—that was only fair. After all, they'd chosen to survive; they had a whole life ahead of them to live now, together, in their own silence, separately.

Spring 2012

Kids

Luke Mogelson

By that time every local knew that Kansas—the wide track of barren earth and upturned trunks surrounding the patrol base, where we'd bulldozed the trees and razed the bushes to deprive would-be waylayers of cover—was a no-man's-land across which, absent permission, one did not proceed. Nonetheless, according to Dupree, the kid climbed right over the berm of logs, which the bulldozer had pushed to the edge of the clearing, and the locals, accustomed to burning dry cow patties in winter, had immediately ransacked, leaving smooth poles like driftwood heaped along a tide line. He climbed over the logs, said Private Dupree, set down the object, looked at the tower, and waved. Dupree raised his weapon and peered through the scope. The kid was skinny, barefoot.

"But the object," I said. "The object."

"Like . . . a lunch pail?" said Dupree.

We were in the box, a converted shipping container that served as our tactical-operations center, huddled over Murray, the contractor from Raytheon.

"Show me Kansas," I said.

"Kansas, coming up," said Murray, toggling the joystick that controlled the camera.

"Go get Sergeant Parker," I told Dupree.

"Ain't no lunch pail," Murray said.

I leaned to the monitor. There, smack-dab in the middle of Kansas, equidistant between the logs and the entry-control point, sat a five-liter jerrican.

"Is that?"

"Ain't no lunch pail," Murray said. He chuckled to himself, and I could tell it was going to become a thing with him. Next time we heard gunfire on the ridge—"Ain't no lunch pail." Next time a scorpion skittered across the tent—"Ain't no lunch pail." Next time someone pulled a six-inch hair from his instant eggs or the helicopters strafed or a mortar or a ZPU round whistled overhead—

"Fuck's that?" Sergeant Parker said.

I preempted Murray. "Looks like someone brought a present for you, Bruce." Like the mustaches, using their first names was something the bomb techs did to remind everybody else that they were special. I went along. They were special. "Dupree says a kid just set it down and walked away," I said.

"And waved," said Murray.

"And waved," I said.

Bruce Parker scowled at the monitor.

"Empty, I bet."

But after he'd suited up, ventured out to Kansas, packed some C-4 around the jerrican, and uncoiled a detonation cord back to the ECP, Bruce had his game face on.

"Not empty," he said.

At first, when we arrived in the village and erected the patrol base, we traveled everywhere by vic. They were magnificent machines, a locomotive's worth of steel on wheels, the awesome apogee of our desperate, decade-old pursuit of superhuman invincibility. And yet: if you sparked enough potassium chlorate under one of them, the effect was comparable to wrapping a stick of dynamite in tinfoil. Within a month, I had the platoon moving exclusively on foot. An engineer with a metal detector would walk point while the rest of the squad followed in a line, stepping in one another's boot prints or tight-roping down a trail of baby powder. Tactically, single file has to be the least desirable formation into which infantrymen can organize themselves. But we were getting blown up, not bushwhacked, so fuck tactical, was my thinking.

It didn't matter. Soon they learned to employ components with a low enough metallic signature not to register on our equipment—clothespins and rubber bands, entire trigger devices whittled out of wood—while daisy-chaining them together with lamp cord and speaker wire. Early days, before we gave up going into town, we traveled via rooftop, humping ladders to lay across the alleys like a bridge. That worked until it didn't—until they started mining ceilings.

We'd lost three men, all to bombs, before this business with the kid.

Corporal Kahananui had been killed just two weeks prior. Kahananui had signed up under the relaxed enlistment standards of the late aughts, between surges, when the army was desperate for bodies and taking any man or woman who could fog a mirror. What I mean to say is he was fat. It wasn't his fault. He hailed from fat people—fat was in his blood. His broad skeleton, good humor, and squat neck all seemed specially designed to accommodate the inheritance. How he'd made it through basic was the subject of much chow-hall speculation. No way could he have qualified in the push-up, let alone the sit-up, let alone the run. Rather, some drill with a quota must have fudged his score a point or ten. That drill, turned out, did us a favor: Kahananui was the greatest, most casualty-producingest machine gunner I'd ever commanded. He'd fallen for the SAW the first time he felt it chugging in his arms, spraying metal down the range at Benning. Call it an affinity, like the fat kid who chooses tuba. During a tiff, he could fix a jam, reload a belt, or jury-rig a broken drum with hardly a hiccup in his surgically directed devastation. He had achieved that intuitive communion with his weapon that every rifleman aspires to. It was humbling—it was truly a delicious treat—to watch him work.

Still, though: fat. And so, between patrols, I ran him ragged. Suicide drills with a MOPP suit and gas mask; calisthenics in a rock-filled rucksack; mountain climbers, bear crawls, cherry pickers, duck walks. Kahananui welcomed the abuse—he genuinely wanted to lose. At some point he started calling me "Coach," an impropriety I allowed. You made allowances for Kahananui.

Then one day I caught him skulking out of the supply trailer, his cargo pocket stuffed with Pop-Tarts. I marched him straight to the NCO tent, where we found McPherson, my platoon sergeant, reclining on his cot with a laptop balanced on his tattooed torso.

"Now on, Kahananui gets the radio," I said.

McPherson tugged off his earbuds (which, from his pillow, continued to emit small sounds of screwing), that scar on his face like a continuation of his frown.

"He's got the SAW."

I shrugged. "Tough titty."

The SAW, with a full ammo drum and all the extra rounds Kahananui liked to carry, weighed a good thirty pounds—the radio, with spare batteries and antennae, at least twenty. On top of his flak jacket, hydration system, I-FAK, and Kevlar, it was a load. But Kahananui, in true Kahananui fashion, accepted his punishment without complaint, laughing with everyone else each time he geared up, piling that massive kit onto himself, heave-hoeing, and lurching like a warhorse out the gate.

According to McPherson, that's what killed him: weight. The device had been buried under the doorway of a compound they were searching. Although three men had entered the compound ahead of Kahananui—the third man having been Private Dupree—it had been set too deep for any of them to compress its plates, close the circuit, and ignite the charge. Only Kahananui was heavy enough. Later, while debriefing me at the base, Sergeant McPherson said, "With the radio and everything . . ."

He didn't finish. Didn't need to. By the time the kid pulled his stunt in Kansas, I was sure I could sense it: a suppressed hostility disguised as the strict adherence to enlisted-officer etiquette, a respect that was the opposite of respect—no one calling me "Coach" anymore, that's for sure. I'd begun interpreting any friction, any hesitation or hint of dissent, as having to do with Kahananui. I imagined knowing looks behind my back, privates whispering in the tents, a growing camaraderie, among the NCOs, built on shared contempt for me. They were all in this together, was the gist—all lumbering through the same goddamn minefield every day, struggling to survive the whims of the same goddamn lieutenant.

I felt betrayed. Didn't they realize, big as he was, Kahananui might have triggered that mother walking buck naked, hungry, through the door?

A few days after Dupree first spotted him, the kid appeared again, again put down a bomb in Kansas, waved, and disappeared into the trees. Bruce set the binos on the sandbags, pressed his finger against his right nostril, and ejected something from his left. "Why do I feel like there's a spring-loaded bar behind that piece of cheese?" he said.

"Sometimes," I offered, "maybe a piece of cheese is just a piece of cheese."

Bruce looked at me. By then, I'd become adept at hearing what people were saying without saying. What Bruce was saying without saying was: "Then why don't you go blow it up, asshole?"

Kahananui's replacement, a Specialist Feldman, arrived with the next resupply. McPherson brought him to the box, said, "New guy," and turned to leave.

"McPherson," I said.

He stopped. I thought I saw him sigh.

"That'll be all."

After McPherson was gone, I glanced from Feldman to Murray, who seemed as puzzled as I was. We were both trying to figure Feldman out. The shadow of a fully receded hairline encircled his pale scalp, and his face looked like something thrown against a wall, sliding down. He appeared to have had the wind permanently knocked out of him, an unsoldierly absence of any pectoral definition whatsoever. His nose was honeycombed with capillaries; impressed lines from spectacle frames linked his temples to his ears. I'd seen generals who looked sprightlier.

"How long have you been in the army, Feldman?" I asked.

"Six months, sir."

Murray let out a kind of disbelieving whoop, turned it into a cough. Feldman, who evidently was already used to having to explain himself, said, "I was a teacher, sir. High school mathematics, eleven years. If you want to know the truth, sir, the truth is I hated every second of it. Then my wife left me, took the kids. I'd always wanted to serve. It's always been a dream of mine. I thought I'd missed my chance—but when they raised the age limit . . ."

"Right," I said. "What's it now?"

"Forty-two, sir."

"Forty-two," I said.

"Good God," said Murray.

"I'm not that old, sir."

"No, no," I said, even though he could've been, even though forty-two would not have surprised me in the least.

"Anyway, here I am," Feldman said. He seemed as surprised as Murray and I.

"Here you are," I said.

In the dark, even with the goggles, you couldn't see the baby powder. Night ops, what we'd do was we'd break open light sticks and pour the viscous fluid over cotton swabs. The swabs, in the green world of the goggles, would smolder brightly, like radioactive mice. Not long after Feldman joined us, we followed one of the engineers, Corporal Sanchez, as he led us into the green, one hand working the detector and the other, like a wizard's, sprinkling a trail of emerald luminescence for the rest of us to walk on.

Sanchez had come to America on giant tractor tires lashed together with rope and cable. Once, at Fort Knox, while we were waiting in the bleachers for our turn at the range, he'd told us how, after four days drifting at sea, as his raft approached the beaches of Florida, a Coast Guard skiff attempted to intercept him. Sanchez and his raft mates dove into the water. Sanchez could see the sand, the resort guests outstretched under colorful umbrellas—then he heard the high gunning of the outboard and looked up at a silver hull, a man in a life vest reaching to grab him. At this point in the story, in the bleachers at Knox, Sanchez held out his own hand, fingers splayed, and, after a brief pause, closed it in a tight fist. Just as the Coastie was about to seize him, Sanchez said, shaking his fist, a wave peaked between them, pushing the skiff back to sea and lifting Sanchez aloft, conveying him as if on wing to shore.

That wave had left Sanchez with a pretty fatalistic worldview, which was why he remained unbothered by the fact that after two combat tours he still had not been naturalized, and why he didn't mind walking point at night.

We worked our way through the woods, down the valley, and to the river, where a large compound, identified by surveillance drones as the site of frequent comings and goings, was suspected of caching ordnance. We were just about to breach when the new guy, the old man, Specialist Feldman, dropped his rifle. The clatter roused a pack of dogs, whose barking roused the cats, whose caterwauling roused the jackals—none of which was as jarring as what Feldman did next. What he did was whisper, loud enough for all to hear, "I'm sorry."

Back at the base, after we found nothing and no one in the compound, Sergeant McPherson took Feldman aside and spoke to him. Light was breaking. On my way to the box, I saw Feldman standing beside the entrance to one of the tents. He held his carbine high above his head, as if fording a river. To every soldier who ducked through the flaps, Feldman said, "I'm sorry." Around noon, I stepped out for chow. Feldman was behind the serving table, holding up the carbine. As the platoon filed by, heaping food onto their trays, he again told each of them, "I'm sorry." Feldman's arms were shaking violently; his face was an alarming shade of purple. A couple of privates ahead of me were laughing. They must have been twenty years younger than Feldman, at least.

"I'm sorry," Feldman told them. "I'm sorry . . . I'm sorry . . . I'm sorry . . ."

Eight hours later, he was back out there for dinner. It was an unfortunate way to have to introduce yourself.

In the week following the night op, the kid returned twice more. The second time, I saw him for myself. Private Dupree was on duty again. He radioed me as soon as he spied him scaling the logs. I sprinted for the tower. The kid was smaller than I'd expected. He had to sort of hug the jerrican rather than hold it by the handle. After he set it down, he wiped his nose with his sleeve. I focused the binos. His *kameez* featured an intricate pattern stitched across its chest in white and gold. He wore a brown prayer cap. He waved.

According to Bruce Parker, the outsides of the cans had all been marked with soil. This would have seemed to indicate that the kid was digging them up. Bruce went on to argue, however, that it would be easy enough for a person to rub on some dirt precisely for the purpose of giving that impression.

"Mousetrap," Bruce declared.

I admit I was inclined to disagree. The kid, after all, was the only good thing that had happened to us since we'd arrived in that fucking village. Within the platoon, he'd come to be viewed as a kind of a win. Moreover, since Dupree had been the first one to spot him, and the only one who'd seen him twice, a degree of the kid's juju extended to the private. In our minds, Dupree was connected to the kid, and this connection was in turn connected to Dupree also having been the last person to walk through the last door Kahananui walked through. Via Dupree, in other words, the kid was connected to Kahananui.

It was partly for this reason that I asked Bruce to keep his theories to himself. Another reason, I confess, was that ever since the kid I'd personally sensed less resentment from the men.

Specialist Feldman might also have had something to do with that. It was as if, with so much enmity focused on the math teacher, none remained for me. Every day his difficulties seemed to increase. For starters, after the night op, nobody called him Feldman; he was known by everyone as "Sorry." McPherson's relentless hard-on for the specialist further estranged him from the platoon. Once, during chow, I heard McPherson say, "Who let this fucktard into my army?" and watched him march across the yard to where Feldman sat alone with a book.

"What is that?" McPherson demanded.

Feldman pushed his glasses up his nose and smiled. Somehow under the impression that the sergeant's interest was genuine, he began talking with enthusiasm about the book, a history of Afghanistan, saying things like, "It's actually quite interesting . . ." and "Says here the mistake the British made when they installed the shah was . . ."

A few hours later, when McPherson had finished with him, I summoned Feldman to the box. He was sweating so heavily that the salt stained his uniform in thick white bands. I tossed him a water bottle, and he turned it upside down, bobbing his Adam's apple until it was empty.

"I guess it's not for everyone," I said.

"Sir?" Feldman said.

I waved in a general way. "Why didn't you go officer? You have the degree. Army needs officers. How is it your recruiter let you enlist?"

"I insisted, sir."

Over at the monitor, Murray shook his head. I tossed Feldman another water. "You were expecting something a little different?"

Feldman shrugged. He was reluctant to acknowledge how poorly things were developing for him. When I suggested that McPherson would back off in time, it was nothing personal, he laughed and said, "Beats teaching!" He gulped at the bottle, wheezing through his nose. "Beats my empty condo! Beats having to see Brad Drexler every day. Drexler in the break room, Drexler in the halls, Drexler in the—"

"Brad Drexler?"

Again Feldman laughed. "Nobody, sir. A social studies teacher. My wife . . ."

He was smiling in an ugly, crooked way, lips curled against his teeth, eyes wrenched wide. It took me a minute to realize he was trying not to cry. When I did I understood why Feldman so disgusted McPherson. Quickly, to avoid saying something cruel, I pointed at his rifle. "Just show them you know how to use that thing. That's all that matters."

Feldman's mouth remained twisted in its mocking rictus. When he replied, "Yes, sir, I'll show them," it was plain that we were talking about different people, he and I.

A few days later, while we were alone in the box, Murray said, "When I was in Iraq there was this squad leader. Sergeant Walsh. Not my squad leader. Not even my platoon. But everybody in the unit knew him. Walsh was the darling. High speed, Ranger-qualified, born for the uniform. Imagine Kahananui not fat. That was Walsh. So one day Walsh and his squad are kicking down doors. They're in this building where every time we pass it, somebody fucks us from the roof. They come around a corner—standing in the hall, minding his business, there's this kid. Young kid, like yours."

"Mine?" I said.

"Only no man jammies. No week's worth of moon dust on his face. This is Baghdad. Oh, and he's not carrying an improvised explosive device; he's got that going for him.

"So Walsh halts the squad. The kid, he points at one of the apartment doors. He points at the door, says something to Walsh, and then he runs away. Interesting. Thing is, we're talking early days—Walsh doesn't have no terp with him. But he thinks, Walsh does, There must be some baddies in there. Sure. Why else point it out? Why else run away?

"You know what happens next. It happens the instant they hit the door. Blast nearly brings the building down. Dude from the QRF told me a flying TV almost killed some bitch five blocks away. Walsh's guys? Our guys? Two of them are dead.

"Two guys in the first month of our deployment. Meaning guess what? That platoon had an entire year to get theirs. I mean these yahoos were notorious. Sure, maybe the lieutenant was a fucking psychopath. But still: it all started with that kid. Kid's what set it all in motion."

Murray raised his eyebrows.

"You're saying you're with Bruce on this," I said.

"Hold on," said Murray. "The story's not about the kid. It's about Walsh. Walsh had a problem. His problem was: he thought about things. That way, he was kind of like you."

That way, I thought. Not the born-for-the-uniform way. Not the darling-of-the-unit way.

"One thing Walsh thought about," Murray continued, "one thing he couldn't *stop* thinking about, was what if the kid hadn't set them up? What if what the kid had done was warn them?

"Good question. A few days after the attack, Walsh visits the terps. He finds their hooch, knocks on the door, is like, 'How do you say, "Don't go in there"? How do you say, "Go in there"?' He says every line he can think of, every possible thing the kid might have said either to set them up or warn them. But of course none of it is ringing any bells. It all sounds the same. It all sounds like fucking gibberish.

"OK. Night after night, Walsh lies awake, he replays the scene. The kid appears in the hall, he points at the door, he speaks to Walsh. Everything is clear—*too* clear—everything except when the kid opens his mouth, what comes out? Fucking gibberish. So Walsh, what does he do? He starts hanging with the terps. He starts taking lessons. He starts trying to learn the fucking lingo. Now he's got to know, right? It's like this kid's words, whatever the fuck they were, are the key to the whole shitty mess. Like if Walsh can't understand them, he won't ever understand anything. He figures, Walsh does, if he can learn some of the lingo, maybe then the words will come.

"Well, what do you think? We're getting contact almost every day, losing guys, and our star NCO, our main dude, is spending all his downtime with the *terps*? Nope. By the end of the deployment, nobody wanted anything to do with fucking Sergeant Walsh."

Murray turned back to the monitor and began fiddling with the joystick.

"That's the end of the story?" I said.

He shrugged. "I got out after that tour and started working for Raytheon."

"Jesus, Murray," I said. "You're telling me you don't know what happened? You don't know if Walsh ever figured out what the kid said?"

Murray looked at me and grinned. What he was saying without saying was: "You dumb son of a bitch, of course he never figured it out."

The drones had spotted more comings and goings, and we had orders to return to the compound by the river. It was daytime. Sanchez was working the detector. He was midway across a wide, dry creek bed when he got a hit. I pulled the squad back onto the bank, and then farther back, into a small grove where a spring fed moss and trees. While we waited for Bruce to join us with the robot, there came the scream of a shell and its breathtaking thunderclap near enough to wash debris across our backs as we pressed into the earth wishing she would open up. Almost immediately a second shell impacted on the opposite side of the grove, and the panic, the awareness that the mortar team was adjusting in, arrived at the same time as a barrage of small arms from our six, the bullets so close we could hear them whining shrilly, vibrating the air.

We spread out, returning fire every which way, bracing for the next mortar round to land. Sergeant McPherson yelled at the men to identify targets, locate muzzle flashes, movement, kill holes in the compound walls. I took a quick inventory and noticed, among the frazzled grunts, one soldier lying comfortably in the prone, rifle propped on a log. He was scanning a distant stand of pines while squeezing off precise, methodical bursts. The unhurried way the soldier was shooting and reloading—the way, at one point, he expertly cleared a jam without removing his eyes from those pines—stood in stark contrast to the existential alarm taking hold of the men around him.

McPherson saw it too, low-crawled over, and shouted, "What do you got?"

To which Specialist Feldman, ejecting an expended magazine and inserting a fresh one, responded, "Two o'clock. Tree line."

Today, no matter how hard I try to transport myself back to that grove, I can't say for how long Feldman's little moment lasted. Half a minute? Half an hour? I suppose it doesn't matter. For a short while, anyway, the old man was doing what he'd come there to do. He was showing them.

I was so distracted that I didn't notice Private Dupree until he hollered in my ear.

"He's here, sir."

"Who?"

Dupree pointed at a patch of chaparral midway between our position and the pines. I raised my rifle. The kid was squatting in the bushes, eyes clinched, covering his ears. Clearly, he didn't want to be there. The little bastard must have been following us, I realized, ever since we'd left the base.

Before I had a chance to consider what it might mean, or to alert Sergeant McPherson, the kid did a jerky half spin, as if an invisible assailant had whipped him around from behind. I saw, through the scope, the spray. He landed face-flat in the dirt.

I looked up. The only soldier aiming his weapon that way was Feldman. He had no scope—I hadn't issued him one yet—and he was squinting down the iron sights, trying to see his man.

The first thought that occurred to me was what a remarkable shot he was.

It took us until sundown, availing ourselves of close air support, to exfil home. There was no hope of recovering the kid, who in any case had been a goner before he'd hit the ground. As soon as we got back inside the wire, Private Dupree jumped Feldman. He got in several vicious punches before anyone tried to pull him off. I sent Feldman to the aid station, where he stayed for the rest of the evening. Later,

I brought him some food. He was sitting on the floor, holding a cold pack to his swollen brow. After muttering some bromides about collateral damage, the nature of combat, I said, "Don't worry about the report."

For a moment I thought Feldman was going to object; to insist on suffering some consequences for his actions; to say, "I killed that child, and I need to pay." I could see the noble temptation flickering like a loose bulb behind his eyes.

Then it went out.

I didn't really talk to Feldman for several weeks after that. None of us did. If before he'd been a minor nuisance, unfortunate but innocuous enough, now the old man was a bona fide pariah. McPherson no longer put forth the effort to find excuses to rebuke or punish him, and the rest of the platoon, understanding this to be a still harsher form of rebuke and punishment, followed suit. Feldman was considerate. He made avoiding him as easy as he could.

A month or so after the ambush at the creek, I received word that the chaplain was making the rounds and would be at the patrol base in the morning. That night I waited until Murray hit the shower, and then I called Feldman into the box.

His appearance disturbed me. What little hair he had was way too long—far exceeding regulation. It made him look even older, more incongruous in that place, and less like a soldier. I could only imagine what McPherson, in the past, would have done to him. Now, it seemed, no one had noticed.

I said, "I was thinking it might be a good idea for you to talk to someone, Feldman."

There was evident relief in his eyes. Evident gratitude. "I appreciate that, sir," he said.

"Good. So you agree."

Feldman vigorously nodded. "If you want to know the truth, sir, the truth is that if it weren't for my kids, I might just go ahead and . . ." He laughed. "But then, I can't even *think* about my kids without thinking about . . ."

I cleared my throat. "What I was going to say is the chaplain will be here tomorrow, and he'd probably be a good person to talk to."

Feldman blinked.

"Better than me, probably," I added.

He had the same stupid, befuddled look on his face as when he'd thought that McPherson really wanted to hear about the book he was reading.

"I'm sorry, sir."

"They're trained in this stuff," I said. I picked up a stack of papers from the table and began flipping through them, stopping occasionally to set one face down on a different stack.

"Should I go now?" Feldman asked.

I glanced up as if surprised to find him still standing there. "Sure, Feldman," I said. "And do me a favor, will you? Cut your fucking hair."

The next morning Corporal Sanchez was the only soldier at mass, and Feldman steered clear of the chaplain for the rest of the day. It was only much later that I learned that Feldman was a Jewish name—although, by then, I knew that no priest, rabbi, or other person could have helped him anyway.

Ours was a war that offered few opportunities, aside from getting killed or wounded, to distinguish yourself. There were no hills to charge, peninsulas to hold, bridges to seize. There was only the patrol: a year's worth of mine-littered walks ending where they started. Maybe this is why it was with a kind of horny impatience that we kept waiting for the big one, some mad battle in retribution for Feldman's crime.

As usual, when it came it was a letdown.

We were finally returning to the compound by the river, which we'd postponed doing since the ambush. We'd made it past the grove and the creek bed, the chaparral where the kid had died. We were almost there, about a dozen meters from the property, when a slot in the metal gate slid open, a muzzle poked out, and someone from inside opened fire.

It lasted maybe five seconds. Neither of the two shots came anywhere near us. The gate was flimsy tin, and before the gunman could get off a third round we'd riddled it with holes. We fanned out and readied for the others. Incredibly, there were none.

"The hell?" McPherson said.

Bruce and Sanchez opened the gate. As they swung it wide, we all braced in anticipation, weapons raised. What they revealed was a shot-up corpse slumped in a wheelchair. The man had taken several bullets in the face; it was difficult to judge his age. Both of his feet were missing. Not his legs—just his feet. A Kalashnikov lay across his lap.

Sanchez patted him down. He shrugged.

"The hell?" McPherson said.

Once again, we found nothing suspicious in the compound. There were only a few mud rooms, cell-like, each with a narrow entrance obstructed by a tacked up sheet. The sheets were floral patterned.

I peeked into each of the rooms after they'd been cleared. All but one held farm equipment, engine parts, hay, and chickens. The sole space dedicated to human living was crammed with bedding and pillows. Colorful tapestries hung from the walls. A wooden chest stood in a corner. The soldiers had yanked out all the drawers: clothes lay in messy piles atop the cushions and blankets. I noticed that some were the clothes of a child. I sifted through them with my boot. Did I know what I was looking for? Was I surprised when I found the brown prayer cap, the *kameez* with the familiar pattern stitched across its chest in white and gold?

Sanchez was calling me on the radio: "You better come and see this, sir."

I joined him behind the compound, where we'd neglected to search during the night op, under the shade of a pomegranate tree. He stood at the lip of a yawning hole in the ground. The hole looked like the mouth of a small volcano, sloping gently, and then vertically, into a pit of uncertain depth. It was a karez: part of a labyrinth of subterranean passageways built millennia ago to transport water from desert aquifers. The system had long since dried up, leaving beneath the village a complex network of tunnels, some big enough to drive a truck through. These tunnels obsessed the CO, who was convinced that the enemy used them to travel from village to village, stash matériel, and convene *shuras* undetected by the drones. He'd once confided in me that he wouldn't be surprised if there was a whole "Taliban city" down there, complete with power and roads. Of course, the implied image was the CO descending with a flame-thrower, hordes of screaming gooks running out on fire. Like I say, though, ours was a lackluster war: rarely did it yield such lurid satisfactions. We'd searched dozens of these caverns, and not once had we ever found anything.

Sanchez turned on his flashlight.

"Merry Christmas," he said.

What we discovered, after Bruce rappelled to the bottom, was a burlap sack containing almost two hundred pounds of ammonium nitrate, some blasting caps, and a couple dozen carbon rods. No Taliban city, exactly, but a haul.

I found Specialist Feldman pulling security near the gate, brought him to the wheelchair, and made him look.

I explained how this fucking hajji—who'd attacked us, who'd been hiding enough shit to blow up half the village, who'd lost his own feet during some mishap in the workshop, and who, for all we knew, had been responsible for Kahananui and the others—this fucking hajji was the father of the kid. "Or grandfather," I said. "Or brother. Point is, the kid lived here. They lived here together."

Before I'd even finished I regretted it. Feldman gazed down at that brutalized corpse, and I could see him working it out. He was smart, after all, in his way. Too smart for the infantry, anyhow—although, fatally, not smart enough to have seen that in the first place. Just as I'd told Feldman one story, another was telling itself. I mean the story in which the kid was exactly who we'd wanted him to be; the story in which he'd tried to help us with the bombs because it had been a bomb that maimed his father, grandfather, brother, or whoever; the story in which the kid had followed us not just that day of the ambush at the creek but every day, ever since we'd arrived in the village and erected the patrol base; the story in which he saw for himself what happened to Kahananui, and he pitied us; the story in which this footless, faceless person had volunteered the use of his karez and launched his pathetic little kamikaze raid only after we had killed the kid; and the story in which Specialist Feldman, far from forestalling a catastrophe, as I'd suggested, was in a sense responsible for two deaths now, not one.

This story was as plausible as mine, mine as plausible as this one, and who could say how many other variations there might be, or which of them, precisely, Feldman was contemplating then.

It didn't matter. He had the rest of his shitty life to attend to all of them. The rest of his shitty life: and still he'd get no closer to knowing. No closer than Sergeant Walsh will get to knowing whether that boy in Baghdad set him up or warned him. No closer than I will get to knowing whether the weight of that radio was the weight that killed Kahananui.

One day, toward the end of our deployment, Murray told me he had something he wanted to show me. He reached into the gym bag he kept under the monitor and brought out an unopened can of Dr. Pepper. It was the first Dr. Pepper I'd seen since my leave, nine months ago. He'd been squirrelling it all this time.

"It's going in my first machine," Murray said. Then he went on to explain how he intended to use the money he'd earned in Afghanistan to invest in the "pop-vending racket." "There's only one word you need to know to make your fortune," said Murray, "and I'm about to tell you what it is." He tossed me the Dr. Pepper can, and I held it in my palm, feeling its heft, its promise. "Location," Murray said.

Back at Knox, I pinned the new ribbons on my dress blues, spoke at the memorials, completed my contract, and took the discharge. I saw the old platoon once more, about six months later, at a bar in Louisville. McPherson had organized a party to celebrate Sanchez getting his citizenship. When I arrived, Sanchez was parading around in a cardboard Uncle Sam hat. I'd been apprehensive about seeing McPherson, but as soon as I walked in, he threw his arm on me, yelled for everyone's attention, and proposed a toast. He called me the best lieutenant he'd ever had the privilege to serve under, and all of the men duly agreed.

I sat in a booth with Rob Dupree. He was a corporal now, a budding McPherson. You could see the sergeant's influence on him. He told me they'd already been put on alert again, and he seemed pleased. A few minutes later, he said, "Look who it is."

I turned to find Feldman stepping through the door. He wore a plaid shirt tucked into pleated slacks. He still looked like a math teacher.

"How's he been doing?" I said.

Dupree shrugged. Then he told me something strange. He told me that Feldman had re-upped, extending his contract for another four years.

"He's not so bad," said Dupree.

I watched Feldman navigate the crowd. I could see that things had improved for him. No one turned his back or snubbed him; no one called him "Sorry." Still, after a few polite greetings, silent nods, Feldman was at the bar, on a stool, by himself.

Eventually, I headed that way. Just before I reached him, I glimpsed Feldman's face in the mirror above the taps. It stopped me cold. I was standing there, a foot or two behind Feldman, when someone yelled "Sir!," and I seized the chance to turn around, away from him, into the middle of a war story. It was a familiar one, a story we'd all heard and told a dozen times but that we still laughed and shook our heads at, even though it wasn't true.

Winter 2016

Those Who Burn

Lara Prescott

At the center of a city nearly emptied of its people, in a country already gone half dark, a young woman leaned her elbows against the deli case of a butcher who'd been her father's closest friend.

"Nothing?" she asked the butcher again.

The butcher, a man with jowls that wobbled equally when he laughed and when he yelled, held up his hands and shrugged.

"No more of that tripe I got from you last Tuesday?"

"Gone Wednesday."

"Any fat?"

The butcher made a show of cinching the ties of his starched, white apron. "Even that's going." He rested his hands on his once-robust belly. "Quickly."

"Bones?"

"Someone's soup by now."

The woman opened her canvas bag with the faded insignia of a foreign university on its side. She removed her wallet. "Any rations?" she asked, her voice a whisper, her gaze on the wallet not the butcher.

"I'd have given them to you, Yarah."

She put her wallet away. "Tomorrow, maybe?"

Radi reached for a rag on the hook behind the counter and started buffing an invisible spot on the deli case. "If I were a betting man, I wouldn't take those odds."

"Why then?"

He hung the rag back on its hook. "Why what?"

"Why open your doors if you have nothing left to sell?"

Radi stared at the counter; the silence hung. "On the bright side," he looked down the front of his apron then up at Yarah, "have you ever seen a butcher's apron so white?"

Yarah turned to the two large windows at the shop's front. The early evening sunlight reflected off broken glass scattered on the sidewalk next to a bus stop. A man wearing a makeshift camouflage uniform poked his head out of a doorway across the street. He looked left then right, then ran in a zigzag across to an empty office building that used to house an insurance company. Yarah watched, puzzled. *The snipers were in the villages. They hadn't come this far into the city. Not yet, anyway.* She turned back to see Radi sitting on a wooden stool, a newspaper spread across his lap. "How was the weather four months ago, uncle?" she asked.

"Let's see," he said, flipping the pages. "Ah, yes. June 12th.

Lovely day that was. Lots of sun. A hot one."

"And what did dear President have to say on June 12th? Are we still winning?"

Radi turned back to the front page. "Peace is on the horizon, Yarah." He held up a finger. "And with peace, comes meat."

"Speaking of which," Yarah turned her head slightly away from Radi, "is El-Hashem's shop still open?"

Radi closed the newspaper.

"I have no choice," Yarah said.

Radi's cheeks grew as red as his apron on a good day. El-Hashem had once threatened to tell the secret police Radi was passing along information with his cold cuts. "I know you have no choice." He sighed like a bellows. "If your father were alive—"

The thought made Yarah's chest tighten. Her father had been dead just over a year. Two years earlier, she had arrived home from class to a message her roommate had written on the chalkboard in their kitchen:

Call your father!
You have a father?

When Yarah called, her father told her, in a way akin to saying he didn't want anything for his birthday, that he had *the cancer* and not to worry or come home. He repeated: *Do not come home.* So she came home. She told her roommate she'd be back next semester, that she'd see her in the spring. It wasn't until she was in the deserted baggage claim of an airport in which the departures greatly outnumbered the arrivals that Yarah realized just how impossible that would be.

Her father Fareed was a hard man, made harder when his wife died shortly after Yarah's birth. He was also an impatient man with high expectations. He would accept nothing but the best from his only child. The day Yarah received her acceptance letter to a university two plane rides away was the only time she ever heard him say he was proud.

So when she knocked on the door of the apartment she grew up in, Yarah expected Fareed to tell her to get back on those two planes and return to school. Instead, he answered and stood back for a moment, silent. When he finally embraced her, Yarah could feel the bones in his back, how the top of his head felt like peach fuzz. "You came," he said, pressing his face against her shoulder. "You came."

"But alas," Radi continued, his face now back to its olive hue, "El-Hashem's butcher shop is closed. He's long gone."

"*Gone*, gone?" Yarah asked.

"Not that gone."

Yarah's right hand reached for the back of her head. She pulled on a hair until it came out in her fingers. "What am I going to do?"

"That's easy," Radi said, taking off his black hairnet. He crumpled it into a ball, then tossed it toward the trash bin, missing. "You leave."

As she turned the corner onto her street, no meat in her bag, Yarah looked up and saw her apartment building—a black silhouette against the evening sky. A scattering of tiny lights flickered in the windows of the few people she knew still lived there: Abdul-Malik and his young family in 3C, the widow Mrs. Farhi in 10D, and Dr. Zaman and his wife in 4B.

She scaled the six flights to her apartment with the feeling of cold stones rattling in her stomach. At the door, a white paw reached out from underneath, latching onto the doormat. "Just a minute, Sasha," Yarah said, fumbling for her keys in the dark hallway. She opened the door and made her way to the kitchen, the small grey and white cat with a beige spot next to her nose running ahead. Yarah lit a candle, opened the cupboard, and took out the second-to-last dented can of tuna. "Just half tonight," she said to the cat rubbing against her leg. Then she pulled out a box of stale cereal and poured herself a bowl.

Outside, the streets were quiet, the early moon framed between two empty buildings. Curfew was at eight, so Yarah had to get to the square and back quickly. En route, she passed only one person: a kerchiefed woman with a prominent nose she could spot from a half a block away.

At a distance, Yarah mistook her for a former classmate's mother. In the space of a few seconds, her heart leapt then fell when she realized the woman was a stranger. They nodded to each other as they passed.

The square was vacant except for a small diamond-shaped arrangement of abandoned tents, a scattering of overturned metal tables that once displayed herbs and spices and bronze-plated trinkets, and the rubble from a statue of someone whose name Yarah had long forgotten. A newcomer, if there had been any newcomers, wouldn't have known the statue was ever a statue, except for the head—perfectly intact but three meters away from its crumbled base, lolling on its side as if chopped from a guillotine.

Yarah made her way toward the bench in the square's northeast corner. It was the same bench where she'd sat with Amir six months prior. On the back of the bench was a small, gold plaque: *To Ula, My Heart.* Yarah had memorized the inscription; it was where she looked, instead of at Amir, when he told her he was leaving with his family. He said other things too, but Yarah stayed focused on the plaque. *Who was Ula? And was the person who dedicated this bench still here? And if he was, did he still come and sit and think about Ula?* Yarah's concentration broke when Amir placed his hand on her left knee. She pushed it off.

Yarah knelt and pulled the last of the tuna from her bag. At the sound of the can opener, cats emerged from their hiding places. They were all shapes and sizes and colors, but Yarah could tell which had been strays from the start and which had been pets—the former house cats cried louder. They knew what it felt like to be loved, to be full, and they howled at the memory.

A week after Amir met Yarah in the square to tell her he was leaving, he asked her to come to his apartment. Yarah usually came weekday afternoons to tutor his daughter, Mina, but Amir had asked her to come on a Saturday morning. The apartment was quiet, except for the refrigerator's hum. They were alone.

"No," she told Amir for the second time.

"I have no choice," he said.

Yarah pulled on a curly, brown strand until it came out. She held it, then let it drop. "You do have a choice. I'll take the cat."

Amir got up from the table and poured more hot water into his teacup. "And who will take her in when *you* leave?" he asked, his back to Yarah.

"I told you." She started picking at her hair again but stopped herself. "I'm not leaving."

Amir stared out the window above the sink. He watched a pigeon catch an updraft of wind and coast from one rooftop to another. "You will."

Yarah wanted to ask if he had an extra ticket, an extra set of papers, but stayed quiet. She knew to whom Amir's three airplane tickets and new IDs belonged: one for him, one for Mina, and one for his wife.

Amir raised his teacup and drained it in two gulps. He set it in the sink. "I have something for you." He left the kitchen. Yarah heard him open and close a drawer in his bedroom. He returned and sat across from her, placing an envelope on the table.

Yarah stared at the envelope but didn't move to take it. She could see the outline and bulge of money inside. "What's this?"

Amir pushed it toward her. "It's for you." Yarah pushed the envelope back.

"Please," Amir said. "You *will* go someday, and I don't want you walking out when you do. There are other ways. Safer ways."

"I'm not leaving," Yarah said again.

Amir sighed. "There's nothing left here for you."

Yarah heard someone get off the elevator and walk down the hallway. She held her breath until the footsteps passed.

Amir buried his face in his hands.

"I'll take good care of her. Let her lick yogurt off the spoon like she likes. Throw her bottle caps to fetch."

Amir looked up. "She can do that?"

Yarah stood and got a Coca-Cola from the refrigerator. She popped the cap off on the corner of the countertop and took a sip. Sasha, a small grey and white cat with a beige spot next to her nose, left the sunbeam she'd been lying in and ran into the kitchen. Yarah threw the cap into the adjacent room and Sasha barreled after it, almost crashing into a coffee table. She batted it around, then brought the cap back to Yarah in her teeth. "See?" Yarah said.

Amir gave a half-smile, which was quickly replaced with a grimace. "I just . . . I don't want anything to happen to you."

Yarah didn't break her gaze from Sasha, who had dropped the cap at her feet and was waiting for her to throw it again.

"I care for you," Amir said. "Deeply. If we had met—"

"Why not just let her outside?" Yarah interrupted. "She'd be a fine little hunter." She bent down and scratched the cat's chin. "Wouldn't you?"

"I don't know what else to say."

Yarah wanted to ask what he remembered of the night they'd spent together. It had been so clear in her mind at one point. She had even gone to a café the next morning to sit and sip her tea and try to cement it all in her memory. But fragments came and went regardless, operating under some will of their own. While drawing a bath: *how his beard felt pressed against her stomach.* Waiting in line for rations: *was the small scar next to his left eye or his right?* Cleaning the toilet: *how he slept without a pillow. Who sleeps without a pillow?* But as she sat in that café, going over each moment frame by frame, she'd already known it would never happen again. Amir told her the next day it couldn't. The only way Yarah could stomach the shame was to put it aside, somewhere separate from her, as if it were in a safe deposit box she knew she would have to open and unpack someday.

Yarah walked over to Amir and touched his right shoulder. Their eyes met for a moment. She reached for the envelope. She put it in her jacket pocket, then picked up Sasha. "I don't know what else to say either." She walked out of the apartment with the cat.

Years later, Amir's daughter would email him, asking if he remembered their cat Sam. She'd be taking a creative writing class and want to write about her home country. Amir would respond, saying that the cat's name was Sasha, not Sam. *She had grey and white fur and a small beige spot next to her nose. Don't you remember?* Mina would reply: *Are you sure? I'm positive it was Sam. Didn't my tutor—Yarah?—didn't she teach him to fetch bottle caps? Or did I make that part up?* Mina would remember having a cat, but not her name. She'd remember her tutor's name, but not what she looked like. She'd remember what her mother looked like, but not the sound of her voice. Mina had been so young when they left, and her mother had died in transit, never making it to their new home. She would rely on her father to fill in the blanks. He'd maintain an almost photographic memory of what happened, because he'd often spend his days going over all he had done, and all he hadn't.

After the envelope money was spent, after the electricity stayed off and the city grew darker still, after Radi boarded up his shop, Yarah spent her days scavenging food and candles and batteries from abandoned apartments. She looked in people's cupboards, their pantries, their refrigerators, underneath their bathroom sinks. Sometimes she found a can of pears or the metal shell of a used tea light. Most of the time she found mold, cockroaches, the occasional rat. Once, in an apartment in her building that used to house a young family, Yarah found two young girls looking for toys. The older girl was holding a stack of books; the younger, a stuffed giraffe with a missing eye. The two girls froze when they saw Yarah. She wanted to tell them that it was OK, that she was doing the same thing herself, but the taller girl dropped the books, grabbed her friend's hand, and ran.

One afternoon, after another unsuccessful morning of scavenging, a knock came at Yarah's door. Radi stood on the other side, holding a large cardboard box. Yarah opened the door, and he set the box at his feet, wiping the sweat from his forehead with the back of his hand. "I want you to have this," he said.

"What is it?" Yarah asked.

Radi squatted and opened the box with the jagged edge of his key. Inside were stacks of brown plastic packages. He held one up, inspecting the label. "Dried chicken *catch-a-tore-ee*."

"Where'd you get this?"

"Fell off the back of a truck."

"Where'd you get *that*? *The Godfather*?"

"*Scarface*." He picked up the box and followed Yarah into the apartment. "It's food. It's yours."

"I can't take it," she said, trying to give it back. "Your family—"

"I'd rather starve than eat the kind of meat you have to," Radi lowered his voice, "*add water to moisten*." He put his hands behind his back and surveyed the living room. He hadn't been inside the apartment since Yarah's father was too sick to leave it. Everything was just as it had been. It was as if Fareed would come out of the kitchen at any moment with a tray of tea. "Besides, we're leaving tomorrow, Yarah."

"Tomorrow?"

"Tomorrow, yes. You know this." He scratched the back of his neck with his key. "And we still want you to come."

Yarah caught Sasha, who was trying to run into the hallway. "She's always doing that."

"Did you hear what I said?"

She looked at the man who'd been her father's closest friend, the man who'd become her friend. "Tomorrow's so soon . . ."

"You have other plans?"

"I can't."

"No," Radi said. "You *won't*."

"I won't," she repeated.

"And there's nothing I can do or say?"

Yarah nodded.

Radi tightened his lips.

"Thanks for the food, Radi." Yarah embraced him before he could reply. "For everything." Radi squeezed Yarah for a moment, then backed into the hallway. Yarah closed her door, waiting by it until she heard his footsteps. After she heard the stairwell door close, she finished scraping the melted wax from the previous night's candles off her tables and counters and began melting it into jars for the night to come. When she finished, Yarah took a bottle cap from her cardigan pocket and tapped it on the counter. Sasha, lying in the corner, looked up, then laid her head back down.

Yarah looked over to her lamp—gold with a blue lampshade, now useless. Her father had placed a yellow sticky note on its side, noting the price he thought she should sell it for. "You can start selling the furniture now if you'd like," he'd told her. She'd watched as he'd hobbled across the apartment, placing notes on the belongings she'd grown up with: four thousand pounds—a pittance—for the footstool with wooden lion's paws for legs; three thousand for the oversized freezer in need of a new motor; one thousand for the lamp.

At the time, Yarah didn't acknowledge the sticky notes. Instead, she'd put her energy into ensuring her father took his medication at the right time, that he'd finish his bowls of broth, that he'd wash his face and brush his teeth.

A year after the funeral, Yarah had to remind herself to wash her face and brush her teeth and get out of bed. She never sold the furniture or touched her father's sticky notes, and the longer she stayed in the apartment, the harder it became to leave.

Her thoughts went to Radi and his offer, and her heart felt like it was being pressed between two books. She had a feeling she would never see the butcher again.

Radi and his family would settle in a new country, where, thanks to a cousin-of-a-cousin, he'd secure a part-time job in a kosher butcher shop in a part of the city people described as *up and coming*. Where they were coming up to, Radi would never know. He'd struggle at first with the language and high customer volume but would quickly improve with the aid of old Western films. He'd become fluent, albeit with an occasional expression unheard since the stagecoach era, be promoted to full time, and eventually made a partner with the small Jewish man who had inherited the butcher shop from his father and would live above it his entire life. When a restaurant serving charcuterie with hard-to-pronounce cheeses and olive oils that cost more than Radi charged for a shank of lamb opened its doors, he and the Jewish man would have to close theirs. But by that time, Radi would be ready to retire. He'd tell his wife he could use a rest, and he'd look forward to spending his days watching old films, walking on the treadmill at the gym, and calling his two grown sons on the phone, asking when he could expect grandchildren.

Two weeks after Radi left, four days since Yarah had a candle to burn, and three days since she'd scavenged anything worthwhile, she knocked on Dr. Zaman's door. Dr. Zaman was a veterinarian, although it had been almost a year since he'd addressed himself as such. His office had closed when more people sought his medical assistance for themselves than for their pets. He couldn't blame them: People were dying in hospital waiting rooms after waiting days to be seen by a doctor, a nurse, an aid worker, anyone. So when they started showing up at his office with shrapnel wounds and concussions and appendicitis, he'd wanted to help them—he did—but felt he wasn't qualified. Eventually, the office was ransacked—people pushed past his receptionist and took painkillers, dewormer tablets, plaster meant for tiny casts, even the medicated food for cats with bladder infections. When all was gone, Dr. Zaman sat on the edge of a metal exam table, staring at a canine anatomy poster while his receptionist rubbed her bruised elbow. Neither said a word.

"Yarah," Dr. Zaman said, opening his door. The doctor looked at Yarah, then the cat poking her head out of the top of Yarah's coat, and invited them in.

She took a seat on the couch, and Dr. Zaman disappeared into his bedroom. "Will it hurt at all?" Yarah asked when the doctor reappeared with his medical kit.

"A slight burn with the needle. Then she'll sleep."

Yarah took a deep breath. Her voice struggled to pass her lips. "She's just so small. She won't make it. These other cats . . . they're different."

Dr. Zaman put his hand on top of Yarah's. "It's the right thing to do."

Yarah nodded but wasn't sure she believed him.

The remorse and shame that would plague Dr. Zaman for not helping his city's people when they needed him would take years to ease, and would never disappear. He'd open a new practice in a country that would take him decades to call home. On his first day of business, he would hang the same dog anatomy poster in his new reception area, so that when he'd arrive at work each morning, he would see it and remember.

A tuxedo cat followed Yarah as she approached the square. An orange tabby ran ahead, her tail vibrating with excitement. Yarah set the cardboard box down, and a calico with a nub for a tail licked her right shoe.

More cats encircled Yarah as she opened the box, their cries reaching a fever pitch. Yarah crouched down and opened a bottle of water and one of the brown plastic packages Radi had given her. She poured in two capfuls, waited for the Styrofoam-like meat to plump into something that appeared edible, and flicked the pieces into the crowd. An all-white male jumped at her hand, nipping her thumb. Yarah put the bloody thumb in her mouth and continued.

An aggressive black cat leapt and caught the last of the meat from Yarah's last package—a feat of acrobatics only a recently abandoned cat could have mustered. With the meat gone, the cats continued caterwauling. Yarah turned the box over, showing them she had nothing left to give. A Siamese with a crooked tail took off with an empty package. Others followed, and a fight broke out.

Yarah stood and straightened her back. She was alone in the square, under the low moon's light in an otherwise darkened city. The catfight faded into the distance, and the quiet sank in. She reached into her jacket pocket and removed the yellow sticky note she'd taken off the gold lamp with the blue lampshade. She rubbed the paper between her fingers, folded it in half, and put it back. She cut through the square and continued walking straight ahead. It wasn't until she reached the line of people waiting at the first roadblock near the city's edge that Yarah realized she wouldn't be going back.

Four years would pass before Yarah would make it back to the university she had once left to care for her father. During that time, she would lose her right pinky toe to frostbite and spend the night with an Italian aid worker who'd tell her she was one of the *harraga*—those who burn. She'd liked the word and would repeat it as he kissed the dimples in her lower back.

Yarah would think she'd seen Amir's wife in a camp while waiting in line for the small toiletry bags distributed during entry. She would remember the photograph Amir had kept on his bedside table—of the couple taken at the ocean, their backs to the camera. She'd remember how she could tell, although she had been unable to see their faces, that they were happy at that moment. She'd remember holding the photograph close to her face, inspecting it for a sign that never came.

The woman Yarah would think was Amir's wife wouldn't give her a second glance as she'd pass and disappear back into the crowd. Yarah would wonder if Amir had taken the photograph with him, if he had removed the frame and folded it in half for easier travel.

In her second year of graduate school, Yarah would date an associate professor from the School of Engineering. Once, after a dinner of Thai food, he'd show her *before* and *after* photos of her home country taken at night, by satellite. *Before*, an array of speckled lights, clustered in cities, lit up the photo. *After*, a country gone dark—just a few pinpricks of light near the borders. Yarah would think of the little grey and white cat with a beige spot near her nose, of the cats in the square, of Radi, and Amir. She'd think of her home, of that stool with the lion's paw legs. She'd think of her father and his sticky notes—how she would have traded both pinky toes for one more day with him. And she'd think of the burning candles, melted over and over until there was nothing left.

But she would look at the satellite images for only a moment, before glancing down at her phone to check her email.

"What do you think about that?" the associate professor would ask. "Such mindless devastation."

Yarah would look up from her phone. "You've never been."

"Yes, I know," he'd reply, clicking away from the photos. "I can hardly imagine what it was like."

"No," Yarah would agree.

Autumn 2016

The Bridge

Cary Holladay

> When your enemy is fleeing,
> give him a bridge of silver.
> —Spanish proverb

Rapidan, Virginia

Bonnie Hazlitt can't remember how it ended, her stint as bridge guard. Like the others, she was hired by Henry Fenton, who was directed by the Orange County Court to employ "four to six discreet persons" to defend the short span over the Rapidan River. Strolling along the bridge, Bonnie gazed down into the water, oh, watching and listening for the Yankee army, for spies and traitors, reading the sky for clues, believing the hawks and buzzards wheeling in the sky would warn her of enemies' approach. There was plenty of traffic over the bridge, neighbors and tradesmen and rebel soldiers. Bonnie had the morning hours, starting at sunrise. She had a baby at home; her mother took care of him. Bonnie was not respectable, but Henry Fenton saw beyond that, and she was grateful to him.

It made sense that Henry Fenton was in charge. His mill sat on the riverbank.

Even then, Bonnie must have known she didn't accomplish a damn thing. And she must have got the bighead. That was what her mother said, her mother who believed it was nonsense for a girl to guard the bridge. "You'll be gettin' the bighead," her mother said, and they would laugh. Was it all in vain, those hours of scanning the bridge, the water below it, the road to and fro? Maybe she did keep the Yankees away, her vigilance forestalling the marauders who would have pillaged and killed, swept down on Rapidan and routed them all from their homes, farmers and housewives, children and old folks, the coloreds, the whites, the dogs and cattle. Finally, of course, the Yankees came anyway.

Years later, in her fifties, her sixties, Bonnie just doesn't remember how it ended. "Musta been knocked on the head," she tells her canaries, "the bighead," twittering back at them, the glosters and fancies, agates and isabels, their feathers silken in her hands. Buyers come from Washington, Richmond, Wheeling to buy her birds. She has a wonderful memory. A knock on the head is the only thing that would interfere with it. She remembers when Henry Fenton's mill was burned in 1864, by the Yankees. She recalls which bird a customer purchased years ago. Keeps up with her birds, since her children are gone away. "Still alive, far as I know," she observes as she cleans cages. "Bonnie's Beauties" says the wooden sign on her house, the same little house she grew up in. A tramp carved the bird-shaped sign for her, painting it yellow. "Purty thing," he said of the canary she supplied as a model, and by then, the war was long over and her mother was dead.

As bridge guard, she had a gun loaned to her by Henry Fenton, but she never used it. Her eyes and ears were her best defense, and her strong legs could sprint a warning, miles if need be. Henry Fenton had a telegraph in his mill office. He knew before anybody, about the moving armies. What you had to watch for were strays, outsiders. Horseman, swimmer, fisherman. You would not know him, when you saw him.

She did not hesitate to question strangers. Three times, heart in her throat, hand on the gun, she took someone to Henry Fenton's office. Each time, Henry greeted the man by name. "Don't *she* look sheepish," one man chuckled, but Henry praised her. How much was she paid? She can't remember that either, all those years later, when her thoughts are all for her canaries. A few dollars, she guesses, paid by Henry Fenton in his mill office. She put the money down her dress and didn't care who saw.

One day she spotted a white squirrel in a tree. It made her happy, that flash of exotic fur high in the trees along the river, something natural that yet did not belong. She was glad for the war, for it meant there were fewer men and boys to hunt the squirrel, to kill it. "Mens is so cruel," said the Negro midwife who delivered Bonnie's baby. The woman told tales of the colored world, of a wife killed by her husband and found with eyes open and hands in front of her face as if to push her murderer away. The teller demonstrated, lying on the ground with hands up and eyes wide for the benefit of Bonnie and her mother. Everybody knew it was poison, the woman said, because of the staring eyes and a white line like salt on her lips.

Flash, scurry. The white squirrel showed itself only to Bonnie. It is her most vivid memory of the war, and maybe of her life, what she would see if she died. Not her long-ago first baby who went to Mexico; not Henry Fenton whom she loved sort of, though she'd have died if he'd guessed it; not those morning hours when she was a vital shield protecting Rapidan; not even her canaries so soft in her hands. But a white squirrel, glimpsed in a stand of box elder by the Rapidan River—her best memory. She likes to think the squirrel is still there. The same one.

Henry Fenton's own wife, Mary Jane, is the most discreet person he knows. He would deploy her to the bridge, and she would gladly go, but since the birth and death of their daughter, she has been sick. Mary Jane suggested who the guards might be, after careful thought, speaking the names clearly from her bed.

Because of her being sick, he need not go to war.

In the afternoons, while she tries to sleep, she imagines the pattern that leaves and pine needles would make on tent canvas, with sunlight above them. As a young girl, she toured the Shenandoahs and the Blue Ridge with her cousins, an uncle, and an aunt; the aunt was her father's sister. Mary Jane's sister Beth didn't go; Beth was married by then. Beautiful, what Mary Jane saw from the knolls and in the woods. They slept at inns, some none too clean. She begged the others to camp, to sleep in the wilderness. She longed to look up through a roof of canvas and see pine needles on the thin cloth of a tent, making shade, a kaleidoscope of shifting shadows. Back then, she was strong enough to climb the Peaks of Otter. Now her middle's been blasted out of her, feels like.

"Tell me everything," she says to the bridge guards, as one by one they visit her room and sit in her slipper chair. "Tell me who you saw."

That's what her mother used to say to her, every time Mary Jane stepped out the door and returned. It drove her crazy, as a young girl. "Who did you see?" her mother asked. "Who did I see?" Mary Jane repeated furiously, for there were so few neighbors. Mary Jane and Beth bewailed their loneliness. Beth married young and moved to Richmond. Their mother expected the world would come to their Spotsylvania County farm, but Mary Jane in bitter triumph knew that it would not. Her parents were Scots living in Ireland when they fled for their lives, changing their name from Livingston to Boggs. Such an ugly name, Mary Jane thinks, as two of the bridge guards, the old Pratt twins, begin their recitation.

"We stopped a horse and wagon," they say, "and searched it. What was in the wagon was all lumpy, under some old rugs."

"Let me guess," says Mary Jane. But everything is lumpy under old rugs. Her fever is coming back, and that sensation of her body slipping out of itself, silencing her.

"It was ornaments," a Pratt says, fumbling for the word. "Decorations. Lanterns, stars, all different colors. For a party, the man said."

"How old are you?" asks Mary Jane. Sometimes, pain jolts her in mid-sentence, taking her to a place she thinks of as *hold-still, bear it.*

"We are seventy," responds one man, as if the age is permanent.

"What is it like?" she asks, and they think she means not their twinship but their duty.

"It's all right," they say together.

"I can't tell the two of you apart," she says. "Can anyone?"

"Yes, ma'am," they say. "We can tell us apart."

"Now listen," she says. "The way I see it, there won't be just one battle, been and gone. Our soldiers and the Yankees will be all through here, the whole time this war lasts. This will be contested territory." The Pratts couldn't scare crows from a cornfield. "We can't let them have it. To guard the bridge, you have to love it. Do you?"

Miz Fenton is scarier than the Federals. "Yes, ma'am," the Pratts chorus. They've never said the word love in their lives, except about apple butter, the way their mother made it.

The boy, Burrell, has the dead-of-night watch. He relishes it. Animals come by then, trotting, lolloping, slithering, flying, padding, powered by their invisible hearts, their eyes bright as coins. He had never known that they too use the bridge, not just the wild and tame dogs that cross it during the day, but possums and deer, foxes and bobcats, as if to say, Why not, it's here. He thinks he's dreaming when herd animals appear: goats and sheep, one or two as if ark bound. They have business to tend to. He could reach out and pet their flanks, their fur, their hides, the tips of their whiskers. He tries, and they swerve out of reach. Porcupine, bear, turkey, squirrel, and pig. Their nighttime travels have a dapper purpose and camaraderie. Snakes move fast at night, and toads jump high as Burrell's shoulder. Tortoises, he swears, just about gallop. The animals have no fear of him, this boy crouched at one end of the bridge, proud of missing his sleep.

He has only one eye. When he recites the list of creatures, he grows insistent, turning his good eye toward Mary Jane Fenton, cocking his head.

"I believe you," says Mary Jane. "I know they are there. I've heard them."

Her house overlooks the mill and the river. She herself would be the best guard of all.

"It's not like people think it is," Burrell says, meaning the animal world, the night world. He unwraps his sketchbook. He has drawn them, the creatures. Among their figures float faces and forms of humans, caught in his lantern light as he hailed and detained them, then let them pass. Mary Jane barely glances at those.

"Here's an owl riding the back of a mule," she says, delighted. "They came by 'bout three o'clock," says Burrell.

It's early in the morning, and he's sleepy, his shift having ended with sunrise, when Bonnie Hazlitt swung down the road wearing a yellow apron over her dress. He longs to be dashing and witty in her eyes but believes she dislikes him.

"Go home," Mary Jane tells the boy, "and rest."

"How can you hear 'em? The animals."

"I often sleep with the windows open. Sounds carry at night, and over water." She blushes, for this is Henry's room, too.

Burrell folds his sketchbook and lopes away.

All over the South, there are bridges, and some with guards. Are they all like this, busy at night with animals in transit? Mary Jane has seen the army, Southern soldiers. When men are coming, Henry often has word. From her window she watches the long assemblage with its music, its shouts, drumbeats, a cavalcade and parade. Men find their way to her door, and her cook feeds them. Commanders stop at the mill, and Henry greets them. The bridge holds them all, men, horses, wagons. For miles after they pass, she can glimpse them on the rising road as the column winds through farms and up into the hills.

"Throw him back like an ugly fish," says Henry, his eyes twinkling, when the guards ask what they should do if they apprehend a Yankee. He expects, before the war ends, that they may all have to fight, at least the old men and the one-eyed boy. That girl, Bonnie Hazlitt, could nurse her baby and fight at the same time, don't put it past her.

Don't ever say goodbye on a bridge. You'll never see the other person again. Henry's grandmother used to say that. Henry is thirty-six years old. From the top floor of his mill, the bridge and the river look as far away as the Grand Canyon.

Miller, landowner, horse breeder, husband, yet he is helpless, powerless. Their little girl lived two years, during which she and Mary Jane were usually sick.

His wife will die too. Then he'll go to war. *She'll die, and I'll fight.* The realizations slice through him while he bargains with two farmers. He speaks and smiles, but he is wood. Can't they see it? He and the farmers have reached some agreement. They shake hands, there on the top floor of his mill where he set up his office, with the view of river and mountains and trees. Oh, the old mill's got mice in the walls, mice clever and swift on tiny feet, mice running for their lives up and down the steep stairs, riding the lift. In Henry's dreams, they work the machinery. Mice know Henry could not for the life of him say what he and the farmers have agreed on. The farmers are telling jokes, pleased with the deal. When he says, *I don't remember a word I've just said to you*, the men's laughter is a roar. *That Henry Fenton*, they'll say.

Most of his horses are gone to war. The army took them, even his favorite, Bessy Bedlam, the best steeplechaser in five counties. A painting of Bessy Bedlam hangs on the wall of the room he shares with his wife. *Go get 'em, Bessy*, he says when he looks at the picture. The painter made Bessy's coat too brown. She is bay.

He is alone in his high office with a chunk of petrified wood on his desk as a paperweight on a stack of orders and bills. The farmers are gone, and it is evening, time for supper. His wife is sick and their daughter dead. His workers are silent, if they are here at all. Did he send them home already? Down on the bridge, the two old Pratts, bowlegged as wishbones, face away from each other, one picking his nose, the other scratching his stomach. Never say goodbye, his grandmother said, on a bridge. His wife is a Scot. Building cairns is in her blood. The sun moves toward setting. The war surprised him, threw him. Thrown, as if from a horse. He can't get up from his chair. The mice must be striking all kinds of crazy positions in the walls, on the stairs, in the piles of grain, mocking him. It would have taken him forever to choose the bridge guards. The war would have ended before he decided. So Mary Jane, cairn builder, did it. She'll be having her supper on a tray, watching the sundown birds.

Bessy Bedlam threw Henry once, deep in the woods, worst fall he ever took. Lying on the thick leaves, the hard damp ground, he'd thought of this chunk of petrified wood on his desk, timber to rock, its thick plugged veins that once held sap, its sawed-off level base. Bessy Bedlam was not contrite or faithful. Stepping high, she took off through the trees, empty stirrups jingling like a woman's earbobs. He had to admire that.

Lanterns and stars, the old men said, for a party. Mary Jane does not believe they would know a party decoration from a hound dog. Lanterns and stars hidden in a wagon, lumps beneath a coverlet, suspicious heaps that the old men examined. *Whose party was it? I want to go.* It's fall and so warm outside, the river might evaporate and nobody would need the bridge.

Henry does not know what it's like to feel so alone you could die of anger. He has two brothers, Joe and Lawrence. One knows locks, the other, ice. That is their business, locks and ice. Both brothers are gone to war, and the shop is closed; the stucco building by the river, not far from Henry's mill, stands empty. You can go and stare through the cloudy windows. Would it not have made more sense to stay here, running the business? Lawrence and Joe wanted to go. Loud, showing off, betraying locks, forgoing ice.

Their wives visit Mary Jane on Sundays, bringing their sewing. She longs for her sister. *Why don't you write to me, Beth? Why should I keep pouring out all my news, my heart, in letters to you, and you don't answer?*

In the empty stucco building, ice melts, locks rust. Yet the sewing sisters-in-law chat about a new style of collar. They will edge the collars with crocheted lace. War has fueled a fever of fashion, a need to create daily a different aspect of face, figure, and hair. The sisters-in-law are as caught up in it as young girls. Mary Jane, well enough to be out of bed, digs her elbows into the sofa pillows. "You're looking better today," her sisters-in-law say. They would write to her, if they were apart, letters about weather and visitors and any little gifts the visitors bring: jelly, peaches. She loves these women for the mundane letters that they will never have to write to her. She does not understand why her own sister, whom she knows to be alive and presumably in possession of paper, does not. Henry wrote Beth, explaining that Mary Jane is sick, asking Beth to visit Mary Jane, but Beth hasn't answered, and she hasn't come. Mary Jane last saw Beth five years ago, when she and Henry journeyed to Beth's home on a foggy, cobblestoned Richmond street. Beth and her husband were aloof, directing most of their attention to their children. *That was before I had my little girl. Would that have made a difference?* When after a few days, Mary Jane announced their departure, Beth's face showed relief.

Mary Jane keeps on writing but holds some things back and finds pleasure in that: the owl riding on the mule, the lanterns and stars hidden in a wagon. *I don't have to give you everything.* Surely Beth will feel something missing, will pine for what is no longer there. Mary Jane would stop writing entirely if she could. The withholding of bits of news takes all the energy she has, the keeping back and the staving off of what is too terrible to admit: *Beth doesn't care if I die. She won't miss me, and she won't mourn. Does my life press down on hers in some bad way?*

She has Henry's arms around her at night, but still there is the blowing out of the candle and the sense of failure that darkness evokes in her. The doctor has brought sleeping medicines, malodorous, the colors of dark jewels, but they no longer have an effect. She could swig laudanum by the bottle and still stare wide-eyed at the ceiling all night, flexing her ankles and pointing her toes, as if she is swinging on a branch, about to be born. "Swinging on the moon," her mother used to say, of time before Mary Jane arrived on this Earth, "that was way back, darling, when you were still swinging on the moon."

She has a lock that she likes to play with, given to her by Henry's brother Joe, for Joe is Locks and Lawrence is Ice of FENTON'S LOCKS AND ICE. The lock is her toy, small and heavy with a whole universe of tumblers and ratchets within. She knows the combination by heart, she just enjoys twirling the dial, hearing the mechanisms fall into place. She has in fact a whole cabinet full of locks and keys of all kinds, assorted metals and shapes.

She had thought her child would play with them.

One balmy night, at two in the morning, she rises and gets dressed. She hasn't worn these boots in a long time, nor this shawl. The garments' scent, her own smell of skin and hair, says welcome back, hello Mary Jane. Henry stirs but doesn't wake.

In minutes, with a lantern in her hand, she is out of the house, down the drive, and on the road, covering the brief ground to the bridge, where she finds the boy, Burrell, asleep.

She flies at him with whip-sharp words. His waking is a spasm, a contortion of face and body that strikes Mary Jane as funny, and her ire subsides. He is young, after all, and she recalls with a pang that he lost his eye to a bully's rock.

When Bonnie Hazlitt arrives at dawn, she finds Mrs. Fenton earnestly consulting with the boy. Bonnie has trouble remembering his name: Burrell, rhymes with squirrel. Bonnie is amazed to find Mrs. Fenton out of bed. "Has the war ended?" she asks, for this is the only event she can imagine that would bring Mary Jane Fenton here to the bridge. Bonnie is hoping for fireworks, a celebration, the hundred people of Rapidan converging to kiss and cheer.

Mary Jane Fenton and the boy laugh. The war is not over, Bonnie infers, as Mary Jane and the boy double up so violently they might be sick.

Later that day, Mary Jane *is* sick, and there is blood. Dr. Stover tears the stethoscope from his ears and says, "Mary Jane. Stay in this bed. No more running off in the night, hear me?"

It's Henry he's talking to, and Henry nods.

She sees a woman put a hand on Henry's arm, observes this from her obedient bed, through the window that a servant polishes weekly with vinegar and water. There on the road, the woman is conferring with Henry. The woman has short red hair and, Mary Jane guesses, the frank brown eyes and freckled skin that go with that, and she does not know better than to wear brown with that hair and skin. Puts out her hand and lays fingers on Henry's arm.

I will die, and he will marry her.

Fannie Porter. That is who the woman is, a friend of Mary Jane's sisters-in-law. She came to church with them one time, but she lives at a distance, over toward Madison. Lives with her brother. They teach music, and what good is that with a war on? They will eke and starve, brother and sister, fainting away with their fiddles in their arms, their piano strings snapping, hoping somebody might need them to play at a wedding. They probably practice war marches for something to do, praying their solitary hen might lay an egg. Maybe Fannie Porter is asking Henry for a loan. No, she is consoling him. In the dip of her head, there is the practiced strength of a woman steadying a violin with her chin, a sturdiness and patience that Henry will grow to prize, forgiving those ham colors of her. Doesn't he see the stubbornness of that chin? Consoling him for what? Mary Jane squints through the window. For having a sick wife?

Henry's stance is straight. The woman's attention means something to him.

You were a little too sharp for him, Mary Jane's father said once, at a time when Henry's budding interest had seemingly waned. Mary Jane recognized her father's compliment. Sharp women were admired in her family. She was sharp, Beth was not.

Henry's younger brother Joe had come calling a time or two. Joe and Henry were the only suitors she ever had.

A walking stick proceeds along Mary Jane's window, its black feet attaching to the glass, the jaunty pencil of its body impossibly thin, carried high. You never see but one at a time, strange creatures, you never see them arrive and then where do they go? She'll forget about it for just a moment and then it will be gone—

Too sharp for him. A little too—

Fannie Porter lifts her hand away. A buggy approaches, slowing down and stopping in the road beside her. Henry might be conscious of warmth on his arm, through his sleeve. Fannie climbs into the buggy with clumsy efforts that emphasize her backside, beneath the ugly brown dress. Mary Jane checks the mantel clock: 11:02 in the morning. There is an untouched pot of cold tea by her bed, and all of the medicine jars, stinking as bad as the fluids of her own body. She'd do better to drink whiskey. Most of those potions are just alcohol anyway. Her head swims, the nausea closing in on her the way it does, fast, with light pulsing at the sides of her face, a fanning heat. The walking stick, she has got to remember to check—

She won't have you. I won't allow it. Red and brown, you'd get so tired of her looks and of the children she would bear. Fannie Porter, bumpkin, would sing at her own wedding, and Henry might be embarrassed, but he would be proud too, and afterward, that evening, there would be silence, bare arms, and firelight, here in this very room or out in the field, on the grass, with Fannie's brother sending a few last notes of fiddle and flute their way as he took his leave. Sweet notes that ride the air, *hold still and listen, he is playing for us, the old song I told him you love.* Fannie will whisper to her new husband, "Do you remember one day on the road, right out here? You were not free, but somehow I knew then that I, that you . . ."

I will get well, Mary Jane decides.

I will live.

Lady fair, Henry used to say, catching her hair in his mouth.

"It is a waste," she tells Henry, "to let the lock and ice shop go. Who knows how long the war will be? People need locks and ice. It should have stayed open, even with them gone."

"Now, now. Joe and Lawrence believe they can better serve our country this way."

"This is why we will lose. You know that, Henry. Melted ice and rusted locks, men running off to kill each other and ignore the very business that would give them a future."

Henry says, "When the war's over, they'll pick up where they left off. My brothers'll be rich men. Me, I'll still be just a poor miller, but I reckon we'll do all right."

Mary Jane won't let him off so easy. "But now, you're saying, Lawrence and Joe need to fight." She's going too far; the crimp in

Henry's eyelids tells her so. She can't help it. Poor-miller talk annoys her enormously. And Fannie's hand on his arm, she can't forgive that. Poor-miller talk is not attractive, she longs to say. Fannie will grow to hate it, too. Fannie will go and get the rolling pin, and I don't blame her, wave it at your head.

"I can't manage it all," Henry says, "not the mill and the other too. We talked about it, Joe and Lawrence and I."

The wives, the collar-makers, could run the business and better than the men. What are locks and ice, compared to making lace? You chop, you store. You forge ahead. You listen to the tumblers falling in a lock, with a sound like faraway applause. You pray the lock will open, *click*, right in your hand, its scent of oil the breath of surrender.

Joe, the youngest of the Fenton brothers, will live the longest. Mary Jane expects this. He will outlive all of the other members of the family who are now alive, and that includes his son and daughter, his nieces and nephews. In 1906, he will take a notion to visit San Francisco, where he will be saved by a stray dog that wanders into the bar where he is drinking beer. The dog tugs on his pant leg till he follows it outside, where moments later, the sky crashes down and the street rolls in waves beneath his feet. "Everybody in that bar was killed," he tells a reporter, who puts his story on the wire worldwide, "and that dog, some little mutt that picked me out to save, I got to thank him, but I can't find him."

Home in Virginia and restless, he will close his eyes, circle his finger above a map, and move to the spot he touches: Memphis, Tennessee. Mary Jane does not, cannot, know that Joe will step into the best society and be elected Cotton Carnival King. Even into the 1920s, when Mary Jane and Henry and Lawrence have been dead for a long time, Joe will be riding high, literally, on a float in a Cotton Carnival parade, saluting crowds on a hot June night, Joe, the man to call in Memphis if you need something locked up tight and forever. *Joe Fenton, he'll make you a safe nobody can crack, where'd he come from, Virginia, well, he's one of us.*

During the war, he'll tell you, he thought about locks all the time. He figured out some things. He had to get away from locks to learn them right, he'll say.

He'd courted Mary Jane before his brother Henry did. She was a distant cousin, and he called on her twice, even called once on her sister Beth, but Beth spooked him a little, something kinda mean about her. It was Henry whom Mary Jane encouraged. Joe sometimes wonders, well, if things might have been different.

Even in the twenties, on a motorized float shedding dyed carnations, with cornet music blaring in his ears and a Cotton Carnival Princess on either side of him, he misses Mary Jane. She used to play with those locks he gave her, not like a child plays but as if she were solving a puzzle far beyond sport. *Oh, Mary Jane. One time I said, You hold that lock like it's somebody's heart, and you smiled and said, It's not that easy.* The Cotton Carnival Princesses aren't nothing but tacky little girls, all rouged up, hair whacked off, grimacing, offering gum. "Want a stick of Juicy Fruit, Pops? I'm carsick as hell." With his cracked old teeth, he doesn't dare chew it, but he loves the way it smells. Women used to be prettier. His Clara, so modest, always sewing. Mary Jane, oh, *it's not that easy.* You were still right young when I was off at war, and you were so sick. I used to hope for news of you in letters from my wife.

He still has a letter Clara wrote about making a pie out of crackers and cloves to substitute for apples. The float turns a corner a mite too fast for a clumsy chassis on wheels, and a gum-smacking Princess knocks against him, squealing. Substitutes: oh, all those substitutes for coffee during the war, and none of them much good, were they? He and Henry used to laugh about that, once they were home, with all the coffee and good meat they wanted, all the roast chicken and hot rolls and bacon. They came back scarecrows from the war and got barrel-chested once they had enough to eat. Lawrence, well, he didn't make it home. Joe and Henry looked after his widow, and Joe learned ice as well as locks. He and Henry rebuilt the burned mill. Henry and his second wife, that red-haired woman Joe could never quite warm up to, raised a passel of children. Joe gave her some locks, and she tossed 'em in a drawer, didn't appreciate 'em the way Mary Jane did. Back in Rapidan, people still talk about the night the mill burned, how you could see the fire for miles and hear the commotion of flames and shouts. But the Yankees left the bridge alone. It's still there, after all this time.

Joe kept meaning to ask Clara to make him a cracker pie, then forgot about cracker pies till after she died.

Clara lost a crochet hook in the backyard during the war, and he was so proud the day he found it for her, oh years later, after a hard spring rain, the silver hook a tiny winking eye in the earth. She wiped the dirt from it and kissed him. "I just happened to look down," he told her.

Funny: he's never raised cotton in his life.

He is ninety-eight years old.

He waves, and his arm stays high.

Early one morning, a deer ambles to the river, wades in, and swims toward Bonnie, who holds her breath. The deer crosses at a slight zigzag, making up for the current. Bonnie has heard that deer can swim for miles, crossing the greatest rivers, far broader than this. How must it feel, head high above the water, your four slim legs churning, and what if you were pregnant, a doe swimming for your life, fixed on reaching that opposite shore, running from hunters maybe or a hungry dog, you can't stop? The middle of the river, shadowed by clouds, must feel so big.

The deer emerges downriver, clambering onto the bank and breaking into a run for the trees. Bonnie lets out her breath with a moan. Her baby is safe at home with her mother, who is making potato candy. But Bonnie's heart is wide open, lost. If the deer had floundered, she'd have gone into the water herself. Died trying to tow it in and save it. Loved it better than anything else in the world, her whole life—

Henry has engaged a man to make a daguerreotype of himself and Mary Jane. "There are newer methods," Mary Jane says. "Photographs."

"This will do for now," Henry says. Mary Jane sits on a horsehair sofa that has been dragged onto the porch. Henry stands behind it. The sofa smells stale, stable-like. She touches the cameo at her throat, yes, it's still there; it was hard to pin the brooch to her dress. Beads of sweat gather on her forehead, and pain slides razor-thin through her middle.

"Hold," the man says. Mary Jane doesn't like his beard, which sticks out spoon-like from his chin. Daguerreotypes unnerve her, the amber light, people's frozen, spread-out expressions. She could hold her breath forever. Henry's watch ticks loudly behind her ear. If she turns around, she'll see the silver fob and chain, marked by their daughter's teething.

"There, I've got it," the man says.

Henry says, "Someday I'll get picture-making equipment of my own and take a picture of my shadow on grass. Long grass."

Packing up, the man says, "That would be right pretty."

Mary Jane has no photographs of their daughter, but after the child's death, she commissioned a portrait, which hangs in the parlor. The painter was the same one who had painted that horse Henry loved, Bessy Bedlam. From Mary Jane's own drawings and descriptions, and furnished with a lock of the child's hair, the artist got the little girl's arms and hands, even her neck, but not her face. The expression is skeptical, adult, lips and teeth hooked in a pruney way as if saying *future*. Though Mary Jane made the artist do the face over, the expression did not improve. Henry said, "It's close as it'll ever be," and paid the man. The portrait is slowly erasing Mary Jane's memory of how her daughter really looked. *Just because you can paint a horse, with an ugly jockey in the saddle, does not mean you can paint the sweetest child in the world.*

"Have you made pictures of the soldiers?" Henry asks the daguerreotypist.

"Many times," the man says, in a salesman's voice. "Everybody needs their picture made. For the family, the sweetheart."

Mary Jane smells old leaves, and the dusty, familiar scent heartens her. She'll banish that portrait to the attic, that canny, false face.

To whom will she and Henry give this picture of themselves? Why are they having it made? They heard the man was in the area, and Henry summoned him. Her mother is dead, father dead. Her cousins Ginny and Dan, with whom she traveled to the Peaks of Otter, died of scarlet fever. And their parents, her aunt and uncle, went out West, Nebraska she believes.

The pain returns, hand-shaped inside her, each finger probing, wand-like, jointed as the walking stick. Two of her cats chase across the porch, too thin, must have worms, she must do something about that. In the distance, a train whistles. It'll be stopping in every town to the south, as far as Blacksburg and into Carolina. She could send Beth a copy of the picture—*here is my face, my husband*—but Beth does not care. The picture will wind up in a drawer, and red-haired Fannie will lift it out and hold it to the light, working out for herself whether Henry was happier with Mary Jane.

What was it the boy, Burrell, said the night she found him sleeping on the bridge, the night she raged at him and stayed down there so long, talking with him? He told her he had always wanted to be in a club, that the books he read as a child talked about clubs, and that as a guard, he felt he was in a club. Somehow that made them laugh, and they kept on laughing, because it felt so good. She likes the boy, likes the pictures he draws. She should get back to sketching, to keeping a diary, and she will, once she is well again.

She is suddenly convinced that she has bled all over the horsehair sofa, through her clothes. She might look down and find blood pooling on the floorboards of the porch, runnels of it about her feet, deltas of blood at the edge of the porch. From the corner of her eye, she sees only clean floorboards, cats, blowing leaves.

The men are talking about the war. Mary Jane is twenty-eight. The daguerreotype will show a childless couple, of indeterminate age, holding on. She couldn't speak if she wanted to.

Bonnie's mother does not know what to do. Bonnie has always been the sensible type, and now all this crying, blubbering and crazy talk. Some nonsense about a swimming deer, a white squirrel. Bonnie's mother puts the baby in its dresser drawer. Bonnie has never done this before, falling apart, not when that no-good left her nor even when one of the critters died that she was always bringing home, Lord, all them rabbits and hoptoads and such. Bonnie's the only person could keep wild baby birds alive, feeding them off the tip of her finger, raised a baby crow that way and a little jay, that flew off by theirselves when they got grown.

Bonnie raises her apron to her face to catch her wet, messy sobs. Her mother hands her a cup of water, but Bonnie pushes it away. So her mother settles down opposite Bonnie at the table where they do all their eating and sewing and where Bonnie nurses the baby, and waits out Bonnie's storm. Why, even in a crying jag, her daughter is still pretty.

Deep in the mother's heart burns a secret hope. Mr. Fenton's wife is known to be sick. What if she dies, and he chooses Bonnie? Men always marry again. Women, well, *she's* been better off since her husband died, Bonnie's father, a drinking man who fell off his mule and broke his neck. This morning, after getting the potato candy in the stove, using up the sugar and last year's potatoes though she should have kept some back, she haphazardly cleaned her yard with a broken rake, and the idea came to her: Bonnie as Mr. Fenton's new bride. Oh, she don't wish Mrs. Fenton ill. Hasn't never spoke to her, only glimpsed her, beautiful with that dark hair. Bonnie has visited with her on account of the bridge. It don't do to be so sorrowful about losing one child. She herself lost a daughter before Bonnie and a son after.

Dreaming, she stopped in the middle of her overgrown yard, the rake having uncovered a rusty pot—why, in last summer's dry spell, she'd stuck it out here to catch rainwater; if she scrubs it, it'll be good as new—and she imagined Bonnie taking lunch to her husband at the mill, yes, a covered basket for Mr. Henry Fenton, and Bonnie and the baby living in the big house by the river. Oh, it's sad about the Fentons' little girl, but Bonnie'll make Mr. Fenton forget all that. Bonnie can turn out babies one after another, children to farm the land and ride Mr. Fenton's horses. Once he's married to Bonnie, he won't even remember his first wife's face, the way Bonnie can't hardly remember that boy who got the baby on her and then went off to Manassas. He'd a-married me, Bonnie says, but a mother knows that's just talk.

So this won't do, all this blubbering.

"It's being a guard, gol-durnit," Bonnie's mother tells her. "That's a man's job."

"No, it's not," Bonnie chokes out.

"Well, what is it, then?" her mother asks. Two women in wartime, poor as Job's turkey, and the potato candy burned in the stove. She'd given up cleaning the yard and was chopping kindling when she smelled burning and let the ax fly right out of her hands. The candy was black rocks, which she threw out on the grass. Not even the birds wanted it. She tried to eat some, but it was ashes. Back of her tongue, she still tastes it. That's what hardship tastes like. Here she is getting old, trying to take care of this girl and this baby. And winter coming. Bonnie might end up like this forever, and her too, poor and crying and all the sugar gone. "Bonnie, what is the matter? Don't do this way. You got a child to tend to, and I'm not so young anymore—"

Raising her head, Bonnie rubs her fist across her cheeks. There's her baby in the drawer—her boy, asleep in a heap of rags—and her mother, whose biscuit face looks exactly as Bonnie suspects her own will look in twenty years. From her mother, she inherited hambone arms and restlessness. Neither of them can concentrate long enough to finish a prayer, unless they hurry to the amen. They break off in the middle of a conversation, their thoughts leading them to some chore that needs doing. A phrase bursts into Bonnie's mind, words she heard a preacher say: *storm petrel.* Some kind of bird maybe? *Storm petrel.*

The dresser where the baby sleeps is warm from the sun, and the deer made it to the trees.

Mother and daughter regard each other. "I found that pot we lost," her mother says.

Bonnie blows her nose and says, "I'm happy, is all." She hugs her startled mother.

"Law, Bonnie." Her mother squeezes Bonnie's ample back, her thoughts already moving away, raking through her day the way she'd raked brush. Mr. Fenton probably wouldn't marry Bonnie in a thousand years. She sighs. "I got to pay more mind when I'm cooking."

Touring the mountains with her aunt, uncle, and cousins, Mary Jane at eighteen kept a journal, recording the towns where they stayed: Waynesboro, Wytheville, Roanoke. In her diary, she described notable characters: a woman in Boone's Mill who wore too much jewelry, all her thunder and lightning, Mary Jane's uncle said, and an old man gathering hay near the Peaks of Otter who thrust his pitchfork in the ground when they waved to him, as if that were his reply. The trip was one her aunt and uncle had always wanted to make. Having recovered from a recent stillbirth, the aunt was quiet, even when her children Dan and Ginny, Mary Jane's cousins, told jokes and clung to her.

Her aunt was too old for babies, Mary Jane thought, with a son twelve and a daughter almost as old as Mary Jane.

Ridge after ridge of wavy blue land. Mary Jane sees it in her dreams. That day, on the Peaks of Otter, they were struck dumb by the beauty of it, all five of them, out of breath from the ascent. Mary Jane's arms were scratched from a fall in briers on the way up. Her aunt unpacked a picnic of deviled eggs, ham sandwiches, lemonade. There were no other hiking parties in sight and no sound except their voices and the wind. It was July, but the air was cool, then cold.

They had expected that, had been warned. Yet why had they all worn such thin clothes?

Ridge after ridge of beauty, oceans of mountaintops and forests. A blowing hollow, Mary Jane thought, wondering where that phrase came from. She and Dan and Ginny stood shivering with their arms around each other, leaning over the edge, far enough for the wind to take them away.

Are there animals in all the woods? Dan asked. Do people live there? I can see a thousand miles. Is that California?

His voice was a seashell pressed against Mary Jane's ear. He found a lizard among the rocks and declared he would take it home.

They stayed as late as they dared. These were not peaks to descend in the dark. When the uncle insisted it was time to leave, Cousin Ginny cried and begged. It's heaven, she said.

Mary Jane tried to draw what she saw, but her pictures did not come close. She did not write anymore in her diary, after that day. It seems to her—as she is dying, on a December afternoon in 1861—that as they shouted to hear their echoes, they stood on a grassy spot mere inches wide, above the unfurling earth.

More than we can see, her uncle said, sweeping his wife's windy hair from her face with his hands. Mary Jane saw that the baby-grief would never go out of her aunt's eyes. Her uncle said, There are caves down there and rivers, and cities in the valleys.

I can't see them, said Dan, and I want to.

Mary Jane hugged Dan and Ginny, pretending they were her children, needing the warmth of them. Dan's lizard escaped beneath a boulder. *This is summer*, Mary Jane thought. *I will come back here every summer of my life.*

She thought with excitement of Henry Fenton, who had asked to court her.

Oh, that was back when she believed she would live a long time.

Henry is with her now, beside her bed, and the doctor is in the room. She never expected to die on a beautiful day, with the trees such colors. She wants to look at the trees again and at Henry's face, but she has time, hasn't she, to close her eyes?

It was hard to climb the Peaks of Otter, but she was strong. Her arms tingled from the brier scratches.

Henry holds her hands to his face and cries, his tears hot on her skin, while she scrambles up and up.

"Echo!" she called from the Peaks of Otter, and the mountains answered, "Oh, oh, oh."

Her aunt gazed into the sky—not a bird, only blue—with her husband holding back her hair.

Winter 2004

They stayed [illegible] late [illegible] they danced. Those who [illegible] peeled [illegible] [illegible] the cold [illegible] [illegible] [illegible] covered and hugged [illegible] [illegible]

Mary [illegible] [illegible] [illegible] her place [illegible] [illegible] [illegible] her diary [illegible] [illegible] [illegible] a December afternoon in 186[illegible] [illegible] [illegible] them their boots, they stood on a grassy [illegible] [illegible] wide, looked [illegible] earth.

[illegible] and sweeping his wife's wine [illegible] with [illegible] Mary [illegible] [illegible] [illegible]

[illegible]

Copyrights and Credits

Allen, Brooke. "Don't Forget the Butterfly Effect." Reprinted by permission from *The Hudson Review* 73, no. 3 (Autumn 2020). Copyright © 2020 by The Hudson Review, Inc.

Balaban, John, and Donka Farkas, trans. "Préface en Prose," by Benjamin Fondane. Reprinted by permission from *The Hudson Review* 70, no. 4 (Winter 2018). Translation copyright © 2018 by John Balaban and Donka Farkas.

Bennett, Joseph. "A Cambodian Diary." Reprinted by permission from *The Hudson Review* 24, no. 3 (Autumn 1971). Copyright © 1971, renewed 1999, by The Hudson Review, Inc.

Berry, Wendell. "A Desirable Woman." Reprinted by permission from *The Hudson Review* 61, no. 2 (Summer 2008). Copyright © 2008 by Wendell Berry.

Bogin, Nina. "Halabja," "Yugoslavia in Ruins." Reprinted by permission from *The Hudson Review* 47, no. 2 (Summer 1994). Copyright © 1994 by Nina Bogin.

Caistor, Nick, trans. "Hunting in July," by Julián Ríos. Reprinted by permission from *The Hudson Review* 64, no. 1 (Spring 2011). Translation copyright © 2011 by Nick Caistor.

Farkas, Donka, and John Balaban, trans. "Préface en Prose," by Benjamin Fondane. Reprinted by permission from *The Hudson Review* 70, no. 4 (Winter 2018). Translation copyright © 2018 by Donka Farkas and John Balaban.

Finlay, John. "The Night of Alcibiades." Reprinted by permission from *The Hudson Review* 47, no. 1 (Spring 1994). Copyright © 1994 by the Estate of John Finlay.

Gullans, Charles, and Franz Schneider, trans. "Last Letters from Stalingrad." Reprinted by permission from *The Hudson Review* 14, no. 3

(Autumn 1961). Copyright © 1961, renewed 1989 by The Hudson Review, Inc.

Hoffman, Daniel. "On First Looking into Lattimore's Homer." Reprinted by permission from *The Hudson Review* 53, no. 2 (Summer 2000). Copyright © 2000 by Daniel Hoffman.

Holladay, Cary. "The Bridge." Reprinted by permission from *The Hudson Review* 66, no. 4 (Winter 2004). Copyright © 2004 by Cary Holladay.

Holladay, Cary. Quotation included in foreword. Permission granted to use it by the author in an email of September 5, 2023.

Kumin, Maxine. "Red Tape and Kangaroo Courts I," "Red Tape and Kangaroo Courts II," "Old News." Reprinted by permission from *The Hudson Review* 64, no. 4 (Winter 2012). Copyright © 2012 by Maxine Kumin.

Mason, David. "Introduction." Reprinted by permission from *The Hudson Review* 74, no. 4 (Winter 2022). Copyright © 2022 by The Hudson Review, Inc.

Mogelson, Luke. "Kids." Reprinted by permission of the author from *The Hudson Review* 68, no. 4 (Winter 2016). Copyright © 2016 by Luke Mogelson.

Morgan, Frederick. "Editorial." Reprinted by permission from *The Hudson Review* 21, no. 1 (Spring 1968). Copyright © 1968, renewed 1997 by The Hudson Review, Inc.

Nelson, Marilyn. "Aborigine in the Citadel." Reprinted by permission from *The Hudson Review* 53, no. 4 (Winter 2001). Copyright © 2001 by Marilyn Nelson.

Pais, Abraham. "'The Impossible Real.'" Reprinted by permission from *The Hudson Review* 46, no. 1 (Spring 1993). Copyright © 1993 by Abraham Pais.

Patton, Jr., George S. "The Moon and the Dead." Poem excerpt in Marilyn Nelson's "Aborigine in the Citadel." Used by permission of the George S. Patton Jr. Historical Society.

Pevear, Richard, and Larissa Volokhonsky, trans. "The battle of Austerlitz," "Natasha's first grand ball," and "The brief career of Petya Rostov," from Leo Tolstoy's *War and Peace*. Excerpt(s) from *War and Peace* by Leo Tolstoy, translated by Richard Pevear and Larissa Volokhonsky, translation copyright © 2007 by Richard Pevear and Larissa Volokhonsky. Used by permission of Alfred A. Knopf, an imprint of

Knopf Doubleday Publishing Group, a division of Random House LLC. All rights reserved. From *War and Peace* by Leo Tolstoy published by Vintage Classics. Translation copyright © Richard Pevear and Larissa Volokhonsky 2007. Reprinted by permission of The Random House Group Limited.

Prescott, Lara. "Those Who Burn." Reprinted by permission from *The Hudson Review* 69, no. 3 (Autumn 2016). Copyright © 2016 by Lara Prescott.

Ridland, John, trans. "Sir Gawain and the Green Knight, Part IV." Reprinted by permission from *The Hudson Review* 62, no. 4 (Winter 2010). Translation copyright © 2010 by John Ridland.

Ríos, Julián. "Hunting in July." Reprinted by permission from *The Hudson Review* 64, no. 1 (Spring 2011). Copyright © 2011 by Julián Ríos.

Schneider, Franz, and Charles Gullans, trans. "Last Letters from Stalingrad." Reprinted by permission from *The Hudson Review* 14, no. 3. Copyright © 1961, renewed 1989 by The Hudson Review, Inc.

Serizawa, Asako. "Allegiance." Reprinted by permission from *The Hudson Review* 65, no. 1 (Spring 2012). Copyright © 2012 by Asako Serizawa.

Simpson, Louis. "Soldier's Heart." Reprinted by permission from *The Hudson Review* 49, no. 4 (Winter 1997). Copyright © 1997 by Louis Simpson.

Stevenson, Anne. "The Miracle of Camp 60." Reprinted by permission from *The Hudson Review* 52, no. 2 (Summer 1999). Copyright © 1999 by Anne Stevenson.

Terrone, Maria. Epigraph, quotation from the chef Moshe Basson, by permission.

Terrone, Maria. "Knives." Reprinted by permission from *The Hudson Review* 63, no. 3 (Autumn 2010). Copyright © 2010 by Maria Terrone.

Williams, Tennessee. "In Spain There Was Revolution." Copyright © 2003 by the University of the South. Reprinted by permission of Georges Borchardt, Inc., on behalf of the author's estate. All rights reserved.

Notes on Contributors

Brooke Allen (Winchester, Virginia, b. 1956) is a contributing editor of the *Hudson Review*, where she writes on literature, history, and film. She was on the literature faculty at Bennington College and now teaches in the Bennington Prison Education Initiative. Her two most recent books are *The Other Side of the Mirror: An American Travels Through Syria* (Paul Dry Books, 2011) and *Benazir Bhutto: Favored Daughter* (New Harvest, 2016).

John Balaban's (Philadelphia, Pennsylvania, b. 1943) books of poetry have received the William Carlos Williams Award from the Poetry Society of America, the National Poetry Series, and the Lamont Prize from the Academy of American Poets. His translations from Vietnamese and preservation work in Vietnam were awarded a medal from Vietnam's Ministry of Culture.

Joseph Bennett (Pittsburgh, Pennsylvania, 1922–72) was a founding editor of the *Hudson Review* in 1947, served as an editor until 1966, and then continued by serving on the magazine's editorial board. He was valedictorian of the Princeton University class of 1943. Following, he was a lieutenant (jg) in World War II. After his discharge in 1946, he joined Wellington and Co., a New York banking concern, retiring as partner in 1966. He was the author of *Baudelaire: A Criticism* (Princeton University Press), *Decembrist*, a collection of poetry, and *Luxury Cruiser*, a novel.

Wendell Berry (Port Royal, Kentucky, b. 1934) is a native of Henry County, Kentucky, where he is still living. "A Desirable Woman" belongs to the imagined history of Port William, begun in the mid-1950s and still in progress. His latest book is *How It Went: Thirteen More Stories of the Port William Membership* (Counterpoint, 2022).

Nina Bogin (New York, New York, b. 1952) has lived in France since her mid-twenties, based near the Swiss border in the foothills of the Vosges Mountains. A recipient of an NEA grant for poetry in 1989, her collection *In the North* was published that same year by Graywolf Press, followed by two books with Anvil Press (UK), *The Winter Orchards* and *The Lost Hare*. Her most recent collection is *Thousandfold* (Carcanet Press, 2019).

Nick Caistor (Manchester, England, b. 1946) is a British translator from Spanish and French. He has translated more than one hundred works of fiction. As well as Julian Ríos, he has published translations of works by Juan Marse, Eduardo Mendoza, Manuel Vazuez Montalban, and many others.

Donka Farkas (Timişoara, Romania, b. 1952) is professor emerita of linguistics at the University of California, Santa Cruz. She emigrated to the United States in 1976. She has published extensively in semantics, her subfield of specialization.

John Finlay (Ozark, Alabama, 1941–91) was a poet and essayist. He taught at the University of Montevallo before entering Louisiana State University in 1970 to pursue a doctorate. Among his many books are *The Wide Porch and Other Poems* (1984), *Between the Gulfs* (1986), *The Salt of Exposure* (1988), *Mind and Blood: The Collected Poems of John Finlay* (1992), *Flaubert in Egypt: Essays on the Gnostic Spirit in Modern Literature and Thought* (1993), and *Hermetic Light: Essays on the Gnostic Literature and Thought* (1994).

Benjamin Fondane (Iaşi, Romania, 1898–1944), born Benjamin Fundoianu, was a poet, critic, and philosopher, celebrated as a symbolist and surrealist. Early on, he wrote, "only poetry could succeed where morality and metaphysics had failed." He moved to France in 1932 and became a leading figure in existentialism. Among his books were *Ulysse* (Ulysses, 1933) and *Titanic* (1937). He served in the French army against Nazi Germany, was taken prisoner in 1940, eventually returned to Paris but was arrested by the French police in March 1944, and was deported from France. He was killed in a gas chamber in Birkenau in October 1944.

Gawain Poet (fl. c. 1375–1400) is the unknown author to whom scholars ascribe the poems *Sir Gawain and the Green Knight*, *Pearl*, *Patience*, and *Cleanness* (or *Purity*). The author's name and life are unknown; the language of the surviving manuscripts has been traced to southeast Cheshire, close to the Staffordshire border.

Charles Gullans (Minneapolis, Minnesota, 1929–93) was a poet who taught English at the University of California at Los Angeles for more than six decades. His books of poetry included *Arrivals and Departures* (1962) and *Letter from Los Angeles* (1990). *Last Letters from Stalingrad* was one of his translations. In 1978, Gullans founded the Symposium Press, which published limited editions.

Daniel Hoffman (New York, New York, 1923–2013), a poet, scholar, and critic, was the US poet laureate from 1973 to 1974. He was the Felix E. Schelling Professor of English at the University of Pennsylvania. His first collection, *An Armada of Thirty Whales*, was selected for the Yale Series of Younger Poets by none other than W. H. Auden. In addition to *Brotherly Love*, his narrative poem about William Penn (2000), collections included *Makes You Stop and Think: Sonnets* (2005), and *Hang-Gliding from Helicon: New and Selected Poems 1948–1988*, which won the Paterson Poetry Prize. His numerous prizes included *Sewanee Review*'s Aiken Taylor Award and the American Academy of Arts and Letters' Arthur Rense Poetry Prize.

Cary Holladay (Richmond, Virginia, b. 1958) is the author of eight volumes of fiction. She has received an O. Henry Prize and a fellowship from the National Endowment for the Arts. "The Bridge" appears in her collection *Horse People: Stories* (Louisiana State University Press, 2013). Her most recent book is a nonfiction pictorial history, *Images of America: Glen Allen* (Arcadia Publishing, 2022). She lives in Rapidan, Virginia.

Maxine Kumin (Philadelphia, Pennsylvania, 1925–2014) was the US poet laureate from 1981 to 1982 and the poet laureate of New Hampshire from 1989 to 1994. In 1973, she won the Pulitzer Prize for *Upcountry*, her fourth book of poetry. Among her nearly twenty volumes of verse are such titles as *Halfway* (1961), *The Retrieval System* (1978), *Our Ground Time*

Here Will Be Brief (1982), *The Long Marriage* (2001), and *Where I Live* (2010). She was known for her political poems as well as those on pastoral subjects.

David Mason (Bellingham, Washington, b. 1954) served as Colorado poet laureate from 2010 to 2014. His many books include the verse novel *Ludlow*, four collections of essays, and several anthologies. Collections of poetry also include *The Country I Remember*, *Sea Salt*, *The Sound*, and *Pacific Light*. His most recent book is *Incarnation and Metamorphosis: Can Literature Change Us?* ((Paul Dry Books, 2023). Mason is also an opera librettist whose work is available on CD from Naxos. He now lives in Tasmania. He is an advisory editor of the *Hudson Review*.

Luke Mogelson (St. Louis, Missouri, b. 1982) has written for the *New Yorker* since 2013, covering wars in Ukraine, Afghanistan, Syria, and Iraq. Previously, he was based in Kabul for the *New York Times Magazine*. He is the author of *These Heroic, Happy Dead* (Tim Duggan Books, 2016) and *The Storm Is Here: An American Crucible* (Penguin Press, 2022).

Frederick Morgan (New York, New York, 1922–2004) was a native New Yorker and graduate of Princeton University. During World War II, he served in the Tank Destroyer Corps of the US Army. A founder of the *Hudson Review* in 1947, he edited it for fifty years until 1998 and remained affiliated with it as founding editor until his death. He published eleven books of poems, two collections of prose fables, and two books of translations. His final collection *Epilogue: Selected and Last Poems* was published posthumously in 2022 (Red Hen Press). In 1984 he was made Chevalier de l'Ordre des Arts et des Lettres by the government of France. In 2001 he was named the winner of the Aiken Taylor Award for poetry.

Marilyn Nelson (Cleveland, Ohio, b. 1946) is an American poet. A professor emeritus at the University of Connecticut and the former poet laureate of Connecticut, she is also a winner of several important awards, among them the Ruth Lilly Poetry Prize, the NSK Neustadt Prize for Children's Literature, and the Frost Medal. In spring 2000, a fellowship in Contemplative Practices sponsored by the Center for Contemplative Mind in Society, funded by the Fetzer Institute, allowed her to teach two sections of

"Poetry and Meditation" to two groups of cadets at the US Military Academy at West Point.

Abraham Pais (Amsterdam, the Netherlands, 1918–2000), a physicist and science historian, was the author of *"Subtle Is the Lord": The Science and the Life of Albert Einstein* (1982), among other books. Einstein, Niels Bohr, and J. Robert Oppenheimer numbered among his immediate colleagues. For many years he was the Detlev W. Bronk professor at Rockefeller University.

Richard Pevear (Waltham, Massachusetts, b. 1943) is a poet, essayist, and translator. He has published two collections of poetry, a number of essays on various subjects, and translations from French, Italian, and Russian. He is well known for his collaborative translations with Larissa Volokhonsky of the classic authors of Russian literature.

Lara Prescott's (Pittsburgh, Pennsylvania, b. 1981) debut novel *The Secrets We Kept* was published by Knopf in 2019 (and has been published in thirty countries). Years after writing "Those Who Burn," she thinks not of the horrors of war, but of her protagonist Yarah feeding stray cats in the square at night, bending down to give them her last can of tuna. She thinks of this small act of kindness among the ruins. Prescott currently lives in Portsmouth, New Hampshire.

John Ridland (London, England, 1933–2020) was the author of *In the Shadowless Light* (1978), *A Brahms Card Ballad* (2007), *Happy in an Ordinary Thing* (2013), *The Lincolniad: An Epic Poem Honoring the Memory of President Abraham Lincoln* (2014), and *Epitome and Epiphany* (2017), among others. His verse translation of the Hungarian folk epic *John the Valiant* (Corvina Press, Budapest, 1999) contributed to his winning the Balassi Sword Award for his translations of Hungarian literature in 2010. He taught for over forty years at the University of California, Santa Barbara. He retired in 2005.

Julián Ríos's (Vigo, Spain, b. 1941) story "Hunting in July" is from his collection *Procession of Shadows* (Dalkey Archive Press, 2011). US editions of his novels include *Larva: Midsummer Night's Babel* (Dalkey Archive Press,

1990, 2004), *Loves That Bird* (Knopf, 1998; Vintage, 1999), *Monstruary* (Knopf, 2001), and *The House of Ulysses* (Dalkey Archive Press, 2010). The French translation of his novel *Pont de l'Alma* won the Prix Laure-Bataillon 2010 for the best book and translation of the year.

Franz Karl Schneider (Wiesbaden, Germany, 1928–2021) was a well-regarded poet, translator, and literary critic. He was a greatly respected professor of comparative literature at Gonzaga University in Spokane, Washington, where he taught from 1957 to 1993. His book of poetry, *The Roof of Stone*, was published in 1982. He was born in Germany and earned his US citizenship in 1957.

Asako Serizawa (Kanagawa, Japan, b. 1974) was raised in Singapore, Jakarta, and Tokyo. Her debut book of fiction *Inheritors* (Anchor Books, 2021) won the PEN/Open Book Award and the Story Prize Spotlight Award, was a Massachusetts Book Awards Honors Book, and was longlisted for the PEN/Robert W. Bingham Prize. A recipient of grants from the National Endowment for the Arts and the Mass Cultural Council, her work has been awarded two O. Henry Prizes, a Pushcart Prize, a Rona Jaffe Foundation Writers' Award, and various fellowships, including a MacDowell.

Louis Simpson (Kingston, Jamaica, 1923–2012) was a Pulitzer Prize-winning poet. During World War II, he served as an Army combat infantryman, first with the tank corps and then with the 101st Airborne Division in France, the Netherlands, Belgium, and Germany. He was injured during the war and suffered from post-traumatic stress syndrome. He was a professor at the University of California, Berkeley, in the 1950s and '60s before moving on to Stony Brook in 1967, where he served on the faculty into the 1990s. His poetry collection *At the End of the Open Road* won the Pulitzer Prize in 1964. His two autobiographies were *North of Jamaica* (1972) and *The King My Father's Wreck* (1995).

Anne Stevenson (Cambridge, England, 1933–2020) was a prominent poet whose many awards included a lifetime achievement award from the Lannan Foundation in 2007. She published sixteen poetry collections, including *Completing the Circle* in 2020. She was widely known for her controversial 1989 biography of Sylvia Plath: *Bitter Fame: A Life of Sylvia Plath.*

Maria Terrone (New York, New York, b. 1951) is the author of various poetry collections including *Eye to Eye* (Bordighera Press, 2014) and the forthcoming *No Known Coordinates* (The Word Works). Her creative nonfiction debut *At Home in the New World* (Bordighera Press, 2018) focuses on her changing life as a New York City native. She is poetry editor of the journal *Italian Americana*.

Tolstoy, Count Leo Nikolayevich (Yasnaya Polyana, Russia, 1828–1910) was one of Russia's most famous novelists. His *War and Peace* was composed between 1863 and 1869. *Anna Karenina* was written between 1874 and 1876. Other novels included *The Death of Ivan Ilyitch* (1887) and *Resurrection* (1899), the latter helping to earn him excommunication from the Holy Synod in 1901. The essay *What Is Art?* (1898) is one of his celebrated books.

Larissa Volokhonsky (Leningrad, b. 1945) graduated from Leningrad State University with an MA in linguistics. She has translated works by the prominent Orthodox theologians Alexander Schmemann and John Meyendorff into Russian and is now working on a Russian translation of stories by Isak Dinesen. She and Richard Pevear have collaborated on translations on over thirty years of Russian literature and have twice been awarded the PEN Book-of-the-Month Club Translation Prize.

Tennessee Williams (Columbus, Mississippi, 1911–83) was an award-winning playwright whose accolades included the New York Drama Critics' Circle awards and Pulitzer Prizes. His many plays included *The Glass Menagerie* (his first success), *A Streetcar Named Desire*, *Cat on a Hot Tin Roof*, *The Night of the Iguana*, *Orpheus Descending*, *The Rose Tattoo*, and *Sweet Bird of Youth*. He wrote two novels, including *The Roman Spring of Mrs. Stone*, screenplays, poetry, and a book of memoirs, called *Memoirs*.

Printed in the USA
CPSIA information can be obtained
at www.ICGtesting.com
CBHW020553060624
9643CB00004B/14

9 780815 611677